Praise for
THE TRIDENT DECEPTION

"A terrific thriller debut. Campbell does an amazing job, balancing character interaction with high-octane action, all the while keeping the technical jargon to a level understandable by nonmilitary readers. This is the best novel about a submarine since Tom Clancy's classic *The Hunt For Red October*."

—*Booklist* (starred review)

"Fans of submarine thrillers who are saddened by the demise of Tom Clancy will welcome Campbell's debut."
—*Publishers Weekly*

"No one puts the reader inside a submarine like Rick Campbell does in *The Trident Deception*. I couldn't put it down. Compelling and thrilling, this novel is a must read." —Jack Coughlin, *New York Times* bestselling author of *Shooter* and *Time to Kill*

"*The Trident Deception* is a fistfight of a thriller. A masterpiece." —Dalton Fury, *New York Times* bestselling author of *Kill Bin Laden* and *Tier One Wild*

TREASON

RICK CAMPBELL

St. Martin's Paperbacks

This is a work of fiction. All of the characters, organizations, and events portrayed in this novel are either products of the author's imagination or are used fictitiously.

Published in the United States by St. Martin's Paperbacks, an imprint of St. Martin's Publishing Group.

TREASON

For information, address St. Martin's Publishing Group, 120 Broadway, New York, NY 10271.

www.stmartins.com

Library of Congress Catalog Card Number: 2018044449

ISBN: 978-1-250-25279-1

Our books may be purchased in bulk for promotional, educational, or business use. Please contact your local bookseller or the Macmillan Corporate and Premium Sales Department at 1-800-221-7945, ext. 5442, or by email at MacmillanSpecialMarkets@macmillan.com.

Printed in the United States of America

St. Martin's Press hardcover edition / March 2019
St. Martin's Paperbacks edition / February 2020

10 9 8 7 6 5 4 3 2 1

To loving friends Denise and Jason, our hearts feel for yours.
To their daughter Rachel, may each memory calm the storm.
To their daughter Whitney, whose heart now beats for two.
To Josh—their son, brother, and twin—who was called to
return before his story was fully written.

*Goodbyes hurt when the story is not finished and
the book has been closed forever.*
—Author Unknown

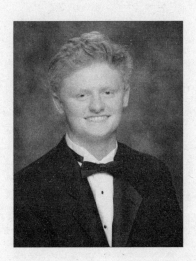

MAIN CHARACTERS
·COMPLETE CAST OF CHARACTERS
IS PROVIDED IN ADDENDUM·

UNITED STATES ADMINISTRATION
KEVIN HARDISON—chief of staff
DAWN CABRAL—secretary of state
BILL DUNNAVANT—secretary of defense
CHRISTINE O'CONNOR—national security advisor

MILITARY COMMANDERS
OKEY WATSON (General)—Chairman, Joint Chiefs of
   Staff
BRIAN RETTMAN (Admiral)—Chief of Naval Operations
ANDY WHEELER (General)—Supreme Allied
   Commander, Europe
BOB ARONSON (Admiral)—Commander, U.S. Strategic
   Command
DUSTY RHODES (Vice Admiral)—Director, Strategic
   Systems Programs

USS *MICHIGAN* (OHIO CLASS GUIDED MISSILE SUBMARINE)–CREW
MURRAY WILSON (Captain)—Commanding Officer
JOHN MCNEIL (Commander)—SEAL Team Commander
JAKE HARRISON (Lieutenant)—SEAL Platoon Officer-
   in-Charge
JEFF STONE (Special Warfare Operator Senior Chief)

RUSSIAN FEDERATION ADMINISTRATION

Yuri Kalinin—president

Josef Hippchenko—director of the Foreign Intelligence Service (SVR)

RUSSIAN MILITARY COMMANDERS

Sergei Andropov (General)—Chief of the General Staff

Alexei Volodin (Colonel General)—Commander-in-Chief, Aerospace Forces

Viktor Glukov (Colonel General)—Commander-in-Chief, Ground Forces

Oleg Lipovsky (Admiral)—Commander-in-Chief, Navy

WASHINGTON, D.C.

It was just past two in the afternoon when the president's motorcade sped down 17th Street NW toward the White House. In the center of the convoy, the president rode in the back of Cadillac One, a hybrid vehicle built on a truck frame and extensively modified with armored plating and bulletproof windows. As the motorcade approached the President's Park South, commonly called the Ellipse, Cadillac One screeched to a halt, as did the rest of the motorcade.

The president's door was yanked open and he was pulled from Cadillac One by his Secret Service detail. They surrounded the president, shepherding him toward the nearest building as the head of the president's detail explained.

"We're under attack—ballistic missile!"

Atop several buildings surrounding the White House and Capitol Building, surface-to-air missiles streaked upward. The president followed the white exhaust trails, spotting five reddish-orange objects descending toward the city. He almost froze when he realized what they were.

There had been no warning.

How was that possible?

Neither NORAD nor the Joint Air Defense Operations Center had provided a warning, which should have arrived twenty or more minutes ago.

Through a gap in the Secret Service detail, the president spotted the Navy officer carrying the Presidential Emergency Satchel, sometimes referred to as the nuclear football, containing the nuclear launch authentication codes and attack option matrix, sprinting toward him. But there was neither the time nor the necessary information—who had attacked—for a response.

As the missiles streaked upward, the president knew the probability of destroying the descending warheads was minuscule. Not even the most sophisticated antiballistic missiles in the American arsenal could consistently intercept nuclear warheads traveling in the descent phase.

A few seconds before warhead detonation, the president and his security detail had just begun climbing the steps toward the nearest building. They weren't going to make it. The head of the president's detail reached the same conclusion. He forced the president to the ground and ordered the agents to cover him with their bodies. As the president was smothered by his detail, one question in his mind stood out from the others.

How could this have happened?

THREE WEEKS
EARLIER

MOSCOW, RUSSIA

Russian President Yuri Kalinin entered the Kremlin conference room, joining his advisors seated around the table. The six men stood, then returned to their chairs after the president took his position at the head of the table. To the president's right sat Defense Minister Anton Nechayev and Foreign Minister Andrei Lavrov. On the other side of the table were four military officers: Chief of the General Staff Sergei Andropov, joined by the commanders of the Russian Ground Forces, Aerospace Forces, and Navy.

Kalinin had assembled his senior civilian and military advisors to review the results of their disastrous initiative—Russia's invasion of Ukraine and Lithuania, along with their blackmail attempt to prevent NATO from intervening. Their effort had failed, however. The Americans had soundly defeated the Russian Navy and NATO had begun preparing a counterattack into Lithuania and Ukraine. Russia had withdrawn its troops and peace now prevailed across Europe, but the sting of Russia's failure remained.

Diplomatic relations had returned to normal and it was time to discuss the way forward. Kalinin turned first to his new minister of defense. "Proceed."

Nechayev began with his prepared summary. "The Navy has finished its assessment. The water depth where the battle occurred is too deep to raise the sunken ships; they are a complete loss. Fortunately, the battle cruiser *Pyotr Velikiy* and aircraft carrier *Kuznetsov* remained afloat after the battle. Both restored propulsion and have arrived at our nearest shipyard. However, they are heavily damaged and it will take at least two years to return them to service."

Now that the bad news had been delivered, Nechayev shifted gears. "Our submarine fleet remains a viable asset, especially in light of the American losses during their war with China and the additional casualties they suffered at our hands. Although we lost most of our guided missile submarines, we still have thirty-five diesel and nuclear-powered attack submarines, while America has only eighteen fast attack submarines remaining in service. However, the United States raised twenty-seven of the submarines lost during their war with China, and the first of those will begin exiting the shipyards within the year. Our submarine advantage will not last long.

"We are in an even better situation regarding our land and air forces. The army suffered only minor losses in Ukraine, so we are in excellent shape on the ground. In the air, we lost all tactical fighters assigned to the Middle East, but the bulk of our Aerospace Force remains intact. After factoring in our anti-air assets, we can deny any NATO attempt to achieve air superiority."

With his update complete, Nechayev sat back, letting Kalinin absorb the information.

General Andropov, Kalinin's senior military advisor, joined the discussion. "Our basic strategy was sound. NATO cannot defeat our land and air forces without the United States. What failed was our strategy to keep the United States from intervening. If we fix that, we will succeed next time."

"Next time?" Kalinin asked.

Andropov's eyes narrowed. "America humiliated us. The images of our warships adrift and on fire have been shown repeatedly on the news, and public support for your administration is at an all-time low. If you want to be reelected next year, you'll have to make a bold move."

Kalinin replied, "It was the bold move you and Defense Minister Chernov recommended that created this situation. The plan failed, and I shouldn't have to remind you that Minister Chernov was assassinated by the Americans." He eyed his new defense minister, who shifted uncomfortably in his seat.

"It was a flawed plan," Andropov insisted. "We were supposed to blackmail the United States, keeping them from entering the conflict, but they blackmailed us instead. If we correct this flaw, we will prevail next time. The Zolotov option is finally ready to implement, and if the updates to the Alexander submarine class are adequate, America won't dare risk intervening."

Turning back to his new defense minister, Kalinin asked, "What is the status of the Zolotov option and the Alexander class?"

Nechayev responded, "As General Andropov mentioned, the Zolotov option can now be fully implemented. But, as you know, it is a high-risk, high-reward plan. Regarding the Alexander class, the equipment aboard *Alexander* has been upgraded and is scheduled for another test this afternoon. If it performs as intended, I'd have to agree with General Andropov. The American fleet would be at our mercy. Even if they chose to intercede in Europe, they couldn't risk transporting their troops or equipment by sea. Any effort to oppose us would be seriously hampered."

"*Alexander*'s test is this afternoon?"

Nechayev nodded. "Yes, sir."

"We will meet again tomorrow," Kalinin said, "and then I will decide."

K-561 *KAZAN*

Standing in the Central Command Post of his Yasen class attack submarine, Captain Second Rank Anatoly Mikhailov surveyed his crew. They were at Combat Stations, tracking Hydroacoustic two-one, a submerged contact lurking off *Kazan*'s starboard beam in the Barents Sea. It was quiet in the command post as Mikhailov stood near one of the two lowered periscopes, occasionally glancing at the admiral beside him. Admiral Leonid Shimko, commander of Russia's Northern Fleet, displayed no hint of what he was thinking as he watched *Kazan*'s crew prepare to attack.

Captain Third Rank Erik Fedorov, *Kazan*'s First Officer, stood behind two fire control consoles, peering over the shoulders of the two operators, each wearing the rank of michman on their uniform. He tapped one michman on the shoulder. "Set as Primary." The michman complied and Fedorov announced, "Captain, I have a firing solution."

Mikhailov examined the target parameters. The enemy submarine was six kilometers off *Kazan*'s starboard beam, headed west at ten knots. It was mirroring *Kazan*.

"Prepare to fire," Mikhailov announced, "Hydro-acoustic two-one, tube One."

"Solution updated," Fedorov called out.

"Torpedo ready," the Weapons Officer reported.

"Countermeasures armed," the Watch Officer announced.

Mikhailov examined the target solution again. Satisfied it was accurate and all torpedo search settings were optimal, he gave the order.

"Fire tube One."

The torpedo was impulsed from the tube, and Mikhailov's ears popped when the impulse tanks were vented, refilling them to supply water for another shot. He moved behind his Weapons Officer, monitoring the status of their outgoing torpedo as it descended to the estimated target depth of 150 meters. The torpedo closed on its target, and at the predetermined range, went active.

"Torpedo One has enabled," the Weapons Officer announced.

The torpedo began pinging, and not long thereafter the Weapons Officer reported, "Detect!"

The next report arrived seconds later, once the torpedo verified the detected contact was indeed a submarine.

"Homing!"

On the Weapon Launch Console, the parameters updated as the torpedo increased speed.

Mikhailov's eyes shifted to the nearest fire control console, looking for indication their target had begun maneuvering. The contact remained steady on course and speed. This, of course, was expected. The contact they had fired at was *Kazan*'s sister ship *Alexander,* a modified Yasen class, built and launched in secrecy from the Sevmash shipyard in the White Sea.

The torpedo *Kazan* had fired was an exercise version, its warhead explosive replaced with inert material. This was the fourth time *Kazan* had tested its torpedoes against *Alexander,* and Mikhailov wondered whether leadership suspected there was a problem with their torpedo inventory. After launch, the torpedo's artificial intelligence controlled every aspect of target prosecution. It wouldn't be the first time a software bug had rendered their torpedoes ineffective in some way. Thus far, however, *Kazan*'s torpedoes had performed as designed. This one appeared to be functioning properly as well.

"Exploder armed," the Weapons Officer announced.

The exploder had rotated into the firing position, preparing to detonate the warhead. This torpedo wouldn't explode, however, since the explosive had been removed.

Mikhailov watched the torpedo close the remaining distance to *Alexander,* then the Weapons Officer made the expected report. "Exploder has fired!"

There was no explosion, though. Instead, Hydroacoustic reported, "Weapon impact."

Normal exercise torpedoes had a turn-away feature or depth interlocks so the torpedo didn't impact the submarine and break into pieces, or even worse, damage the submarine's propulsor or screw during a shot from astern. However, the torpedo Mikhailov had fired against *Alexander* ran to termination, smashing into the submarine's hull.

The result was anticlimactic. The torpedo had operated perfectly. When Mikhailov turned to Admiral Shimko, he was surprised to see a frown on the admiral's face.

"Return to port immediately," Shimko ordered.

CAMBRIDGE, MASSACHUSETTS

Seated in his cubicle on the fourth floor of the Clark Curtain Laboratory building, Steve Kaufmann stared at his computer display, doing his best to stay focused. It was almost quitting time, in more ways than one. After replying to the latest email, he heard his division director's voice, calling for everyone's attention. Kaufmann looked over his cubicle, joined by several dozen other heads popping above the matrix walls. Jacinta Mascarenhas was exiting the elevator. Her executive assistant, Rich Underwood, followed behind, pushing a cart filled with champagne bottles and glasses.

Mascarenhas headed to an open area in the center of the cube farm, stopping beside a conference table where Underwood hastily unloaded additional glasses from beneath the cart.

"Gather round, everyone," Mascarenhas said. "We have some celebrating to do."

Kaufmann joined his colleagues, forming a semicircle around Mascarenhas. Kaufmann, tall and gangly, towering above most of his coworkers, watched from the last row of the crowd.

"Today marks the final shipment," Mascarenhas began, "the last set of spares for a decade-long project. Many of you have been here since the beginning, and Clark Curtain Laboratory thanks you for your dedication and hard work." She lifted a champagne bottle, peeling the foil and wire muselet from the cork. "I want to congratulate you on a job well done, completed on-schedule and on-budget, a rare accomplishment in the defense industry."

Mascarenhas popped the cork from the bottle, bouncing it off the ceiling. Underwood caught the overflowing champagne in a glass, which he handed to Mascarenhas, who raised it high.

"Here's to the successful end of one contract and the beginning of many more."

Underwood filled the champagne glasses, and several employees passed them through the crowd until everyone had one. Kaufmann took a sip of champagne, savoring the bittersweet achievement.

The current contract expired at the end of the month and Clark Curtain Labs hadn't won enough new government contracts to keep everyone employed. Kaufmann looked around, figuring that over half of those present would be looking for work by the end of the month unless the oft-promised replacement contract materialized. Kaufmann reckoned he'd be among those unemployed.

For the last ten years, Kaufmann had been assigned to the contract, developing the initial software, then tweaking the middleware as various microprocessors and other components went obsolete and were replaced with new versions. As the effort drew to a close, he'd seen the writing on the wall and had asked to be transferred to another contract, but Mascarenhas had disapproved each request. Kaufmann was far too valuable; no one knew the software code better than he did.

Kaufmann tilted his head back, emptying the glass. He hadn't been happy, stuck to a dying contract. But at least he'd gotten a glass of champagne out of it.

WASHINGTON, D.C.

The mid-afternoon sun filtered through the windows of his West Wing corner office as Chief of Staff Kevin Hardison reviewed the document on the table. Across from him, also reviewing a copy of the proposal, sat his White House nemesis, Christine O'Connor, the president's national security advisor, while an aide on Hardison's right took notes. Hardison braced himself for Christine's rejection of his latest recommendation. Instead, she nodded her agreement. Hardison pulled back slightly, examining the woman across from him—the only person from the opposite political party on the president's staff—more closely.

During the past three years, Christine had opposed him on almost every key proposal. The perennial thorn in his side was an incredibly obstinate woman. Even more irritating, her attempts to persuade the president to her point of view were quite effective. Hardison had stopped tracking who the president sided with more often once the trend became clear. However, during the past two months, Hardison had experienced a reversal of fortune. Christine had suddenly become agreeable.

Following the events at Ice Station Nautilus, Christine had buried herself in her work, staying late into

the night and working every weekend. After she returned from Russia, however, the pattern had reversed.
She left early when possible and no longer worked on
weekends unless the matter was urgent. Her interactions with Hardison and the rest of the president's staff
had grown distant, and Christine had surprisingly
agreed to several proposals Hardison was certain
she'd vehemently oppose. Hardison took advantage of
Christine's unusual pliability this afternoon, circling
back to a proposal she'd refused to endorse three years
earlier: a reorganization of the nation's numerous
intelligence agencies.

As much as Hardison relished his newfound success,
he missed the old Christine. Without her infuriating
opposition on almost every issue, coming to work
each day had become less . . . fun. As he reviewed
the document before him, he realized he'd scheduled
this meeting for opposing purposes. If Christine's
new trend held, he'd obtain her endorsement for a key
policy proposal—one the president would be sure to
push forward with Christine on board. However, she'd
made her position on the issue clear during previous
meetings, practically throwing Hardison out of her
office the last time he brought it up. He was certain
Christine's bona fides would surface this afternoon
when he pressed the matter.

"So," Hardison said. "I take it you agree with the
restructuring?"

"I'll consider it," Christine replied, with no hint of
the icy tone he expected.

Hardison contemplated his next move as the aide
typed notes into her laptop. He focused again on
Christine, who was staring out one of the triple-paned,
bomb-resistant windows in his office. The fresh scar
across her cheek was faintly visible. His eyes went
to her wrists; the cuts had likewise healed. Although

Christine hadn't shared the details, the CIA report had painted a clear enough picture: Christine handcuffed to a pipe above her head as she was tormented by Semyon Gorev, the director of Russia's Foreign Intelligence Service. Hardison wondered what Christine had thought when Gorev slid his pistol barrel into her mouth. The emotions that must have flooded her body as he slowly squeezed the trigger.

There had been no bullets in the pistol, part of Gorev's sadistic torment. A few hours later, Christine had somehow reversed the roles, jamming a gun into Gorev's mouth. Then she blew his brains out.

The aide finished her notes and looked up. Christine was still staring out the window.

Hardison turned to the aide. "Excuse us for a few minutes. I need to talk with Miss O'Connor privately."

The aide pushed back from the table and the movement caught Christine's attention, interrupting her reverie.

When they were alone, Hardison said, "Are you okay?"

"I'm fine. Why do you ask?"

"You haven't been yourself the last few weeks."

She folded her arms across her chest. "I'm fine." This time, her voice had an edge to it.

"You're not fine. It's obvious you're still dealing with what happened in Russia. It's affecting your work."

"I don't have time for this." Christine's eyes went to the aide's empty seat. "Are we done?"

"We're *not* done. I know you don't consider me a friend—"

"Because you're not."

"—but I do care about you a tiny bit. You need to take some time off. Clear your head."

Christine leaned forward, placing her hands on the

edge of the table. "I don't need your psychoanalysis. I'm doing just fine."

Hardison collected his thoughts. It was pointless to continue. There was too much animosity between them. Deservedly so, he had to admit.

"You're right," Hardison said. "You're doing just fine. That's all I have for today."

Christine stood and grabbed her notepad, then left without a word.

Christine tossed her notepad on her desk, then settled into her chair. She stared at the dark computer display for a moment, reviewing her conversation with Hardison. She hadn't realized it was so obvious. Her thoughts turned to what had occurred in Russia, then to Ice Station Nautilus. To what she'd done to her good friend Captain Steve Brackman, the president's former senior military aide. Former, as in deceased. Thanks to Christine. She went back even further to her imprisonment in the bowels of China's Great Hall of the People, then to her townhouse where she lay on the floor as a man tried to drive a knife through her neck.

This wasn't what she had signed up for. She was supposed to be a White House advisor whose confrontations were limited to those across a conference room table. Not those requiring a semiautomatic pistol, especially one shoved into her mouth or someone else's. What had occurred in Russia, along with her pending trip to Moscow in two weeks—she was the primary U.S. nuclear arms negotiator—weighed heavily on her mind.

She woke the computer, then selected her personal folder. Her hands hovered over the keyboard as she examined nine versions of an almost identical document, each one beginning with—*Letter of Resignation*. She opened the latest one, read it twice, then hit

Print. She signed the letter and placed it in a folder. After a moment of indecision, she took a deep breath, then headed down the seventy-foot-long blue-carpeted hallway toward the Oval Office.

The president's secretary looked up when Christine entered her office. "Is the president available?" Christine asked.

The secretary checked the president's schedule. "He's open for the next ten minutes. Will that be enough time?"

Christine nodded. The secretary knocked on the president's door and inquired. After his response, the secretary stepped aside and Christine entered the Oval Office.

The president was at his desk, framed by towering colonnade windows providing a view of the Rose Garden and South Lawn. He put down the document he was reading.

"Afternoon, Christine," he said, gesturing toward the three chairs in front of his desk.

Christine took one of the proffered seats, gripping the folder on her lap with both hands. There must have been something in her body language, because the president leaned back in his chair and pushed his glasses above his forehead, studying her carefully. He waited for her to begin.

"I apologize for the interruption," she said, unsure of how to broach the subject. After a quick reflection on the issue, she decided to start at the beginning.

"I want to thank you for the opportunity you provided, choosing me as your national security advisor. I appreciate your faith in my ability and your willingness to look beyond my party affiliation. I've thoroughly enjoyed working for you and I hope you'll consider me again if another opportunity arises in the future."

There was no response from the president, so she continued. "In the last three years, I've ended up in situations that go far beyond what I expected. I've done things that violate my core principles. I'm not sure what I stand for anymore."

Her eyes went to the folder, then she handed it to him.

After reading the letter, the president said, "I must admit that you've been forced to make difficult decisions. But I think you're being too harsh on yourself. I can't express how impressed I am with how well you've handled yourself in these challenging situations." He paused for a moment, then said, "Let's work on keeping you out of trouble from now on."

The president closed the folder and pushed it across the desk toward Christine. "I'd like you to reconsider."

Christine leaned forward, pushing the folder slowly back to the president.

"Are you sure about this?" he asked.

She wasn't sure, but Hardison was right. She needed to step away for a while.

"I am, Mr. President."

The president leaned back in his chair again and folded his hands across his waist. "You've provided a two-week notice. I have another idea. You've worked hard on the new nuclear arms reduction treaty with Russia, establishing important personal relationships. I'd like you to continue as my national security advisor until the final details have been hammered out."

"That could take months," Christine replied.

"How about this: two months or when the agreement is final, whichever comes first?"

Christine contemplated the offer. The rationale was sound, but the meetings alternated between the two countries. After what she'd done on the shore of the Black Sea, returning to Russia didn't sound like a good idea.

"Can we conduct all future meetings in the United States?"

"That could be arranged," the president replied, "but I think we can leave the venue unchanged. I don't believe there's anything to worry about if you meet in Russia. Diplomatic relations have returned to normal and Russia is currently on their best behavior. Plus, President Kalinin assured me there will be no retribution for what you did in Russia."

"I wasn't aware of Kalinin's assurance."

"I considered mentioning it, but since you've avoided the subject, I decided not to."

Christine appreciated the president's thoughtfulness, but the issue had never been far from her mind.

"Two months?" Christine asked.

"Two months. And if you happen to change your mind in the meantime, you may withdraw your resignation."

"You're just stringing me along, hoping I'll change my mind."

"I am." The president smiled.

Christine stared at the folder on the president's desk as she contemplated his offer. Two months. It gave the president plenty of time to hire a new NSA, plus it provided an opportunity to finish what she'd started—a new nuclear arms reduction treaty with Russia.

"I agree," she said. "Two months or a new treaty, whichever comes first."

"Excellent," the president replied. "Now why don't you spend some time annoying Hardison. You've been far too amenable lately."

It was Christine's turn to smile. "I'll see what I can do."

5

MOSCOW, RUSSIA

Russian President Yuri Kalinin took his seat at the head of the Kremlin conference table, populated by the same men who had joined him the previous day: Defense Minister Nechayev, Foreign Minister Lavrov, plus Chief of the General Staff Sergei Andropov and the commanders of the Russian Ground Forces, Aerospace Forces, and Navy.

"What is the status?" Kalinin asked.

Defense Minister Nechayev replied, "*Alexander* failed the test."

"What is the prognosis for correcting the issue?"

Nechayev looked to Fleet Admiral Oleg Lipovsky, who answered defensively, "We are pushing the boundaries of both physics and technology. The challenges are significant and we've overcome most of them."

"I understand the issues," Kalinin replied. "Will there be a solution anytime soon?"

Lipovsky shook his head. "The next proposal will require dry-docking *Alexander* to retrofit some of the components. That will take several months."

General Andropov joined in. "We do not need the Alexander class. The Zolotov option is sufficient. We have the opportunity to demonstrate our capability in three weeks, and we must take advantage of it. We don't know when the next opportunity will occur."

"I'm uncomfortable with the Zolotov option," Kalinin replied. "We don't know how the Americans will respond, and if the situation spirals out of control, the consequences would be dire."

"The Americans *won't* respond," Andropov insisted. "That's the point of the Zolotov option. They will be paralyzed, providing an opportunity to reestablish our border security."

Kalinin replied, "Perhaps we should be content with our current border situation."

Disapproving looks formed on each man's face. Kalinin contemplated the issue and the events that had shaped his advisors' perspectives.

The painful memories of World War II, referred to as the Great Patriotic War within Russia, weighed heavily on the Russian psyche, something the West seemed incapable of understanding. The United States, for example, extolled its Greatest Generation—those who fought in World War II—along with their enormous sacrifice: over 400,000 dead. A sacrifice that paled in comparison with the Soviet Union's: seven million military personnel killed, along with twenty million civilians as the German Army exterminated ethnic groups during their occupation and razed entire cities to the ground as they retreated.

Twenty-seven million.

And those were the casualties from just the last invasion by a Western European power. First the Poles in the seventeenth century, followed by Napoleon's army in the nineteenth century, with both armies sacking Moscow.

Following World War II, the Soviet Union took precautions to ensure it would never again endure the genocide of its people or the destruction of its cities, establishing a buffer zone of friendly Eastern European governments. The next time the West invaded Russia, there'd be advance warning as troops moved through the Eastern European countries on Russia's border. Next time, the war would be fought on another country's soil. Unfortunately, the buffer zone had eroded since the fall of the Soviet Union.

The Baltic States had joined NATO, and now Ukraine and Finland, also on Russia's western border, were considering joining the Alliance. Numerous Russian experts were sounding the alarm. It was time Russia re-created a buffer zone of friendly provinces to the west, even if that meant employing its military. Two months ago, Kalinin had authorized a bold move, seizing portions of Lithuania and Ukraine, implementing a plot to keep NATO from intervening. The plan had succeeded at first, but America had reversed the table, forcing Russia to withdraw in humiliating fashion.

"Doing nothing would be a mistake," Andropov said. "NATO will continue to encroach on our borders and you will lose the election. Bold action is required to rectify both situations."

Kalinin considered the general's words. Andropov wasn't the first person to leverage the nation's fears of a NATO invasion, as well as Kalinin's election concern. Former Defense Minister Chernov had done so, convincing him to authorize the invasion of Ukraine and Lithuania. It hadn't gone well. Andropov was insisting on a second round, implementing a different strategy to prevent the United States from intervening.

The proposed plan was too risky. A cornered animal with no chance of escape would often lash out. That was something Russia—and the rest of the world—could not afford. Kalinin was convinced the

West didn't understand Russians, and after Russia's attempt to blackmail the United States had backfired, it was clear that Russians didn't understand Americans. There was simply no way to know how the American president would respond. Finally, Kalinin made his decision.

"We will not proceed. The Zolotov option is too drastic, and without the Alexander class to provide additional insurance against an American response, the scenario is too volatile."

Kalinin pushed back from the table. "Thank you for your input."

6

ARLINGTON, VIRGINIA

It was after midnight when Christine pulled into her townhouse driveway, only a few miles from the White House. She'd been out later than planned. A quick call to share the news of her resignation with her best friend, Joan, had turned into an impromptu dinner and drinks. The evening had slipped by while they discussed Christine's future, from both professional and personal perspectives. The topic of Jake Harrison eventually arose, and how she'd blown both opportunities to be with the only man she'd truly loved.

Harrison had proposed twice, once during their senior year in high school and again after she graduated from college. She'd accepted his ring the first time, but returned it the next morning. She wasn't ready for marriage, headed to college on a gymnastics scholarship the first time he proposed, and embarking on a life in Washington politics the second. She'd asked him to wait, but apparently ten years was too long. By the time Christine was ready, Jake had proposed to another woman.

Harrison was a Navy SEAL now and their paths had unexpectedly crossed during the last few years. The time they'd spent together had rekindled her feelings for him, but unfortunately it didn't matter. During their last opportunity to talk privately, she'd asked if he was happily married. Looking into his eyes as he answered, she'd seen his love for Angie and realized he would never leave her. It was a bitter acknowledgment; Jake was no longer an option. The time off from work after resigning would provide an opportunity to reevaluate her life.

Christine headed up the walkway and retrieved her mail, then entered her townhouse and stopped in the kitchen, placing her purse on the island countertop. As she opened her mail, her sixth sense tugged at her, drawing her eyes toward a kitchen drawer not fully closed. She examined her surroundings more closely. The pantry door was slightly ajar. Goose bumps formed on her arms. She put down the mail and checked the other rooms. In the living room, a couch pillow was askew. She stopped at the dining room entrance and flicked on the light. A man was seated at the table, staring at her.

"Good evening, Miss O'Connor."

Christine froze, evaluating whether the man was a threat and whether to flee her townhouse. If it became a race to the front door, however, the man had a more direct route. She examined him more closely: medium height and weight, wearing a dark gray business suit and tie, with the jacket unbuttoned.

"Have a seat," he said.

Christine detected a faint accent, one she immediately recognized. An image of her mom flashed in her mind, sitting on her sofa alongside Jake Harrison's mother as Christine and Jake played in the living room, the two women talking while they drank tea. Both women were from Russia, and although the man's accent was barely discernible, it matched the women's.

He gestured to a chair on the other side of the table. "Please, have a seat."

She eased into the chair, her mind churning; who was he, why was he here, and what were her options if he intended her harm?

"I have a new director," the man said, "who sends his greetings."

Christine pieced together the clues: the Russian accent and reference to a new director. He was an agent in Russia's Foreign Intelligence Service—the successor to the First Chief Directorate of the KGB—referred to as the SVR due to its Russian spelling, *Sluzhba Vneshney Razvedki*. Christine hadn't been aware that President Kalinin had selected a replacement director.

"And the new director is . . . ?" Christine asked.

"Josef Hippchenko, promoted after Gorev's unfortunate accident."

"Accident?"

"A horrible boating tragedy on the shore of the Black Sea, claiming both Chernov and Gorev. Of course, you and I know what really happened, but it would not reflect well on the SVR if the public or our adversaries learned that our director was assassinated. We'd be held in even lower regard if they learned the killer was a complete . . . amateur."

"I wouldn't call it an assassination. It was more of a—"

"The exact terminology isn't important. What's relevant is that you killed Director Gorev. What's even more relevant, and the reason I'm here, is that within the SVR there is a sacred code. Anyone who kills an SVR agent must pay the price."

As Christine processed the agent's words, she did her best to remain calm. "And that price is?"

"Quid pro quo." He slid his hand inside his jacket and retrieved a pistol, which he leveled at Christine.

Christine's pulse quickened, her thoughts racing

through her options. She was unarmed and her gun was upstairs. There were knives in the kitchen, but it was unlikely she could get her hands on one, plus the adage—*never bring a knife to a gunfight*—flashed through her mind. She quickly concluded she had no viable option. Perhaps she could talk her way out.

"Gorev was a cruel, sadistic man. He deserved what he got."

"I don't disagree. However, it does not absolve you of your sin." The man leaned back in his chair. "Fortunately for you, President Kalinin has directed us to refrain from retribution."

"Why did he do that?"

The man's eyes moved over her body, coming to rest on her face. "You are even more attractive in person, and your resemblance to Kalinin's deceased wife is remarkable. I see why he is enamored with you. But none of that will matter once Kalinin leaves office."

"Why is that?"

"Kalinin's order is valid only as long as he is president. The day he steps down as Russia's president will be your last day alive."

Instead of the agent's threat spawning fear, Christine's anger began to simmer. Her eyes went to the pistol, still pointed at her. "Last I heard, Kalinin is still president. So why are you here?"

"To deliver a message from our new director. He appreciates your role in his promotion, but he is bound to the code. He—" the agent paused, then spread his hands out to his sides,"—*we* will enjoy watching you live your remaining days in fear."

"That's it? You came here to scare me?"

"Actually," the man said, "I was hoping for more." He placed the pistol on the table and pushed it toward Christine, stopping when it was within her reach. He leaned back in his chair.

"If the situation were to get out of hand today, ending in your unfortunate death . . ."

Christine examined the pistol; it was halfway between them.

"Go ahead. Take it."

Even if she reached it first, did he have another gun? She surveyed his jacket for another bulge, seeing none. Her eyes went back to the gun, which she suddenly recognized: a Glock 26, the same type she'd been given outside China's Great Hall of the People. The same type she'd bought and was upstairs in—

The gun on the table was *hers*.

The realization must have played across her face, because the agent admitted, "Yes, Christine. It's your pistol. You should take it."

She looked at the gun again. The magazine was inserted, but there was no way to know if he'd stripped the bullets. Plus, if the gun on the table was hers, his was undoubtedly within easy reach. As she debated her odds of survival if she went for the gun, something the man said earlier echoed in her mind.

Fortunately for you, President Kalinin has directed us to refrain from retribution.

She didn't need the gun.

Christine leaned forward. "Get out. And if you step foot in here again, I'll put a bullet in you."

The SVR agent stood and retrieved the pistol, releasing the magazine onto the table. It was loaded. "You should have taken the gun. You would've had a chance, however slim."

Christine pointed toward the door. "Get out!"

The man slipped the magazine into his pocket. "Good night, Miss O'Connor."

After the man left, Christine moved swiftly to the door and locked it, then evaluated her predicament.

Despite her resignation, it appeared she couldn't walk away from what she'd done in Russia. She grabbed the gun and headed upstairs, entering her bedroom closet. After retrieving a case from the top shelf, she lifted the lid and verified the Glock was hers; it was missing from the case, as was one of the two magazines. She pulled back the pistol's slide, verifying the chamber was empty, then inserted the magazine and released the slide, chambering a round.

As she held the pistol, she took a deep, shaky breath and tried to focus. What happened in Russia wasn't her fault. Gorev had tormented her, telling her she'd be fish food at the bottom of the Black Sea by morning. What was she supposed to have done? Let him put a bullet in her head and toss her into the sea? After what she'd been through, the danger she found herself in now was decidedly unfair. A rage began to build, her face becoming flush with anger. She placed the pistol in the top drawer of her nightstand and slammed it shut, knocking over a portrait of her mother.

Christine righted the picture, studying her mom's features. She took after her mother more than her father, her mom's Russian genetics dominating. She couldn't argue with the agent's comment about her resemblance to Kalinin's wife, who had died of cancer not long after he was elected president. When Kalinin had shown Natasha's picture to her in his Kremlin office, it was like looking into a mirror.

She was grateful Kalinin had intervened, delaying the SVR's retribution. However, it appeared he didn't have firm control of his SVR, with the new director sending one of his minions to torment her. Perhaps Kalinin should be informed. During her last visit to Moscow, he'd given her his personal cell phone number after inviting her to spend the weekend, hoping for a favorable answer. She'd declined the invitation, but still had the number. She checked her watch; it was 8 a.m. in Moscow.

Christine returned to her kitchen and pulled her cell phone from her purse. She scrolled through her contacts, selecting Kalinin's personal number, then hit *Send*.

The phone went immediately to voicemail.

She selected Kalinin's work number—his Kremlin office. As the phone rang, she realized she should probably be polite, but her anger was boiling over.

When the call was answered, Christine said, "This is American National Security Advisor Christine O'Connor. I have a message for President Kalinin. You tell him—"

"One moment please." The secretary placed her on hold.

Christine's frustration built further at the rude interruption, and she paced around the kitchen island while she waited.

The secretary spoke again. "Miss O'Connor?"

Christine picked up where she left off. "You tell President Kalinin—"

"You can tell him yourself. He is on the line."

Christine's words caught in her throat. Before she could continue, Kalinin spoke.

"This is President Kalinin."

Christine collected her thoughts, deciding it was best to tamp down on her anger. "President Kalinin, thank you for taking my call."

"It is my pleasure. How can I help?"

"One of your SVR agents broke into my house and threatened me tonight." After providing the details, she said, "I want to thank you for intervening, sparing my life for now. But if another agent breaks into my home again, I'll either kill him myself or have someone do it for me. I'm sure there are a few people in Langley," Christine said, referring to CIA headquarters, "who'd be happy to oblige."

There was silence on the line. As Christine awaited a response, she worried that she'd come across too strong. Kalinin had intervened to save her life after all, and perhaps she should have been more grateful.

Finally, Kalinin spoke. "Thank you for informing me. I apologize for this incident and will address the matter."

Christine let out a slow breath. This had gone much better than it could have.

Kalinin then said, "Let me make amends for today's unfortunate event. The next round of nuclear arms reduction negotiations is in Moscow in two weeks. Afterwards, I'd be delighted if you joined me for the weekend at my summer residence in Gelendzhik."

It was Christine's turn for silence. Kalinin was an attractive man and only ten years older than her. Age wasn't an issue, but Kalinin was Russia's president and Christine was America's national security advisor. She had trouble wrapping her mind around the complications created by a liaison between them, much less an intimate relationship, even if it began after she resigned.

After a short wait, Kalinin said, "This is the third time I have extended an invitation. I will not ask again."

On the other hand, in light of what she'd just learned, keeping Kalinin in the *friends* column seemed like a really good idea. But a weekend with Kalinin wasn't something she could agree to on the spur of the moment. She stalled for time.

"I'll have to discuss this with the president and his legal counsel first."

"I understand. I look forward to hearing from you."

The line went dead, and Christine exhaled between pursed lips. The elation she'd felt after handing in her resignation had evaporated. She'd been handed a death sentence, to be executed on Kalinin's last day in office. She searched her memory for details on his term as president, recalling that the next Russian presidential election was less than a year away. A knot formed in her stomach.

7

MOSCOW, RUSSIA

President Kalinin hung up the phone, his eyes going to the man seated on the other side of his desk, who was wearing a disapproving frown. Kalinin addressed Josef Hippchenko, the new director of the SVR, whose meeting with Kalinin this morning had been interrupted by America's national security advisor.

"Did you direct a visit with O'Connor?" Kalinin asked.

"I may have mentioned it to a subordinate."

"I believe my order was clear."

"It was," Hippchenko admitted. "What's also clear is the price she must pay. You are only delaying the inevitable. When you step down as president, I—or my successor—will give the order."

"I will deal with that when the time comes. Until then, you will not harm her."

"Why do you protect her? You barely know this woman."

"That's something I intend to rectify."

"She killed your defense minister and SVR director, and not only are you going to let her waltz back into our country, you're going to take her to dinner.

If you establish a relationship with her and the public finds out what she did, you're finished."

"Then I recommend you ensure they don't find out."

Hippchenko chose his words carefully, trying to keep the frustration from bleeding through. "Do you remember one of the first mantras you learned when you joined the SVR? How to obtain leverage against your opponent? *When it comes to sex, don't underestimate a man's stupidity.* Men will risk their marriage, their career, and a lifetime's reputation for a few minutes of pleasure."

"I'm not talking about a few minutes of pleasure," Kalinin replied.

Hippchenko slammed his hand on the president's desk. "But the outcome will be the same!" He stood. "I will not be part of this folly."

Kalinin glared at his SVR director. "Sit down." When Hippchenko remained standing, Kalinin repeated, "Sit down!"

Hippchenko sank into the chair, his gaze locked on Kalinin.

The Russian president stared at Hippchenko for a moment, then pushed back from his desk, retrieving a bottle of cognac and two glasses from the credenza behind him. He placed the glasses on his desk and poured two drinks. He pushed one to Hippchenko. The SVR director took a sip, as did Kalinin.

Hippchenko spoke first. "I know how much you miss Natasha and that Christine somehow fills that void. But it is unwise to pursue a relationship with an American woman."

"Christine is half Russian."

"She's *American*. She doesn't even speak Russian."

"Still," Kalinin said, "her being half Russian provides an avenue for public approval should our . . . *friendship* be discovered. Besides, Russia has a long history of its leaders marrying foreigners. Peter the Great married a Polish-Lithuanian woman, Alexander III married a Dane, and most of the later Russian rulers, including the last tsar, married Germans."

"The last tsar was executed."

Kalinin stared at Hippchenko. "Bad example. But I believe I've made my point. A relationship with a foreigner would not be unprecedented."

Hippchenko shrugged. "You are not a tsar, and things are different today. Public opinion is fickle, and it could easily turn against you."

"I'm not planning on marrying the woman," Kalinin replied. "I'm interested in a few social visits. Get to know her better. Afterwards, if we decide to pursue a relationship, I'll reevaluate the matter."

Hippchenko took another sip as he assessed the situation. "You have many political enemies, and some of them know that Christine killed Chernov and Gorev. They will use that against you if they learn you've established an intimate relationship with her. I recommend we keep your *friendship* with Christine discreet for now."

"I agree. I've invited her to join me at Gelendzhik. I'd like you to make the travel arrangements so her detour to the Black Sea isn't discovered."

Hippchenko nodded. "It's your political future."

8
MOSCOW, RUSSIA

In his office in the Ministry of Defense headquarters in Moscow's Arbat District, General Sergei Andropov studied the three men seated on the other side of his desk. Colonel Generals Alexei Volodin and Viktor Glukov, commanders-in-chief of the Aerospace and Ground Forces, respectively, along with Fleet Admiral Oleg Lipovsky, would have to commit their support for Andropov's plan to succeed. Although he didn't know how they'd respond, he was sure their discussion today would remain confidential.

The four men shared a common bond. They had dedicated their lives to protecting the Motherland, and all options to achieve that goal were worthy of discussion. Andropov's plan would not be shared with the new defense minister, however. Andropov didn't know Nechayev well enough to judge his reaction to today's proposal, plus Andropov didn't trust politicians anyway. Only the men who wore the uniform could be trusted to act in Russia's best interest, unfettered by political ambition or public opinion polls.

With the three officers waiting patiently for Andropov to begin, he launched into his prepared remarks. "The opportunity to demonstrate the Zolotov option occurs in eighteen days. We will then have a long window of opportunity during which the United States, and by extension NATO, will be paralyzed. It will take years for America to undo what we've done. By then, the actions we'll have taken along our border will be ancient history. NATO will realize we pose no threat to Western Europe."

"The Baltic States will not agree with your assessment," Admiral Lipovsky said.

"They should not be part of NATO to begin with!" Andropov snapped. "They provide no value to the Alliance, but NATO was eager to add them for the sole purpose of irritating us. Ukraine and Finland have expressed interest in joining NATO, leaving Belarus as our only ally to the west. NATO will not stop until they have turned all of our neighbors against us. We will then be at the West's mercy, like we were at the beginning of the Great Patriotic War. Everything we've achieved since then will be for naught."

After none of the three men disagreed with his assertion, Andropov continued. "We are at a crossroads, presented with an opportunity that may not occur again. We've spent ten years implementing the Zolotov option, but without demonstrating its capability, we gain nothing from it."

General Volodin reminded him, "It was supposed to be an insurance policy. It was not meant to be used offensively."

"Times are different today. Our border security has eroded even further than when the Soviet Union dissolved. We must do something to keep NATO from encroaching on our doorstep. We can no longer leave it to the political whims of our neighbors. Regrettably, we must be more forceful."

General Glukov replied, "You presented this option to President Kalinin, and he declined to pursue it."

"Kalinin is weak. Chernov convinced him to proceed last time, but Nechayev is too new, unwilling to guide the president toward the correct answer. That leaves the four of us. We must make the decision *for* Kalinin."

"What is your plan?" Glukov asked.

"We will demonstrate the Zolotov option, then secure our borders. The Zapad war games have been scheduled to coincide with this opportunity, providing over one hundred thousand mobilized troops that can immediately pivot to the west. NATO generals will still be drinking their morning coffee by the time we've seized our objectives, and additional Russian forces will flow into the seized territories within forty-eight hours. With the Zolotov option preventing the United States from interfering, NATO will have no choice but to cede the territory."

Volodin replied, "You do not have a Zolotov controller. There are only ten units and they are tightly controlled, manned twenty-four hours a day. Not even I have access."

"I've made the necessary arrangements," Andropov said. "I will have a control unit by the required time."

General Glukov said, "You're proposing we execute the plan without Kalinin's authorization? You're proposing a coup?"

"Not exactly," Andropov said. "We will merely make a few decisions for Kalinin, until the matter is beyond his control."

The three men displayed no emotion as they processed Andropov's proposal and its implications. If they succeeded, they'd stabilize Russia's deteriorating security posture, restoring the crucial buffer zone to the west. If they failed, they'd all go to prison.

Finally, Glukov responded. "I cannot commit to this today. I need time to assess."

The other two men nodded their agreement.

"I understand," Andropov said. "You have two weeks to decide."

9

WASHINGTON, D.C.

Seated in the Oval Office between Chief of Staff Kevin Hardison and a staffer from the Office of the Director of National Intelligence, Christine awaited her turn during the president's national security brief. As the daily intelligence highlights were provided, her thoughts occasionally fast-forwarded to the last topic on today's agenda, the nuclear arms reduction treaty with Russia and the related personal matter—Kalinin's request she join him for the weekend afterward.

The intelligence staffer departed and Christine delivered her morning update, finishing with a reminder. "I head to Moscow in two weeks for the next round of nuclear arms reduction negotiations. If things go well, we should be able to agree on the remaining terms."

"I look forward to reviewing the final document," the president said. "Anything else?"

Christine preferred that Hardison not be present when she discussed the final issue; she was certain he'd find some way to use it against her. But Hardison would find out soon enough, so she proceeded.

"President Kalinin has invited me to join him at Gelendzhik after my next trip to Moscow."

The president leaned back in his chair, a grin on his face. "Cavorting with the enemy?"

"Not exactly," Christine replied, failing to see the humor in the situation. "He's asked me to join him for the weekend twice before and I declined both times. He made it clear this was his final request."

Hardison turned to Christine. "All this time in Moscow, I thought you were slacking off. It turns out you were working overtime."

Christine overrode the urge to slap him, delivering an icy stare instead.

"You're taking Kalinin up on his offer this time?" the president asked.

"I haven't decided," Christine replied, turning her attention back to the president. "I wanted to run it by legal first to make sure there isn't a prohibition."

"Yes, of course," the president said. "I'll have Hardison run it past Brooks. I think you're fine, though. A social visit with Kalinin after you wrap things up in Moscow is well within the bounds of propriety. I've met Russian dignitaries at Camp David before. It's a fair quid pro quo."

When the president mentioned *quid pro quo,* Christine's stomach tightened, recalling the death sentence the SVR agent had delivered. She considered bringing that topic up but decided otherwise. She had a year to sort through *that* issue.

10

SAN JOSE, CALIFORNIA

In a sparsely populated parking garage on the outskirts of San Jose's Japantown, Keith Vierling waited nervously in his car. As directed, he had parked on the fourth level, devoid of other vehicles at this time of night, overlooking the Guadalupe Freeway. A pair of headlights appeared in his rearview mirror, stopping after climbing the third-floor ramp. A moment later, the car moved slowly toward him.

Vierling glanced at the briefcase on the backseat. Over the past few years, he'd delivered ten identical units per the original contract. A few days ago, an eleventh unit was requested, along with a rapid delivery. Vierling had finished assembling the components this afternoon.

A black sedan parked beside him and the driver stepped out. Vierling's passenger door opened and the man slid inside. He went by "Ed Sutton," although Vierling was certain it wasn't his real name. Vierling never bothered to research the issue; it wasn't like Sutton paid by check. Since their agreement ten years ago, Vierling had scheduled several trips to Vegas each year, returning noticeably richer each time.

Sutton looked over his shoulder, examining the briefcase. "Same design as the others?"

Vierling nodded. "Same operating procedures too. I've included a set of instructions inside this unit as well."

Sutton reached back and retrieved the briefcase, opening it on his lap. After inspecting the components inside, he asked, "Is there a range limitation?"

"No," Vierling replied, trying to not sound irritated. He'd just told him the unit was identical to the previous ones, and the contract was clear: *Operable from anywhere on the planet.* "The signal gets routed through several satellite networks, so it'll work anywhere." Vierling added, "As a reminder, once you activate the algorithms, it cannot be undone."

The man glanced at Vierling.

Vierling held his hands up. "Hey, that's what you guys ordered. I just want to make sure you don't forget."

Sutton closed the briefcase. "We are aware."

He opened the car door and Vierling grabbed the man's forearm. Sutton stopped and slowly turned his head toward Vierling, who quickly released his grip.

"What about compensation?" Vierling asked. "This is an extra unit, not part of the original deal."

"You will receive a ten percent bonus. Pick it up via the usual process, anytime within the next year."

Without waiting for a response, Sutton stepped from Vierling's car. A moment later, his sedan disappeared down the parking garage ramp. Vierling took a deep breath, then let it out slowly. He had fulfilled his part of the deal and then some. He hoped he never saw Ed Sutton again.

11

MOSCOW, RUSSIA

Christine O'Connor peered out the window of the C-32 executive transport, the military version of Boeing's 757. Designated Air Force One when the president was aboard, or Air Force Two when the vice president was being flown, it had no designation today, since it was transporting Christine to Moscow. Before departing Washington, D.C., she had accepted Kalinin's offer to join him at his summer residence on the shore of the Black Sea. Kalinin had been pleased, and he'd requested she add a stop in Bucharest during her return trip. Transportation to Gelendzhik would be arranged from there. Christine had an inkling as to why she wasn't heading directly to the Black Sea from Moscow, but Kalinin didn't elaborate.

The C-32 began its descent, passing through the clouds to reveal a sprawling metropolis—the capital of the Russian Federation and home to twelve million. The aircraft touched down at Moscow's Vnukovo International Airport, and Christine descended the staircase onto the tarmac. She was preceded by two Diplomatic Security Service agents and followed by her aide, plus a subject matter expert who would assist with the more detailed aspects of the nuclear arms reduction treaty as it neared its final version.

Christine spotted her Russian counterpart, National Security Advisor Sergei Ivanov, leaning against a black sedan. Christine was handling the negotiations from the American side due to her assignment as the president's national security advisor—combined with the experience she'd gained as the director of nuclear defense policy—while Russia defaulted to the Ministry of Foreign Affairs, which had negotiated New START. Beside Ivanov stood Mark Johnson, Christine's interpreter for the negotiations, supplied by the American embassy in Moscow.

After exchanging greetings, Christine and Johnson joined Ivanov in the back of his sedan, while the rest of her entourage followed behind in another car. By the time the vehicles pulled up to Hotel National, not far from the Kremlin, darkness had enveloped the Russian capital. While the bellhops collected her luggage, Christine entered the hotel lobby where she was met by Barry Graham, an aide to the U.S. ambassador to Russia. He handed Christine the keycard to her room on the tenth floor.

Weary from the long flight, Christine looked forward to a good night's sleep. After entering her room and receiving her luggage, she went to draw the curtains, stopping to gaze out the window; her room offered a stunning view of the five palaces and four cathedrals enclosed within the Kremlin walls. After surveying the impressive sight for a moment, she pulled the curtains shut.

Daybreak arrived quicker than Christine had hoped. After stopping for a cup of strong coffee in the lobby, she stepped into an embassy sedan waiting at the hotel entrance. Inside the car was her interpreter, Mark Johnson. The two DSS agents, along with Christine's aide and nuclear arms expert, followed in an identical car. Moments later, the sedans passed within the six-hundred-year-old Kremlin walls, pulling to a halt in front of the triangular-shaped Kremlin Senate, the Russian version of the White House, with its distinctive green dome.

National Security Advisor Sergei Ivanov was there to greet her again. He escorted Christine and her staff to the third floor of the building, entering a twenty-by-sixty-foot conference room containing a polished ebony table capable of seating thirty persons. As before, on one side of the table sat Maksim Posniak, director of security and disarmament in Russia's Ministry of Foreign Affairs, who had negotiated the previous nuclear arms reduction treaty for Russia. Also present was Posniak's aide, who'd take notes, plus a Russian interpreter, although neither side had needed one for the previous discussions. Posniak's accent was thick, but his English understandable.

Also waiting in the conference room was Russia's new minister of defense, Anton Nechayev. The three men at the table rose as Christine entered.

Christine had reviewed Nechayev's file during the flight. He had a similar background as Chernov, having spent a few years in the Russian Ground Forces. He'd left military service after his first tour and entered politics soon thereafter. Due to an unexpected vacancy in Kalinin's administration, thanks to Christine, Nechayev had become Russia's new minister of defense.

Considering she had killed his predecessor, Christine wasn't sure how to interact with Nechayev. Russia and the United States were technically at war at the time and Christine had simply played her part in the conflict. But that didn't lessen the gravity of what she'd done. She felt uncomfortable in Nechayev's presence, and she wondered if he was too. However, if the new defense minister felt awkward, he didn't let on.

"Welcome back to Moscow, Miss O'Connor. I hope you had a pleasant flight." He extended his hand, shaking Christine's firmly, adding a smile. It was as if nothing unusual had occurred during her last trip to Russia.

After a short discussion, Nechayev ended with, "I leave you in Director Posniak's capable hands. But before I go, I must ask. Will you be attending the state dinner Friday night?"

"Yes," Christine answered. "Thank you for inviting me. I'd be honored to attend." The last part was a lie. The state dinner was in honor of Belarusian President Alexander Lukashenko.

Since the establishment of Belarus following the dissolution of the Soviet Union, there had been only one president, and Lukashenko's five-term presidency along with accusations of voter fraud had led some Western journalists to label Belarus "Europe's last dictatorship." Then there was Lukashenko's supportive role in Russia's invasion of Ukraine, which was undoubtedly the reason for the state dinner.

Christine had considered declining the invitation but decided to follow protocol. The way Russia and the United States were behaving was simultaneously maddening and comforting. Both countries carried on as if nothing unpleasant had recently occurred.

Nechayev and Ivanov departed the conference room.

Christine turned to Posniak as she settled into her chair. "Let's get started, shall we?"

12

THE BLACK SEA

USS *MICHIGAN* (SSGN 727)

With his submarine at periscope depth, Captain Murray Wilson sat in his chair on the starboard side of the Conn listening to the speaker, which was broadcasting intercepts from the submarine's Electronic Support Measures sensor. A few feet away, the submarine's Officer of the Deck circled on the port periscope, scanning the horizon for contacts. This afternoon's trip toward the surface had been uneventful, and the only scheduled tasks were a radio broadcast download and a satellite position fix for the submarine's inertial navigators. After the tense battles following Russia's invasion of Eastern Europe, Wilson welcomed the calm scenario.

During the short but intense conflict with Russia, Wilson had sunk four frigates left behind in the Black Sea, and no surface combatants had returned from the larger battle in the Indian Ocean. However, three of the Black Sea Fleet's five Kilo class submarines had been spotted heading up the Turkish Straits from the Mediterranean. They were currently in port, getting refitted and rearmed, as had *Michigan*.

Following the conflict, *Michigan* had stopped in Guam for a weapons loadout. Fully rearmed, and after being vectored under the polar ice cap into the Barents Sea for a short mission, the formidable guided missile submarine had returned to the Black Sea, taking station on Russia's southwest border in case President Kalinin got another bright idea.

Although *Michigan* was built as a ballistic missile submarine, it was a far different ship today than when it was launched three decades ago. With the implementation of the Strategic Offensive Reductions Treaty, the Navy had converted the four oldest Ohio class submarines into guided missile and special warfare platforms. Twenty-two of *Michigan*'s twenty-four missile tubes had been outfitted with seven-pack Tomahawk launchers, with the remaining two tubes providing access to two Dry Deck Shelters attached to the missile deck. For this deployment, one shelter carried a SEAL Delivery Vehicle—a mini-sub used to transport Navy SEALs miles underwater for clandestine operations—while the other shelter contained two Rigid Hull Inflatable Boats.

During the conversion from ballistic to guided missile submarines, *Michigan* and her three sister ships had received a slew of tactical system upgrades. The combat control consoles were now the most modern in the submarine fleet, as were *Michigan*'s new sonar, electronic surveillance, and radio suites. The torpedoes aboard were also the newest in the Navy's arsenal: MK 48 MOD 7 torpedoes, the most advanced heavyweight torpedo in the world. *Michigan*'s most valuable assets, however, were in the Missile Compartment. Aboard *Michigan* were two platoons of Navy SEALs, ready should their services be required, along with sixty tons of munitions stored in two of *Michigan*'s missile tubes: small arms, grenade launchers, limpet mines . . . anything a SEAL team might need.

"Conn, Nav. GPS fix received," the Quartermaster announced.

Wilson's thoughts returned to the reasons for their trip to periscope depth as the first of the expected reports arrived—a satellite fix of the submarine's position.

"Nav, Conn. Aye." Lieutenant Victor Clark, the Officer of the Deck this afternoon, acknowledged the Quartermaster.

A moment later, Radio completed its task. "Conn, Radio. Download complete."

Clark announced, "All stations, Conn. Going deep. Helm ahead two-thirds. Dive, make your depth two hundred feet."

The watchstanders acknowledged and *Michigan* tilted down toward the safety of deep water. When the periscope optics slipped beneath the sea's surface, Clark reached up and twisted the locking ring, and the periscope slid silently downward.

Not long thereafter, a radioman entered Control and handed Wilson the message board. Wilson flipped through the messages, skimming the contents.

When he finished, he handed the board to Lieutenant Clark.

"Any orders, sir?" Clark asked.

"Nope," Wilson replied. "All quiet on the Russian front."

13

MOSCOW, RUSSIA

"It is done," Director Posniak announced, adding a rare smile. He reached across the Kremlin conference table, extending a hand to Christine. The week had flown by as Christine and Posniak hammered out the remaining details to the new nuclear arms reduction treaty. There'd been a few sticking points, which had taken until Friday afternoon to resolve, but the timing was perfect. Russia's state dinner was tonight, then Christine would head to Kalinin's summer residence in the morning. Christine glanced at her watch. It was 5 p.m., leaving just enough time to return to her hotel and change from a business suit into a formal evening gown.

Christine thanked Posniak for his assistance and bid farewell, and it wasn't long before she stepped into her room at Hotel National. She donned a high-neck, open-back turquoise dress with lace sleeves, accessorized with diamond earrings, matching pendant, and turquoise heels. She returned to the hotel entrance, where a black limousine waited, along with Christine's interpreter, Mark Johnson, who had switched from a business suit into a tuxedo.

After the car passed through the Kremlin's Borovitskaya Gate, it pulled to a halt not far from the Kremlin Senate, stopping behind a procession of limousines depositing their guests for the evening's event. As the men and women stepped from their cars onto a red carpet, they were welcomed by Kremlin officials who escorted them into the green-domed building.

Christine's car inched forward, eventually reaching the red carpet. Stepping from the sedan, Christine and Johnson were escorted by a young man to the building's third floor, entering a ballroom with crystal chandeliers illuminating a glossy parquet floor. The room was faced with white marble, with two walls decorated with floor-to-ceiling paintings. Moscow was depicted on one wall and St. Petersburg on the other, symbolizing the centuries-long rivalry between the historic and "northern" capitals of Russia.

There was a receiving line just inside the ballroom, where Russian President Yuri Kalinin and Belarusian President Alexander Lukashenko greeted their guests. Christine wasn't thrilled about shaking hands with President Lukashenko, a man who accumulated power and profit at the expense of his countrymen, and who had joined forces with Russia to invade Ukraine.

Christine reached Lukashenko, who was first in line, and his greeting was cold. He offered no smile and a brief handshake, moving Christine along quickly. In contrast, Kalinin smiled warmly and his handshake lingered, and he took a moment to talk with her. The usual pleasantries: how was her trip and had she taken advantage of her evenings off, taking in Moscow's sights?

Kalinin was a handsome man, about six feet tall

and two hundred pounds, and quite charismatic. In a different time and place, Christine could envision a relationship with him. But as Russia's president and considering his recent transgressions, the prospect of a romantic involvement seemed impossible. However, establishing a strong friendship with him had its advantages—like staying alive—even if the relationship failed to develop further.

Kalinin released his handshake and offered a final smile before turning to the next guest. With Johnson's help, Christine mingled with the exclusive crowd while additional dignitaries worked their way through the receiving line. On the other side of the ballroom, Kalinin's chief of the general staff, General Andropov, talked with several other military officers, including the commanders-in-chief of Russia's Ground and Aerospace Forces and Fleet Admiral Lipovsky. Waiters in tuxedos carried silver platters of drinks and hors d'oeuvres through the crowd, and Christine selected a glass of champagne when one was offered.

Several Russian dignitaries advanced and introduced themselves, with most needing the help of Christine's interpreter. The conversations covered nothing of substance, as if she were a tourist visiting Moscow. She was talking with two men when they glanced over Christine's shoulder, then suddenly excused themselves. Christine felt a presence behind her. She turned to find Josef Hippchenko, Russia's new SVR director.

"May we speak in private?" Hippchenko shifted his gaze to Christine's interpreter. Like Gorev, Hippchenko spoke excellent English.

Christine nodded to Johnson, who looked around, spotting the American ambassador. "I'll be with the ambassador when you need me."

Johnson left quickly, leaving Christine alone with the SVR director. Unlike Defense Minister Nechayev, Hippchenko made no effort to gloss over what Christine had done during her last trip to Russia.

"It is remarkable that you are allowed to set foot on Russian soil without being arrested."

Christine forced a smile. "Diplomatic immunity."

But then she recalled her conversation with the SVR agent in her townhouse, about the story the Russian administration had fabricated for the public.

"Actually, why would I be arrested for a boating accident? It was a horrible tragedy, claiming both Chernov and Director Gorev."

"An excellent point," Hippchenko replied. "You were fortunate you weren't aboard. Of course, I'd have preferred you were."

She took a sip of her champagne. "Are you always this charming?"

"Usually, I make an effort. I've made an exception in your case."

Christine considered stepping away. It was clear Hippchenko's only goal was to intimidate her. But then she decided to make the best of the situation.

"I had a visit from one of your minions the other day."

"You don't say," Hippchenko replied. "Did you enjoy the conversation?"

"The next time an SVR agent steps foot in my home—"

"I know Christine," Hippchenko interrupted. "I was in Yuri's office when you called, and he put you on speakerphone. If another SVR agent breaks into your home, you'll kill him yourself—good luck with that, by the way—or have one of your lackeys at Langley do it."

Christine was taken aback. She hadn't realized

Kalinin and Hippchenko were that close. Then again, Kalinin was a former SVR director and had undoubtedly handpicked Hippchenko.

"You've known Yuri for a while?"

"We joined the SVR at the same time and spent a few years in the field together. We are good friends."

Hippchenko's eyes moved to the scar on her cheek. It was thin and would fade over time, she'd been told, but not completely. While wearing makeup, the blemish was barely discernible, and she wondered why Hippchenko had noticed it.

"I'm not a sadistic animal like Gorev," he said. "But we share one trait. I will do what is in Russia's and Yuri's best interests, removing any obstacle that threatens either. Do you understand?"

Hippchenko *was* like Gorev, in more ways than one. But Christine wasn't going to be intimidated by him either.

"I'm a little unclear," Christine replied. "Could you spell it out for me?"

He gritted his teeth for a moment, then smiled. "I see why Kalinin likes you so much. You are a lot like Natasha." The SVR director leaned closer, lowering his voice. "However, there are other influential people in Russia, me included, who *don't* like you. Be careful."

Christine was about to respond when President Kalinin approached. Hippchenko pulled back as Kalinin eyed him.

The Russian president turned to Christine. "I see Director Hippchenko has been bothering you, despite my direction."

"Actually," Christine replied, "he's been quite helpful, suggesting places in Moscow to visit when I have free time. He even recommended I ask you to take me to the Bolshoi Theatre." She smiled at Hippchenko.

"He did?" Kalinin turned to the director.

Hippchenko replied, "Of course. I recommend *Anna Karenina*. I was thinking of a balcony suite, in full view of everyone in attendance. I'm sure there'd be a cell phone video clip of you two, holding hands, on the evening news."

The smile faded from Kalinin's face. When he turned back to Christine, Hippchenko's eyes narrowed.

Christine reached toward Kalinin's arm, running her hand along his forearm. "So you're saying I shouldn't wrap my arm around Yuri's waist right now?"

Hippchenko turned and left.

Kalinin watched him disappear into the crowd. "You'll have to forgive Josef. SVR directors can be a bit overzealous at times."

"You were the SVR director."

"And I was a bit overzealous at times." He smiled. "But Josef has a point. Our friendship must remain discreet for now. He's made the necessary travel arrangements so your detour from Bucharest to Gelendzhik isn't discovered."

"Hippchenko is in charge of my travel arrangements?"

"You have nothing to worry about."

Christine took another sip of champagne, unconvinced by Kalinin's assurance.

The ballroom lights flashed, signaling it was time to enter the dining room.

"I will probably not have an opportunity to talk with you again tonight," Kalinin said. "But we'll have time at Gelendzhik."

"I'm looking forward to it."

14

MOSCOW, RUSSIA

It was almost midnight when General Andropov entered his office in the Ministry of Defense building. The state dinner at the Kremlin had dragged on longer than he'd hoped, but he and the other leaders of Russia's military had finally slipped away. Before departing his office this afternoon, he'd drawn the curtains so no one with the interest, and ability, would notice the late night meeting. He sat at his desk as the two colonel generals and admiral took their seats opposite him.

"Have you decided?" Andropov asked.

Colonel General Volodin replied, "Do you have a Zolotov controller?"

"I do. We now have the ability to activate the option ourselves. Based on the timing of the American exercise, we must implement the option tomorrow night. Everything is ready, aside from your commitment."

There was no immediate response from the three men until General Glukov raised the critical issue.

"And what of President Kalinin?"

"He will be detained, kept sequestered so he cannot countermand our orders. To the public and the rest of the military, it will appear as if we are executing the president's desires."

"And the long-term plan for him?"

"After we gain control of the objectives and verify the United States will not intervene, we will return Kalinin to power. Once he sees what we've accomplished, he will take full credit for the operation. He won't reveal it was initiated without his authorization. The revelation that he lost control of the military would be politically disastrous. All will be forgiven."

Of the last part, Andropov wasn't certain. However, since he had no intention of returning Kalinin to power, the issue was moot. There would be no repercussions.

Glukov glanced at the two men beside him. Colonel General Volodin was the first to nod, followed by Admiral Lipovsky.

Turning back to Andropov, Glukov declared, "We will support all efforts related to this operation, with or without Kalinin's authorization."

Andropov suppressed a smile. "I appreciate your support. Operational plans will be provided to you by courier in the morning. I will need you at your command centers by nightfall."

After a short pause, Andropov said, "Kalinin is scheduled to spend the weekend at Gelendzhik. I will visit him tomorrow evening."

15

GELENDZHIK, RUSSIA

Atop a three-hundred-foot-high plateau overlooking a pebble-sand beach, with the scenic Caucasus Mountains rising to the east, lies the forty-acre Residence at Cape Idokopas, often referred to as Putin's Palace. Dominating the complex is an Italianate mansion, similar in design to the tsars' Winter Palace in St. Petersburg, completed at a cost of over one billion dollars. The sprawling compound has its own church, casino, and three-pad heliport, along with a summer amphitheater, courtyard swimming pools, teahouse, and staff apartments.

Just before noon, under a clear blue sky, a black limousine approached the massive granite facade surrounding the complex, stopping before wrought iron gates crowned with a golden double-headed eagle. The gates slowly parted, and the sedan pulled forward to complete the last leg of Christine O'Connor's journey.

After departing Moscow this morning, her C-32 transport had stopped in Bucharest. After descending onto the airport tarmac, she'd boarded a Dassault Falcon executive jet and was airborne minutes later, landing at Gelendzhik Airport, a few miles from Kalinin's residence on the shore of the Black Sea.

As the limousine coasted to a halt in the inner courtyard, Christine spotted three men waiting at the base of the steps leading to the mansion entrance. She recognized one man as Andrei Yelchin, Kalinin's executive assistant. When Christine stepped from the limousine, Yelchin greeted her while the other two men attended to her luggage.

After exchanging pleasantries, Yelchin escorted her up the steps, where two servants opened towering French doors. Christine entered a stunning two-story foyer lined with white marble, illuminated by a triple set of chandeliers hanging from a ceiling painted in the High Renaissance style, with scenes reminiscent of Michelangelo's work in the Vatican's Sistine Chapel. Directly ahead were two curved staircases spreading up in a "Y" design, leading to the second level of the three-story mansion.

Yelchin led Christine up the right staircase to a row of bedroom suites, opening the door to an exquisitely furnished room with gilded ceilings, complete with a king-size canopy bed with white drapes. He informed her they'd be heading out on Kalinin's yacht, then waited outside while Christine changed into an outfit she'd packed for the weekend: tan capri pants and blue blouse.

After she rejoined Yelchin in the hallway, he led her down to the main floor and through a set of French doors into a study lined with mahogany bookshelves and paneling. Russian President Yuri Kalinin, wearing khaki slacks and a collared sport shirt, rose from his chair behind a matching mahogany desk.

"Christine, welcome to Cape Idokopas." He circled around his desk and offered a warm, two-handed shake. "I'm glad we are finally able to get together." He checked his watch. "Are you hungry? We will have lunch aboard my yacht as we enjoy the beautiful weather."

The weather was indeed beautiful, and Christine was hungry as well.

"Lunch aboard your yacht sounds great."

Kalinin escorted Christine through the mansion's passageways, joined by four black-suited presidential security service agents along the way, then entered an elevator and descended several hundred feet, exiting into a tunnel. They emerged from the base of the cliff onto a dock, where Christine and the five men boarded the president's yacht.

Kalinin showed Christine around *Sirius,* a 177-foot-long, five-deck ship, complete with a cinema, two whirlpools, a glass-encased waterfall, and wine cellar, able to accommodate eleven overnight guests and twelve crew members. They stopped by the bar, where a crewmember poured Kalinin a glass of cognac and made a White Russian for Christine. The aroma of rosemary and thyme filled the air as Kalinin led Christine past the kitchen, where a chef was preparing lunch. After climbing to the top level of the yacht, Christine and the Russian president settled into cushioned seats on the starboard side of the flying bridge. Crewmembers took in the lines and *Sirius* angled out to sea.

The weather couldn't have been better, with the temperature in the low eighties and a light breeze kicking in as *Sirius* picked up speed, cutting through the Black Sea. They cruised southeast down the coast as Kalinin pointed out the sights along the shore. In the distance, rolling green hills ascended toward the Caucasus Mountains.

After they passed Sochi, Russia's largest and most popular resort city, a cove drew into view, containing a villa atop a rock outcropping overlooking the water. Christine examined the rubble of what once was a flagstone patio, and her pulse quickened. Her eyes shifted to the boathouse by the shore, and her thoughts took her into a dark room where she'd been handcuffed to an overhead pipe; a room where Semyon Gorev had jammed a pistol into her mouth.

Kalinin was talking, but Christine seemed oblivious to his comments, staring toward an alcove along the shore. Her complexion had turned pale and her breathing shallow.

She stood without a word and descended the staircase, disappearing into the level below. Kalinin studied the distant alcove, realizing it contained Chernov's villa. He recalled what Christine had been forced to endure, then realized how insensitive he'd been. He had directed *Sirius*'s captain to head southeast, past Chernov's villa.

Kalinin headed below, spotting Christine leaning against a credenza, staring at her reflection in a mirror. He stopped behind her and placed his hands gently on the side of each shoulder. "I'm sorry," he said. Her eyes shifted, catching his reflection in the mirror. He added, "I should have been more thoughtful."

Christine turned toward him. "It's okay." Her voice was listless and she failed to make eye contact. As Kalinin searched for appropriate words, he watched emotion play across her face. Then her features suddenly hardened and her eyes locked on to his.

"No, it's not okay," she said, her words sharp. "It's *your* fault this happened." She pointed her finger at him, poking him in the chest with each sentence. "*You* invaded Ukraine and Lithuania. *You* blackmailed the United States and NATO." Kalinin stepped back, creating space between them, but Christine advanced. "It's *your* fault I ended up in that alcove."

The pitch of her voice rose, her face turning red with anger. Kalinin continued retreating, nearly tripping over an ottoman before his back hit the bulkhead. Christine jabbed him in the chest again. "It's *your* fault that I—" She stopped, her hand frozen in midair.

It was Christine's turn to search for words, but Kalinin spoke first. "I did what I thought was best for my country. I intended you no harm." He waited for a response, but Christine remained quiet, the color slowly fading from her face. Kalinin said, "Please accept my apology."

She stared at him for a moment, then headed toward one of the guest staterooms, closing the door behind her.

Kalinin took a deep breath, running a hand through his hair. Hippchenko was wrong. A relationship with Christine would be *far* more complicated than he'd predicted.

He returned to the flying bridge, unable to enjoy the beautiful weather, his thoughts dwelling on Christine as he lingered over his cognac. His shoulders were tense and he stared more into his glass than upon the scenic shore sliding slowly by. Lunch was almost ready, and there'd been no sign of Christine.

She suddenly reappeared, a refilled drink in her hand. She sat on the sofa beside him, a bit closer than normal.

"I'm sorry," she said.

Her words seemed sincere, but her voice remained flat. Kalinin tried to decipher the mixed signals, concluding she hadn't completely worked through the issue. He decided the best tack was to put the matter behind them for now.

"You have nothing to apologize for," he said.

Christine looked up. "You do," she said, her eyes catching his. Then she added, "But I accept your apology," and she smiled.

The tension faded from Kalinin's shoulders and he returned the smile. He decided to take a chance and draped his arm along the top of the cushion, behind Christine. She leaned back into his arm. Kalinin felt warm, unsure whether it was from the cognac or Christine's proximity. Perhaps their relationship would develop further after all.

He'd find out tonight.

16

KUBINKA AIR BASE, RUSSIA

Sixty kilometers west of Moscow, General Sergei Andropov stood on the tarmac beside the Ilyushin IL-76 aircraft, its jet engines spinning up as Colonel Vagit Savvin motioned for his handpicked men to board. Andropov waited impatiently while the 120 armed soldiers boarded the troop transport. A short distance away, twenty armored personnel carriers and infantry fighting vehicles were loaded aboard Antonov An-124s. Although Andropov expected no resistance from Kalinin's servants and was confident the president's security detachment would be quickly overwhelmed, he was taking no chances.

Colonel Savvin approached. "The communication equipment is aboard," he reported, referring to the jammers that would disrupt all cell phone signals within a one-hundred-meter radius of Kalinin's mansion. Prior to commencing the operation, the landline would also be cut. Although Kalinin's security detail would be quickly overrun once Andropov's men stormed the residence, he had to be sure no one was notified of the situation. Andropov would arrive at Gelendzhik accompanied only by his aide, with the rest of the men held back until Kalinin was in custody.

The last of the armored personnel carriers were loaded aboard the An-124s and the ramps lifted slowly shut. The most important piece of equipment, however, was in Andropov's hand. A briefcase delivered to his home several days ago. After the last soldier boarded the Ilyushin IL-76, Andropov followed Savvin into the transport for the ninety-minute flight south.

17

GELENDZHIK, RUSSIA

The orange-reddish sun hovered only a few degrees above the horizon by the time Kalinin's yacht returned to Gelendzhik, coasting to a halt alongside the pier. The conversation during lunch and the rest of the afternoon had been light and the time had passed quickly, accompanied by quite a few laughs while Kalinin tried to teach Christine a few Russian words. Despite several mispronunciations, she was a quick learner and had virtually no accent, which wasn't surprising since she'd spent her childhood listening to her and Jake's moms speaking in Russian over tea.

Kalinin escorted Christine onto the pier, joined by his presidential security service detachment, and they soon reached the dual staircase in the foyer leading to the bedroom suites. Dinner would be at eight, giving Christine enough time to freshen up and change into an elegant evening gown. She ascended one staircase while Kalinin climbed the other.

After washing her face and redoing her makeup, Christine slipped into a one-shoulder, sleeveless, red satin dress that hugged her curves, with a slit to the middle of her right thigh. It was a dress she hadn't worn since before her last visit to China's Great Hall of the People. Tonight, however, she would no longer avoid it, putting her blemishes on full display; the three bullet hole scars on her arm, shoulder, and thigh.

She made one final assessment in the bathroom mirror, then headed down the hallway. When she entered the foyer, she spotted Kalinin waiting at the bottom of the stairs wearing a blue suit jacket over an open-collared white dress shirt. His gaze surveyed her body as she descended the stairs, but if he noticed the scars, he didn't comment. He extended his arm as his eyes locked on to hers.

Christine intertwined her arm in his and he escorted her toward dinner. To Christine's surprise, they passed the dining room and kept going, emerging onto a poolside patio containing a candlelit table for two. Kalinin helped Christine into her chair, then slid into his.

A sommelier appeared within seconds, and after learning what type of wine Christine preferred, Kalinin selected a bottle of Cabernet Sauvignon. The sommelier returned a moment later with the wine, pouring a sample for Kalinin. After a short swirl and taste, Kalinin nodded his approval. The sommelier poured two glasses as the first serving of a five-course dinner arrived. The meal was delicious and the wine exquisite.

The conversation remained light and the wine flowed freely, and after Christine's second glass, she began to feel the alcohol's effect. Her thoughts wandered, touching on several issues but always returning to Kalinin and why she had agreed to spend the weekend with him. Notwithstanding the SVR death sentence and the value of remaining in Kalinin's good graces, she had trouble reconciling her feelings for him. Personally, he was charming, but how could she overlook his sins: invading two countries and attempting to blackmail the United States from intervening?

Eventually, the topic came up. Kalinin was unrepentant, defending his actions to reestablish a zone of friendly countries along Russia's western border, even if it required military force. It became clear that in Kalinin's mind, this buffer zone was essential, and Christine's frustration mounted as she failed to convince him he was wrong. As she pressed the issue, Kalinin shifted gears.

"Additionally, there are many Russians trapped inside other countries. The borders of European countries have been fluid for two millennia, and the current borders do not recognize the desires of the people. Russians should be in Russia, not Ukraine or the Baltic States, simply because some king traded away land that wasn't his to begin with. Rectifying past wrongs, placing Russians in Russia, is not such a terrible thing."

"Great idea, Yuri. You should give it a try. Oh, wait. You did, and we sank most of your Navy."

Displeasure flashed across Kalinin's face. He reached for his wineglass. "There is an edge to your personality that I hadn't detected before this weekend."

Christine took a deep breath. Hardison wasn't the only one who'd noticed the change. It had begun in China's Great Hall of the People, when Jake Harrison, the left side of his chest drenched in blood, placed a pistol in one of her hands and a flash drive in the other. Although she took several bullets in the process, she'd emptied the pistol magazine with a corresponding body count. At Ice Station Nautilus, she'd jammed an ice pick in one man's temple and through another man's throat. But those deaths were unavoidable. Her life and the lives of others had hung in the balance.

What she'd done at Chernov's villa was different. She'd crossed the line. She was about to slip away, undetected, when she chose instead to place a gun in Gorev's mouth. On the shore of the Black Sea, she'd killed a man for no other reason than . . . she *wanted* to.

Since that moment, she'd been struggling with who she was, the principles she stood for, and had been unable to reconcile her action with her values. An image appeared in her mind—of her standing above Gorev, looking down at his vacant eyes, his blood and brains splattered on the upholstery. She felt a lump in her throat as tears formed in her eyes.

Christine placed her napkin on the table. "Coming here was a mistake." She stood and turned to leave.

Kalinin caught her wrist.

She faced him and he released her.

"Stay," he said. "You must stop running away from what you've done."

Christine vacillated, unsure if she could continue the conversation, much less wanted to. Finally, she asked, "Have you killed in cold blood?"

"That is a complicated question," Kalinin answered.

"I don't think it's complicated at all."

Kalinin countered, "Your problem is that you are too idealistic, your values too open-ended. They need to be constrained inside a framework that helps you distinguish between right and wrong." As Christine contemplated his words, he said, "I am not guided by personal gain. I do what is in Russia's best interest. That is what forms my values and shapes my actions."

"So that's how you sleep at night after invading two countries?"

Kalinin leaned back in his chair. "Yes."

He gestured toward her chair. "Please."

After a moment of indecision, she returned to her seat.

Kalinin refilled her wineglass. "I realize a relationship between us will be difficult, if not impossible. But let's put the past behind us, at least for the weekend, and focus on the future." He held his glass up for a toast.

Christine's eyes went from his glass to hers. Burying the past seemed like a good idea. She touched her glass against his. "To the future."

President Kalinin's executive assistant approached. "I apologize for interrupting," Yelchin said, "but General Andropov and his aide are here. The general says he needs to talk with you about the Zapad war games. There has been a terrible incident."

Kalinin's eyes shifted to Christine. "Where is General Andropov now?"

"He is waiting in the foyer."

After considering things, Kalinin said, "I'll meet him in my study. Do not mention Miss O'Connor."

When Yelchin departed, Kalinin turned to Christine. "I don't want General Andropov to see you. He isn't pleased with some of my recent decisions, and I don't want to arm him with information he could use against me. You can't stay here, nor can you return to your room undetected. Come with me."

Christine joined Kalinin, matching his pace as he strode toward his study. Once inside, he stopped beside a mahogany panel in the back. He flipped a rosette to the side, revealing a security pad. He punched in a code and the adjacent mahogany panel slid sideways, revealing a dark opening. Kalinin guided her inside.

"Wait in here. I'll get you once Andropov is gone."

Christine stepped through the opening and a heavy metal door slid shut behind her.

18

GELENDZHIK, RUSSIA

Yuri Kalinin settled into the chair behind his desk, waiting for General Andropov. Footsteps echoed off the marble floor, growing louder until there was a knock on the study doors. Kalinin acknowledged the knock and the doors opened, revealing his executive assistant standing between General Andropov and an Army colonel Kalinin didn't recognize. Andropov gripped a briefcase while the colonel carried a sealed classified courier pouch. Kalinin tried to read the two Army officers. Andropov's face was an impassive mask, whereas tension registered from the colonel.

Before Kalinin could assess further, Andropov spoke. "President Kalinin, we need to discuss an issue in private." The general glanced at Yelchin.

Kalinin waved his executive assistant away, and Yelchin closed the doors as he left. "What is the issue?" Kalinin asked.

Andropov glanced at the colonel, who placed the courier pouch on the edge of Kalinin's desk and entered its combination. After opening the pouch, he slid his hand inside and withdrew a pistol, which he leveled at Kalinin's head.

Kalinin assessed the situation, then turned to Andropov. "What do you want?"

General Andropov placed the heavy briefcase on Kalinin's desk.

19

OFFUTT AIR FORCE BASE

Just south of Omaha, Nebraska, within the confines of Offutt Air Force Base, lies the United States Strategic Command or USSTRATCOM, one of nine unified commands in the U.S. Department of Defense. Established in 1992 as the successor to Strategic Air Command, USSTRATCOM is responsible for nuclear strategic deterrence, global strike, and operating the Defense Department's Global Information Grid.

Deep beneath the surface inside USSTRATCOM's new $1.2 billion headquarters building, Admiral Bob Aronson sat in his chair in the command bunker, a facility encased in a concrete shell inside a thick steel cube. Large displays were affixed to the far bulkhead, displaying the status of America's nuclear assets. Every console in the five-row command center was manned, with supervisors pacing behind them, occasionally stopping to look over an operator's shoulder.

About to commence this afternoon was a rare combined strategic deterrence exercise, testing the response of all three legs of America's nuclear triad. In a few minutes, USSTRATCOM would simulate a nuclear attack from country *Orange,* and Admiral Aronson's staff would assess the *Blue* force response.

Simulated ICBM launches would occur and B-2 bombers loaded with dummy warheads would sortie. The exercise also included an FCET—Follow-on Commander's Evaluation Test—an actual launch of a Trident II missile from a submarine. The missile's nuclear warheads had been replaced with inert instrumented payloads that would record data through every phase of the missile's flight, all the way until impact far out in the Atlantic Ocean.

Admiral Aronson's eyes shifted from the main screen, displaying the status of America's nuclear assets, to a live video feed from just off the East Coast. It was a bland video, displaying the Atlantic Ocean with whitecaps cresting the swells in the brisk wind. Lurking several hundred feet below the surface, however, was USS *Maryland,* an Ohio class ballistic missile submarine, with its communication buoy deployed, floating a few feet below the surface.

When the clock struck 14:00:00, the exercise began.

Warnings flashed on several consoles in the first row, and a supervisor shifted the main display screen to country *Orange,* which was the same size and shape as the Russian Federation and in the same location. Triangles appeared at several dozen ICBM silo locations in *Orange,* and red lines began arching westward. The command center's computer algorithms took over, calculating the warhead destinations. White circles appeared in the United States around several major cities and military bases. As the red traces arched toward their apex, the circles contracted as the algorithms calculated the aim points more accurately.

The information was passed to the National Military Command Center in the Pentagon, where the watch captain in the Operations Center would simulate contacting the president and secretary of defense, who for this exercise were two Air Force colonels filling in. The faux president would be informed of the attack and after providing his authentication code, would authorize a nuclear response and select an attack option. For this exercise, the American response would mirror the *Orange* attack.

An Emergency War Order arrived on Admiral Aronson's console display, simulating the release of nuclear weapons. Not long thereafter, Emergency Action Messages were transmitted over all circuits, executing the training attack option specified in the War Order. Although ICBM launches would be simulated today, four B-2 bombers would sortie and the submarine leg of the nuclear triad would launch a Trident II missile.

Aronson watched a video feed from Whiteman Air Force Base in Missouri, observing four B-2 bombers take off, then shifted his attention to the Atlantic Ocean. A moment later, a Trident II missile emerged from the depths, its first-stage engine igniting once it cleared the surface, leaving behind a white trail as it raced upward.

20

GELENDZHIK, RUSSIA

Minutes earlier, after the heavy metal door closed behind Christine, low-level lights flickered on in the six-by-eight-foot room, growing brighter until fully lit. One wall was filled with a dozen video displays, all dark, with several rows of buttons beneath each monitor. On the counter beneath the displays were four backpacks, sitting beside four semiautomatic pistols in a stand, along with eight loaded magazines. Beside the pistols were four smartphones—green ruggedized military versions, each in a charging stand.

There was a single chair in front of the displays, and on the other end of the room was another closed metal door. The walls were made of concrete as were the ceiling and floor. After examining her surroundings further and finding nothing additional noteworthy, she rummaged through the backpacks. Each contained an identical assortment of items: a flashlight, dry food rations, and water bottles.

There was a button beside the far door, which Christine pressed. The door slid open, revealing a dark, musty passage. After retrieving a flashlight, she illuminated a staircase leading down until it disappeared in the darkness. She turned off the flashlight and closed the door.

Christine sank into the chair. After staring at the dark monitors for a while, she pressed one of the buttons beneath the far-left display. It energized, providing a view of the mansion entrance. She hit a different button beneath each display and was soon looking at eleven different sections of the mansion and surrounding grounds, plus one Russian television news feed. Her eyes were drawn to the monitor showing the study on the other side of the wall.

An Army colonel was pointing a gun at Kalinin's head.

Christine sucked in a sharp breath. Her eyes went to the four pistols, evaluating whether she should intercede.

Kalinin didn't seem fazed, though, sitting calmly at his desk as he spoke, but there was no sound from the video. Christine found what looked like a speaker button, selecting it to the desired monitor. The speaker energized as General Andropov placed a briefcase on Kalinin's desk.

Andropov opened the briefcase, revealing a Frankenstein version of a laptop, cell phone, external display, and trackball, wired into a custom-made circuit board. He looked up at Kalinin, then explained his plan.

He spoke in Russian.

Christine cursed quietly, wishing she had learned Russian. She listened as Andropov elaborated, trying to pick up a key word here or there, but nothing registered.

General Andropov reached into his uniform jacket, retrieving a handheld military radio, which he spoke into. Moments later, Christine noticed movement on one of the displays; twenty armored vehicles streaked toward the mansion gates. Kalinin answered the speakerphone on his desk with the Army colonel still pointing a pistol at him. The mansion gates opened and the vehicles streamed into the inner courtyard. After they ground to a halt, over a hundred men surged toward every entrance. Christine watched as some of the president's security detail tried to repel the soldiers and were gunned down in a fusillade of bullets. Others realized the futility of resistance and surrendered. It took only a few minutes before the entire mansion was under military control.

An Army officer entered the study with two other soldiers, weapons drawn. Andropov issued an order and the two soldiers approached Kalinin. The president stood and was escorted from the study by the three soldiers. Christine followed along on the monitors until Kalinin was placed in a bedroom suite on the second level. Two armed guards were posted outside.

After Kalinin departed the study, General Andropov took his seat behind the desk, placing the briefcase before him. He energized the laptop and a map of North America appeared on the screen, with several dozen symbols in the United States and western Atlantic Ocean. Andropov stared at the display, his forearms resting on Kalinin's desk, fingers interlaced. He kept checking his watch, but otherwise did nothing. As Christine wondered what was going on, a blue trace appeared on the map, originating in Missouri.

General Andropov magnified the display and the single trace separated into four. Andropov selected each trace, then entered several commands into the laptop. A moment later, another blue trace appeared in the Atlantic Ocean, just off the U.S. East Coast. Andropov selected that trace and the external display energized. A world map appeared and Andropov zoomed in toward the East Coast of the United States. He then clicked on a location in Washington, D.C., then hit *Enter*.

He closed the briefcase and left the study with it, accompanied by the Army colonel. Christine watched on the monitors as they descended several floors and entered an underground command center.

21

THE SPIRIT OF KITTY HAWK

High above Missouri, headed east, Air Force Major Carole Glover sat on the left side of the two-seat B-2 Spirit, one of the U.S. Air Force's long-range stealth bombers, monitoring the computer's automatic adjustments of the aircraft's flight control surfaces. The aircraft Glover was flying today was *The Spirit of Kitty Hawk,* the trailing bomber in a four-plane diamond formation, with each aircraft carrying sixteen bombs with inert payloads. For today's mission, the four B-2s would fly halfway across the Atlantic Ocean before turning around.

Glover examined the communication settings and additional cockpit electronics, including the new fully digital navigation system with terrain-following radar and GPS guidance, part of the B-2's once-a-decade cockpit modernization. After completing her assessment and assured that everything was operating satisfactorily, her eyes skimmed over additional components painted yellow, signifying emergency use only. Glover surveyed the yellow components more than usual, considering she was flying the bomber nicknamed *Christine.*

The complex flying-wing bombers sometimes had system failures during flight, and some of the aircraft were more reliable than others. *The Spirit of Missouri,* flying directly ahead, was the most reliable B-2, even though she was the oldest. Glover's aircraft, however, had its issues. Years earlier, while the bomber was in a maintenance hangar, its engines had ignited on their own. Other unusual failures had occurred and maintenance crews had nicknamed this B-2 bomber *Christine,* after the possessed homicidal Plymouth Fury in Stephen King's novel.

Glover glanced at the yellow ejection seat lever on her left.

Everything was operating perfectly today, and Glover settled in for the long flight. She turned to her copilot, Captain Bill Houston, planning to catch up on her friend's summer plans, when the B-2's engines extinguished and the cockpit went dark. The B-2 tilted downward and plummeted toward earth.

Glover reacted quickly, taking manual control of the flight surfaces via battery backup, trying to keep the flying-wing aircraft stable. She was about to curse at *Christine,* who had lived up to her reputation, when she noticed the other three bombers were also falling from the sky.

Houston tried a warm start of the engine electronics. When that failed, he rebooted the entire system.

No response.

He tried again. Still no response.

Without cockpit electronics, Glover had no idea what altitude they were passing through. Fortunately, it was daytime and a quick glance at the horizon told her they didn't have much longer. Houston tried a cold restart one final time. When there was no response, he informed Glover of the obvious.

She reached for the yellow lever.

22

OMAHA, NEBRASKA

In the back of USSTRATCOM's command center, Admiral Aronson monitored the nuclear-defense exercise. The initial response had gone as planned, with all three legs of the nuclear triad responding. Every ICBM silo had simulated its missile launch, B-2 bombers were aloft, and USS *Maryland* had launched a Trident II missile from just off the East Coast.

Aronson's attention was drawn to commotion on the left side of the command center, where two supervisors had gathered around one of the consoles, with the two adjacent operators leaning in. One of the supervisors spoke into his headset, and the command center's watch captain, also wearing a headset and seated beside Aronson, turned to the admiral.

"Sir, all four B-2s are losing altitude and we've lost communication with the crews."

Aronson was about to ask if he had any idea about what was going on when he was distracted by a disturbance on the other side of the command center. A supervisor shifted the main display to the western Atlantic Ocean; the Trident II missile had changed course, angling west.

The watch captain reported, "Sir, the Trident missile has altered course."

"I can see that," Aronson replied. "Where is it headed?"

"Don't know yet, sir. The missile's third-stage engine has resumed firing, altering the ballistic trajectory. The tracking algorithms aren't designed to—"

Admiral Aronson stood as red alarms began flashing on numerous control consoles.

What the hell is going on?

23

WASHINGTON, D.C.

It was just past two in the afternoon as the president's motorcade sped down 17th Street NW toward the White House. As the motorcade approached the Ellipse, the president spotted the forty-foot-tall Colorado blue spruce, transformed each winter into the National Christmas Tree. As his thoughts drifted back to the first winter he and his wife lit the tree, the motorcade screeched to a halt.

Seconds later, the president's door was yanked open and he was pulled from Cadillac One by a Secret Service agent. As the Secret Service detail surrounded him, shepherding him toward the nearest building, the head of the president's detail explained.

"We're under attack—ballistic missile!"

Atop several buildings surrounding the White House and Capitol building, surface-to-air missiles streaked upward. The president followed the white exhaust trails, spotting five reddish-orange objects descending toward the city. He almost froze when he realized what they were.

A U.S. nuclear response exercise was planned for today, which included a submarine-launched ballistic missile, and his thoughts went in several directions at once.

Could the Russians have misinterpreted the test launch and counterattacked?

There had been no warning.

How was that possible?

Neither NORAD nor the Joint Air Defense Operations Center at nearby Joint Base Anacostia-Bolling, with the latter in charge of safeguarding the skies above the national capital region, had provided the expected warning, one that should have arrived twenty or more minutes ago.

Along 17th Street NW, pedestrians were looking skyward or scurrying for cover, following the president's example. Unfortunately, against nuclear warheads, nothing in the area would provide sufficient protection. Neither Cadillac One nor the basement of the sturdiest building in the vicinity could withstand the carnage of a nuclear detonation, much less five, from such a close range. It looked like the warheads were headed toward the White House, only three blocks away.

The probability of destroying the descending warheads was minuscule. Nuclear warheads in the descent phase traveled at twenty times the speed of sound; not even the most sophisticated anti-ballistic missiles in the American arsenal could consistently intercept nuclear warheads traveling in the final phase.

A few seconds before warhead impact, the president and his security detail had only just begun to climb the steps toward the nearest building. They weren't going to make it. The head of the president's detail reached the same conclusion. He forced the president to the ground and ordered the agents to cover him with their bodies. As the president was smothered by his detail, one question in his mind stood out from the others.

How could this have happened?

24

WASHINGTON, D.C.

The ground trembled and a deafening roar filled the president's ears, followed by debris billowing past the president and his security detail. As the rumble faded, what surprised the president the most was—he was still alive. The descending warheads hadn't been nuclear.

Secret Service agents helped the president to his feet and he turned toward the White House. When the dust cleared, he was amazed to see the building still standing. But if the White House hadn't been the target, what had been attacked? His eyes went to the Capitol building in the distance; there was no apparent damage.

Abandoned vehicles and chunks of upturned earth littered the street. People slowly emerged from buildings, examining their surroundings and the sky. The wail of first responder sirens filled the air, and a violent crash caught the president's attention as a car sped through a red light at the nearest intersection, smashing into another vehicle whose driver was just as desperate to exit the city.

He started walking toward the White House, but the head of his security detail intervened. "Mr. President.

You should return to Cadillac One and we'll take you to an alternate location until we verify you're safe."

The president considered the recommendation, then asked, "Are there additional attacks?"

"No reports at the moment, Mr. President. But we can't be sure more won't occur."

"If whoever did this wanted me dead, I'd be dead," the president said. "Contact NORAD and JADOC. If it's clear, I'm heading to the White House."

The president stood alongside the street, surrounded by his detail, until he received the requested information. "NORAD and JADOC report no further attacks. Admiral Aronson at STRATCOM has requested a videocon as soon as possible."

"He knows who attacked us?"

"Yes, Mr. President. But he wouldn't share that information with me."

The president nodded, then headed toward the White House on foot, not bothering to brush the dust from his suit.

The White House grounds appeared in the distance; there were three large craters in the South Lawn, evenly spaced in an arc curving around the White House. After passing through the West Wing security gates, the president spotted two additional craters in the White House front lawn. The warheads had landed in a circle around the White House.

A message had been sent.

The president's anger began to simmer, his mind racing. Who was responsible? What was their objective? How had they accomplished the attack without warning?

Kevin Hardison was waiting at the West Wing entrance. "Mr. President, we have a conference with STRATCOM ready to go in the Situation Room."

The president entered the crowded Situation Room

and surveyed those present. The two persons he was most interested in joining him—SecDef and SecState—weren't there; Hardison informed him that the secretary of defense was in the National Military Command Center in the Pentagon, and although the secretary of state was only a few blocks away, the roads were gridlocked.

The president took his seat at the head of the table and fixed his eyes on the display on the far wall. Hardison announced to the microphone on the table, "Proceed with the videocon."

Admiral Bob Aronson, Commander of U.S. Strategic Command, appeared on screen. "Good afternoon, Mr. President."

It was afternoon, but decidedly not a good one. Whether from his poor choice of words or seeing the dust-covered president at the head of the table, Admiral Aronson winced.

"Who is responsible?" the president asked.

Aronson didn't immediately respond. It seemed he was choosing his words carefully after his poor greeting. Finally, he answered, "*We* are."

There was silence in the Situation Room as all eyes remained fixed on Aronson, who clarified his response. "We were conducting a nuclear response exercise today, testing all three legs of the nuclear triad. The exercise involved B-2 bomber sorties, simulated ICBM launches, and the Navy's annual test firing of a Trident missile."

"I recall being briefed on this exercise," the president said. "I don't recall an attack on Washington being part of it."

Aronson replied quickly, "The Trident ballistic missile veered off course. Fortunately, it was loaded with inert warheads for the exercise."

"Have you seen the impact craters?" the president

asked. "A perfect circle around the White House. This wasn't an accident."

"I concur, sir. In addition to the Trident missile issue, four B-2 bombers aloft during the exercise lost power and crashed. The situation is serious. Two legs of our nuclear triad have become unreliable, and the third is suspect until we determine the causes."

After the president digested the information, he said, "I understand, Admiral. Do you have anything else to add?"

"Not at the moment, sir."

"Keep me and SecDef informed when you learn anything new."

"Yes, sir."

The president leaned forward, selecting the video technician button on the conference table speakerphone. "We're done here."

The display went dark and the president turned to Lars Sikes, the White House press secretary. "Give me something in fifteen minutes. Leave out the B-2 bomber part for now. We'll figure out how to address it after the press connects the dots. They'll be fixated on Washington for a while."

It looked like the meeting had drawn to a close when the video technician's voice came across the Situation Room speakers. "Mr. President. Russian General Sergei Andropov, Chief of the General Staff, has requested a video conference with you, immediately. He says it has something to do with the incident in Washington today. He's using one of President Kalinin's communication portals."

Hardison surveyed the dust-covered president. "Do you want to clean up first?"

"I'm fine," the president said. "Establish the link."

The screen energized again, this time displaying a

Russian general seated at a control console. Andropov spoke first.

"Thank you for taking my call, Mr. President. I know how busy you are." The president detected a hint of sarcasm in Andropov's tone.

"Why are *you* contacting me, instead of President Kalinin?"

"President Kalinin is temporarily indisposed."

"Indisposed? Can you be more specific?"

"Kalinin won't be giving orders for the foreseeable future."

"I assume I'm speaking to the man who will?"

Andropov smiled. "You're quite astute."

"Get to the point, General."

The Russian's eyes narrowed for a moment, then his features relaxed. "I can see you've had a rough day. I will be brief." A monitor on the wall behind the general energized, displaying a satellite image of the White House surrounded by five craters. "I believe you know what happened to your Trident missile today. A most unfortunate *mishap*." The image shifted to another satellite image, this one displaying the burning hulks of four B-2 bombers, with aircraft debris scattered across the landscape. "I assume you are also aware of what happened to your strategic bombers."

"I am," the president said.

"If you haven't already realized, you have no nuclear deterrence. Your nuclear triad has been disabled. We have the ability to retarget your ballistic missiles, both submarine and land-based, and your bombers will never make it to Russia."

Andropov waited for a response, but the president just stared at the screen. The Russian general continued, "I want to assure you that although you are defenseless and at our mercy," he paused for effect, "we intend you no harm. However, we expect the United States to be on its best behavior."

"What do you want?" the president asked.

"We are going to try this again," Andropov replied, "and this time America will do nothing. Russia will take control of the eastern region of Ukraine, along with a corridor through Lithuania, connecting Russia proper with Kaliningrad Oblast. Additionally, we will install new governments in the Baltic States, removing the NATO cancer from our borders. If America intervenes, your country will pay a heavy price. You will have to explain to your people why meddling in Russia's border security was worth the destruction of dozens of cities and the death of millions. Do I make myself clear?"

"Crystal," the president said, displaying no emotion.

A confused expression worked across the general's face. He looked to the side as a Russian spoke offscreen. When the man finished, Andropov turned back to the camera and smiled. "I'm glad we understand each other."

The screen went dark.

A morbid silence hung over the Situation Room. After a long moment, the president slammed his fist on the table, rattling the water glasses. "Son of a bitch!"

No one spoke while the president seethed. After gathering his anger, he turned to Hardison. "Have the Joint Chiefs of Staff and appropriate cabinet members at the Pentagon in two hours. Get SecState on the line now. We need to inform NATO of Russia's pending assault."

"Yes, Mr. President."

The president turned to his press secretary. "Mention nothing about Russia. What happened today was an accident, a test missile veering off course."

The president excused everyone except his chief of staff. When the two men were alone, the president reached forward again, pushing the button for the video conference technician.

"This is the president. You said the Russian general used one of President Kalinin's lines. Do you know which one?"

"Yes, Mr. President. He used the portal at President Kalinin's residence in Gelendzhik."

The president asked Hardison, "Isn't Christine visiting Kalinin at Gelendzhik?"

Hardison nodded. "She is. I'll try her cell phone in a minute, but I suspect she's caught up in whatever happened to Kalinin."

The president took a deep breath, then released it slowly. "That doesn't surprise me."

25

GELENDZHIK, RUSSIA

In President Kalinin's underground command center at Cape Idokopas, General Andropov stared at the dark monitor. The videocon with the American president had gone as planned, and now it was time to put the next phase of his plot in motion. NATO would have advance notice, as alarms would begin flashing in command centers once the American president informed the Alliance of their conversation. Not that it mattered. NATO had only a single brigade deployable within twenty-four hours. Russia, on the other hand, had twenty-two mobilized brigades as a result of the Zapad war games.

Andropov selected different contacts for the three monitors at his console. The displays energized and a man appeared on each: Colonel Alexei Volodin—Commander-in-Chief, Aerospace Forces; Colonel General Viktor Glukov—Commander-in-Chief, Ground Forces; and Admiral Oleg Lipovsky—Commander-in-Chief of the Russian Navy.

"I assume you've reviewed the operational plans delivered today," Andropov said. "The initial ground campaign is similar to last time, so there shouldn't be any surprises. Our fleet, of course, will be employed differently. Do you have any questions?"

After three negative responses, Andropov issued the order.

"Commence operations."

26

THE PENTAGON

Forty feet underground in the Pentagon basement, the president strode down the hallway with Kevin Hardison and Colonel Bill DuBose, the president's senior military aide. Upon reaching the end of the corridor, DuBose swiped his badge and punched in his passcode, and the door opened to the Current Action Center of the National Military Command Center. The CAC dropped down in increments, with workstations lining each tier, descending to a fifteen-by-thirty-foot electronic display on the far wall. Unlike the adjacent Operations Center, which focused only on nuclear weapons, the CAC handled all aspects of the country's conventional military operations around the world.

DuBose led the way to a conference room on the top tier, where the president took his seat at the head of the table. Joining him on one side were the Joint Chiefs of Staff, while on the other side sat Vice President Bob Tompkins and members of the president's staff and cabinet—Secretary of Defense Bill Dunnavant, Secretary of State Dawn Cabral, Kevin Hardison, Colonel DuBose, and CIA Director Jessica Cherry. The mood in the conference room was somber, the faces around the table dour.

Dunnavant began, "Two hours ago, one hundred thousand Russian troops participating in Russia's annual Zapad war games pivoted west. Another ten brigades from Russia's Central Military District are mobilizing, and we expect them to begin transit within twenty-four hours. Also mobilizing are seven Spetsnaz and thirteen airborne brigades. That brings the total number of Russian troops committed to about two hundred and fifty thousand. Russia's initial objectives seem clear. They plan to annex Eastern Ukraine and establish a corridor through Lithuania, connecting Kaliningrad Oblast with Belarus."

The president reflected on Russia's obsession with buffer states to their west, along with the perennial problem of Kaliningrad Oblast, Russian territory on the Baltic coast. Home to Russia's Baltic Fleet, Kaliningrad Oblast is surrounded by Lithuania to the north and Poland to the south, with ground transit to and from the oblast controlled by the two NATO countries.

The situation infuriated the Russians, being forced to obtain the permission of foreign governments— NATO ones at that—to travel between two autonomous regions of their country. Years earlier, when Russia announced its intention to station additional military units in Kaliningrad Oblast, NATO had objected, blocking transit. Russia's military, still reeling from the disintegration of the Soviet Union, was too weak to force the issue. That was no longer the case.

Dunnavant continued, "It's still early, but what's different so far is the Russian force distribution. Russia's last invasion of Lithuania utilized only two brigades for the initial assault and a total of eight once reinforcements arrived. This time, eleven brigades have already been committed, half of the troops mobilized for the Zapad war games.

"The higher concentration of Russian forces in

Lithuania is partly to be expected, as there isn't much left of the Ukrainian Army after Russia's last incursion. Russia destroyed most of the Ukrainian Army equipment, reducing the remaining Ukrainian troops to riflemen at this point, easily overwhelmed by Russian mechanized forces. They won't be able to stop Russian troops from reaching the Dnieper River, seizing the eastern portion of Ukraine.

"What Andropov plans to do with the additional troops in the Lithuanian corridor is a concern. It could be a defensive move, placing troops where a NATO assault is most likely. A NATO offensive in Ukraine would have to cross Western Ukraine first, giving Russia time to redeploy units, while the Lithuanian corridor is very close to Poland. NATO could strike quickly once sufficient forces are assembled."

The president replied, "Andropov said he intends to install Russian-friendly governments in the Baltic States. That could be why there are more troops headed toward Kaliningrad."

"It could be a ruse," General Okey Watson, Chairman of the Joint Chiefs of Staff, said. "You don't need that many troops to control the Baltic States. Lithuania has only four thousand combat-ready troops. Estonia and Latvia are in a similar position. Fully mobilized, the Baltic States can field twenty thousand combat troops at best."

"What about the rest of NATO?" the president asked.

Dunnavant answered, "For immediate response, there's NATO's Very High Readiness Joint Task Force, deployable within twenty-four hours, but it's a single brigade of five thousand troops. It's a component of the NATO Response Force, with another thirty-five thousand troops, deployable in five to seven days. We also have two U.S. combat brigades in Europe under

Operation Atlantic Resolve, established after Russia's previous attempt to seize territory in Ukraine and Lithuania. We're talking fifty thousand troops, which isn't near enough. It will take several weeks before the necessary forces are mobilized."

"I understand the situation in Europe," the president said. "What else is Russia up to?"

Admiral Brian Rettman, Chief of Naval Operations, replied, "Russia's Northern, Baltic, and Black Sea submarines are sortieing to sea. We think Russia will try to blockade the entrances to the Baltic and Black Seas and eliminate any NATO submarines within. This would force NATO Navy strikes to occur from farther out to sea, putting some targets out of range."

Dunnavant added, "So far, the Russian strategy appears straightforward: blockade the Baltic and Black Seas and annex Eastern Ukraine and part of Lithuania, installing friendly governments in the Baltic States in the process. NATO can't intervene without the U.S., and we can't respond until we have a remedy for what Russia did to our nuclear triad. Until then, I recommend no military action on our part."

The president asked, "What do we know about the Trident missile and B-2 bomber issues?"

"The B-2 pilots ejected," Dunnavant replied, "and we've learned that all four aircraft lost power. The crews tried every method to restore power and failed. Regarding the Trident missile, we know almost nothing so far. Only that new warhead aim points were somehow inserted. Whether those aim points were dormant within the missile or transmitted from another source, we don't know yet. We're just now beginning to peel the onion apart. NCIS is taking the lead, with OSI—the Air Force's version of NCIS—in a supporting role. They'll focus first on common elements between the bombers and Trident missile."

The president reflected on the information provided, then made his decision. "I want a three-pronged effort. The top priority is figuring out what Russia has done to our nuclear triad and how to correct it. Until we've addressed this issue, I have to agree with SecDef—there will be no observable movement of U.S. forces. In the meantime, mobilize all conventional units and have them deployable within a day's notice. Move transportation assets into place at the air bases and ports, but keep the military units where they are."

The president added, "Note that I said *observable* movement. Deploy all submarines to wherever makes sense, but don't attempt to penetrate the Baltic or Black Sea blockades if they're established."

To SecDef Dunnavant, the president said, "Take the lead on both of these.

"On the diplomatic front, we need to organize support for a military response once we've addressed the issue with our nuclear triad." To SecState Dawn Cabral, the president asked, "What's the status within NATO?"

Cabral replied, "An emergency meeting of the North Atlantic Council will occur within the hour, but the council representatives won't have authorization to commit NATO to a war with Russia. That's going to take a meeting with the heads of state from all twenty-nine nations. I expect NATO to schedule that meeting for tomorrow. I'll keep you informed as I learn more, but you should plan to travel to Brussels tonight."

The president nodded his understanding, then asked, "What do we know about the Russian coup?"

CIA Director Cherry replied, "It's not clear what we're dealing with yet. General Andropov is issuing orders under the pretense they're coming from President Kalinin, but we don't know what's happened to him. We've reviewed satellite imagery and as best we can tell, Kalinin hasn't left Gelendzhik. Russian military forces have taken control of his summer residence, but whether he is alive or dead is unknown. Andropov stated he intends to transfer power back to Kalinin, but there's no way to know his true intent."

"Anything on Christine O'Connor?" the president asked.

"She has not left Gelendzhik either," Cherry replied. "We tried to contact her, but cell phone signals are blocked."

The president studied the grim faces around the table. "Any questions?"

There were none, and the president said, "Time is of the essence. The longer Russia has to dig in, the tougher our job becomes. And I shouldn't have to point out how vulnerable we are without nuclear strike capability. This needs to be a full-court-press, twenty-four/seven effort."

27

FORT BLISS, TEXAS

It was approaching 6 p.m. as Major General Dutch Hostler stood before the mirror, knotting his tie. Not far away, his wife, Megan, was putting the final touches on her makeup as the pair looked forward to celebrating her birthday with friends. After one final tug of his tie, Hostler deemed the operation a success. He reached for his coat, his eyes catching a copy of his division's insignia framed on the wall: a triangular blue, yellow, and red patch representing the three basic components of mechanized armor units—infantry, cavalry, and artillery—with a large "1" at the top of the triangle.

1st Armored Division—*Old Ironsides*—had a distinguished history. It was the first armored division of the U.S. Army to see battle in World War II and it spent much of its existence in Europe, stationed in West Germany in 1971 during the Cold War. In 2011, the unit returned to the United States and its new home at Fort Bliss.

Hostler found it particularly satisfying to be in command of the 1st Armored Division. His dad served in the Air Force, stationed at Birkenfeld Air Base in West Germany. There was a playground adjacent to the base's military housing complex and he fondly remembered the times he'd be playing outside with the other kids, their games interrupted by a deep rumble coming from the adjacent road, which disappeared into the forested hills. They'd run to the street to catch a sight to behold—a tank convoy leaving the Baumholder Troop Drilling Ground; tanks from the 1st Armored Division when the unit was stationed in West Germany.

His life had come full circle, from a kid watching 1st Division tanks alongside the road to a major general commanding America's only armored division.

As Hostler shrugged his suit jacket on, the doorbell rang. He opened the front door, surprised to see his aide, Captain Kurt Wise, on the doorstep, carrying a classified courier pouch.

"I apologize for interrupting, General, but this just came in, IMMEDIATE priority."

Hostler ushered Wise into the foyer, where the captain extracted the classified message and handed it to the general.

After reading the message, Hostler said, "Cancel all leave. Get everyone back on base and get the division packing."

"Where to?"

"Nowhere at the moment."

Hostler's thoughts drifted to his first few months in the Army, when he'd learned a basic Army practice, something every soldier first experienced in boot camp. Drill instructors ran recruits in formation from one event to another, only to have them wait for a half-hour once arriving. It was almost an inviolate Army principle.

Hurry up and wait.

They weren't shipping out yet, but when they did, it looked like 1st Armored Division would return to Europe.

28

USS *MICHIGAN*

"Raising Number Two scope."

Standing on the Conn, Lieutenant Carolyn Cody lifted her hands in the darkness, grabbing the periscope ring above her head, rotating it clockwise. As the periscope slid silently up from its well, she held her hands out beside the scope barrel. When the folded periscope handles hit her hands, she snapped them down and pressed her face against the eyepiece.

Cody called out to the microphone in the overhead, "All stations, Conn. Proceeding to periscope depth. Dive, make your depth eight-zero feet."

The Diving Officer directed the two watchstanders seated in front of him, "Ten up. Full rise, fairwater planes."

The Lee Helm complied, pulling the yoke back, and five hundred feet behind them, the stern planes—large flat hydrodynamic control surfaces—rotated, pushing the stern down until the submarine was tilted ten degrees up. The Helm also pulled the yoke back, pitching the sail planes to full rise.

"Passing one-five-zero feet," the Dive announced.

Cody peered into the periscope, looking up through the dark water, scanning for evidence of ships above, their navigation lights reflecting on the water's surface.

As *Michigan* ascended, it was silent in Control aside from the Dive's reports. There would be no conversation until the periscope broke the surface and the Officer of the Deck called out *No close contacts* or *Emergency Deep*.

Submarines were vulnerable during their ascent to periscope depth, with the surface contact picture only an estimate. Occasionally, ships were closer than the algorithms calculated and collisions occurred. The surface ships, oblivious to the threat rising from below, plowed on, while the submarine, operating at slow speed during the ascent, couldn't move out of the way fast enough. Even the smallest U.S. fast attacks in service, the Los Angeles class, were over a football field long, displacing seven thousand tons. USS *Michigan,* on the other hand, was almost two football fields long—560 feet, displacing eighteen thousand tons.

Sitting on the Conn in the Captain's chair, Murray Wilson monitored his submarine's ascent. As Cody peered through the dark water, the Dive called out the submarine's depth in ten-foot increments, and Cody gradually tilted the scope optics down toward the horizon. As the Dive called out eight-zero feet, the scope rose above the water's surface. Cody performed several rapid circular sweeps, searching for nearby contacts bearing down on them.

After scanning the horizon, Cody called out the report everyone was hoping for.

"No close contacts!"

Conversation in Control resumed, and a moment later Radio reported over the speaker, "Conn, Radio. Download in progress."

The Quartermaster followed with his expected report, "GPS fix received."

After the usual two-minute wait, Radio confirmed *Michigan* had received the latest round of naval messages. "Conn, Radio. Download complete."

They had accomplished the two objectives for their trip to periscope depth, so Cody ordered *Michigan*'s descent. "All stations, Conn. Going deep. Helm, ahead two-thirds. Dive, make your depth two hundred feet."

Each station acknowledged as *Michigan* tilted downward.

"Scope's under," Cody announced, then lowered the periscope into its well.

The lights in Control flicked on, shifting from Rig for Black to Gray, allowing everyone's eyes to adjust, then shifted to White. As *Michigan* leveled off at two hundred feet, a radioman entered Control, message board in hand, delivering the clipboard to the submarine's Commanding Officer. Wilson reviewed the messages, scrutinizing one message in particular. When he finished, he turned to the Officer of the Deck.

"Have the XO and Commander McNeil meet me in the Battle Management Center."

Cody ordered a Messenger to inform the two men as Wilson headed behind Control into the Battle Management Center. A fire team of four SEALs, plus one of the two platoon leaders, Lieutenant Jake Harrison, were clustered around a console, reviewing mission plans. Harrison was much older than the standard SEAL lieutenant; the prior enlisted man had reached the rank of chief before receiving his commission as an officer. Even though he was over forty now, he was still the prototypical SEAL: tall, lean, and muscular.

The submarine's Executive Officer, Lieutenant Commander Al Patzke, arrived shortly after Wilson, followed by Commander John McNeil, head of the SEAL detachment aboard *Michigan*. With the arrival of the three senior officers aboard the submarine,

Lieutenant Harrison pulled away from the fire team and approached the three men.

"New orders," Wilson said, handing the message board to McNeil. "The Russians are trying to annex parts of Ukraine and Lithuania again."

"What's our mission?" Patzke asked.

"We've been directed to reposition off the coast of Odessa, putting additional targets within range of our Tomahawk missiles."

"Anything for us?" McNeil asked as he flipped through the message.

"Not yet. But we'll be off Ukraine's coast not far from the Dnieper River. I imagine there are a few potential scenarios."

McNeil nodded as he passed the board to Patzke.

"Also," Wilson said, "the three Kilo submarines stationed at Novorossiysk have sortied to sea. The Russians know we're in the Black Sea due to our transit up the Turkish Straits, so I want to shift to a modified battle stations watch rotation, effective on the next watch relief." To his Executive Officer, Wilson said, "Until further notice, one of us will be in Control at all times."

29

CAMBRIDGE, MASSACHUSETTS

Steve Kaufmann leaned against the break room counter, arms folded across his chest, his eyes glued to the TV across the room. It was dark outside, and Kaufmann was the only person on the fourth floor of the Clark Curtain Laboratory building. There'd normally have been a dozen other employees working late, but after the news broke, everyone else had scurried home to watch events unfold in Europe.

Kaufmann had been about to do the same when Rich Underwood, Director Jacinta Mascarenhas's aide, stopped by, directing him to stay at work. Mascarenhas would meet with him later tonight. Underwood hadn't elaborated, but Kaufmann harbored hope that his oft-requested transfer to another program had been approved. His thoughts about the matter had been shelved, however, once the first images appeared on TV: Russian tanks and armored vehicles pouring across the borders into Ukraine and Lithuania.

Rich Underwood appeared beside Kaufmann. "Mascarenhas will see you now." Underwood's complexion was pale and there were beads of sweat on his upper lip. His fingers fidgeted with a leather notepad in his hands.

"What's up?"

"Just come with me."

Underwood escorted Kaufmann to the top floor, into a conference room filled with Curtain Lab's top management; Director Mascarenhas was the low person on the totem pole. Along the side of the room were a half-dozen men and women in suits whom Kaufmann didn't recognize. It was silent in the room and Kaufmann immediately registered the tension.

Underwood pointed to an empty chair and Kaufmann slid into it uneasily, eyeing the room's occupants. Nothing was said as four other Curtain Lab employees arrived—experts from other divisions. Kaufmann connected the dots. They all worked on the same contract.

The door closed and Diane Traweek, the company's CEO, rose. "Before we begin, I want to stress that the topic we'll be discussing this evening is Top Secret, Sensitive Compartmented Information. Each of you has a Secret clearance, which is being upgraded to an interim Top Secret, SCI clearance, effective immediately. You'll be briefed and sign nondisclosure agreements tonight."

Kaufmann considered Traweek's words. They weren't being given an option.

Traweek continued, "This issue is extremely sensitive and will not be discussed with anyone not in this room. NCIS Special Agent Joe Gililland will brief you on the matter."

One of the six strangers stepped forward. "As Miss Traweek mentioned, I'm Special Agent Joe Gililland, in charge of this investigation. This afternoon, during a nuclear response exercise, four B-2 bombers lost power and crashed. At the same time, a submarine-launched ballistic missile changed course in mid-flight, releasing its instrumented warheads onto new aim points. We're still early into the investigation, but there's one thing the B-2 bombers and Trident missiles have in common. Both recently had their navigation systems modernized. Those new navigation components were designed and built by Clark Curtain Laboratory."

Gililland paused to let the implication sink in. Several Curtain Lab employees looked around the room, casting uneasy glances.

"I'm not accusing anyone in this room of wrong-doing. You're here because we need your help. You have to figure out how the navigation upgrade is interacting with the B-2 power system and Trident missile targeting."

Gililland added, "We're not certain the navigation upgrade is the culprit, but it's the leading candidate. I want you to assume it's responsible and find the software or hardware bug. Once that's accomplished, you'll have to figure out how to fix it.

"Time is critical, as is the classification of this project. I regret to inform you that until this investigation is complete, you will not leave this building. There's a gym and locker facility in the basement where you can shower, and you can have someone bring whatever clothes and personal articles you need or we'll send an agent out for you."

There were protests from two Curtain Lab employees; each had important family events. Kaufmann also had plans and considered objecting too, but Gililland stared at the two men until they fell silent. Kaufmann decided it was pointless to complain, his mood souring as he considered the prospect of being cooped up in an office building for who knows how long.

Gililland continued, "You'll be moved into a secure location on the top floor where you'll work on this issue, and as Miss Traweek mentioned, you will not discuss this with anyone not in this room. Your new workspace is almost ready, and once you've completed your security in-brief, you can collect whatever you need from your current workstation and report back here. From now on, each of you will be assisted by an NCIS agent, who will accompany you whenever you leave your new workspace."

Gililland pulled a sheet of paper from his jacket pocket and unfolded it. He read two sets of names: a Curtain Lab employee and an NCIS agent, the two pairing up each time.

"Steve Kaufmann."

Kaufmann raised his hand and Gililland read off the NCIS agent's name.

Kelly Lyman, an attractive woman in her late twenties, stepped forward.

Kaufmann's mood lifted. The situation wasn't entirely bad after all.

30

GELENDZHIK, RUSSIA

Christine O'Connor stood at the edge of the console in the six-by-eight-foot concrete room. Hours earlier, her eyes had been fixed on the monitor as a Russian colonel held a gun to Kalinin's head. She'd been up all night, her mind racing through Kalinin's apprehension and General Andropov's intentions. As she considered her options, she glanced frequently at the four pistols in the stand, looking away quickly each time.

As the time approached 6 a.m., her eyelids had grown heavy, but it was no time for sleep. She couldn't stay in the room forever. Sooner or later, she'd have to exit through one door or the other. She decided to explore the rear passage. The back door opened to reveal a staircase leading down fifty feet, then the passage leveled off and ran straight into the distance; as far as Christine's flashlight would illuminate.

Rather than flee through the tunnel to who-knows-where, her thoughts pulled her back into the mansion. After Kalinin was arrested, it was clear General Andropov was up to no good. One of the monitors Christine watched through the night was a television news feed, and her suspicion was confirmed. Russian troops had invaded Ukraine and Lithuania. Whether

Andropov intended to stop there was unknown. Somehow, Kalinin had to be freed and returned to power. As the night wore on, a plan to accomplish the first part had slowly formed.

Christine glanced at the pistols again, then her eyes returned to the displays she'd been watching all night. The distribution of the Russian soldiers involved in the coup had become clear. Most were outside the mansion, patrolling on foot and in armored vehicles. Inside the mansion, along with General Andropov and the Army colonel, were a dozen men: two outside Kalinin's room, with four more making rounds, plus six other soldiers forming another shift, who were currently sleeping in the upstairs bedrooms. After watching the soldiers make their rounds, Christine had determined their routes and timing, as well as the mansion layout.

The servants had been sequestered in the staff apartments, also patrolled by guards. For her plan to succeed, however, she'd have to convince the Russian soldiers outside Kalinin's room that she was a maid. Unfortunately, she was wearing a red evening gown, which wouldn't do. But she had a black business suit and white blouse in her luggage. If she ditched the jacket, it should work.

The clothes were the easier part. Not understanding or speaking Russian was the more difficult problem. She'd pondered the issue through the night, making a mental list of the few Russian words she knew, with the image of her and Harrison's moms chatting and drinking tea vivid in her mind. Then the obvious answer dawned on her. She knew the Russian word for *tea*.

Christine checked her watch. It was sunrise, and she was certain the two guards outside Kalinin's room would welcome a maid delivering a tray of tea. Of course, there'd be a surprise beneath the tray. Cursing under her breath, she grabbed two pistols and inserted a magazine into each, then chambered a round in both. She had finally decided to walk away from this life, handing her resignation to the president. Yet here she was, *again,* with a pistol in her hand.

Returning her attention to the displays, she examined the path between the study and her bedroom. The route was clear. She opened the heavy metal door and entered the study, then moved to the French doors. Opening one slowly, she peered down the hallway, seeing no one. She hurried down the corridor while listening for footsteps, stopping to look around the corner. It was clear. After heading down the deserted hallway, she stopped where it opened into the foyer and checked her watch. A soldier would be passing through the foyer anytime now.

Christine looked around the corner, spotting a soldier enter the far end of the foyer. She pulled back, watching the seconds tick by on her watch as the soldier continued on his rounds, then turned right. Christine peered around the corner again, spotting the soldier heading away. A moment later, the foyer was clear.

She raced up the stairs and slipped into her bedroom without being seen. After stripping off her dress and donning a black skirt, white blouse, and black heels, Christine looked in the mirror and decided she could pass for a maid. She retrieved her purse from the dresser drawer and checked her cell phone. There was no signal and it was almost dead. She considered taking the phone and charger with her, but she had no pockets. She already had two pistols and would soon be carrying a tray as well. She returned the phone to her purse, leaving it on the bathroom counter.

With a pistol in each hand, she headed downstairs

and entered the kitchen. She found a teapot and two cups and saucers, which she placed on a silver tray. She checked her watch, and convinced that the path to Kalinin's room was clear, headed out with the tray in both hands, holding each pistol flat underneath with her fingers.

In case a soldier spotted her, Christine walked at a measured pace. She made it to the second floor unnoticed, then headed toward Kalinin's bedroom. As she approached the final corner, she slowed and took a deep breath, then made the turn. Her pulse began racing when the two soldiers noticed her.

The Russian soldiers posted outside Kalinin's bedroom were facing the president's door, leaning against the wall. Upon spotting Christine, they stood erect. The Russians eyed her as she approached, the way many men do when encountering an attractive woman. Christine smiled. When she was two-thirds of the way there, one of the soldiers spoke.

She had no idea what he said, but responded in Russian, "Tea."

He gave her a curious look and Christine tried not to wince. She must have pronounced it incorrectly. But the man's eyes went to the teapot and there was no further reaction while Christine closed the remaining distance.

This next part could play out in a couple of ways, but Christine hoped they took the bait. She stopped in front of the nearest soldier, said *tea* again, then pushed the tray toward him. She had no idea how to tell him she would pour the tea for him, but he got the idea. He took the tray and Christine stepped back, leveling the pistols at the two men.

Both soldiers froze, one with the serving tray in his hands. Christine took another step back, beyond both men's reach, and gestured toward the pistols on their hips. Slowly, each man pulled the gun from its holster, then set it on the carpet, along with the tray. Christine pointed to the ground with both guns, but neither man understood. She tried again, accompanied with, "Lie down," in English. Whether they understood English or figured things out the second time, they complied, lying prone on the floor.

Christine kicked their guns away, then opened Kalinin's door. Kalinin was awake and dressed in the clothes he'd worn the previous evening, minus the blue suit jacket, sitting in a chair, staring into the distance. When he saw Christine, he surged toward her. He stopped at the door and surveyed the hallway, spotting the soldiers on the floor.

Kalinin took one of Christine's pistols, then aimed it at the nearest man as he spoke in Russian. The soldier pushed himself onto all fours, then Kalinin delivered a crushing blow to the man's head with the butt of his pistol, knocking him unconscious.

It was impressive, the way Kalinin knocked the man cold with a single blow. Christine wondered what other tricks the former SVR agent had up his starched white sleeves, hoping a few of them would help keep them alive. At the same time, she shivered involuntarily. As civilized and charming as Kalinin appeared, there was a cold, hard side to him.

Kalinin repeated the process with the second soldier, who was hesitant at first. After a stern warning from Kalinin, the soldier complied and was also rendered unconscious. Kalinin dragged the men into the bedroom, along with the serving tray and dishes, then closed the door.

"What is the status of security?" he asked.

After Christine explained the distribution of Russian soldiers, Kalinin said, "We must return to the study."

Christine nodded, recalling there were two guards

patrolling the mansion between them and the study, but had lost track of where they were on their rounds. She explained the problem to Kalinin.

"We will deal with them if necessary," he said.

Kalinin moved down the hallway toward the stairs, with Christine close behind. There was no one in view and they descended quickly. They had almost reached the end of the foyer when Christine heard a man shout behind her. She glanced over her shoulder, spotting a soldier entering the foyer, reaching for his gun. Kalinin sprinted toward the exit, as did Christine, turning the corner as a bullet splintered a fluted column beside her. The gunshot echoed through the foyer and Christine heard the man talking into his radio.

They were still a distance from the study and Kalinin continued at a full sprint, slowing at the end of the first corridor. Christine caught up, and after pulling off her heels, kept up with Kalinin during the sprint down the second hallway. The soldier turned the corner behind them and fired his pistol.

Kalinin and Christine made it into the study just in time. Kalinin dropped to one knee and swiveled around the study entrance, firing three times, and Christine heard a man's body thud onto the floor. Kalinin then went to the back of the study, where he flipped the rosette aside and punched in the security code. The mahogany panel slid aside and Kalinin pushed Christine into the dark chamber, then followed.

The lights flicked on as the door closed. Kalinin surveyed the equipment on the counter. He grabbed two backpacks, stuffing a ruggedized smartphone in each, along with the six remaining pistol magazines, three in each backpack.

"We must move quickly," he said. "They will figure out where we've disappeared to and won't be far behind."

Christine glanced at her heels, which she still held in one hand, then broke off the spikes on the counter edge.

Kalinin handed Christine a backpack and grabbed the other, retrieving a flashlight from his, as did Christine. He tossed his backpack over his shoulder, then opened the far door and turned on his flashlight, illuminating the tunnel. Christine slipped into her shoes and shrugged into her backpack, then followed Kalinin into the musty passageway.

31

GELENDZHIK, RUSSIA

General Andropov strode down the hallway, passing the dead soldier sprawled on the floor with only a glance. He turned into Kalinin's study where Colonel Savvin awaited, while several other soldiers searched the room's bookshelves, lighting fixtures, and decorations.

"How did this happen?" Andropov asked.

"We're not sure, General. The guards posted outside Kalinin's room were found inside his bedroom, unconscious. They haven't been revived yet. All we have is the report from Danilov," Savvin glanced in the direction of the corpse in the corridor, "saying Kalinin had escaped and that he was pursuing both of them."

"*Both* of them?"

"Kalinin was with a woman."

Andropov's anger began to build. "You were supposed to keep the staff sequestered for the night, letting only those required for essential services return to the mansion in the morning. How did this woman get inside?"

"She wasn't a servant," Savvin replied. "They are all accounted for."

Andropov's face turned crimson. "You were supposed to search every room before setting security. How did you miss her?"

One of Savvin's men entered the study, holding a purse. He handed it to Colonel Savvin. "We found luggage in one of the bedroom suite closets and this in the bathroom. We missed it the first time; the room was neatly made up."

Savvin opened the purse, finding a wallet. He pulled out a government ID card.

Christine O'Connor.

"How did we not know America's national security advisor was here with Kalinin?"

Savvin was about to answer when one of the soldiers called out. He had flipped a rosette to the side, revealing a security pad. Other soldiers began tapping on nearby wood panels, identifying one with a distinct, heavy sound. Tools were brought in and the paneling stripped, revealing a metal door.

"Blow it," Andropov ordered.

Explosives arrived and were placed along the seams. Andropov and the other men waited in the hallway while the explosives were detonated. Upon reentering the study, they found the door still intact, but slightly ajar. Several soldiers pushed the heavy door aside, creating an opening into a small, concrete room. A soldier entered, weapon drawn. Lights flicked on, illuminating another door at the far end. The soldier pressed the door control and it slid open, revealing a dark passage.

Andropov turned to Colonel Savvin. "Kill both of them, then we will frame O'Connor. After what she did to Chernov and Gorev, it will be easy."

Savvin called for more men on his radio. A moment later, two dozen soldiers arrived and disappeared into the tunnel.

"I will return to Moscow," Andropov said, "to over-see the military campaign from the National Defense Control Center. Keep me informed."

32

KRASNODAR KRAI, RUSSIA

They'd been running for fifteen minutes, their flash-lights illuminating a tunnel that seemed to stretch on forever. They had passed through several intersections where Kalinin consulted a map on his ruggedized smartphone, selecting a path each time. The tunnel began to slope upward, rising each time a new path was selected, and the temperature dropped as time wore on. Kalinin, who held the lead, remained quiet, his breathing steady even though they maintained a brisk pace. Although Christine no longer spent six hours a day training for gymnastics meets, she still worked out three times a week and had no problem keeping up.

The tunnel turned sharply and when they rounded the corner, Christine spotted a pinprick of faint white light in the distance, growing larger as they continued. They soon reached the end of the tunnel, a gated opening partially overgrown with vines.

Kalinin pulled back the gate and pushed his way through the vegetation. Christine followed, stepping onto a narrow ledge cut into the side of a cliff above a narrow river. They worked their way along the ledge until it widened to a hillside rising from the cliff.

Christine followed Kalinin, who kept close to the river for about an hour. Fatigue began to set in, and Christine realized she'd been awake for over twenty-four hours. Kalinin, however, showed no signs of tiring.

He kept glancing up the hillside, with Christine wondering what he was looking for, until he turned and headed up the slope. He slowed and walked carefully, stepping on vegetation instead of bare dirt so he didn't leave footprints. Christine did the same, following Kalinin until they reached a small bump in the hill, overgrown with brush. Kalinin pried the vegetation apart, revealing a dark recess beneath a rock outcropping, which he examined with his flashlight.

"This is one of my hunting hideouts," he said, then he crouched down and slipped through the opening, disappearing as the vegetation closed behind him.

Christine followed him through the brush, entering a small recess about the size of a phone booth on its side. Kalinin sat against the wall, the ceiling a few inches above his head, then propped his flashlight up like a miniature lamp. The hillside below was visible through a few gaps in the foliage. Christine sat beside Kalinin, mimicking his flashlight placement.

Kalinin pulled the three spare pistol magazines from his backpack, inserting a new one in his pistol and the other two in his pants pockets, then placed the partially full one he'd extracted from the pistol in his backpack. He examined Christine. She had no pockets, either in her skirt or blouse. Her extra magazines would have to remain in her backpack. Kalinin rummaged through his backpack some more, pulling out a water bottle and a package of dry rations.

"Eat and drink," he said.

"Then what?" Christine asked. "What's your plan?"

"I have none at the moment. Our immediate priority is to stay alive. We must minimize movement during the day. There are no reconnaissance satellites assigned to this area, but Andropov will reassign one if he's smart. We can move at night. Although we will be detectable by infrared, there is enough wildlife in the area to blend in.

"I must figure out who I can trust," he said, "which is a catch-twenty-two problem. Until I know who I can trust, I cannot contact anyone. But to learn who I can trust, I must reach out. I must decide quickly, though. If we do not obtain assistance soon, we will be killed."

"Killed?"

"As a hostage, I was a valuable asset and would have been kept alive for a while. Our escape has accelerated Andropov's long-term plan for me. He knows I'll have his head if I regain control and I am certain he has ordered my execution. He will not let you live to serve as a witness."

Christine contemplated their predicament and decided to keep her response light. "I have to hand it to you, Yuri. You really know how to show a girl a good time. What do you have planned for our second date?"

Kalinin laughed. "If there is a second date, I'll take you wherever you want."

"I'll think on that," Christine said. "In the meantime, is there anyone at all you can trust?"

"Director Hippchenko is the only one on the list at the moment. But there are many SVR commanders he must work through to come to my aid, and I am not sure about their loyalty. There is no telling to what extent Andropov's treachery extends, and I cannot underestimate the measures he has taken to strip me of allies."

Christine pondered the situation for a moment, staring at the ground. Then she looked up, realizing there was one potential ally Andropov would not have considered.

"We'll help," she said.

"We?"

"The United States. We'll rescue you and take you someplace safe where you can figure out how to defeat the coup."

Kalinin wrinkled his nose as he considered Christine's suggestion. She added, "You have nothing to fear from us. But I'll call for help on one condition. Once you are back in power, you'll pull your military back to Russia."

"Back to Russia?"

Christine briefed Kalinin on what she'd learned from the Russian news feed in the safe room. Russian troops were invading Ukraine and Lithuania. Andropov was replicating Kalinin's plan, hoping this time for success.

Kalinin considered her offer of assistance, for way too long as far as Christine was concerned. "I agree," he finally said.

But then he considered the issue further and asked, "Can I keep part of Lithuania?"

"No!"

Undeterred, Kalinin made his case. "It would solve a long-standing problem of having to obtain permission from NATO countries to move military units into Kaliningrad Oblast by land."

"What part of *no* don't you understand? The *n* or the *o*?"

Kalinin smiled. "As you wish. I will withdraw all troops to Russia."

Christine added, "And you won't try this again. No more invasions, security operations, or whatever you want to call your attempts to take control of another country's land or government."

Kalinin folded his arms across his chest. "You drive a hard bargain."

"Agreed?"

After a lengthy wait, Kalinin replied, "Agreed."

Christine pulled the Russian cell phone from her backpack. "Can they track our phones?"

"It's possible," Kalinin replied. "I don't know the colonel assisting Andropov—how capable he is or the resources at his disposal. These phones use satellites, so they can't be pinpointed using cell towers. But with the right equipment, they might be able to track the call.

"We don't have a choice, however. We need to make arrangements. Make the call."

Christine turned the cell phone on and entered the president's number.

33

AIR FORCE ONE

Minutes earlier, as Air Force One and two F-22 Raptors cruised at 36,000 feet, almost at the end of its overnight trip to Belgium for NATO's heads of state meeting, the president entered his office on the main deck of the VC-25 aircraft, a military version of Boeing's 747. SecDef Bill Dunnavant, SecState Dawn Cabral, and Colonel DuBose followed the president into his office for his morning brief, settling into a brown leather couch opposite the president's desk.

Dunnavant was the first to speak, briefing the president on military developments. Russian forces had entered Lithuania and Ukraine. Eleven brigades had taken position along a fifty-mile-wide corridor on Lithuania's southern border, creating a transit lane between Kaliningrad Oblast and Belarus, Russia's staunch ally. There had been no combat, as Lithuania's president had wisely decided it was pointless to send the country's four thousand combat-ready troops against fifty thousand Russians.

Ukraine's government had taken a similar tack. Their armor and mechanized assets had been destroyed during Russia's previous incursion, and Ukrainian leadership had likewise concluded that resistance, without NATO or at least U.S. support, was futile. Russian units in Ukraine were continuing on to the Dnieper River as expected, with airborne units already seizing key bridges.

On the diplomatic front, Lithuania had submitted a resolution to the Alliance authorizing military force to repel Russian units. However, there was a common misperception regarding NATO's responsibility, and Cabral reminded the president of the specifics.

"Lithuania isn't as cut-and-dried as it appears. Article Five of the North Atlantic Treaty states that an armed attack on one or more members shall be considered an attack on all, and that all members will assist, taking actions deemed necessary. However, the treaty doesn't spell out what *assist* means, nor the *actions deemed necessary*. The wording keeps NATO's options open, with the possible responses ranging from nuclear retaliation to a simple diplomatic protest. Even though Lithuania has been invaded, there is no obligation to engage Russia militarily."

"We've been down this road before," the president said. "We'll take it one step at a time. Do you have the resolution for Ukraine drafted?"

"Yes, Mr. President. Same language as last time, authorizing NATO military action to repel Russian forces. Do you want me to submit it upon arrival?"

"What do you recommend?"

"I recommend we hold off for a while. We submitted it too early last time, creating a pressurized situation, trying to hold off any *no* votes before the deadline. Ukraine is a more complicated problem since it's not a NATO member and the Alliance has no obligation to intercede. There are several countries that may balk even when it comes to Lithuania, not wanting to risk war with Russia, and Ukraine is an even tougher sell."

"I agree," the president replied. "Hold off on the

resolution, but start working the issue with your counterparts once we arrive in Brussels. I'll do the same."

Turning back to Dunnavant, the president requested an update on the nuclear triad.

Dunnavant replied, "We've identified a common navigation electronics upgrade to the B-2 bombers and Trident missiles. NCIS is working with the company that designed and manufactured the new equipment. The bad news is that our ICBM missiles received the same upgrade as the Trident missiles, so if this upgrade is the culprit, it seems General Andropov's claim is accurate; all three legs of our nuclear triad have been compromised."

"Compromised is an understatement," the president said. "Russia's invasion of Lithuania and Ukraine is insignificant compared to this. Our entire country is at risk." The president leaned forward. "There is nothing more important right now."

"I understand, Mr. President. We're working the problem as fast as we can."

The president was about to inquire further when his phone buzzed, then his secretary's voice came across the speaker.

"I apologize for interrupting, Mr. President, but Christine O'Connor is on the line."

The president raised an eyebrow. "Where is she?"

"She didn't say. Should I put her through?"

"Yes, of course."

There was a click and the secretary spoke again. "Miss O'Connor, you're connected."

The president spoke first. "Christine, where are you?"

"Under a rock."

"A rock?"

Christine explained what had occurred: General Andropov's coup, Kalinin placing her inside a safe room, and how they had escaped and were currently hiding under a hillside rock.

She continued, "President Kalinin doesn't know who to trust, and I took the initiative to offer U.S. assistance. We need an extraction to someplace safe. If we can also return him to power, he'll withdraw all military forces back to Russia."

"What about the nuclear triad issue?"

"What issue?"

It was the president's turn to explain. When he finished, Christine said, "Just a minute." The icy tone of her response was unmistakable.

The president listened as Christine discussed the issue with Kalinin in hushed voices. He couldn't follow along, although he was certain Christine was cursing at the Russian president.

"I understand now," Christine said, with an edge still in her voice. "President Kalinin says he declined to implement this option and he believes that's one of the issues that led to Andropov's coup."

The president asked, "Is there a way to safeguard our systems or countermand what Russia has done?"

"There is not." It was President Kalinin who answered. "It was designed to be foolproof. Once implemented, the commands cannot be overridden, and there is no way to shield your systems from the signal during flight. It will take a significant engineering design change and hardware upgrade."

"Can you tell us anything about the signal or the hardware involved?"

"I cannot. I do not know the specifics."

Christine joined in. "I believe I watched General Andropov send the commands. I was in the safe room when Andropov arrested Kalinin, and I watched what he was doing through one of the cameras. He used equipment inside a briefcase: a laptop, cell phone, external display, and a trackball, all wired into a circuit board."

Colonel DuBose scribbled notes as Christine spoke.

"Thanks," the president said. "We'll see if it helps."

The president looked to his cabinet members. "Any other questions?"

Dunnavant spoke. "Christine, this is Bill. I'm here with Dawn and Colonel DuBose. We'll start working on an extraction plan. Where are you and how can we reach you?"

Christine conferred with Kalinin, then provided their latitude and longitude, along with two phone numbers.

Cabral joined in. "How are you two holding up?"

"President Kalinin seems okay, but I'm beat. We've been up all night and on the run since first thing this morning. We'll take turns sleeping, and plan to stay put until nightfall."

"Anything else?" the president asked his advisors across from him. After all three shook their heads, the president said, "Any questions on your end, Christine?"

"Not at the moment," Christine replied. "But Kalinin says Andropov's forces will be searching the area for us. We need help as soon as you can arrange it."

"I understand," the president said. "We'll be in touch soon."

He hung up the phone, then said to Dunnavant, "I want a rescue plan by the time we wrap up the NATO meeting today."

34

BRUSSELS, BELGIUM

Seven hours after departing Joint Base Andrews, Air Force One descended through gray, overcast skies, landing at Zaventem Airport, a few miles northeast of Brussels. The president was met on the tarmac by the U.S. ambassadors to Belgium and NATO, along with senior NATO staff and Belgian government representatives.

After the requisite greetings, the president slipped into the back of Cadillac One, which had been transported to Brussels during the night with the rest of the president's motorcade and backup vehicles. The motorcade headed into Brussels, arriving at NATO's new headquarters, signified by a twenty-three-foot-tall oxidized steel star, symbol of the North Atlantic Treaty Organization, in front of the building.

The president and his entourage were escorted to a lobby outside the Alliance's main conference room, where the leaders of NATO's other twenty-eight countries were already gathered. British Prime Minister Susan Gates was the first to greet the president.

"I received your message," Gates said, "and have reserved a conference room."

The two leaders entered a private room not far from

the lobby. Gates spoke first. "In light of the resistance we encountered to the previous resolutions, I've held preliminary discussions with those who supported the use of NATO force. All remain on board. Additionally, I've reached out to the new German chancellor."

Although the president hadn't yet met Lidwina Klein and she was new to the council, her hard-liner reputation was well known.

Prime Minister Gates continued, "Klein has pledged her support. With Germany on our side, we should be able to overcome French and Italian resistance to the resolution, convincing them to either support or abstain."

"Good work," the president said. "But we have a problem. I can't support the resolution at this time."

Minister Gates was taken aback. "Why not?"

The president explained the Russian coup and the nuclear triad issue, then finished with, "Don't press forward with the resolution during the meeting. I'll handle things. Also, I'd like you to keep the compromise of our nuclear deterrence confidential for now. No one else can know, not even within your government."

"I understand," Gates said. She checked her watch. It was almost time. "This is going to be an interesting meeting."

The president and Prime Minister Gates returned to the lobby as the conference room doors opened. The twenty-nine NATO leaders took their seats at a large round table with thirty chairs; one for the leader of each NATO country, with the final chair for the secretary general. After inserting a wireless earpiece into his ear, the president listened to the English interpreter as the secretary general, Johan Van der Bie, a well-respected diplomat from the Netherlands, gave a short introductory speech. An update on Russia's dual invasions followed, with the information displayed on a dozen video screens mounted along the circumference of the conference room.

It was quiet in Lithuania and Ukraine, with Russian units digging in along the corridor cut through Lithuania, while additional Russian forces streamed toward the Dnieper River in Ukraine. As far as NATO intelligence could infer, it appeared that Russian forces would stop at the Dnieper.

Following the secretary general's update, there was a somber silence until he recognized Lithuania's president, ceding the floor to her. Dalia Grybauskaitė delivered a passionate plea for NATO intervention, ending with a reminder of NATO's obligation under Article Five of the North Atlantic Treaty. At the conclusion of her speech, she announced that Lithuania had submitted a resolution authorizing the use of Alliance military force to expel Russian units from her country.

Following Grybauskaitė's speech, several council members looked to the American president, who had taken the floor after Grybauskaitė during the last heads-of-state meeting, pledging the United States' support. The president remained quiet, and an uneasy silence gripped the council.

Emboldened by the American president's silence, French President François Loubet requested to speak next and was recognized by the secretary general.

"We must consider our options carefully," he began, "as well as the extent of Russia's infraction."

President Grybauskaitė interrupted. "Infraction? You call Russia's invasion of a sovereign country an *infraction*? This isn't a game of futbolas, where you can red card Russia for a rule violation."

"I agree," Loubet replied, "but to use your football analogy, we can penalize Russia accordingly. Considering the extent of Russia's *infraction*, war is not the answer. We should implement economic sanctions instead, crippling Russia until it vacates the occupied territories."

Grybauskaitė replied, "Sanctions, sanctions, sanctions. That is all NATO is good for these days. We imposed sanctions after Russia annexed Crimea. What has that achieved? Nothing. Which is exactly what additional sanctions will accomplish."

The Italian prime minister requested to be recognized, then backed France's position. "Despite your disdain for sanctions, the alternative is war. Should that not be held in even higher contempt? Considering the number of Russian troops we'll be facing and Russia's formidable air-defense and land-attack missile systems, the cost to NATO countries will be extremely high. We must ask ourselves, is war with Russia, which could escalate into the use of tactical nuclear weapons, worth a few square kilometers of sparsely populated countryside? Let Russia take this meager strip of land, and let us respond in ways that don't threaten the very existence of our countries."

German Chancellor Lidwina Klein joined the conversation. "I realize this is my first council meeting, but I am shocked at the backbones missing from some Alliance members. That is the root of our problem.

"When Russia last invaded Lithuania and Ukraine, NATO failed to take action, unable to reach consensus in response to the most flagrant violation, an invasion of an Alliance country. We did nothing and the Russians took notice. They sensed our fear. I see it in your eyes as I look around the table. If we do not take action, the Russians will press forward, taking whatever land they want. They will carve up Lithuania, annex Ukraine, install puppet governments in the Baltics, and they won't stop there. Russia will not deem itself safe until there is no Alliance left to oppose it."

Klein's gaze swept across the NATO leaders gathered

this morning. "We must act, and act quickly. I propose the resolution be put to a vote within twenty-four hours."

When Klein finished, the American president glanced around the table, noticing numerous nods. The resolution was gaining momentum with the German chancellor's forceful backing. He pulled the microphone toward him and requested to be recognized. The secretary general turned the floor over to the president.

"There are two things I must relay to the council," the president began. "The first is that there has been a military coup in Russia. President Kalinin is no longer in control. Kalinin's Chief of the General Staff, General Andropov, is calling the shots."

There were murmurings around the table following the revelation. The president debated whether to reveal Kalinin had escaped and that the U.S. was planning a rescue, then decided against it. He couldn't risk the possibility that the information might leak out.

"The second issue is—regarding Lithuania's resolution, I cannot commit at this time. There are matters I must resolve first, and I request as much of an extension on the vote as possible."

There were surprised expressions around the council table, and numerous conversations between the heads of state followed. The secretary general gaveled the meeting to order, pounding the wooden strike plate repeatedly until silence was achieved. All eyes returned to the American president, awaiting an explanation for the requested delay. When the president offered none, Lithuanian President Grybauskaitė spoke.

"Time favors the Russians. The longer they have to dig in, the more difficult our task."

The president replied, "Even if we approved the resolution today, the Russians would have weeks to prepare. It will take that long for adequate American forces to arrive. An extra week or two won't make a significant difference. I have my reasons for requesting an extension, which I cannot share at this time."

President Grybauskaitė started to object again and the American president cut her off.

"Do not press the matter. If you do, I will be forced to vote *no.*"

Grybauskaitė said nothing further, and silence gripped the conference room.

After a long moment, General Secretary Van der Bie took control. "The United States has requested a delay. I propose two weeks. Does anyone object?" When no one did, Van der Bie said, "All votes must be received within two weeks. Any country that objects to the resolution must do so in writing by the stipulated date."

With a thud of his gavel, the meeting was adjourned.

Upon departing NATO headquarters, the president stepped into the back of Cadillac One, joined by Dunnavant and Colonel DuBose, for the return journey to Air Force One.

After the doors shut, Dunnavant said, "We have a plan to extract President Kalinin and Christine."

Colonel DuBose provided the details, then Dunnavant said, "It will take a few hours to move forces into place, but our best estimate is that we'll begin the mission just after nightfall. If you approve, I'll inform Christine and President Kalinin."

The president nodded his concurrence. "I approve."

35

KRASNODAR KRAI, RUSSIA

Christine woke to find a hand clamped over her mouth. When the haze cleared from her mind, she realized it was Kalinin's hand. He was lying beside and facing her, looking over her shoulder through the foliage. He placed an index finger on his lips, instructing her to remain quiet, then removed his hand from her mouth.

He pointed over her shoulder. Christine rolled over, peering through gaps in the vegetation covering their hiding spot. She spotted a Russian soldier moving quickly across the hill, following the river, and another soldier farther down. A third man, higher and much closer, came into view.

Kalinin retrieved his pistol and placed Christine's in her hand, then whispered, "Do not shoot unless we are discovered. Follow my lead."

He reversed positions so that his head was at Christine's feet. He lay perfectly still, pointing his pistol at the nearest soldier. Christine verified her pistol safety was off, then took aim on the next closest man. All three men walked a parallel line twenty feet apart. As the closest soldier crossed in front of the recess, Christine heard another set of footsteps. There was a fourth soldier, closer than the others. Based on the spacing between the three soldiers below, Christine estimated the fourth man would pass a few feet above them.

The footsteps grew louder and Christine held her breath. There was no change to the man's pace as he approached. Then the sound of his footsteps began to fade. As the Russian soldiers continued on, first one soldier disappeared from view, then a second, and finally a third. Christine rested her forehead on the ground. That'd been close. Kalinin had selected a secure hideout indeed.

As she let out a deep breath, her cell phone vibrated. She answered it quickly, bringing it to her ear.

It was Secretary of Defense Bill Dunnavant. A rescue had been arranged. Tonight, shortly after dark. Dunnavant provided the time and location—a hilltop clearing four hundred yards above and thirty degrees to the right of their current position.

36

CAMBRIDGE, MASSACHUSETTS

Seated at his desk in the darkened office, Steve Kaufmann rested his head on his forearms, debating whether to call it a day. Not that it hadn't been a long day already—it was 4 a.m. Thirty hours ago, he'd been pulled into the meeting at Clark Curtain Labs with the NCIS agents. He'd been at it for twenty-six of those thirty hours, grabbing four hours of sleep the previous night on one of the two cots beside his desk, with NCIS agent Kelly Lyman taking the other. But the end had been near tonight and he had pressed forward, checking the last software subroutines loaded onto the navigation circuit card attached to his computer. Everything was as he'd written it, not a single line of code changed.

Lyman was seated beside him, the glow from Kaufmann's computer display illuminating her features in the darkness. She nudged his shoulder. "We should get some sleep. We can plan the next step in the morning."

Kaufmann lifted his head, his computer screen slowly coming into focus. He'd answered the easy question, obtaining the answer he expected. It wasn't the software. That meant it had to be one of the microprocessors on the circuit card. Unfortunately, they were black boxes to Clark Curtain Labs. Most of the chips were commercial microprocessors performing specific functions, which Kaufmann's software tapped into. Thus far, every chip had performed properly. But without knowing the code inside each chip, there was no telling what algorithms lay dormant.

"I want to take a look at the data packets before calling it a day," Kaufmann replied.

He launched a test algorithm and put the circuit card through its paces, simulating a navigation update after launch. It took only a few seconds as the data scrolled down his screen, and the card executed its task perfectly. After a cursory review of the data packets, the port status grabbed his attention. It was still open.

"What the . . . ?"

The circuit card port should have shut after completing the task, but Kaufmann's computer was telling him it was still open. From a security standpoint, it was like leaving the front door of your house wide open.

Agent Lyman noticed the same issue. "Oh, yeah," she said. "We got a problem."

Kaufmann rubbed his head. "It's one of the chips on the card, then. But which one?"

"Decapsulate them," Lyman said, "and compare them to the engineering samples."

Kaufmann scrunched his eyes together. Hardware wasn't his expertise, but he knew enough to follow her. Before going into production, Curtain Labs and other defense contractors would put each microprocessor selected for a circuit card through extensive testing, and once it was certified, they'd slice off the top layer of each chip and examine the circuitry with a scanning electron microscope, taking a master photo. You had to trust that the source company provided identical chips during the manufacturing process, but one way to check was to slice off the tops and compare what was actually installed to the engineering sample.

It was an excellent recommendation by Lyman. It hadn't taken Kaufmann long to realize she knew her stuff, and not much longer to realize she wasn't by his side every minute of the day just to offer pointers. She was watching him, ensuring he ran the proper tests and didn't disguise the results. She was there to make sure he wasn't the guy responsible.

"Where did you get your degree?" Kaufmann asked.

"Bachelor's from Cornell and master's from MIT."

Yeah, she knew her stuff. Then he wondered why she wasn't curious about him. "Don't you want to know where I got my degrees from?"

She smiled. "Carnegie Mellon and MIT."

Kaufmann refrained from smacking himself in the head. Of course she'd know. She probably knew everything about him: his friends—whom NCIS was probably interviewing—what car he drove, his favorite foods, and every woman he'd dated. He tried not to let his eyes wander when he talked with her. Despite her expertise, she didn't look like the bookworm type. She was pretty hot as far as he was concerned.

The discovery of the open port invigorated Kaufmann. He was wide awake now and he focused on the next step. Decapsulating the chips was important, as it would identify which microprocessor had been modified and the company who did it. There were more pressing questions, however. How were the Russians triggering the missile flight alteration and B-2 bomber power problem, and how could the meddling be prevented or corrected?

After talking things through with Lyman, Kaufmann settled on an obvious answer for the missile issue.

Part of the navigation upgrade included the ability to communicate with GPS satellites. With the port still open, a command could be transmitted back to the circuit card, activating a routine inside one of the chips that would either modify where the missile thought it was starting from or provide replacement aim points. Given that the output from the circuit card was an updated, more precise position—the aim points were stored elsewhere—Kaufmann figured the Russians were simply telling the missile it was starting from a different spot. The flight algorithms would then calculate a new path to the target, taking the missile in an incorrect direction.

The challenge was—what command was triggering the chip? Kaufmann knew the software language inside and out. Although the number of commands was extensive, it was finite, plus it would have to be one not used by Kaufmann's software. He'd have to go through each unused command, one by one.

Kaufmann busied himself creating a software routine carrying the same data transmitted by the GPS satellites, then prefaced the routine with one of the commands most likely to activate the chip. When he finished, he held his finger over the keyboard, then looked at Lyman. She nodded and he hit *Enter*.

Nothing happened.

It wasn't unexpected, as there were hundreds of commands, and the odds of selecting the correct one on the first try were minuscule. Kaufmann updated the routine with another command and tried again. Then again, and again. Still no result. Then something happened.

After executing the latest routine, the circuit card fried itself and Kaufmann's computer, the display flashing bright white before going dark. The odor of burnt electronics wafted up from the circuit card and computer. An examination of the card revealed a melted power supply. The latest command had triggered a power surge, which the card sent through the port, destroying his computer. He now knew how the circuit card was frying the B-2 electronics.

Kaufmann called Director Mascarenhas, relaying what he'd learned, while Lyman updated agent Gililland. Kaufmann also requested another circuit card and computer, which arrived ten minutes later, along with an entourage. Mascarenhas and agent Gililland were now looking over his shoulder. Kaufmann rebuilt the software routine and picked up where he left off with new commands, watching the data on his computer. One of the algorithms eventually triggered the circuit card, which sent the new navigation position back out the port.

"Bingo," Kaufmann said. "Now we know what the Russians are doing and how to combat it."

"How's that?" Lyman asked.

"Easy," Kaufmann said. "If the Russians mess with a missile, we transmit the original navigation coordinates."

"The Russians are one step ahead of you," Lyman said, pointing to the circuit card. One of the microprocessors had melted. "It looks like the position update is a one-use routine, destroying the chip at the end."

Kaufmann tested Lyman's supposition, which proved correct. The circuit card ignored subsequent commands. Once the Russians altered the missile flight, there was no way to override it.

"Crap," Kaufmann said. "We're toast."

"Wrong answer," Lyman said. "Find a way."

37

THE BLACK SEA

The faint beat of a helicopter's four-bladed rotor reflected off the dark water as an MH-60M Black Hawk skimmed fast and low across the Black Sea. There were only four soldiers aboard the helicopter piloted by two Night Stalkers, members of the U.S. Army's 160th Special Operations Aviation Regiment. Unseen but not far behind, a second Black Hawk—empty aside from the pilots—serving as backup transport in case something happened to the primary MH-60M, followed an identical flight path northeast toward the Russian coast.

In the lead helicopter, strapped into their seats, were Army Captain Joe Martin and three other members of the 1st Special Forces Operational Detachment-Delta, commonly referred to as Delta Force, an elite U.S. Army unit trained for hostage rescue, counterterrorism, and missions against high-value targets. Although tonight's mission didn't involve hostages, it was certainly a rescue mission involving a high-value target: Russian President Yuri Kalinin.

Under the illumination of a full moon, the Russian coast appeared in the distance. The two helicopters skimmed low across the beach, then angled upward as the terrain rose toward the Caucasus Mountains. A Night Stalker's voice came across Martin's headset, announcing they were approaching their destination. Martin and the other three men pulled their night vision goggles on and retrieved their weapons. As the Black Hawk began its descent, Martin peered out the window toward their destination: a small clearing in the forest.

38

KRASNODAR KRAI, RUSSIA

Crouched together at the edge of the clearing, a few feet within the tree line, Christine O'Connor and President Kalinin searched the dark sky. A few minutes earlier, they had crawled from their hillside hiding spot, then climbed toward the rendezvous location. Christine still held her pistol in one hand and the Russian cell phone in the other, although neither had been used since her earlier communication with Secretary of Defense Dunnavant. There was no wind and the forest was still, but the night sounds filled her ears while she waited tensely for their transport.

She finally heard something, barely audible above the chirping crickets. The faint sound grew louder until she spotted a Black Hawk helicopter plummeting toward the clearing with alarming speed. The helicopter slowed its descent as it approached the ground, landing softly in the meadow grass. Not far away, a second Black Hawk touched down.

Four soldiers exited the nearest helicopter, taking defensive positions around the Black Hawk, down on one knee and weapons pointed outward. Each man's rifle swung slowly left as they surveyed the tree line. When one man's rifle was pointing directly at Christine, he halted, keeping his aim on her. Another soldier swung his weapon around, locking on to Kalinin. The first man beckoned with his arm, urging Christine and Kalinin forward.

Christine led the way, with Kalinin pulling up alongside, as both soldiers kept their weapons trained on them. When they closed to within range of the helicopter's rotors, Christine ducked and approached the man who waved. He lifted his night vision goggles and scrutinized Christine and Kalinin, then lowered his weapon as he stood.

"President Kalinin, Miss O'Connor," he said, then pointed toward the Black Hawk cabin.

Christine and Kalinin climbed in, joined quickly by the four soldiers. The helicopter lifted off as they took their seats, barely clearing the treetops as it raced toward the Black Sea. Not far behind, the second Black Hawk followed.

In the dark cabin, faintly illuminated by the green cockpit controls, the first soldier extended his hand to President Kalinin. "Captain Joe Martin, Delta Force, *U.S. Army*." Martin put emphasis on *U.S. Army*, then added a grin. "Welcome aboard."

Kalinin returned the smile. "I appreciate your assistance."

"Buckle in," Martin said. "It'll be an hour before we land at Bartin Air Base in Turkey."

Christine shrugged out of her backpack, then let out a deep breath. Their ordeal was almost over.

As she reached for the seat harness, the night sky lit up with an orange flash, accompanied by a loud explosion and debris pinging off the Black Hawk's metal skin. The helicopter tilted suddenly, making an evasive maneuver, throwing Christine from her seat. As she grabbed on to the nearest fixture, she spotted the other Black Hawk engulfed in fire, falling from the sky. Christine pulled herself onto her chair and was searching for the seat harness when she spotted a red trail racing up from the forest toward them.

Flares and chaff were ejected from the Black Hawk, then the helicopter turned sharply down and left, almost throwing Christine from her seat again. The missile locked on to the decoys and passed by as the Black Hawk leveled off above the treetops. Christine buckled herself in just before the helicopter tilted on its side and swerved right. She looked out the windows, spotting the forest through one side and moon through the other. The helicopter righted itself, but only for a second before zigging left.

Another round of flares and chaff were dispensed, then Christine's stomach leapt into her chest as the Black Hawk dropped into a rocky clearing. Another missile streaked overhead, distracted by the decoys as the helicopter plunged toward jagged rocks.

The helicopter leveled off, but was now racing toward towering pines directly ahead. The Black Hawk tilted upward at the last second, leveling off again after barely clearing the treetops. Christine twisted around in her seat, looking out the windows for other inbound missiles. She spotted another one closing from behind, but the helicopter took no evasive maneuvers.

Through the cockpit window, Christine spotted two more missiles speeding toward them, from thirty degrees on either side. The pilots were having a terse conversation, deciding what to do. The conversation ended and decoys were ejected again, then the Black Hawk maneuvered radically to the left, followed by another round of chaff and flares. Blinking red lights on the countermeasure panel indicated they had expended their decoys. Christine didn't have much time to think about it, as she was whiplashed by another maneuver.

The decoys fooled two of the missiles but not the third, which adjusted course toward the evading helicopter. Only a few seconds remained as the missile closed the distance, and the Black Hawk swerved left again, pitching Christine against her seat harness.

An explosion roared through the helicopter, ripping its tail off. The Black Hawk spun as it tumbled from the sky, the rate of rotation increasing as it fell, ejecting two Delta Force soldiers into the darkness. The forest rushed up toward them, and then there was the sound of splintering tree branches and crumpling metal.

39

AIR FORCE ONE

It was mid-afternoon as Air Force One made its descent toward Joint Base Andrews, just outside Washington, D.C. The president was seated at his desk, reviewing the latest intelligence report detailing the Russian troops committed to the invasions of Ukraine and Lithuania, when there was a knock on his door. After he acknowledged, Dunnavant, Cabral, and Colonel Dubose entered, with Dunnavant carrying a thin folder. Their expressions told the president they were about to deliver bad news.

"What do you have, Bill?"

"I've got two updates," he said as he sat on the couch across from the president. "I'll start with our nuclear triad. We found the problem.

"Curtain Labs discovered two dormant programs in a microprocessor chip in their navigation upgrade, activated by an external message. One routine creates a power surge strong enough to destroy the connected B-2 electronics, and the second program relays a position update to the Trident missile flight algorithm, altering the flight path. The bad news is that there doesn't appear to be a way to prevent the Russians from interfering, short of replacing the navigation circuits, which will take time."

"How much time are we talking about?"

"Curtain Labs is working on a revised circuit board. Their production line is still warm, so it should be only a few weeks before we have new cards. The B-2 upgrade should be easy, but the missile upgrade can't be done while the missiles are in their tubes or silos. They'll have to be returned to the refurbishment facilities. It'll be at least a year before a respectable percentage of our nuclear missiles are upgraded and returned to service, and much longer to fix the entire inventory."

The president asked, "Is there a way to address the missile issue faster? Can we jam the Russian signal that activates the dormant programs?"

"There's no way to block all satellite communications during the missile's entire flight path. The only viable way is to block the transmission at its source. But we have no idea where they're transmitting from, and it could be from multiple locations. I'm afraid the only way to address this issue is by replacing the navigation circuits. Curtain Labs is trying to develop a more immediate solution to restoring our nuclear deterrence, but the odds are slim."

The president nodded his understanding.

"In other bad news," Dunnavant said, "the extraction of President Kalinin and Christine didn't go as planned. We lost contact with both Black Hawks during their return trip."

"Do we know what happened?"

Dunnavant pulled a photograph from his folder and handed it to the president, who examined a satellite image of two helicopter wrecks ablaze in a thick forest.

"Any survivors?" the president asked.

"Unknown," Dunnavant said. "We slewed a satellite

onto the area ten minutes after we lost contact with the Black Hawks. No one has emerged from the wreckage since then. If there were survivors, they had already departed the scene. However, there's not much left of either helicopter. The odds of survival are low."

40

KRASNODAR KRAI, RUSSIA

An hour earlier, Christine's helicopter had plummeted toward the forest, its rapid descent ending with a crescendo of splintering tree branches, crumpling metal, and helicopter rotor blades disintegrating into pieces. The dreadful noises had lasted for only a few seconds, followed by silence.

Everything seemed to shift into slow motion after the crash. Christine surveyed the wreckage. What remained of the Black Hawk had come to rest tilted down thirty degrees and heavily to starboard. She was dangling from her seat, still strapped in. Kalinin was on the floor of the mangled cabin, wedged against the starboard bulkhead, his right foot jammed beneath a cargo seat. Fires burned in the cockpit, illuminating the two pilots sitting lifeless at their controls, crushed in the front of the crumpled helicopter. Of the two Delta Force soldiers remaining in the cabin, one was dead and the other, Captain Martin, was badly wounded.

Christine released her seat harness and fell onto the cabin floor, sliding toward Kalinin. He was conscious, but groggy. In the yellow glow from the cockpit fires, she checked him for injuries. He seemed okay except for his right foot, which was at an awkward angle. Kalinin slowly came to his senses, his eyes gaining clarity.

"Can you move your leg?" Christine asked.

Kalinin slid his right foot out from under the seat, wincing immediately. He had either a broken or badly sprained ankle, but otherwise seemed fine.

She turned her attention to Captain Martin, who was sitting on the deck, his back against a cockpit seat. A chunk of the helicopter fuselage protruded from his chest and he was bleeding heavily; his uniform was already saturated. Christine applied pressure to the wound with her hands, but the warm blood still oozed between her fingers. Her eyes searched the wreckage for something she could use as a wound compress after removing the fragment. She was no medic, however, and she worried that the bleeding would worsen if she removed it. Captain Martin deciphered her thoughts.

"Leave it in," he said. "I'll bleed out faster if you take it out. I'm not going to make it either way." He coughed, spraying specks of blood onto Christine's face as he winced. "Go," he said. "It won't be long before they get here."

He pulled his pistol from its holster. The sight of Martin's weapon spurred Christine to search for hers, and she spotted one of the two pistols she and Kalinin had carried aboard, along with one of the Russian cell phones. She retrieved the pistol and phone.

"Leave the phone," Kalinin said as he pushed himself to a sitting position. "This mission was compromised. Andropov's men either tapped into the conversation or traced the signal."

Christine dropped the phone and went to assist him. "Can you walk?"

"Yes," Kalinin said, "one way or another."

He climbed to his feet, grimacing when he put

weight on his right foot. "Let's get to level ground," he said.

Christine slid from the cabin, then helped Kalinin out. He stood on one leg, leaning against the helicopter as Christine found one of their backpacks and took a pistol and night vision goggles from the dead Delta Force soldier, handing the pistol to Kalinin. He gradually put weight on his right foot again. He could stand on his own, but the pain was evident on his face. When he took a step, however, he crumpled to the ground.

She helped him to his feet and he draped one arm across her shoulders. With her arm around his waist, they took a few gingerly steps. He was still in pain, but they could move. She turned to say good-bye to Captain Martin, but his eyes were closed, his face pale. The pistol was still in his hand, resting in his lap. With one final look at Martin and the burning wreckage, Christine headed into the forest, Kalinin limping beside her.

They'd been traveling through the forest for an hour now, their pace slowing as Christine grew tired. She was in excellent shape, but Kalinin leaned heavily on her as they walked. There were no trails to follow and the terrain was uneven, making the transit treacherous. They'd fallen three times already.

Not wanting to risk using her flashlight in the darkness, Christine had slipped the night vision goggles into place, searching for a suitable resting place along the way. As they pushed their way through the dense foliage, they halted abruptly, almost walking into a stack of decaying logs about ten feet high. They took a breather as Christine examined the obstacle in their path. It wasn't a stack of logs; it was a wall. A log cabin wall. She leaned Kalinin up against it and worked her way around the perimeter, finding an opening. Peering inside, she confirmed her hunch.

They had stumbled into an abandoned cabin. The door and windows were missing and half of the roof was caved in. She retrieved the flashlight from her backpack, then lifted her night vision goggles and turned the light on, examining the interior. It was bare.

Christine figured this was as good a spot as any, and definitely better than resting against a tree in the open. The night chill was setting in and she was already cold, wearing only a skirt and thin blouse. Plus, the cabin was well-concealed within the overgrown forest. Ten feet to either side and they'd have passed by without noticing it.

She helped Kalinin into the cabin and leaned him against the wall, helping him to a sitting position. She settled beside him.

"Now what?" she asked.

"Communication," Kalinin said. "You need to obtain a cell phone."

"How do I do that?"

"There are several small towns in the area. I lost track of our location while the helicopter maneuvered, but we can't be more than a few kilometers from the nearest one. In the morning, follow the slope until you reach the hilltop, then climb the tallest tree and look around. You can climb a tree, correct?"

"Of course I can climb a tree."

"Once you spot a village, go there and fetch a phone."

Christine said, "There's an awful lot of *you* and not much *we* in this plan."

"You will leave me here," Kalinin said. "In the morning, it will be even more difficult for me to walk. Go to the nearest town and steal a cell phone. We can then call the American president without being tracked and make arrangements for another rescue."

Christine mulled over Kalinin's idea. She hadn't come up with anything better. She turned to Kalinin, who had his eyes closed.

"Should we take turns on watch?"

Kalinin shook his head, his eyes still closed. "If they find us here, it will not matter."

Christine turned off the flashlight and stared into the darkness, listening to the forest sounds. The cool night was even more noticeable now that they weren't moving, and she slid sideways, beside Kalinin. He wrapped his arm around her shoulders and pulled her close.

41

MOSCOW, RUSSIA

Overlooking the Moskva River, the Main Building of the Ministry of Defense contains the supreme command and control center of Russia's armed forces. With 930 miles of tunnels and communication conduits beneath a thick layer of reinforced concrete, the facility is designed to withstand a nuclear detonation. Deep beneath the protective concrete layer lies the three-level National Defense Control Center. The bottom floor of the control center contains over one hundred consoles arranged in seven rows. The two upper levels are open, framed by balcony stations looking down on the main floor and toward a one-hundred-foot-wide screen dominating the far wall.

In the center of the second-tier balcony, flanked by a dozen of Russia's highest-ranking Ground and Aerospace Force generals, Russia's Chief of the General Staff, General Sergei Andropov, sat behind a frosted glass railing emblazoned with a five-pointed star, assessing the situation along Russia's western front.

Thus far, his plan had worked flawlessly. In Ukraine, Russian forces had reached the Dnieper River and were preparing defensive positions at the bridgeheads and all shallow portions of the river. Russian troops in Lithuania were doing likewise on both sides of the eighty-kilometer-wide corridor stretching between Kaliningrad Oblast and Belarus. Meanwhile, NATO Forces appeared paralyzed. Not a single unit had begun transit, not even the Alliance's Very High Readiness Joint Task Force.

NATO leaders realized that committing their single brigade against the fifty-two Russian Ground, Airborne, and Spetsnaz brigades would have been suicide. It would take America's full commitment and several weeks to mobilize enough troops to attempt an offensive against the fortified Russian positions. Of course, the defensive positions were a ruse. Once the additional brigades from the Central Military District arrived, Andropov would be ready to execute the second phase of his plan. With the United States paralyzed for at least a year, there would be no one to stop them.

Andropov's executive aide approached and leaned close, speaking into Andropov's ear.

"Colonel Savvin has requested a private videocon."

Andropov entered a secure conference room, instructing his aide to activate the video. Colonel Savvin's grainy image appeared on the display, transmitted from a command and control van near Gelendzhik.

"Good evening, General," Savvin began. "We intercepted a signal from one of President Kalinin's communication devices earlier today. Christine O'Connor contacted the American president and arranged a rescue. We determined the approximate location of the transmission and moved anti-air assets into place. An hour ago, we detected two inbound helicopters, which we shot down during their return trip."

"Were Kalinin and O'Connor killed?"

"We inspected the wreckage of both helicopters, and found only their communication devices. It appears they survived and escaped on foot."

Andropov's frustration began to mount. "You need to bring this to a close quickly, Colonel. Kalinin cannot survive."

"Our resources are limited, General. We have only one hundred twenty men. There are additional assets we can task, but we have to be careful about who learns we are hunting President Kalinin. When we are finished, no one outside our inner circle can know he was executed."

"What is your plan?"

"We know where they started from and that they're on foot. They can't get far. We've established checkpoints at every road leading out of the area, which means they'll be contained to the forest. There are a few air reconnaissance and attack units I trust, which I will bring to bear on the matter. I will also coordinate with local authorities, concocting a story about a fugitive on the run. We will mention only O'Connor, as we don't want to reveal we are searching for Kalinin. If we find O'Connor, Kalinin shouldn't be far. It will take time as we sweep the forest and search for clues, but we will find them."

42

CAMBRIDGE, MASSACHUSETTS

Nightfall was creeping across New England as Steve Kaufmann sat at his desk in the Curtain Labs building, staring at his computer display. His fingers rested on the keyboard, his thoughts wandering. A few hours ago, they had decapsulated every microprocessor chip on the navigation circuit board, confirming what they suspected. The chip that melted had been modified from the approved engineering sample. Agent Lyman, still by his side, had informed him that NCIS was opening an investigation into the company that manufactured the microprocessor. But the onus was still on him to find a solution. No one knew the navigation software or circuit card design better than he did.

Unfortunately, the Russian implementation had been flawless. Had they simply locked out the chip after sending the updated navigation coordinates, Kaufmann was confident he could have found a way to break the cycle, allowing the chip to accept additional updates. But the Russians had overclocked the chip, generating enough heat to destroy itself. Without that chip, there was no way to override the Russian command after it was received.

Suddenly, a solution dawned on him. He hit himself

on his forehead. It was so obvious. The answer had been in front of his nose the entire time.

Agent Lyman noticed the eureka gesture. "What's up?"

Kaufmann explained the potential solution to Lyman, who pulled back with a skeptical look.

"Yeah, that could work," she said. "But . . ." She pulled her cell phone out and called Agent Gililland, who arrived shortly with Director Mascarenhas.

After Kaufmann explained his proposal, Gililland asked Lyman. "Will it work?"

"It should," Lyman said, "but it's unconventional."

"I'll say," Gililland replied. He turned to Mascarenhas.

"If Steve says it'll work, it'll work," she said.

Gililland retrieved his cell phone from his jacket and punched in a number. After explaining the situation twice, being put on hold afterward each time, he was connected to someone even higher up the food chain—Secretary of Defense Bill Dunnavant. Kaufmann listened as Gililland explained the proposal yet again, then hung up.

He turned to Lyman. "Take Kaufmann home to pack. We're taking a trip."

"Where to?" Kaufmann asked.

"Washington. You're briefing the president at 8 a.m."

The blood drained from Kaufmann's face.

Lyman said, "Now don't tell me you've never briefed the president before."

"That's not funny," Kaufmann replied.

Lyman placed a hand on his shoulder. "Don't worry. You'll do fine."

43

KRASNODAR KRAI, RUSSIA

Christine woke to find the cabin illuminated by weak morning light filtering through the forest canopy and rotting roof. She was still sitting against the wall, her head nestled against Kalinin's chest, his arm around her. She looked up at him. Kalinin caught her movement and met her gaze.

"Good morning, sleeping beauty," he said quietly, then grinned.

Christine extracted herself from under his arm. "Yeah, right. I bet I've never looked better." She examined herself: her black skirt had made it through without much wear and tear, but her white blouse had seen better days. It was marred with grime from hiding in their hillside recess, and had torn in two places during their nighttime trek through the woods. Plus, her hands were red, stained with Captain Martin's blood. A couple of leaves and a twig in her hair would complete the look. She felt around and found one leaf.

She turned her attention to Kalinin, who had his legs sprawled out before him, her eyes going to his ankle. "Have you taken a look yet?"

He shook his head. "I've been waiting for better light. We can take a look now."

Christine gingerly pulled his pants leg up and pushed his sock down. Kalinin had loosened the shoe-lace but kept his shoe on. His ankle was swollen to twice the normal size, with dark purple bruises.

"Should you take your shoe off?"

"It is best to keep it on. The foot hasn't swollen and the circulation appears good. Plus, putting the shoe back on before traveling would be torturous."

"Do you think you broke something?" Christine asked.

"The bones above the ankle are intact. I'm not sure about the foot, but the lack of swelling indicates nothing is broken. However, I cannot travel without significant assistance. I'll remain here while you obtain a cell phone. Agreed?"

"Agreed," Christine replied. "I'll put my *expert* tree-climbing ability to good use and find a nearby town."

Kalinin gave her a curious look. "I did not mean to insult your tree-climbing ability last night. I did not realize it was a valued skill in America."

Christine did her best to ignore him.

He opened the backpack and retrieved a package of dry rations and a bottle of water. "You should eat," he said.

"I can't," Christine replied. "I can't eat when I'm nervous."

"Drink, then." He pulled another water bottle from the backpack and handed it to her.

Christine quenched her thirst, then returned the bottle.

"I better get going." She eyed her torn, soiled blouse and bloodstained hands. "This is going to be a problem." Even if she found a stream to clean her hands in, there was no way she'd blend in without a change of clothes. Barring a dress in the right size hanging from a clothesline conveniently in her path, like in a Hollywood movie, she'd have to stay out of sight while she stole a cell phone. She grabbed her pistol, then headed out.

"Wish me luck," she said over her shoulder.

Christine followed the slope up the hillside, eventually reaching the crest. It was difficult to assess which tree was tallest, as the tops disappeared in the forest canopy. But after convincing herself she'd found the biggest tree, she hid her pistol under a nearby bush, hiked up her skirt, then began the climb. It felt good to be climbing trees again, and her mind wandered as she pulled herself up through the branches.

Her thoughts drifted to her childhood, remembering fondly the times the two Russian moms got together while Christine played with Jake Harrison and his two older brothers. She couldn't help but smile as she recalled how the older boys always saddled Jake with the *girl,* whether they were playing board games or running around outside. However, she'd made them regret their choice on many occasions; she was quite fast and remarkably strong for a girl, and no one climbed a tree quicker. Anytime the older boys started chasing her with mischief in mind—handfuls of cow dung they planned to rub into her hair, for example—she'd head for the nearest tree, then taunt them from its highest branches.

In the heat of the moment, she didn't always think things through. Escaping to a treetop was a good example. The two boys would look up at her smugly; she'd have to climb down at some point. She'd eventually signal to Jake and he'd be obliged to take on his two brothers, keeping them occupied while she slipped down from the tree and sprinted away.

The two older boys took pleasure in ridiculing her. She remembered the many times they'd be playing a board game in the living room while their moms drank tea, and one of the boys would say something disparaging about her. Jake would come to her defense, which usually involved a fist to his brother's chest. The game would degenerate into the three boys rolling on the floor punching one another. Jake's mom would look over and yell at them in Russian, the same phrase each time, then return to her tea as the boys kept fighting. Although Jake and his brothers spoke Russian, it took a while for Christine to decipher what their mom said each time, eventually translating it into—don't hurt the *girl*.

The *girl* approached the treetop, breaking through the forest canopy. Christine climbed a few more branches, gaining a clear view of the countryside. A road cut through the forest until it intersected a clearing from which light smoke rose. She surveyed the curving landscape, forming a mental picture to help keep her headed in the right direction once she descended.

Before beginning the descent, she took one last look around. The sun had cleared the horizon and was climbing into a clear blue sky. But a brisk wind carrying the scent of rain whipped through the treetops. In the distance, a dark bank of clouds was rolling in from the Black Sea. She figured she had a couple of hours before the rain hit.

Climbing down was always tougher than going up for some reason, but Christine eventually dropped onto the forest floor. Upon retrieving her pistol, she headed toward the clearing. She came across a stream, where she rinsed the blood from her hands and cleaned her face. Still, she figured she had rolled around in the barn with Jake for several hours when they were in high school and emerged more presentable than she was now.

After an hour-long journey, the trees thinned and a clearing appeared. Within it was a village, about a dozen buildings, with several homes alongside the road in both directions. The forest had been cleared some time ago and scattered trees had sprouted up, offering cover as Christine approached. One building was noticeably larger than the rest, with smoke rising from a large chimney, accompanied by the smell of pastries. She figured it was the local pub, which should offer an opportunity to steal a cell phone at some point during the day.

Christine reached the back wall and approached a window, then looked inside. The pub was empty. She checked her watch. It was 9 a.m., a bit late for the morning crowd in this neck of the woods and too early for lunch. She moved along the building perimeter, checking another window, spotting a cook in the kitchen, busy preparing food. No cell phone in sight.

As she approached the end of the building, she heard a man talking. She peered around the corner, spotting two men: one carrying supplies from a van into the pub, while the other talked on a cell phone, occasionally giving directions to the first man. She pulled back, deciding what to do next.

She preferred to steal the phone and slip away unnoticed rather than steal one at gunpoint, so she let things play out. The van door eventually slammed shut and the engine started, then faded into the distance. She looked around the corner again and the van and both men were gone. Waiting might have been a bad idea.

Moving back to the window, she spotted the man

with the cell phone again. He was working behind the bar, putting supplies away, with his cell phone on the counter. Christine waited patiently and was eventually rewarded. The man went into the kitchen, leaving his phone on the bar.

Christine moved quickly to the front door, slipping her pistol inside the waistband of her skirt, snug in the small of her back. She walked into the pub like she owned the place, heading directly to the bar. As she grabbed the phone, however, the man returned.

When he spotted his phone in her hand, an angry expression flashed across his face. He said something in Russian and moved toward her. Christine retrieved her pistol and pointed it at him. The man stopped and raised his hands, palms out. He spoke again, this time in a conciliatory tone.

Christine retreated, keeping her pistol leveled at him. She had almost reached the pub entrance when it suddenly dawned on her—she didn't know the phone passcode. She moved forward and placed the phone on a table between them, then stepped back.

"Passcode," she said.

The man shrugged his shoulders, making a questioning gesture with his hands.

"Passcode," Christine repeated, tapping the air with her finger several times, then pointed to the phone.

This time, the man moved slowly toward his phone, his eyes on the pistol in Christine's hand. He energized the phone and tapped in the passcode, which Christine memorized. She waved the pistol at him and he stepped back. After retrieving the phone, she backed away.

When she reached the pub entrance, she turned and sprinted toward the forest, checking over her shoulder occasionally. When she was a few yards inside the tree line, she stopped and looked back. The man had wisely chosen not to follow.

It took an hour and a half to make it back to the abandoned cabin, finding Kalinin where she left him. She held the cell phone up proudly and smiled, then tossed it into his lap.

"I almost forgot about the passcode. You should have reminded me before I left."

"Obtaining the passcode goes without saying. You clearly don't have much experience stealing things."

Christine folded her arms across her chest. "I *clearly* need to stop hanging out with you."

Kalinin dropped the line of conversation. "Let's call the American president and arrange new transportation, shall we?"

She sat beside Kalinin and entered the phone's passcode, then Kalinin used the map application to determine their location. Christine checked her watch; it was 3 a.m. at the White House. Instead of the Oval Office, she dialed the president's cell phone. The call didn't go through.

Kalinin examined the phone. "It does not have international service. You stole the wrong phone."

Christine grabbed the phone from him. "I did not steal the wrong phone."

She opened the phone's Play Store application, then downloaded and launched a free app. After swiping through several screens, she tapped on a hazy image in the top right corner and a greeting popped up, requesting her user name and password. Christine filled in both fields and pressed *Enter,* and several icons appeared. She pressed the phone symbol and a man answered.

"Name and verification code?" he asked in a monotone voice.

"O'Connor, Christine Taylor. Access code 851051."

There was silence on the other end for a few seconds, then the man said, "How can I help you?"

"I need to talk to the president, immediately."

It took a moment to make the connection.

The president sounded groggy, but his voice cleared once he heard Christine on the other end.

44

WASHINGTON, D.C.

The president entered the Situation Room in the West Wing basement, joining four men around the table: Chief of Staff Kevin Hardison, SecDef Dunnavant, Chief of Naval Operations Admiral Brian Rettman, and Vice Admiral Dusty Rhodes, director of the Navy's Strategic Systems Programs, responsible for the Trident missiles and their launch systems. Although the CNO and Admiral Rhodes were required only for the second topic of this morning's meeting, they had arrived at the original 8 a.m. start time as directed.

Following Christine's middle-of-the-night call five hours ago, the president had set Dunnavant onto the task, directing him to have a rescue proposal by 8 a.m., which they would discuss first.

"What's the plan?" the president asked.

Dunnavant placed a map on the conference table, showing Christine and President Kalinin's location, a few miles inland from the Black Sea. "Following the failed Delta Force rescue, we evaluated whether we should just hide Kalinin somewhere inside the country—we have a CIA safe house in Sochi, for example. But the consensus is we need to get him out of the country as soon as possible. We can't afford to let him fall into the wrong hands.

"Given what happened to the Black Hawks, any new rescue plan must avoid the air. The Russians obviously have capable anti-air assets in the vicinity. That leaves land and sea, and we have the perfect solution. *Michigan* is in the Black Sea, positioned off the coast of Odessa for potential Tomahawk missile support in Ukraine. She's also carrying two platoons of Navy SEALs. We're still finalizing the details, but the basic plan is to send a team of SEALs ashore to retrieve Kalinin and Christine.

"*Michigan* needs to reposition from Odessa, which will take about a day, and the SEALs will head ashore at nightfall. We've considered options to extract them faster, but we think this plan has the highest probability of success."

The president glanced at the Chief of Naval Operations.

Admiral Rettman said, "If there's a way to get them out, our SEALs will get it done."

"Proceed with the plan," the president said. "Let's hope for better success this time."

After Dunnavant acknowledged, the president said, "Let's move on to the second topic."

Steve Kaufmann was one nervous cat, Lyman thought as she watched him pace around the Roosevelt Room. He'd fidgeted in the car during their trip from Ronald Reagan National Airport into Washington, D.C., and his eyes had grown wide as their sedan forced its way through the throng of reporters outside the White House. Despite the administration's denials, the press had connected the dots between the Trident missile issue and the B-2 bomber crashes, and speculation was rampant. Cameras flashed as Kaufmann's car passed by in the dawn, as reporters snapped pictures of the unfamiliar White House visitors.

He was wearing an ill-fitting suit Lyman had borrowed from one of her NCIS buddies last night. She'd taken Kaufmann home to pack for the trip, realizing there wasn't a suit in his wardrobe. His slacks and collared polo shirts were sufficient for Curtain Labs' casual dress policy, but wouldn't do for briefing the president of the United States. A quick call to one of the agents assigned to the Curtain Labs investigation had produced the slightly too small suit for the tall software engineer.

Kaufmann returned to the conference table, slumping into his chair between Agent Gililland and Diane Traweek, Curtain Labs' chief executive officer. Kaufmann tapped his fingers on the folder containing the brief for today's meeting, which he'd quickly put together before departing Curtain Labs last night. He sat still for only a minute before he stood and started pacing again, pausing to scrutinize President Theodore Roosevelt's Nobel Peace medal on the fireplace mantel before moving on. Lyman intercepted the nervous engineer on his route around the Roosevelt Room.

"Take a deep breath," she said, "and try to relax. You're going to do fine. You'll be the expert in the room, so talk with confidence."

"They're gonna think I'm crazy."

"You're not crazy. It's a unique, but solid solution." Lyman straightened his tie. "One more piece of advice. The director of the Navy's SSP—Strategic Systems Programs—is Vice Admiral Dusty Rhodes."

"Dusty Rhodes, like the wrestler?"

"Exactly. Don't make any jokes. He's heard it a million times. I've never met him, but I hear he's a crotchety old fella, a former master chief who started over, working his way up the officer ranks."

"Got it," Kauffman said. "No jokes or sleeper holds during the meeting."

"Not funny."

The door to the Roosevelt Room opened and an aide entered. "The president is ready to see you. Follow me, please."

The aide led the way to the West Wing basement, opening the door to the Situation Room. Waiting inside with the president were two civilians and two admirals, who were introduced after the new arrivals took their seats.

SecDef Dunnavant began by explaining the reason for the navigation upgrade to their nuclear weapons, which they'd spent ten years implementing. In the end, it had to do with hardened targets, but he provided the background first.

Submarine-launched ballistic missiles, while sitting in their launch tubes, were untargeted. They had no idea where they were nor where they were supposed to go. That information was supplied during missile spin-up, with two pieces of information provided to each missile: where it was on the planet, which was provided by the submarine's navigation system, and where the warhead aim points were. Unfortunately, submarine positions weren't always accurate.

Submarines receive satellite position fixes only when surfaced or at periscope depth. While fully submerged, its position is determined by two inertial navigators, which calculate the submarine's position by analyzing the acceleration and velocity vectors as the submarine moves through the water.

The submarine's current position, as calculated by the inertial navigators, could be incorrect by several meters or even more, resulting in a corresponding error in the warhead aim points. A Trident missile takes a star fix during flight, but the new navigation upgrade developed by Curtain Labs took advantage of GPS satellites, updating the missile just after it emerged from the water, further improving missile accuracy. This improved accuracy was crucial, Dunnavant explained. It had to do with hardened targets.

When attacking underground bunkers designed to withstand a nuclear blast, warhead accuracy could make the difference between target destruction and survival. As a result of the Curtain Labs navigation upgrade, combined with the new super-fuze technology controlling the timing of warhead detonation, Trident missiles were now capable of destroying all known hardened targets.

Dunnavant then provided a summary of what everyone already knew: the Russians had compromised America's nuclear deterrence, able to crash B-2 bombers and alter American nuclear missile flight paths. Finally, he arrived at the salient topic of today's brief—the proposed solutions.

"Clark Curtain Labs, which developed the navigation upgrade for all three legs of our nuclear triad, will produce new navigation upgrades for our B-2 bombers. That should take only a few weeks, but twenty bombers are insufficient to guarantee mutual assured destruction, the cornerstone of nuclear deterrence. We need to restore our land- and sea-based missile systems to service. Waiting to replace the navigation circuits in every missile will take too long."

Dunnavant turned to the two Curtain Labs employees. "Diane Traweek and Steve Kaufmann from Curtain Labs have a proposal that, if it works, will immediately restore full nuclear deterrence. Go ahead, Miss Traweek."

"Mr. President, thank you for the opportunity to brief you. As Secretary of Defense Dunnavant said, the solution to the B-2 problem is straightforward and relatively quick. Curtain Labs will manufacture new circuit cards, verifying all microprocessors conform to the certified engineering samples. Addressing the missile inventory is more complicated, as I understand you want a timelier fix than the two to three years it would take to replace the navigation circuits in every missile. Steve Kaufmann, our lead software engineer on this project, has a unique proposal worthy of consideration."

All eyes turned to Kaufmann, who swallowed hard. He opened his folder and passed out copies of his brief, then began.

"Mr. President, thank you for inviting me to brief you on my idea. If you take a look at the first page of the brief, you'll see a schematic of the navigation circuit. The microprocessor with the circle around it is the culprit. The chip's programming leaves the circuit port open after the precision navigation update, which occurs right after the missile clears the water. The Russians then take advantage of this open port, transmitting an updated starting point for the missile, altering its flight path. When trying to address what the Russians have done, the main problem is that this chip self-destructs after it receives the order to send an updated position, which means we can't countermand it. This problem, however, is also the solution."

There were confused expressions around the table before Kaufmann explained. "Basically, if we pretend to be the Russians and order the chip to send a navigation update before launch, it will then self-destruct, making it unavailable to the Russians. The missile will then ignore any attempted interference. However, there are a couple of issues to consider."

Kaufmann turned to the next page of the brief, containing another schematic. "We'll have to connect a device to each missile prior to launch and activate this chip. The software is simple as is the device. We just need to connect to the missile umbilical and send a signal to the navigation card. The chip will send a position update, which the missile will ignore since it hasn't spun up yet, and then the chip will self-destruct. At that point, the missile can no longer be meddled with.

"The drawback is that the precision navigation update after launch will be disabled, but that's not really a big deal as far as I know. You'd be returning the missiles to the accuracy they previously had."

Dunnavant amplified Kaufmann's assessment. "Eliminating the precision navigation update will only slightly reduce warhead accuracy. The impact is that our entire nuclear arsenal won't be hard-target capable. But as Kaufmann mentioned, we'll be back where we started, with twenty percent of our nuclear arsenal having hardened-target capability. All we'd have to do is revert to the previous war plan—or develop a new one, allocating the proper missiles to hardened targets."

When he finished, Dunnavant asked, "Does anyone have any questions?"

Vice Admiral Rhodes looked up from Kaufmann's brief. "You're telling me that you want us to authorize a process where Billy-Bob the missile-man hooks up a homemade contraption built in a lunchbox to every one of our nuclear missiles prior to launch. Are you nuts?"

Kaufmann glanced at Lyman with an *I told you so* expression.

Lyman jumped in. "Actually, Admiral, the device we'd be using is less complicated than a cell phone."

"Well then," the Admiral replied sarcastically. "Why didn't you say so at the beginning? Can you do it with an iPhone? There's an app for that, right?"

Diane Traweek, Clark Curtain Labs CEO, replied, "Admiral, we can put our proposal through whatever testing regimen you desire."

Dunnavant interjected, addressing Admiral Rhodes. "We can't spend the decade the military typically takes to develop and field new technology. I propose we have SSP give the design the once-over. If you can convince yourselves it will perform the required function without unintended consequences, we'll load a new missile with dummy warheads and give it a go."

"We have one other problem," Admiral Rhodes replied, "a significant one. The only way we'll know this solution works is to have the Russians try to alter the missile flight path. That means you'll have to inform them of the test launch and challenge them to affect it. You'll be revealing that we're working on a solution, and if it fails, we'll have an enormous egg on our face."

Dunnavant replied, "I don't think it will be a surprise to the Russians that we're working on a solution. But I agree that we have a conundrum. We don't want to test the solution in front of the Russians until we're certain it will work, but the only way to be certain it works is to test the solution in front of the Russians."

The president asked Kaufmann, "Are you sure this will work? And that the signal you'll be sending into the missile won't have unintended consequences?"

Kaufmann was sure it would work, but the tricky part was knowing for certain that the electrical signal wouldn't interact with other circuity in unexpected ways. Nuclear missile electronics were complicated and the ramifications if something went wrong could be catastrophic. However, he knew the navigation upgrade better than anyone, including its interfaces, and had thought through the issue extensively.

"I'm positive, Mr. President. This solution will address the problem safely."

The president asked Admiral Rhodes, "How long before we can have a submarine ready to launch another test missile?"

"About forty-eight hours to prepare a missile with dummy warheads, pull a submarine in for on-load, then have her in position to launch."

"Validate the design first. Will forty-eight hours be enough time?"

"We'll have an answer by then, sir."

The president turned to Dunnavant. "Let's see if this works."

45

USS *MICHIGAN*

USS *Michigan* owned the Black Sea. From a NATO perspective, that is. She was the only NATO submarine in the area, so colliding with another friendly submarine wasn't a concern. However, three Russian Kilo submarines were also in the Black Sea, and thus far, intelligence messages had provided no information on their locations. Wilson looked up from the electronic navigation chart as Lieutenant Commander Al Patzke, the submarine's Executive Officer, entered the Control Room. Patzke stopped in the Radio and Sonar Rooms for updates on communications and the contact picture—there were only a few merchant ships in the area—then approached Wilson, ready to relieve him.

Two days ago, after receiving reports of Russia's invasions of Ukraine and Lithuania, along with a report that the three Kilo class submarines had sortied to sea, Wilson had augmented the normal watch sections with additional sonar and fire control personnel. Additionally, either Wilson or Patzke would be in Control. Wilson was wrapping up his six-hour evening shift, looking forward to some sleep before returning for another stint in the morning.

After reviewing the submarine's status with Patzke, Wilson stationed him as the submarine's command duty officer, authorized to give orders normally reserved for the Commanding Officer. Wilson then departed Control for his daily tour. With most of the crew asleep in their racks, it would be quiet throughout the guided missile submarine, with the watchstanders going through their hourly routines. Wilson had learned that the mid-watch was the best time to tour his submarine, providing the opportunity to talk with his crew.

Having recently been in Sonar and Radio, Wilson toured the Torpedo Room, then stopped in the Missile Control Center where the submarine's Tomahawk missiles were launched. All were operational. He continued aft, stepping into the Missile Compartment as the submarine tilted upward, proceeding to periscope depth to copy the message broadcast. In the level beneath Wilson, the bulk of the crew slept in nine-man bunkrooms between the missile tubes, while the SEALs and Navy divers slept in berthing installed in the second level during the submarine's conversion into a guided missile submarine.

Wilson traveled down the port side of second level, stopping beside tube Twelve as the submarine leveled off at periscope depth. He knocked on the side of the tube, then pulled back the brown curtain and entered the berthing unit assigned to the three senior SEAL officers aboard: the SEAL detachment commander, John McNeil, and the two platoon leaders. Commander McNeil and Lieutenant Bob Acor were asleep in their racks, while Jake Harrison stood with a towel wrapped around his waist, his hair damp, applying deodorant. The SEALs were workout fanatics, but *Michigan* had limited exercise equipment and they had to take turns. It looked like Harrison had just finished a late evening workout.

"Evening, Captain," Harrison said, tossing his bath kit onto his rack.

Rumor had it that Harrison was considering retiring from the Navy. The prior-enlisted officer had his twenty years in and could move on to a second career at any time. It seemed unlikely to Wilson; Harrison appeared to enjoy being a Navy SEAL.

"I hear you're thinking about getting out?"

"I'm evaluating it, sir," Harrison replied, "but haven't decided. I'm up for lieutenant commander in another year and I'd like to see if I make it. My wife, on the other hand, would prefer I retire sooner rather than later."

Wilson understood Harrison's predicament. He'd had the same discussion with his wife many times. The emotional strain from deployments was tough on a family. Plus, although Wilson took his submarine into danger on occasion, the SEALs dealt with life-threatening situations far more frequently.

Michigan tilted downward and Wilson felt a vibration in the deck. The submarine was increasing speed to at least ahead full. He spotted the Messenger of the Watch hurrying down the side of the Missile Compartment, pulling to a halt as he passed Missile Tube Twelve. He entered the SEALs' bunkroom and handed Wilson the message board. "New orders, sir."

Wilson read the first message, which explained the increased speed. *Michigan* had been assigned a new operating area off the western shore of the Black Sea. The next message explained why. He looked at McNeil, still asleep in his rack. Harrison followed Wilson's eyes and he nudged his boss, waking him up. McNeil swung to a sitting position, rubbing his eyes.

"New orders," Wilson said as he handed the message board to McNeil. "Rescue mission for Russian President Kalinin and Christine."

"Our Christine?" McNeil asked as he accepted the board.

Wilson nodded, then reflected on how the SEALs aboard *Michigan* had taken ownership of Christine O'Connor, having retrieved her off China's coast, assisted at Ice Station Nautilus, and rescued her not long ago in the Black Sea.

McNeil said, "That woman is a blue bug light for trouble."

Wilson laughed. "That much is true."

The SEAL commander finished reading the message and handed the board to Harrison, then poked Lieutenant Acor in the rack below. The platoon leader pulled himself from his bunk and stood in his skivvies, waiting for his turn at the message board while McNeil filled him in.

"Extraction mission; the Russian president and Christine O'Connor, a few miles inland, just north of Sochi. Get with Harrison and come up with a plan."

McNeil asked Wilson, "When will we be on station?"

Wilson did the calculations in his head. "About this time tomorrow."

46

KINGS BAY, GEORGIA

Commander Britt Skogstad stood in USS *Maryland*'s Bridge cockpit, watching as two tugs pushed the ballistic missile submarine slowly toward the explosive handling wharf. It was an evolution he'd done many times to offload Trident missiles for maintenance, replacing them with freshly refurbished ones. This time, however, there would be no offload. Tube Twenty-one was already empty, having launched a missile with inert warheads a few days ago. Unfortunately, the missile had veered off course, breaking the string of 165 consecutive successful Trident missile launches. It wasn't their fault, Skogstad told his crew, but it still left a bad taste in his mouth, being tied to the first Trident missile failure in thirty years.

They would get another chance, however. After entering the explosive handling building, they'd load a new missile into tube Twenty-one. Skogstad spotted the replacement missile on the wharf, lying on a trailer after being extracted from a heavily guarded stowage bunker. It was an eerie sight at times, passing the secure area in the early morning hours on the way to the piers; concrete sentinel watchtowers rising through the fog, searchlights illuminating the bunkers guarded with multiple rings of barbed wired fences, perimeter motion detectors, and controlled access worthy of a *Mission: Impossible* movie set.

The two tugs finished their task, gently pushing *Maryland* against the wharf between the two explosive handling buildings. Lines were attached to the submarine from inside Explosive Handling Wharf Two. Slowly, *Maryland* was pulled into the covered building.

Marines patrolled the wharf and the immediate vicinity, their weapons ready. Trident missile movements were serious business, with the Marines assigned to Kings Bay locking down the transit route between the stowage bunkers and the explosive handling wharf. Also on the wharf were several passengers waiting to embark: the Group Ten admiral, the Squadron Twenty commodore, and three civilians: a tall software engineer with a backpack, a female NCIS agent, and a senior engineer from Strategic Systems Programs.

The missile on-load didn't take long. The wharf crew was proficient and there was only one missile to load, and tube Twenty-one soon had a new occupant. Skogstad watched as the missile muzzle hatch swung slowly shut, sealing the missile inside the tube. As the wharf crew prepared to extract *Maryland* from the explosive handling building, Skogstad ordered the Officer of the Deck to station the Maneuvering Watch.

Several hours later, after transiting the St. Marys River into the Atlantic Ocean, *Maryland* surged east through dark green water. The skies were overcast, the clouds blending into a dull gray haze on the horizon. There was only one contact in the vicinity: a surface ship a few miles away, assigned to provide video surveillance of the missile launch, mirroring *Maryland*'s track.

Steve Kaufmann stood on the Bridge between *Maryland*'s Commanding Officer and Officer of the Deck. Lieutenant Andrew Wells scanned the horizon with his binoculars, as did the two lookouts standing atop the submarine's sail inside the Flying Bridge—a fancy name for a few stanchions with a rope tied between them.

A report echoed from the Bridge box—a carry-on-suitcase-sized communication device plugged into the cockpit. "Bridge, Nav. Passing the one-hundred-fathom curve outbound."

Wells acknowledged the report, then glanced at the Bridge display unit, as did Skogstad, checking *Maryland*'s progress toward the dive point.

"Shift the watch below decks," Skogstad ordered. "Prepare to dive."

A few minutes later, after shifting the watch below decks and securing the Bridge, USS *Maryland* submerged, settling out at a keel depth of eighty feet.

Skogstad turned to Kaufmann. "It's your turn now."

Commander Skogstad escorted Kaufmann and the SSP engineer, along with Lyman, the admiral, and the commodore, into the Missile Compartment. Awaiting them beside tube Twenty-one were the submarine's Weapons Officer—Lieutenant Tom Martin—and two missile technicians: a chief and a petty officer first class.

Everyone had been briefed and the process was straightforward, but the crowded gathering made Kauffman nervous. He wiped his sweaty palms on his pants and opened his backpack, extracting a laptop computer, which he turned on, and a connector with a male USB head on one end and two alligator clips on the other.

Kaufmann plugged the USB end into his computer,

then pointed to a thick black cable attached to the side of the missile tube. "I need you to disconnect the cable."

He waited as a Byzantine series of orders and repeat-backs ensued between the Weapons Officer, chief, and petty officer, and the cable was disconnected.

Knowing this procedure would need to be done to hundreds of missiles by personnel without Kaufmann's background, he'd designed the system to be user-friendly. He had, in fact, built an app for it, which could be loaded onto any personal computer. Additionally, although the connector Kaufmann was using today was crude, they could also design one that plugged into the missile tube connector instead of using alligator clips, simplifying the process even further.

Without a predesigned cap to ensure the computer was connected to the proper missile tube pins, he referred to a schematic that Lieutenant Martin provided. After examining the drawing, Kaufmann connected the alligator clips to two pins, which the SSP engineer verified, giving Kaufmann permission to proceed.

It was about as simple as it got. Energize the navigation card and activate the Russian algorithm, which would then burn the chip out. Kaufmann moved the cursor on his computer over the app, then tapped it.

Data scrolled down his computer screen: the navigation card energized, the Russian algorithm activated, and the chip sent a navigation update to flight control, which the missile disregarded in its current state. The chip should have then burned out, which the app verified by sending an identical command to activate the Russian algorithm. The navigation card ignored it.

Success.

Kaufmann disconnected the alligator clips from

the missile tube. "You should be good to go now. The Russians won't be able to mess with this missile."

The Weapons Officer ordered the umbilical reattached to the tube and for the chief to run diagnostics on the missile. Commander Skogstad led the group back to Control, where they were joined a short time later by the Weapons Officer, who addressed the submarine's Captain.

"Sir, we've verified the missile in tube Twenty-one is operational."

"Very well," Skogstad replied. He signaled another officer in Control, who approached with a message clipboard. As Skogstad reviewed the prewritten message, Kaufmann glanced at the contents, which reported Kaufmann's procedure had been implemented, the missile verified operational, and USS *Maryland* was ready to launch.

Skogstad signed the message, then ordered, "Transmit."

The message was quickly transmitted, then Skogstad ordered the Officer of the Deck, "Increase depth to two hundred feet and deploy a communications buoy."

Lieutenant Wells acknowledged and the submarine tilted downward. Not long thereafter, with *Maryland* steady at two hundred feet, one of the two communication buoys in the submarine's superstructure was released; the doors opened and the tethered buoy floated upward, stopping a few feet below the surface.

A report emanated from the speakers, "Conn, Radio. In sync with the VLF broadcast."

Activity in Control died down as the submarine crew settled into its routine.

"What now?" Kaufmann asked of Commander Skogstad.

"We wait," he replied, "for the launch message."

47

WASHINGTON, D.C.

In the Situation Room beneath the West Wing, the president joined four other men at the table: Kevin Hardison, SecDef Dunnavant, Chief of Naval Operations Admiral Rettman, and Vice Admiral Rhodes. Unlike recent meetings, which had been permeated by a dark, somber mood, there was optimism in the air. They were about to launch a Trident missile again, hoping this time for a successful outcome.

The president directed his first question to Vice Admiral Rhodes. "Are we ready?"

"Yes, sir," Rhodes replied. "A replacement missile with inert warheads and instrumentation packages was loaded aboard USS *Maryland* this morning, and we've disabled the suspect microprocessor in the missile's navigation circuit."

To Dunnavant, the president asked, "Have arrangements been made with General Andropov?"

"Yes, sir. He's been informed that we've inserted a software fix into all of our missiles—although that's untrue at the moment—and that we'll launch one this afternoon. The Russians are undoubtedly awaiting the launch. Andropov is also available for a videoconference at Russia's Ministry of Defense headquarters."

Dunnavant glanced at the video screen on the far wall, split into halves. One side displayed a dull gray ocean with small whitecaps cresting beneath a brisk wind. The other half of the screen was black.

"Let's get Andropov on line," the president said.

Dunnavant spoke into the speakerphone on the table, directing the IT staff to begin the videoconference. General Andropov appeared, sitting at a conference room table flanked by several military officers.

"General Andropov," the president said, "I want to advise you that the United States has restored its full nuclear deterrence. There was a flaw in how you implemented your sabotage, and all three legs of our nuclear triad are again operational. In a few minutes, we'll launch another Trident missile, and I challenge you to alter its flight path."

Andropov displayed no emotion as he listened to the president. When he finished, Andropov replied, "We shall see." The screen went dark.

"Well," the president said, "he's certainly a man of few words."

He turned to Dunnavant. "Send the launch message."

The president waited in the Situation Room as the order was transmitted from the Operations Center in the Pentagon's National Military Command Center. Admiral Rhodes said it would take about fifteen minutes from the time the message was transmitted for *Maryland* to establish launch conditions, spin up the missile, and send it navigation and target coordinates. They watched the display on the far wall, waiting for the missile to emerge from the water.

The minutes ticked by, then a missile rose from the ocean, its first-stage engine igniting once it cleared the surface. It accelerated upward, leaving behind a trail of white smoke, then disappeared into a thick blanket of gray clouds. The video screen switched to a satellite feed, detecting the missile after it penetrated the clouds and continued its climb through the Earth's atmosphere. The missile's programmed aim point, a few thousand miles into the Atlantic Ocean, blinked red, and a data feed from the instrumented missile scrolled across the bottom of the display.

The tension built as the missile shifted to its second-stage engine, continuing on its programmed trajectory. It then transitioned to its third-stage engine burn. When the engine shut down, the missile remained on track. From there, the warheads would land at a location determined primarily by the missile's ballistic trajectory, modified slightly by pulses from the third-stage engine.

No one spoke as the missile continued its descent, with the data feed reporting when each warhead was released from the main bus. There was a collective sigh of relief in the Situation Room when each warhead landed precisely as programmed.

The president turned to Dunnavant. "Begin moving all Army and Air Force assets required for the NATO offensive."

48

MOSCOW, RUSSIA

General Andropov, sitting at his desk across from Generals Volodin and Glukov, slammed the briefcase shut. He wondered if the hastily assembled controller was somehow inferior to the ten units under the control of the Strategic Rocket Forces at their headquarters in Kuntsevo. It had functioned perfectly the first time, however, sapping the power from the American B-2 bombers and altering the Trident missile flight exactly as directed. But a few minutes ago, he'd entered the same commands and the Trident missile had ignored them. The American president hadn't been bluffing; they had somehow neutralized the Zolotov option.

The Zolotov option should have sidelined America for at least a year. By then, with no harm done to the citizens of the occupied countries—merely the installation of pro-Russian governments—NATO's appetite for war would wane. As long as the people prospered, this time under the existing capitalist markets instead of communism, why shed blood to put *their* politicians in power instead of *Russia's*? Politicians as a whole were vile anyway, and the thought of sacrificing the lives of honorable soldiers to put the *right* politicians in power riled his stomach. But now that the United

States was unrestrained, and with the sting of Russia's invasions still fresh, NATO would likely resort to military force.

Andropov examined Colonel Generals Volodin and Glukov, commanders-in-chief of the Aerospace and Ground Forces, respectively. Both men sat stoically in their chairs, their expressions guarded. He knew what they were thinking; was there a way out of their predicament, from both a military and personal perspective?

"Your assessment, Generals?"

Alexei Volodin was the first to respond. "The restraints have been removed from the United States, and their president will no doubt press for NATO intervention as he did last time. When evaluating the path forward, we must minimize the possibility that NATO will resort to military force. If we stop now, holding Eastern Ukraine and only a sliver of Lithuania, leaving the Baltic States independent, NATO would have minimal incentive to wage war."

"A few months ago," Andropov replied, "I would have agreed with you. Our previous invasion of Ukraine and Lithuania served as an excellent test of NATO resolve. There are many members within the Alliance with no intestinal fortitude. But with the right leadership, they will commit. With Germany joining the United States and Britain this time, I believe NATO will resort to military force, even if we take nothing more." Andropov asked Glukov, head of the Ground Forces, "Your thoughts?"

"I believe NATO will intercede militarily," Glukov answered. "We must either withdraw or take the measures necessary to prevail if a conflict ensues."

"What would those measures be?" Andropov asked.

"I need more defendable positions and the continued commitment of the Airborne and Spetsnaz troops. Where do we stand on those forces?"

"General Grachev has pledged his full support, so the Airborne brigades will remain committed. You need not worry about the Spetsnaz, including the GRU brigades. They will follow my orders, although most of the GRU Spetsnaz have been assigned to guard our critical infrastructure sites, so the American president cannot blackmail us like he did last time." Andropov paused, reflecting on Glukov's first point. "You said you need more defendable positions. Explain."

Glukov answered, "We need to advance to the Vistula and Siret Rivers and the Carpathian Mountains."

"You're talking about part of Poland and Romania, plus all of Ukraine."

Glukov nodded. "If we are convinced NATO will attack, we must fight the battle on more favorable terrain. The Vistula and Siret Rivers, combined with the Carpathian Mountains, form a natural defense across the entire continent. It would leave only two small sections on each end of the Carpathians without easily defendable terrain. NATO offensives in either area would be perilous, as they'd be subject to pincer counteroffensives from each side. Additionally, advancing to the Vistula River will free the forces in Kaliningrad Oblast to assist. Their anti-air assets are formidable."

General Andropov repressed a smile. This had been his plan all along; advancing to the Vistula River in Poland and taking the rest of Ukraine and northeast Romania, establishing defendable buffer states between Russia and NATO. Glukov was an astute general and had likely suspected Andropov's endgame.

Andropov met Glukov's eyes briefly, then asked, "If we advance into Poland and Romania, are you certain you can hold what we take?"

Glukov turned to General Volodin. "If we can prevent NATO from obtaining air superiority, my men will hold."

Volodin answered, "As long as my task is to prevent NATO air superiority and not achieve it ourselves, I can accomplish the task. We have adequate anti-air assets to take the sky away from NATO."

General Andropov considered Glukov's plan for a moment, pretending he'd been surprised by the aggressive proposal. Finally, he replied, "Advancing to the Vistula and Siret Rivers and Carpathian Mountains is wise from both a military and political perspective. It offers the best chance of prevailing if the matter devolves into a military conflict, and also provides us with a significant bargaining chip with NATO. If it appears it is in our best interest to withdraw, we may still achieve our primary objective: we'll offer to return the regions of Poland and Romania in our control in return for a sliver of Lithuania and NATO's guarantee not to intercede in Ukraine. Each side gets something they want."

As long as he had a say, however, Russia would keep everything.

Andropov gave the order. "Advance to the Vistula and Siret Rivers and the Carpathian Mountains."

49

KIEV, UKRAINE

Kiev, the capital of Ukraine, is the largest city in the country and seventh most populous in Europe. Although many Ukrainians view Russia favorably and one-eighth of the population believe Ukraine and Russia should unite into a single state, the inhabitants of Kiev are more pro-Western. The city was the primary site of the Euromaidan protests, which railed against government corruption and advocated for closer ties to the European Union rather than Russia. The protests led to the 2014 Ukrainian revolution, during which President Viktor Yanukovych's Russian-leaning administration was replaced with a pro-Western government.

In his temporary headquarters overlooking the Dnieper River, which cut through the center of Kiev, Lieutenant General Dmitry Sokolov, commander of Russia's 4th Guards Tank Division, reviewed the map on his conference room table, scrutinizing his unit's defensive positions along the river's east bank. He found it odd that a tank division would be assigned to such a dense metropolitan area. Armor was ill-suited for urban warfare, as the Germans learned in World War II after sending panzer divisions into Stalingrad. However, there was no better symbol of Russian military might than 4th Guards Tank Division columns entering the Ukrainian capital.

In addition to stationing an armored division in a major metropolis, Sokolov also found it odd that none of the bridges across the river were being wired with explosives. If NATO or the United States attempted to liberate Ukraine by force, Russia would destroy the bridges. However, with fifteen intact bridges spanning the river in Kiev, there was no better place for 4th Guards Tank Division if a march farther west was ordered.

Sokolov's adjutant knocked on the conference room door, then entered carrying a red folder. Sokolov read the message inside. His instinct had been correct; his division's brief stay in Kiev had come to a close. They'd been ordered into southeast Poland, tasked with seizing the main transportation hub of Rzeszów. He read the message further. The entire 1st Guards Tank Army had been assigned to take and hold southeast Poland.

A quick glance at the map explained everything. The Vistula River ran south from the Baltic Sea almost to the Carpathian Mountains, with the two geographic features forming a natural defensive line across Europe. The area in the center, near Rzeszów, was open terrain. If NATO launched an offensive, it would likely occur there, which meant the 4th Guards Tank Division would meet its nemesis, America's 1st Armored Division—*Old Ironsides*.

Sokolov looked forward to the challenge.

50

FORT BLISS, TEXAS

Major General Dutch Hostler, commanding officer of 1st Armored Division, stepped from his office, looking calmly around the hectic headquarters building. His staff was busy on the phones, typing rapidly on their computers, reviewing and signing paperwork, and entering and exiting the building at a brisk pace. He folded his arms and leaned against the doorway. They were polishing the cannonball. 1st Armored Division's preparations to date were good enough, and additional efforts would have no impact on the outcome. Whether you fired a polished or unpolished cannonball made no difference.

However, Hostler took pride in his staff as they attended to the final details of their transport to Europe. All personnel had been recalled; the tanks, armored personnel carriers, artillery, and other vehicles had been fueled, and supplies had been containerized. Transport ships were already docked or en route to the five largest Texas ports, where 1st Armored Division would embark. All that remained was the final order, and *Old Ironsides*' twenty thousand vehicles and supply containers would be on the move.

Captain Kurt Wise, Hostler's aide, emerged from

the communications center carrying a message folder. He handed the message to Hostler, who read the directive. The orders they'd been waiting for had finally arrived.

"Inform all brigades," Hostler said. "We're moving out."

51

CASTEAU, BELGIUM

Five levels underground, the commander of NATO's military force, U.S. Army General Andy Wheeler, stood at the back of the command center, examining the video screens mounted on the front wall. Located just north of Mons, SHAPE—Supreme Headquarters Allied Powers Europe—is the headquarters of NATO's Allied Command Operations. The lighting in the command center was dim so personnel could more easily study the video screens, each displaying a different section of Europe. The maps were annotated with symbols of various colors and designs, each representing a NATO or non-Alliance combat unit— armor, mechanized infantry, artillery, and air defense, to name a few. The red units were on the move.

It had started an hour ago. Russian units digging in on the east bank of the Dnieper River had suddenly surged forward, pouring across the bridges into Western Ukraine. Likewise to the north; the Russian brigades in Lithuania had left their fortified positions behind, moving into Poland. Wheeler searched for the symbols representing Russia's 1st Guards Tank Army, their premier fighting unit. They were in Northern Ukraine, swinging up toward Poland, where they'd connect with the Russian forces heading southwest from Lithuania.

NATO was in no condition to oppose the Russian advance. Throughout NATO, Wheeler had only a dozen brigades ready for combat. In comparison, the Russians had fifty-two. All told, a quarter-million Russian troops were heading west.

There would be no resistance in Western Ukraine, nor in Poland since the Polish Army was still mobilizing. However, even when fully combat ready, Polish forces would total only one-third of the Russian troops advancing into Poland. Without a united, coordinated NATO response, resistance was pointless. To date, the NATO resolution authorizing military force had stalled in the council, and American forces were frozen at their stateside bases. Without the full commitment of the United States and the rest of NATO, repulsing a quarter-million Russian ground troops was impossible.

Retreat was the only option for now, trading land for time. A critical question Wheeler had no answer to was—how far would the Russians advance? Would they stop at the Vistula River? The Oder? Or continue into Germany? The Vistula seemed the most likely for now, as advancing farther west would result in less-defensible terrain and strain the Russian Army's supply lines, which would be vulnerable to insurgent resistance within the occupied territory. Just in case, the Polish Army was wiring the bridges across the Vistula River with explosives, hoping to slow Russia's advance. The bridges had to remain intact for now, providing a retreat path for Polish forces still in the eastern region of the country.

Wheeler needed clarity. What was Russia's objective? When would the United States join the conflict?

How long before sufficient NATO units were combat ready?

A display on the far wall updated, and Wheeler shifted his attention to a map of Western Europe, where new blue symbols appeared, marking the arrival points for U.S. Army divisions. That was good news in what had otherwise been a gloomy day. It would take a while to complete the transit, but American forces were finally on their way.

52

ARLINGTON, VIRGINIA

In the Pentagon's National Military Command Center, the president took his seat at the head of the conference table. The list of those present was similar to the meeting held a few hours after the Trident missile's dummy warheads landed in Washington. On one side of the table sat the Joint Chiefs of Staff, with the other side occupied by Vice President Tompkins and members of the president's staff and cabinet. Dunnavant began the brief, providing an update on Russia's incursions across Ukraine and the dual thrusts into Poland from Lithuania and Ukraine. A summary of NATO forces followed. They were retreating rather than fighting, as NATO hadn't yet constituted sufficient firepower to engage.

"How long before our forces arrive in Europe?" the president asked.

"The first troops will begin arriving at daybreak, and the two Airborne divisions and most Stryker brigades will complete the transit by the fifth day. The rest of our forces will take much longer to complete the transit, with the long pole in the tent being First Armored Division, which will be transported by sea."

"Can we send First Armored Division by air?"

"We can, but we'd have to delay three other divisions. First Armored Division has a lot of equipment, over twenty thousand vehicles and shipping containers, and their tanks are so heavy that only two will fit in our largest transport. From an efficiency standpoint, it makes more sense to send First Armored Division by sea and allocate the airlift to divisions with less equipment."

"How long before every division arrives in Europe?"

"Two weeks, but we're working on pulling the timeline in."

"Two weeks? A quarter-million Russians are on the move now. What if they don't stop?"

Dunnavant turned to General Okey Watson, Chairman of the Joints Chiefs of Staff, who answered the president's question. "General Wheeler will have some tough decisions to make regarding NATO force commitment. U.S. air assets will complete the transit in a few days, and Wheeler can commit those forces early if necessary. That will probably be his last resort, as he'll want to preserve air assets for the offensive. One way or another, Wheeler should be able to stop the Russians or slow them down enough to buy the time we need. The question will be the cost, both in ground and air units. But hopefully the Russians will stop without penetrating deep enough into Europe to force Wheeler's hand."

The president asked Secretary of State Dawn Cabral, "I take it the waffling countries have dropped their objections to the NATO resolution authorizing military force?"

"Yes, Mr. President. The secretary general has moved up the timetable for a vote on the resolution. A decision has been requested by 4 p.m. tomorrow, Brussels-time."

"Submit a *yes* vote for the United States," the president directed.

He looked at General Watson. "If we're forced to engage Russia militarily, I imagine the casualty rate will be high."

"Tens of thousands dead and many more wounded, sir."

The president addressed Dunnavant. "How long until we extract Kalinin?"

Dunnavant glanced at the clock. "*Michigan*'s SEALs will head ashore in two hours."

"Where do we stand on a plan returning him to power?"

"We're working on it, sir. But we're also working with a big assumption. That Kalinin will keep his word and recall his troops."

"If he reneges, we won't be any worse off than we are now."

53

KRASNODAR KRAI, RUSSIA

As night fell across the Black Sea, dark gray clouds had moved ashore, accompanied by strong winds and heavy rain. On the side of a two-lane road of crumbling concrete, rain pelted the windows of Traktir na Petrovke, a local pub in a small cluster of buildings in the heavily wooded oblast. Inside the pub, Danil Vasiliev stood behind the bar serving drinks to his customers. The tavern was busier than normal, with most of the patrons gathered around the bar, their eyes glued to the television mounted on the wall behind him.

Details were filtering in about Russian invasions of Ukraine and Poland, with scenes of Russian tanks and armored vehicles rumbling west. The topic dominated the conversations, with opinions ranging from shock and disapproval to "*it's about time* Russia reasserted control over its belligerent western neighbors."

The pub door burst open with a gust of wind as Georgiy Abramov entered, his coat and hair drenched from the short walk from his car. Abramov hung his coat on a rack, then worked his way through the crowd to the bar. "'Evening Danil. The usual."

Vasiliev greeted his customer and friend, then poured

a glass of his favorite beer. After sliding the drink across the bar, he poured himself a shot of vodka.

Abramov eyed him curiously. "What is the occasion?"

"I was robbed." Vasiliev went on to explain the gunpoint theft, also describing the perpetrator. "Have you seen her around or heard of other incidents?"

Abramov shook his head. "She took only your phone? No money?"

"Just the phone. It does seem strange," Vasiliev admitted.

Vasiliev moved on, serving other customers at the bar, returning to refill Abramov's glass.

Abramov pointed over Vasiliev's shoulder at the television screen. "What did you say the woman looked like?"

Vasiliev turned and spotted a news flash from the local television station, which had taken a break from the Russian invasion to focus on local news. The TV screen was split between a news anchor at his desk and a mug shot of a woman. Vasiliev listened intently as the anchor continued his report.

". . . and is considered armed and dangerous. Anyone spotting her or having information about her location should contact authorities immediately. A reward is being offered for information leading to her apprehension. At the bottom of the screen is the number to call."

Vasiliev wrote the phone number on a napkin as the man continued with details of her alleged crimes.

"Good-looking woman," Abramov said. "You should have invited her to stay for a drink."

Vasiliev extended his hand. "Give me your phone."

Abramov pulled his flip phone from its holster and slapped it into Vasiliev's hand.

After glancing at the napkin, Vasiliev punched the number into the phone and hit *Send*. The next time the woman used her stolen cell phone, authorities would be able to pinpoint her location.

54

USS *MICHIGAN*

Captain Murray Wilson entered *Michigan*'s Battle Management Center where his crew conducted Tomahawk mission planning and coordinated SEAL operations. The BMC was crammed with twenty-five tactical consoles: thirteen on the port side, plus twelve on starboard arranged in four rows facing aft. Mounted on the aft bulkhead was a sixty-inch plasma screen.

Wilson took his seat at one of the twelve consoles on the starboard side, joining his Executive Officer and department heads. Navy SEALs, led by Commander John McNeil, occupied the other consoles, with several more SEALs gathered at the back of the room. Standing beside the plasma display were Lieutenant Harrison and the submarine's Navigator, Lieutenant Ed Lloyd.

McNeil kicked off the mission brief. "As you're aware, we've been tasked with extracting President Kalinin and Christine O'Connor from the Russian countryside. The Nav will brief our approach to the launch point, then Harrison will review the mission details."

McNeil turned to Lloyd, who controlled the bulkhead display with a remote in his hand. A nautical chart of the Black Sea appeared, zooming in on the eastern shore. Lloyd's brief was short and uneventful from a navigation perspective—there were no underwater features interfering with *Michigan*'s approach, but there was another issue to be considered.

"The launch point is twenty-five nautical miles from Novorossiysk, homeport to three Kilo class diesel submarines. Intel reported all three Kilos sortied to sea five days ago and they remain in the Black Sea; SOSUS arrays haven't detected their transit through the Turkish Straits. Although they can refuel at most Black Sea ports, they typically return to Novorossiysk for refueling. That means one or more of the Kilos could be nearby during the mission."

Lloyd handed the remote to Lieutenant Harrison.

"This will be a hot extraction following a failed Delta Force rescue, so the Russians will be on alert. We'll send a squad ashore using the two Rigid Hull Inflatable Boats in the port Dry Deck Shelter. Maydwell, Mendelson, and Brown will join me in the first fire team, while Senior Chief Stone will lead the other team of Rodrigues, Rosenberry, and Stigers."

Harrison shifted the display to a satellite image of the Black Sea coast, annotated with a red dot along the shore. "The coastline in this region is dominated by cliffs, and most points offering easy inland access are too populated for our purpose. There is one suitable spot, just north of Krinitsa, where a small river empties into the Black Sea between two bluffs. We'll head ashore at this location.

"President Kalinin is injured and cannot travel without assistance, so we'll rendezvous with him and Christine O'Connor at a predetermined location. They were last reported about three miles inland. We'll contact them once we're inbound and get an update on their position. Accounting for the terrain, I expect the ingress and egress to take about two hours each, returning to *Michigan* before dawn.

"Weather will be a factor," Harrison added. "A strong front moved in today, bringing heavy rain and wind. The rain will provide additional cover, but may slow our progress. We have an extra two hours as buffer before dawn in case we get delayed.

"Any questions?"

There were a few, delving into the details, then the briefing wrapped up.

Two hours later, with USS *Michigan* at periscope depth, Lieutenant Jake Harrison was outfitted in a black dive suit, rubber booties, and a tank harness, plus a backpack over one shoulder. He stepped into the Missile Compartment, joining three other SEALs by Missile Tube Two: Petty Officers First Class Rob Maydwell and Richard Mendelson, and Petty Officer Second Class Wayne Brown. Although both Rigid Hull Inflatable Boats (RHIBs) were stored in the Dry Deck Shelter attached to Missile Tube Two, Senior Chief Stone's four-man team would enter tube One. With two RHIBs in one shelter, there'd be insufficient room for all eight SEALs. Harrison's team would extract one RHIB while Stone's men exited the other shelter, then grabbed the second RHIB.

Harrison and his fire team stepped through the circular hatch in the side of Missile Tube Two. Maydwell shut the hatch and spun the handle, sealing the four men inside the seven-foot-diameter tube. Harrison led the way, climbing a steel ladder two levels into the Dry Deck Shelter, bathed in diffuse red light.

The Dry Deck Shelter was a conglomeration of three chambers: a spherical hyperbaric chamber at the forward end to treat injured divers, a spherical transfer trunk in the middle, which Harrison had just entered, and a cylindrical hangar section capable of carrying either two RHIBs or a single SEAL Delivery Vehicle—a black mini-sub capable of transporting four SEALs. The hangar was divided into two sections by a Plexiglas shield dropping halfway down from the top, with two RHIBs on one side and hangar controls on the other.

The four SEALs pulled air tanks from stowage racks, then donned their fins and masks, and Harrison rendered the *okay* hand signal to the Navy diver operating the controls.

Dark water surged into the shelter, gushing up from vents beneath them, pooling at their feet and rising rapidly. The hangar was soon flooded down, except for an air pocket on the other side of the Plexiglas shield, where the diver operated the shelter. There was a low rumbling sound as the circular hatch at the end of the hangar moved slowly open to the latched position. Harrison and the other SEALs hauled one of the RHIBs from the shelter onto the submarine's missile deck, then connected a tether line to it from a shelter stowage rail and activated the first compressed air cartridge.

As the RHIB expanded, Maydwell and Mendelson swam aft along the missile deck and opened the hatch to a locker in the submarine's superstructure. They retrieved an outboard motor and attached it to the RHIB, then actuated the second air cartridge. The RHIB fully inflated, rising toward the surface. Maydwell and Mendelson followed the boat up while Senior Chief Stone's fire team, after exiting the other Dry Deck Shelter, pulled the second RHIB from the shelter and duplicated the process.

Mendelson returned a few moments later, rendering the *okay* hand signal, as did a SEAL from Stone's team. Harrison and Stone attached flotation devices to two large duffel bags carrying additional weapons.

They'd be exposed on the surface during their ingress and egress, vulnerable to air attack, and had packed appropriate equipment. Harrison activated the air cartridge, making the heavy weapons neutrally buoyant, then informed the diver inside the shelter that they were proceeding on their mission. The two SEALs disconnected the RHIB tether lines from the shelter and headed toward the surface, with the two duffel bags in tow.

Harrison was the last up, climbing into the RHIB while Mendelson hauled in the duffel bag. The outboard engine was running, but barely audible above the heavy rain pounding the water's surface. Their position updated on Maydwell's handheld GPS display, then he shifted the outboard into gear and pointed the RHIB toward their insertion point on the Black Sea coast. Senior Chief Stone's RHIB followed. Harrison pulled a waterproof phone from his backpack and called the number he'd been given.

55

KRASNODAR KRAI, RUSSIA

As the heavy rain deluged the forest, Christine and Kalinin tried to stay dry inside the dilapidated cabin. The ground had settled since the cabin was built, creating a slight slope in the floor, and rainwater had begun running through the front door. The initial trickle had turned into a small stream, pooling against the opposite wall as it drained through rotted sections of the cabin logs. Christine and Kalinin had moved to the higher corner of the cabin, under the intact portion of the roof. They talked only when required, using hushed voices, afraid they'd be heard by Russian soldiers searching the forest.

The cell phone on the ground beside Christine vibrated and she answered. She recognized the voice on the other end immediately; he was never far from her thoughts. The conversation was short, with Christine relaying their position after checking the smartphone map, and Harrison providing an estimated time of arrival: two hours.

Five kilometers away, seated in a control van parked alongside a narrow two-lane road, Colonel Savvin looked up from his console as Major Lebedev entered.

"We have an intercept," Lebedev said. "We couldn't listen to the conversation but we tracked the signal, pinpointing the source with an accuracy of one thousand meters."

Savvin did the math in his head: they were dealing with a circular area of about three square kilometers. He had hoped for a more accurate position, but it was better than what they'd been working with, not knowing which direction Kalinin and O'Connor had headed after leaving the helicopter wreck. They would cordon off the area quickly, then contract toward the center.

"Employ all available men," Savvin ordered. "Don't let them slip through the perimeter."

56

KRASNODAR KRAI, RUSSIA

Harrison's RHIB was in the lead as they headed toward shore. The SEALs in both RHIBs had shed their scuba gear and donned bulletproof tactical vests, camouflaged rain jackets and pants pulled from their backpacks, plus helmets with built-in communications and attached night vision goggles. As Harrison scanned the dark horizon, cliffs appeared in the distance. Maydwell identified their insertion point—a gap in the bluffs—and adjusted course. Just before reaching shore, he shifted the engine to neutral.

The RHIBs coasted to a halt as they ground onto the pebble-sand beach. The SEALs slid into the water and hauled the boats across the beach into the foliage. After hiding the RHIBs, they retrieved their M4 carbines with attached suppressors, which were loaded with subsonic ammunition to reduce the discharge noise. Harrison then led the squad up the slope into the forest.

After the day-long rain, the ground was soft and their boots sank into the mud in spots, slowing their progress. The two fire teams spread out, remaining within visual distance of each other, with Harrison leading one team and Senior Chief Stone the other.

They had approached to within a half-mile of Kalinin and Christine's position when Stone stopped, then spoke into his headset.

"Movement ahead."

Harrison halted the squad and scanned the forest through his night vision goggles. In the distance, an armed soldier was moving in the same direction as the SEALs. To the left was another man and to the right, a third, the spacing about twenty feet.

Somehow the Russians had located Kalinin and Christine and were tightening the noose. After conferring with Stone, Harrison decided to punch through the Russian perimeter and advance quickly, reaching Kalinin and Christine before the Russians did. Stone brought his M4 carbine to bear on the closest soldier while the snipers in each team, Mendelson and Rosenberry, took aim on the soldiers on either side. Harrison gave the signal and they fired three rounds into each man, the sound of the suppressed shots masked somewhat by the heavy rain.

The three soldiers fell to the ground and the SEALs surged forward, collapsing into a single column to minimize the possibility they'd be spotted by additional Russians on either side. Harrison passed over the middle soldier, immobile and facedown in the mud. The other SEALs passed through the Russian perimeter, undetected in the darkness. Once inside the ring of Russian soldiers, the SEALs spread out again.

As they quickly covered the remaining ground, Rodrigues's voice came over Harrison's headset. "Over here. A cabin."

The eight SEALs converged on the cabin. A stream of rainwater ran down the hillside, through the cabin's entrance. Harrison signaled for a three-man entry, selecting Mendelson and Brown. The three men lined up along one side of the doorway, while Maydwell moved to the other side and Senior Chief Stone's fire team turned outward, guarding against the arrival of Russian troops.

Harrison held up his fingers, counting down the time, then the three men burst inside, Harrison straight ahead, then Mendelson and Brown to each side.

The cabin was empty except for two individuals in a corner. The three SEALs brought their weapons to bear on them. Neither person moved.

Harrison lifted his night vision goggles and illuminated the two persons with a green flashlight, identifying Kalinin and Christine.

"We don't have much time," Harrison said. "Russian soldiers will be here soon." To Kalinin, he asked, "How much assistance do you need to travel?" He glanced at Kalinin's legs, which were extended in front of him, his right pants leg pulled up and his shoelace loosened.

"With one man's help, I can hobble. But if we have to travel quickly, I will need full assistance."

"Brown, Mendelson. Carry him."

The two SEALs helped Kalinin to his feet, each man wrapping one of Kalinin's arms around his shoulders. Kalinin was a tall man, six feet, but when the two SEALs stood fully upright, Kalinin's feet dangled a few inches above the ground.

"That'll do," Harrison said.

Christine pushed herself to her feet, moving close to Harrison. "It's good to see you," she said.

Harrison didn't reply. There'd be time to talk later. He turned off the light and replaced his night vision goggles, noticing that Christine was also donning a set she'd somehow obtained. She slung a backpack over one shoulder and he spotted a pistol in her hand, without a silencer.

"Don't shoot unless we're fired on first."

Christine replied, "I'm not stupid, Jake."

Harrison was going to explain that he was just making sure, then decided to drop it.

After the three SEALs emerged from the cabin with Kalinin and Christine, Harrison decided to head back out the same direction they'd come, hoping the Russians hadn't discovered the gap in their formation.

Harrison led the way again as the SEALs formed a single file, with Kalinin and Christine in the middle. They had traveled only fifty yards before Harrison saw movement ahead. The spacing between the Russian soldiers was now only a dozen feet and there was no longer a gap. They were also advancing more cautiously, continuing to contract their spacing. Harrison ordered the SEALs to stop and cover, and the SEALs dropped down into the foliage as Harrison conferred with Senior Chief Stone.

Stone recommended they hunker down and take their chances as the Russians passed by. If they were discovered, they'd take out the nearest soldiers, then bolt toward the coast. Kalinin was going to be a problem, though. Mendelson and Brown couldn't travel very fast with Kalinin dangling between them.

After Harrison informed the squad of the plan, he contacted the larger of the two SEALs carrying Kalinin. "Mendelson. Carry Kalinin on your back."

Mendelson shrugged out of his backpack and handed his firearm to Brown, then explained the piggyback plan to Kalinin. Harrison then terminated audible communications until further notice; the Russians were almost within earshot. He signaled down the line, assigning each SEAL except Mendelson to an approaching soldier.

As the Russians continued their advance, Harrison kept his M4 trained on the nearest soldier, watching the man's head. It moved slowly back and forth across the forest until it froze, looking directly at Harrison.

The Russian swung his rifle toward him but Harrison fired first. The soldier went down and the other SEALs engaged, killing six more men, three on each side.

Harrison gave the order and the SEAL formation bolted forward, passing through the gap, with Christine in the middle and Kalinin on Mendelson's back. There was a commotion on both sides and bullets whizzed through the foliage. Harrison remained low and checked on Mendelson's speed, reducing his so as to not outpace him. Maydwell was the last in line, and behind him, the Russians were converging in a V formation, gaining ground. Mendelson was doing well, but the unencumbered Russians were traveling faster.

Mendelson's slower pace gave Maydwell the opportunity to stop and fire on occasion. He dropped several Russians, but the others kept coming, their pace unabated. During one exchange, Maydwell took a bullet in his thigh and he stumbled to the ground. Rodrigues lent a hand, and the two men continued on while Rosenberry dropped to the rear to provide cover. It wasn't long before Rosenberry was struck by three bullets: two were stopped by his bulletproof vest and a third dug into his left shoulder. Fortunately, Rosenberry was right-handed and his aim was unaffected.

Harrison crested a ridge and stopped briefly, turning back to assess the situation. The Russians had closed half the distance. They wouldn't make it to the coast. He examined the terrain ahead. The ridge dropped down into a ravine, through which ran a stream. He headed down the ridge, then turned left and followed the stream up the hillside, hoping the Russians wouldn't notice the sudden change in direction. Just before the Russians reached the ridge, he ordered his squad to head ten feet up the slope, then drop into the foliage.

When the Russians reached the ridgetop, they failed

to spot the SEALs and halted. After a short conversation between the lead Russians, the group split into
three formations. About twenty-five men continued
ahead, fanning out into the forest, while a dozen soldiers followed the stream uphill and another dozen
went downhill. The dozen men moving in the SEAL
team's direction proceeded with caution as the other
two Russian formations faded into the darkness.

Harrison assigned two Russians to each SEAL except for Mendelson, who still had Kalinin on his back.
The Russians moved uphill in a single file, hugging the
stream about ten feet below. Harrison peered through
the bushes as they approached. When the formation
pulled even with the SEALs, Harrison gave the order.

It was over in seconds. The SEALs put three bullets
into each Russian—two body shots and a third to the
head. The attack had been barely audible above the
rushing water.

Harrison resumed the trek upstream, and they approached a rock formation where the stream passed
through a path too narrow to follow. Turning right
would take them toward the coast, but also in the same
direction as twenty-five Russian soldiers. Turning left
would head away from the Russians, but away from
their RHIBs as well.

He checked his watch. They'd eaten halfway into
their two-hour reserve. After taking into account a
slower transit due to Kalinin's and Maydwell's injuries
and the need to remain concealed, Harrison concluded
that even if they headed directly toward shore, they
wouldn't make it before daylight. Harrison decided the
best plan was to find shelter and head to the coast the
following evening. He checked his digital map, looking for favorable terrain to their left. There was a river
not far away, which might offer possibilities along the
shore.

Harrison conferred with Senior Chief Stone, who agreed with the plan. Maydwell and Rosenberry were losing blood and their wounds needed to be tended to. Harrison pulled out a radio and contacted Commander McNeil aboard *Michigan,* informing him of the plan. *Michigan* would remain on station, awaiting a rendezvous a day later.

They began moving again, with Harrison leading the squad along the rock formation toward the river. The ground gradually rose as they continued on, then Harrison stopped suddenly. He was on a precipice overlooking a raging river two hundred feet below, swollen with the day's rains. To his right, the rock formation rose even higher, and he spotted an indentation in the cliff about thirty feet up. He climbed up and took a look. It would suffice—a six-foot-wide ledge with an overhang, cut into the rock face, visible only from the cliff edge below. He informed the other SEALs, who then joined him, bringing Kalinin and Christine.

Senior Chief Stone activated a green glow stick, faintly illuminating the recess. Brown and Rodrigues tended to Maydwell and Rosenberry, while Mendelson examined Kalinin. There wasn't much they could do for Kalinin, whose ankle appeared to be badly sprained but not broken. Maydwell's and Rosenberry's wounds were cleaned and dressed, and the bleeding stopped.

Stone developed a watch rotation, assigning Stigers and Rodrigues to the first round, then the remaining SEALs settled in for the night. Mendelson talked with Kalinin, while Stone checked on Maydwell and Rosenberry. They spoke in muted voices, the roar from the river below almost drowning out their conversations. The torrential rain continued, showing no sign of abating.

Harrison sought out Christine. She was sitting by herself at one end of the ledge, her legs hanging over, staring into the rain. The last time he'd seen her was aboard *Michigan* two months ago, her face and wrists still bandaged, as she was transferred off the submarine at Diego Garcia in the Indian Ocean. She hadn't stopped by to say good-bye. He recalled their last intimate conversation a few days earlier, in her stateroom, when she'd asked the only question that seemed to matter—*How were things at home?* He'd seen the disappointment in her eyes when he answered the question truthfully.

He approached Christine and sat beside her. Neither said anything for a while.

Finally, he asked, "How are you doing?"

"I'm good," Christine answered. She didn't continue the conversation, staring into the darkness instead.

"No injuries? It's not like you to be in perfect health." The three previous times she'd been brought aboard *Michigan*, Doc Aleo had removed a bullet from her arm, treated her for severe hypothermia, and tended to her cut face and wrists.

Christine turned toward him. "Miraculously, I'm unscathed." She smiled, and the tension between them melted away.

Harrison pulled his water bottle from its harness and some rations from his backpack, offering them to Christine.

"I have my own," she said, retrieving a water bottle and rations from her backpack. "Vodka," she held up the water bottle, "and Russian vittles."

Harrison glanced at the bottle. "That's not vodka."

"Sure is. Just what I need right now too." She removed the cap and took a sip, then offered the bottle to Harrison. "Want some?"

He brought the bottle to his nose, then broke into a grin. "Nice one. Almost had me."

Christine smiled again, and he remembered the first time they had shared a bottle of vodka, in the barn behind his parents' house. They'd escape there often, sitting in the loft, their feet hanging over the edge just as they did now, and talk. There was always a sparkle in her eyes and her laugh was infectious. When they were kids, she was his best friend. It wasn't until she started developing into a woman that he saw her in a different light. He recalled the day he asked her to be his girlfriend and she said yes; he felt like he was the luckiest guy in the world. By the time he was seventeen, he'd decided they'd get married and spend the rest of their lives together.

When he proposed to her at the end of their senior year in high school, she turned him down, and did so again four years later after she graduated from college. Christine was an intelligent and beautiful woman, intent on climbing the professional and social ladders in Washington, D.C., unencumbered by a Midwestern farm boy. After waiting ten years, he realized he'd never be good enough for her and moved on, proposing to Angie a year later. Christine called the following month, saying she was finally ready. She hadn't heard the news. He loved Angie, but he sometimes wondered how different things would be if he had waited just a little longer.

Christine returned the water bottle and food pouch to her backpack. "What's the plan?"

"We'll hide out here until nightfall tomorrow, then head to the coast and return to *Michigan*."

As they talked on the cliff edge, Harrison's thoughts wandered to the peculiar situation—Christine at President Kalinin's summer residence for the weekend.

"What's with you and Kalinin?"

Christine shrugged.

"Are you seeing him?"

"It's really none of your business," she replied, her voice turning cold.

"Not that it matters," Harrison said. "I'm just curious."

She turned toward him. Even though he could barely make out her features in the faint light of the glow stick, he could tell she was irritated.

"Why do you care?" she snapped. "You're married, I'm not."

"Because I *do* care."

"It's time to stop caring."

She turned away, looking into the darkness as Harrison assessed the sudden tension between them.

"We're going to have to sort this out at some point," he said.

"Sort what out?"

"Us. We need to find a new norm."

"We don't need to figure out anything. We both made our choices in life. It will never be like it was."

"Chris, we can't disregard twenty years of history. Pretend like we were never best friends, that we never dated, were never engaged—"

"We were never engaged."

Harrison pulled back slightly. "You said yes, and the ring went on your finger."

"I gave the ring back the next morning. There's probably a twenty-four-hour rule somewhere."

It was Harrison's turn to become irritated; this wasn't the first time she'd claimed they hadn't been engaged. "Why is our engagement such a sensitive issue for you?"

"Because I follow through on things. When I say yes, I mean it. Unlike you."

Harrison had trouble following her. "What do you mean, 'unlike you'?"

"I asked if you would wait for me, and you said *yes*."

"So that's what this is all about? From the time I proposed in high school, I waited *ten* years, Chris. There was no indication you were interested in getting married, much less to me. You had your sights set on bigger fish."

"I wasn't chasing bigger fish. I was busy. I was working sixty-, seventy-hour weeks. I didn't have time for a relationship, much less marriage. I had a check-list of things I wanted to accomplish before settling down."

"It would've been nice if you had shared that with me."

Christine didn't respond, turning away again.

As Harrison tried to sort through where they stood, he realized the premise of her argument was flawed. "Why are you upset at me for saying yes and then changing my mind, when you did the same thing when I asked you to marry me the first time?"

"I never said yes."

"You're rewriting history now?"

"That's not how I remember it."

Harrison's frustration increased, but he knew it was pointless to argue. Once Christine got something in her head, she'd dig in like a bulldog playing tug-of-war. But he'd get in one last jab. He leaned toward her and softened his voice, whispering in her ear. "It was short, but I enjoyed our engagement."

"We were never engaged."

57

KRASNODAR KRAI, RUSSIA

There was a dull hiss in her ears as she awoke, lying on her side with her back against the cliff wall. As her vision cleared, she realized it was the sound of the unrelenting rain, which seemed to be coming down even harder in the early morning light. She pushed herself to a sitting position, noting someone had covered her with a SEAL camouflage jacket while she slept. A quick look around spotted Harrison without one; he was sitting beside Kalinin, talking with him in Russian. Harrison's eyes caught hers for a moment, then he looked away as he continued his conversation with Kalinin.

Christine took a closer look around. Two SEALs were on watch at opposite ends of the cliff recess, which appeared to be the entrance to an abandoned trail along the cliff face, following the river. Maydwell and Rosenberry were weathering their wounds okay; both had good color in their faces and were talking quietly with two other SEALs. Christine pulled her water bottle from her backpack and took a sip. Senior Chief Stone saw her stirring and moved along the ledge, stopping beside her.

"Do you have food?" he asked.

She pulled the Russian rations from her backpack. "Not the tastiest," she said.

"May I?" Stone asked, reaching toward the pouch.

Christine opened the package and offered him a piece of dried meat.

"That's not bad," he said. "You'll have to wait until we return to *Michigan* for a decent steak, though."

"Do we still plan to wait until tonight before heading to the coast?" she asked.

Stone nodded. "The area is infested with Russian soldiers. Our best bet is to stay put until nightfall, although this miserable weather would provide excellent cover. Even if they chose to fly helicopters in this mess, their visibility would be almost nothing, and their satellites are useless as well. But waiting until darkness, combined with the bad weather, is better."

Chief Stone moved on, conferring with one of the SEALs on watch before checking with the other. Christine chewed a few pieces of meat, then rummaged through her backpack and selected a pouch of dried fruit. As she stared into the gray, dreary weather, her thoughts drifted to her conversation with Harrison last night. She had dropped her guard and revealed the one thing she wished she hadn't.

When she had learned Harrison was engaged, she'd reacted indifferently on the phone, passing it off as— *it's your loss, not mine*. However, the news had been devastating. She'd spent the rest of the weekend curled in a fetal position in bed, crying into her pillow.

He said he would wait.

The years passed and she married Dave Hendricks, their tumultuous marriage coming to an end ten years later. Christine had to admit she was partly to blame. Although she could reason her way through the most complex issues, she sometimes struggled to contain her emotions, and every once in a while, she'd say or do things she'd later regret.

Compared to some of the things she'd done, last night was a minor transgression. But she had finally revealed her true feelings—that she'd been devastated by Harrison's engagement. She didn't know why it was important he not know, but for some reason it was. It was a moot issue now.

She glanced at Harrison again. He was still talking with Kalinin and the two men seemed to be getting along. Christine wondered where their conversations went; whether Harrison was probing Kalinin for information about their relationship, or worse yet—giving him a data dump on her. Although she didn't have any dark secrets, she was bothered by the thought that they might be talking about her. She decided to join them.

Christine approached Harrison, handing him his camouflage jacket.

"Morning, Chris," he said. "Did you get a good night's sleep?"

"Not bad, considering the accommodations." She sat down, the two men clearing a spot between them.

Kalinin noticed that Harrison had used a nickname for Christine. He asked the Navy SEAL, "Do you two know each other?"

"You could say that," Harrison replied. "We were engaged." Then he cracked a sly smile.

Christine's anger ignited. Despite their conversation last night, Harrison had pointed out they'd been engaged, just to spite her. She punched him in the chest as hard as she could, narrowly missing the armor plate in his tactical vest. "Why do you always go there when someone asks about us? Why can't you just say, 'We're friends'?"

"That'd be a stretch."

Her eyes narrowed, then she draped her arm around Kalinin's shoulders. "Yuri is my friend."

"You should choose your friends more wisely. Look at where we are."

She turned to Kalinin. "He's being an ass. Ignore him."

"Well," Kalinin replied, "if I didn't know better, I'd swear you two were married." He glanced at Harrison and spoke again in Russian, and the SEAL laughed.

Christine pulled her arm away. "You're not helping." She folded her arms across her chest and gazed into the pouring rain.

Kalinin offered Harrison a faint smile, which Harrison returned.

Stone hurried toward Harrison, dropping into a crouch. "We got company. North end."

Harrison donned his jacket and helmet, then took his M4 carbine and headed toward one end of the crevice while the other SEALs grabbed their gear and weapons. Stone and Harrison stopped beside Brown at the north end, then the three men pulled back. After conferring with Harrison, Stone moved back down the ledge, updating everyone.

"About twenty Russians below, maybe more. Can't tell through the rain. They've spotted the cutout in the cliff and three men are on their way up. We can't take a stand here. They'd radio in reinforcements before we could eliminate them. We're moving out." Stone pointed to the other end of the ledge, where Stigers was standing watch.

The ledge ahead narrowed to three feet, wide enough for passage in single file only. Her eyes shot to Kalinin and his swollen ankle.

"I will manage," he said.

He didn't have a choice. He'd have to power through the pain until they reached more favorable ground where a SEAL could assist.

Christine grabbed her backpack, then followed the SEALs as they made their way toward Stigers. Rodrigues helped Kalinin to his feet as Harrison issued orders into his headset. Stone took the lead while Christine and Kalinin were placed in the center of the column, Christine in front. While they waited, she turned back toward Harrison and Brown. The two SEALs had their M4s raised to the firing position. Each man squeezed off several rounds, then hustled toward the single-file formation.

Harrison placed himself between Christine and Kalinin, while Brown took up the rear. Harrison spoke into his headset and Stone moved forward, followed by the others. After the single-file column exited the crevice, Harrison directed Brown, "Use a thumper. Close the passage."

Brown pulled a grenade launcher from its holster, then fired a round into the far end of the ledge. The cliff shook from the explosion, partially filling the passage with rubble. Brown fired two more grenades, blocking the route completely. Another order from Harrison and the column moved forward on the narrow path, snaking slowly along the cliff. Kalinin limped along, his slow progress setting the pace.

The rain came down in cascading torrents, hitting Christine and the cliff walls at an angle, accompanied by gusting winds whipping through the gorge. They continued along the winding cliff face, with the ledge narrowing to only two feet. The path eventually widened again, but the ground transitioned from hard rock to loose gravel, sloping down toward a precipitous drop. She peered over the path's edge at the swollen river two hundred feet below. The water rushing through the ravine crashed against the rocks along the way, creating a white mist blanketing the river.

Several of the SEALs ahead lost their footing momentarily before steadying themselves, and the trail gradually deteriorated with each person's transit. Christine continued on, following closely behind Rodrigues when the path beneath her gave way. She tried to catch herself, but both feet slipped through the loose gravel, and she slid toward the cliff edge.

Harrison lunged toward her, grabbing her arm. But his hand slipped down her wet forearm as she fell, until his grip held at her wrist. Christine's weight and momentum were too much, however, and she pulled Harrison toward the cliff edge.

Mendelson dodged past Kalinin and grabbed Harrison's left boot. He dug his feet into the trail, halting Harrison and Christine's momentum. Harrison's lower body rested on the sloping cliff while his upper body hung over the edge. Christine dangled in midair, two hundred feet above the raging river.

In his effort to reach Harrison, Mendelson had knocked Kalinin off balance. His weight ended up on the wrong leg and he lost his footing as well. Kalinin slid down the steep path toward the cliff edge.

Harrison grabbed Kalinin's wrist with his other hand as he slipped off the mountainside, and the Russian swung in the air beside Christine. With Harrison holding both of them, he began sliding down the mountainside; Mendelson's footing was giving way.

Rodrigues joined in, grabbing Harrison's other boot, halting his descent. But Rodrigues and Mendelson were dangerously close to the trail edge. A few more inches and all three SEALs, along with Christine and Kalinin, would plummet over the cliff. Christine looked down and the mist parted for a second, revealing the river surging through the ravine far below.

Stigers and Brown joined in, helping Mendelson and Rodrigues gain better footing before grabbing on to Harrison's legs. With four men pulling, Harrison inched upward. But they had three more feet to go before Christine and Kalinin would be within reach of another SEAL.

The downpour continued, the rainwater running down Harrison's arms and over their hands. As he inched slowly upward, his grip on Christine began to slip, her hand sliding through his. Harrison clamped down even harder, almost crushing the bones in her hand. Then his hold on Kalinin began to slip. Harrison yelled into his headset, urging the four SEALs above to pull faster. His rate of ascension increased, but Christine and Kalinin were still two feet away from help.

Her hand slipped even farther, as did Kalinin's. As the rain streamed down Harrison's face, falling toward her, Christine saw the panic in his eyes. It was a look she'd never seen from him in the thirty-plus years she'd known him.

Harrison would have to choose between them. He could save either Kalinin or the woman he had loved for most of his life.

If there was one thing Christine was certain of, it was that Harrison would save her.

Then he let go.

Of *her*.

Christine's shock was overcome by fear as she fell toward the jagged rocks two hundred feet below.

58

KRASNODAR KRAI, RUSSIA

Kalinin watched Christine disappear into the heavy rain and mist as Harrison grabbed him with both hands. As the two men inched upward, hauled by the other four SEALs, Kalinin listened for a splash, praying Christine hit the water instead of the rocks. But he heard nothing above the roar of the turbulent water. Kalinin saw the anguish on Harrison's face after he released Christine. Then the SEAL closed his eyes for a moment. When they opened, a cold, hard look settled over him and he aimed his gaze at Kalinin.

Slowly, Harrison and Kalinin were pulled back onto the path. The five SEALs and Kalinin rested on the narrow path, sitting with their backs against the cliff, while Stone, Rosenberry, and Maydwell stood watch. Harrison stared into the rain, and no one said a word while they waited for his order to continue. Kalinin's thoughts went to Christine. Even if she survived the fall, she'd be swept through boulder-filled rapids, her body smashed against the rocks. Finally, Harrison stood and gestured forward. Stone began moving again, and the eight SEALs and Kalinin snaked slowly along the cliff face.

Ten minutes later, they reached a break in the cliff,

offering a passage west through the mountains. They turned and ascended a ravine, which led to a grassy plateau. The SEAL formation spread out, with Kalinin in the middle. Mendelson assisted the Russian president, wrapping one of Kalinin's arms around his shoulders. Harrison took the lead while Stone moved to Kalinin's other side. They traversed the plain, then descended toward the sea. The rain began to ease and Kalinin heard the faint beat of helicopter rotors every few minutes passing by in the distance, growing gradually louder each time before dissipating.

The SEALs scanned the forest and the skies as they advanced, and visibility improved as the rain eased. The formation suddenly dropped into the foliage, with Mendelson pulling Kalinin down with him.

"Chopper," Mendelson explained, pointing up and to the left.

Kalinin squinted as he peered into the rain, and a dark object passed slowly by beneath the gray clouds.

After the helicopter melted into the haze, Stone conferred with Harrison, then turned to Kalinin. "Get comfortable. Visibility is improving and they have air assets. We can't risk the transit to *Michigan* aboard the RHIBs in daylight. We'll wait until nightfall."

The day passed slowly, then dusk finally arrived. Kalinin rested beside a tree, with Mendelson and Stone not far away. Kalinin figured they had another hour until it was dark enough to begin moving again when Stone spoke into his headset, concern in his voice. Kalinin listened to the one-sided conversation.

Russian soldiers were advancing toward them, arranged in a line between the SEALs and the shore. The SEALs would have to create a gap in the line like they'd done the previous night. Darkness hadn't yet fallen, so they couldn't slip through unnoticed this time. Once their presence was revealed, it'd be a race to the shore.

Stone approached Kalinin. "How's your foot? How fast can you travel?"

Kalinin massaged his ankle. The tenderness was fading, but it was still stiff and swollen. He could walk unassisted if he had to, but running through the forest was out of the question.

Stone informed Harrison, and a moment later, Mendelson removed his backpack and crouched beside Kalinin. "Hop on."

Kalinin climbed onto Mendelson's back as Senior Chief Stone slung Mendelson's backpack over his shoulder. Stone informed Harrison they were ready. The three men remained stationary, and Kalinin quietly asked Stone what they were waiting for. Stone informed him they were waiting until they were discovered, letting the line of soldiers approach as close as possible before the SEALs burst through toward shore.

"How much farther?" Kalinin asked.

"About a half-mile," Stone answered, then added, "One kilometer for you metric types."

The conversation ceased, and Kalinin waited tensely until Mendelson whispered, "Get ready."

Kalinin tightened his grip around the SEAL's neck, and a few seconds later, Mendelson and Stone bolted forward. As they surged through the forest, Kalinin took in the scene. The six SEALs ahead were arranged in an arrow formation piercing the Russian line, with Mendelson and Stone in the middle. There was a gap ahead and soldiers were falling to the ground on both sides as the SEALs fired.

As the SEALs passed through the Russian line, the remaining soldiers on either side began pursuit. The Russians fired as they followed, their bullets slamming into tree trunks and branches, sending splinters into the air. Two SEALs on either side of the formation slowed occasionally to take out several Russians, keeping them at bay. The strategy seemed to be working; the Russians failed to gain ground. Kalinin figured they had covered half the distance to the shore, leaving only a half-kilometer to go.

A heavy beat of helicopter rotors advanced toward them, then the right side of the SEAL formation was engulfed in a half-dozen explosions. The ground shook and the concussion blast knocked Stone and Mendelson from their feet, but not before Kalinin spotted tree limbs and SEALs flying through the air.

Kalinin remained attached to Mendelson. The large SEAL regained his feet, as did Stone, and the two men sprinted through the forest, changing course forty-five degrees to the left. Stone spoke into his headset, trying to ascertain the status of the other SEALs, but couldn't establish communication with Rodrigues or Stigers. Listening in on the conversation, Kalinin gleaned that Harrison had ordered them forward. With several dozen Russians in pursuit and air assets above, they couldn't afford to stop and search for the missing SEALs.

The forest erupted to the right—another half-dozen explosions. If they hadn't altered course, they would've been killed. Even though the missiles missed, Mendelson and Stone were knocked to the ground by the blast. They scrambled to their feet, with Kalinin still clinging to Mendelson, and altered course again, aiming straight toward shore. They were almost there. Unfortunately, Maydwell could no longer keep up.

He'd taken a bullet to the thigh the previous day, and had done amazingly well thus far. Stone listened on his headset for a while, then joined the discussion, the conversation becoming heated. Maydwell was disobeying a direct order. Harrison had ordered him to continue on as best he could, but Maydwell had decided to make a stand and take out as many Russians as possible, buying valuable time. They'd be vulnerable on the beach as they hauled the RHIBs into the water.

The discussion ended with Stone cursing into his headset. A few seconds later, Kalinin heard the distinctive thump of an M79 grenade launcher as Maydwell fired several rounds. The grenades exploded in the middle of the Russian formation, driving the soldiers to the ground. Maydwell kept firing until he ran out of grenades, then shifted to his M4 carbine. Kalinin listened to the firefight behind him until it suddenly went quiet.

Mendelson and Stone halted abruptly. They were standing beside Harrison and the other two SEALs, standing on a bluff overlooking the beach. Kalinin estimated the height to be sixty meters, with the bluff sloping down at a seventy-degree angle. It'd be a difficult trip down, but they could make it. Unfortunately, while Maydwell had bought them time, it wasn't enough. The Russians would reach the bluff before the SEALs completed their descent. They'd be out in the open, easy targets. They wouldn't make it.

Harrison came to the same conclusion. "Rosenberry, Brown. Stay behind and provide cover."

The two SEALs acknowledged and took up defensive positions behind several boulders. Facing the pursuing Russians, they pressed their M4 carbines against their shoulders and eyes to the sights. Mendelson gently lowered Kalinin to the ground behind him.

"You're going to have to do the best you can," Harrison said to Kalinin, "but you've got to descend quickly."

Stepping over the bluff edge, Harrison slid down

the steep incline. Mendelson went next, followed by Kalinin and Stone, with the four men offset a few feet to each side. Kalinin kept his right foot elevated as he slid down the slope, trying to avoid hitting anything on the way down. But with only one foot and a hand on the ground to keep him stable as he descended, he lost his balance and tumbled down the bluff face. He did his best to protect his head and midsection, clamping his arms beside his head and pulling his knees up, spiraling head over heels until he rolled to a stop on the pebble-sand beach.

Aside from a few tender spots, he'd survived the descent without further injury. The three SEALs joined him and Kalinin climbed onto Mendelson's back again. They hurried down the beach toward a patch of foliage several hundred meters away.

From high above, Kalinin heard rifle fire. The Russian soldiers had reached the bluff and been engaged by the two SEALs. Rosenberry and Brown pinned down a good number of Russians, but a few worked their way around them and reached the bluff edge on both sides. They spotted the fleeing men below and opened fire.

The three SEALs sprinted down the beach as bullets burrowed into the sand around them. After they reached the vegetation, they stopped between the two RHIBs. Mendelson dropped Kalinin and the three SEALs turned their attention to the bluff, spotting several Russians on the way down. The SEALs aimed their weapons and took out the descending soldiers, their prone bodies sliding to a halt on the bluff face.

It was now almost completely dark and Harrison and the other SEALs dropped their night vision goggles into place, scanning the bluff ridge. No additional Russians descended, but they now held the entire bluff; Rosenberry and Brown had been either killed or captured. The Russians kept raking the vegetation with gunfire, forcing the three SEALs and Kalinin to take cover beside one of the RHIBs. When Kalinin thought it couldn't get worse, he heard the sound of approaching helicopters.

Harrison reached into one RHIB and Stone into the other, retrieving two shoulder-fired missile launchers, lifting them into position as four helicopters appeared over the bluff. Harrison and Stone fired, sending two missiles streaking upward. The helicopters weren't far away and the missiles closed within seconds, insufficient time for the helicopter pilots to employ decoys or evasive maneuvers.

The missiles hit two helicopters, engulfing them in flames as they careened downward, one crashing onto the beach and the second into the water. As Harrison and Stone reloaded, the other helicopters turned toward them and fired. Two six-round rocket volleys streaked toward the beach. Mendelson pulled Kalinin to the ground, pushing him against the side of one RHIB, just before their surroundings erupted in flame. The heat and pressure transient was intense. As the fireballs rose skyward, dirt, vegetation, and parts of the other RHIB rained down on them.

Harrison and Stone rose to a firing position and sent two more missiles skyward as the remaining helicopters flew overhead. Each missile plowed into the underbelly of a chopper, and two more burning hulks fell from the sky.

After reloading their missile launchers, the SEALs turned their attention to the bluff. More Russian soldiers were descending. Shifting back to their M4 carbines, the SEALs eliminated the threat. However, the bluff ridge was filled with additional soldiers firing down at them, and Kalinin realized they were in a stalemate. The Russians couldn't descend the bluff, and the SEALs couldn't haul their RHIB across the beach into the water.

Harrison and Stone conferred, and they considered employing their shoulder-fired missiles against the Russians atop the bluff. However, they didn't have many rounds left and decided to preserve them in case additional helicopters or other aircraft arrived. Instead, Harrison pulled a target laser from his backpack and pinpointed two dozen spots along the ridge, then uploaded the coordinates.

59

USS *MICHIGAN*

"Man Battle Stations Missile."

The loud *gong, gong, gong* of the General Emergency alarm reverberated throughout the submarine. As the alarm faded, the Chief of the Watch repeated the order over *Michigan*'s shipwide communication circuit.

Crew members streamed into Control, energizing dormant consoles as they donned their sound-powered phone headsets. Wilson stepped from Radio, a freshly printed message in his hand, then entered the Battle Management Center behind Control, where Missile Technicians were bringing the dual-display consoles to life.

Information scrolled down their displays, matching the data in the message Wilson held. Fire support had been requested from an American military unit ashore, with the request relayed from Pacific Command to the Cruise Missile Support Activity in Camp Smith, Hawaii, to the nearest unit—USS *Michigan*. The entire relay had taken less than two minutes. As Wilson examined the nearest display, containing a map with the target coordinates, he realized the request had come from Lieutenant Harrison's SEAL team.

That revelation wasn't lost on the personnel in the Battle Management Center, and it seemed to add urgency to the target processing. The submarine's Weapons Officer, Lieutenant Trevor Powers, hovered behind the operators as they completed the mission planning for each target coordinate, assigning it to a Tomahawk in *Michigan*'s missile tubes. As they approached the twenty-fourth coordinate, Powers held up a finger, indicating they'd be done in one minute.

Wilson descended the ladder to the second level and entered the Missile Control Center. Like the Navigation Center above, MCC had been transformed during the submarine's conversion to a guided missile submarine. The refrigerator-sized computers had been replaced with servers one-tenth their size, and the ballistic missile Launch Console had been replaced with four workstations: two Mission Planning Consoles, a Launch Control Console, and a fourth workstation displaying a map of the Black Sea, containing a green hatched area.

Stopping behind the Launch Control Console, Wilson looked over the shoulder of a petty officer second class. He glanced at the fourth console, verifying *Michigan* was within the green hatched area—the submarine's launch basket—where *Michigan*'s Tomahawk missiles were within target range.

The Launch Operator announced, "All targets assigned. In the window, salvo One."

Wilson replied, "Very well. Continue."

The Launch Operator clicked the green button, and *Michigan*'s automatic Tomahawk Attack Weapon System took control.

"Opening tube Twelve," the Launch Supervisor reported as the green indicating light for tube Twelve turned yellow. Shortly thereafter, the indicating light turned red. "Hatch, tube Twelve, open and locked."

A few seconds later, the Launch Operator reported, "Missile One, tube Twelve, away."

The first of *Michigan*'s Tomahawks was ejected from the submarine. In rapid succession, another missile followed every five seconds, with the Tomahawk Attack Weapon System automatically opening and closing the missile tube hatches as required.

Michigan's Tomahawks streaked east.

60

KRASNODAR KRAI

The SEALs traded fire with the Russians atop the bluff, pulling replacement ammunition magazines from their backpacks. It became clear that Mendelson was a sniper, as he carried a different weapon than the other two SEALs, and his firing was slower and more deliberate. Even at this distance, he scored an impressive success rate, with a soldier falling down the bluff every few shots.

Kalinin still had a pistol in his hand, but he was too far away for effective fire. In close quarters, however, he could lend assistance. To the left, there was a break in the bluff, through which a river emptied into the Black Sea. Russian soldiers were no doubt working their way along the bluff and would soon descend along the riverbank, approaching from their left flank.

As he wondered how long they could hold out and what the next step in Harrison's plan was, a missile streaked overhead, detonating atop the bluff ridge. Five seconds later, another missile and explosion followed, and another in five seconds more. Kalinin noted the distinctive pattern of cluster munition warheads, spraying the area with deadly mini-bomblets, most likely delivered via American Tomahawk missiles.

With a missile detonating atop the bluff every five

seconds, the remaining Russians dropped back, scrambling for cover, and the bullets raining down from the bluff ridge ceased. Harrison took advantage of the reprieve. As additional missiles streaked overhead, the three SEALs pulled the RHIB across the beach, Kalinin following beside them.

Once the boat was in the water, the SEALs jumped in and Harrison started the engine while Mendelson dragged Kalinin aboard. Harrison engaged the motor and pushed the throttle all the way forward, and the boat's stern squatted down as the RHIB accelerated away from shore.

Water began pooling at Kalinin's feet; the RHIB's hull had been punctured by bullets. Mendelson removed his helmet and started bailing the water out while Senior Chief Stone opened the emergency patch kit, then searched for the holes, sealing each one.

Meanwhile, Kalinin kept his eyes on the sky, scanning for additional helicopters. It was dark by now and the moon was obscured by clouds, so Kalinin was confident they couldn't be detected visually. Infrared was another matter. Stone pulled out several thin, rubbery blankets, handing one each to Mendelson and Kalinin.

"Lie down and cover yourself with this," Mendelson said. "It'll conceal your heat signature. Stone draped a blanket over Harrison, who remained at the RHIB controls, then covered himself with another.

As Kalinin and the SEALs hid under protective blankets, the RHIB continued on at full speed, and Kalinin was surprised at how quiet the engine was. It was probably water-cooled as well to reduce its heat signature. He heard Harrison talking into a radio, connecting with another unit via a call sign, informing them that a single RHIB was returning.

61

MOSCOW, RUSSIA

In the Ministry of Defense headquarters building, General Andropov slammed his hand on the conference room control panel, terminating the videocon with Colonel Savvin. His body trembled with rage. How could they have let Kalinin slip away, much less into American hands? But it wasn't over yet. Kalinin was being taken to an American submarine in the Black Sea. Sink the submarine and their problem would go away. He spoke into the open microphone.

"Establish a connection with Admiral Lipovsky."

A moment later, the Russian Navy's commander-in-chief appeared on the display.

"Admiral Lipovsky," Andropov began. "President Kalinin is in custody of American forces who are taking him to a submarine in the Black Sea. Find that submarine and sink it."

"Yes, General. We detected a missile launch from the Black Sea not long ago. We have three submarines nearby and are drafting orders now."

Lipovsky added, "They may not receive their new orders immediately. If they are at periscope depth, they will receive the message as soon as it is broadcast. Otherwise, they won't receive the order until they download the broadcast, which could be a few hours from now."

Andropov began to fume as Lipovsky wove his web of excuses. "I don't care about your communication issues. You have an entire fleet in the Black Sea. Secure the Turkish Straits so the American submarine cannot escape, and sink it."

Lipovsky started to explain that much of the Fleet had been destroyed in the recent battle with the American Navy, but Andropov cut him off.

"I do not want excuses!"

"Yes, General," Lipovsky replied. "We will sink the American submarine."

B-268 *VELIKIY NOVGOROD*

Velikiy Novgorod, one of the newest submarines in the Russian Fleet and referred to by NATO as an Improved Kilo class, was at periscope depth recharging its batteries with its diesel engines. Captain Second Rank Jozsef Tratnyek leaned over the navigation table in the Central Command Post, examining their location on the electronic chart. Seated beside him was the Electric Navigation Party Technician, who was updating the submarine's position using the latest satellite fix.

After reviewing the submarine's updated position, Tratnyek turned his attention to the center of the command post, where the submarine's Watch Officer supervised his watch section, his eyes scanning each display and the men at their consoles.

The quiet conversations were interrupted by a report from Radio. "Command Post, Communications. Request the Captain's presence. Have received a Commanding Officer Only message."

Tratnyek entered the Communications Post and stopped by the two printers. "Ready."

The radioman hit the *Print* button and a message slid from a printer.

Tratnyek read the message, then read it again. He

took it with him into the Central Command Post, addressing one of the two Messengers. "Request the First Officer's presence in the command post."

The senior seaman acknowledged and departed in search of the submarine's second-in-command. A moment later, Captain Third Rank Grigory Domashev arrived. Tratnyek motioned for Domashev to join him by the navigation table, also requesting the Watch Officer's presence. When the two men approached, Tratnyek pushed the message across the table.

"Read."

Tratnyek waited while they read the directive. When both men looked up, he asked, "Do you have any questions?"

Both responded in the negative.

Tratnyek handed the message to the Navigation Party Technician. "Plot this position."

The technician quickly entered the coordinates and a red X appeared on the chart.

Tratnyek ordered, "Secure snorkeling and proceed to this position at ten knots."

The Watch Officer acknowledged, then gave the requisite orders.

"Steersman, ahead two-thirds. Left full rudder, steady course one-six-zero. Compensation Officer, secure snorkeling."

Tratnyek waited in the Command Post as his submarine turned south and snorkeling was secured. The Watch Officer then ordered the submarine deeper, and *Velikiy Novgorod* tilted downward. Tratnyek's eyes went to the chart again. They weren't far away. At a stealthy speed of ten knots, the American submarine should be within detection range in one hour.

When *Velikiy Novgorod* leveled off at fifty meters, Tratnyek gave additional direction to his Watch Officer. "Man Combat Stations."

63

THE BLACK SEA

A light rain continued to fall as the SEALs sped farther out to sea. Kalinin and the three SEALs remained under their insulated blankets during the transit, hoping to evade detection by aircraft or satellite thermal imagers. So far, there had been no sign of additional Russian forces. Aside from the low rumble of the outboard engine, the journey was quiet; neither Kalinin nor the SEALs spoke. The loss of five men no doubt weighed heavily on the remaining SEALs.

It was clear from Harrison's reaction after he dropped Christine, that she meant something to him. Kalinin had no idea how long they had dated or the current status of their relationship, but it had been easy to discern the strong tie between them. Kalinin could only imagine what had gone through Harrison's mind in those brief seconds before he made his decision, choosing to save his life instead of Christine's. Kalinin felt fortunate; his position as Russia's president had saved his life.

Stone and Mendelson moved to a sitting position, each keeping the blanket over their head and bodies. Kalinin did the same, then moved forward, stopping beside Harrison. The SEAL glanced at him, then returned to a forward gaze.

Kalinin was unsure where to begin, then decided to start with a thank-you. "Lieutenant Harrison. I want to thank you for saving my life. I can tell it was a difficult decision."

Harrison gave no indication he heard him.

Kalinin added, "The cliff was steep and the river swollen. It's possible Christine landed in the water and not on the rocks." He didn't offer his thoughts on her odds of survival, though.

Instead of responding, Harrison checked their position on the GPS display, then idled the engine. As the RHIB slowed, he activated a green glow stick, which he attached to the bow. The RHIB eventually glided to a halt, bobbing in the waves atop the dark water.

A submarine periscope materialized out of the darkness, approaching the RHIB from ahead. The periscope slowed, passing by the SEAL boat a few meters before coasting to a halt.

Mendelson approached Kalinin, handing him a set of scuba gear. "Do you need help?"

"I can manage," Kalinin answered, "except for the right fin."

Mendelson replied, "Don't worry about either one."

Kalinin donned his gear while the SEALs switched into theirs. The SEALs then detached the engine and began to deflate the RHIB. After verifying his facemask was sealed and his regulator was working, Kalinin slipped into the water with Mendelson. The SEAL kept a firm grasp on Kalinin's arm, pulling him downward.

Several green glow sticks appeared in the distance and the shadowy shape of a submarine formed in the murky water. They were headed toward two Dry Deck Shelters attached to the submarine's missile deck. The three-meter-diameter door of the port shelter was open, with two divers waiting nearby. Mendelson guided Kalinin inside, and a few minutes later, the deflated RHIB was hauled into the shelter, joined by the two divers and three SEALs.

The hatch was shut and after the water was drained from the shelter, the SEALs removed their scuba gear, as did Kalinin. Mendelson guided him into the transfer trunk and down through dual hatches into a missile tube, then out through a side hatch, where President Kalinin was greeted by three officers. Kalinin read the name tags on their uniforms.

Lieutenant Commander Haas extended her hand. "Welcome aboard *Michigan,* President Kalinin."

The three officers introduced themselves: Kelly Haas was USS *Michigan*'s Supply Officer, John McNeil was the commanding officer of the SEAL detachment aboard, and Joe Aleo was the physician assigned to *Michigan*'s SEALs. Captain Wilson, the submarine's Commanding Officer, was occupied in the Control Room and would meet with him once *Michigan* was in deeper water.

Mendelson and the other two SEALs followed Kalinin, stepping from the tube into the Missile Compartment. Harrison was the last to exit and he closed the hatch behind him. Kalinin noticed the concerned look on McNeil's face when only three of the eight SEALs returned. Harrison had informed *Michigan* that only one RHIB was returning with President Kalinin, but hadn't provided any details.

Harrison met McNeil's eyes briefly, then moved past him without a word. As he headed down the passageway, Senior Chief Stone quietly filled McNeil in.

Commander Aleo said to Kalinin, "Let's get you to medical. I'll take a look at your ankle and see what I can do, then Commander Haas will get you settled in. You'll be bunking with our Executive Officer."

64

USS *MICHIGAN*

Standing on the submarine's Conn, Captain Wilson surveyed *Michigan*'s progress as it traveled toward deeper water. To minimize the time the returning SEALs spent on the surface, vulnerable to attack, Wilson had ventured into shallow water for the rendezvous. But in shallow water, *Michigan* was also vulnerable, unable to utilize its full depth capability nor employ its most valuable sensor, the towed array. With *Michigan* traveling in water only two hundred feet deep and its keel only fifty feet above the bottom, the array, which drooped behind the submarine at a slight angle when deployed, had been stowed.

The Control Room watchstanders were quiet and focused. The normal watch rotation had been augmented with additional watchstanders, plus the submarine's Executive Officer was in Control monitoring the performance of the fire control technicians. A half-hour earlier, *Michigan* had launched two dozen Tomahawk missiles and the Russians had undoubtedly pinpointed the launch location. It was imperative that *Michigan* vacate the area quickly.

They were proceeding at fifteen knots. Although

the submarine could transit faster, the increased water flow across the submarine's bow dulled the sensitivity of the spherical array sonar. Wilson didn't want to blind the ship by traveling too fast, nor did he want to increase *Michigan*'s detectability due to a higher speed. It was a trade-off—speed versus sonar capability and stealth. At ahead standard it would be about two hours, Wilson figured, before they had cleared the launch point far enough to avoid detection.

The submarine's Navigator was also in Control, monitoring the transit. With a water depth of only two hundred feet and *Michigan* occupying almost eighty feet of it from keel to the top of the sail, the submarine was traveling much closer to the bottom than normal. Nautical charts were notoriously inaccurate, and submarines normally traveled with ample distance between the keel and charted bottom depth. Unfortunately, that wasn't possible at the moment.

The Sonar Supervisor's voice came across the Conn speakers, interrupting Wilson's thoughts. "Conn, Sonar. Gained a new contact on the spherical array, bearing three-five-one, designated Sierra two-seven. Analyzing."

Wilson waited while the two fire control technicians evaluated the contact's bearings to determine its course, speed, and range. Determining an adequate firing solution with sonar bearings alone could take hours; with only a bearing, they had no idea how far away the contact was, which way it was headed, or how fast it was traveling. The combat control system algorithms assisted, but took time.

Determining the type of contact wasn't as difficult. Each submarine emitted unique tonals generated by the equipment aboard, such as the main engines, electrical turbines, and pumps, which could be correlated to a specific submarine class.

"Conn, Sonar. Sierra two-seven is classified submerged, Improved Kilo class."

Wilson turned to the Officer of the Deck. "Man Battle Stations Torpedo."

65

USS *MICHIGAN* • B-268
VELIKIY NOVGOROD

USS *MICHIGAN*

"Battle Stations are manned."

Captain Wilson acknowledged the Chief of the Watch's report. *Michigan*'s Control Room was now at full manning, as was the rest of the submarine. Wilson had taken the Conn from the Officer of the Deck, which meant he controlled the ship's course, speed, and depth, and would issue all tactical commands, while Lieutenant Cody retained the Deck, managing the ship's routine evolutions. Meanwhile, Wilson's Executive Officer, Lieutenant Commander Patzke, had assumed his role as Fire Control Coordinator.

Patzke focused on developing a firing solution on the contact, which had been identified as an Improved Kilo class, the newest and most capable diesel in the Russian arsenal. When operating on the battery, it was as quiet or quieter than American nuclear-powered submarines. The most important question in Wilson's mind at the moment was—had the Russian crew detected *Michigan*. The next report answered that question.

A fire control technician spoke into his sound-powered phone headset. "Possible target zig, Sierra two-seven, based on downshift in frequency."

The technician was monitoring the time-frequency display on his console, noting the decreasing frequencies. Like listening to an approaching train, the pitch of the train's horn was higher as it approached, falling off after it passed. This was due to the Doppler effect, with the sound waves compressing if the source was approaching, or expanding if it was moving away. The subtle change in frequency was detectable by the submarine's sensors, and that change provided valuable information.

Patzke evaluated the frequency change along with the contact's bearing rate, then announced, "Confirm target zig. Target turned away."

Michigan had been detected. The Russian captain had halted his approach, turning away in the hope he could avoid counter-detection while his fire control algorithms determined *Michigan*'s course, speed, and range. Fortunately, *Michigan* had detected the Kilo's approach and could take appropriate action.

Wilson evaluated the scenario. If the Kilo turned west, it'd be paralleling *Michigan*'s path. If the Russian captain turned east, he'd be able to work in behind *Michigan*. Either way, Wilson had to open range.

"Helm, left twenty-degrees rudder, steady course two-four-zero."

Wilson turned southwest, placing the Russian submarine on the starboard stern quarter, still within arc of *Michigan*'s spherical array sonar, so they could monitor the Kilo's maneuvers and listen for torpedo launch transients.

Opening range and slipping away was critical, because USS *Michigan* was still Weapons-Tight. They hadn't received orders to sink Russian surface ships or submarines. If fired upon, Wilson could take whatever actions were required to ensure the safety of his crew.

But it was best if they could slip away, fading from the Kilo's sensors before the Russian crew determined a firing solution.

VELIKIY NOVGOROD

"Possible target maneuver, Hydroacoustic one-three, due to decrease in frequency."

Captain Second Rank Tratnyek listened to the fire control watchstander's report, then evaluated the implications. The American submarine had suddenly turned away. Tratnyek's Kilo had been counterdetected. However, he still had a significant advantage. Russia wasn't at war with the United States yet, and the American captain wouldn't be authorized to shoot just because he detected a Russian submarine. Tratnyek, however, did have authorization to attack. If his crew maintained trail, they could close to within an optimal firing position, leaving the American crew insufficient time to counterfire.

"Steersman, left fifteen degrees rudder, steady course two-two-zero. Increase speed to ahead full."

USS MICHIGAN

"Upshift in frequency, Sierra two-seven. Sonar, Coordinator, aye."

Patzke acknowledged Sonar's report over the soundpowered phone circuit, then announced, "Possible target zig, Sierra two-seven, due to upshift in frequency."

Wilson listened to Patzke's announcement, then waited for the Fire Control Tracking Party to determine the contact's new course and speed. The target could have turned toward them, increased speed, or both. It took a few minutes before Patzke confirmed the maneuver.

"Confirm target zig, Sierra two-seven, contact turned toward and increased speed. Set anchor range at ten thousand yards."

The Kilo's captain had detected *Michigan*'s maneuver and had turned to follow, increasing speed to close to a more favorable firing position. Two could play that game.

"Helm, ahead full."

Wilson considered increasing speed to ahead flank. The Kilo submarine wouldn't be able to keep up, but if there were other Russian subs in the area, the extra propulsion noise at ahead flank would give away *Michigan*'s presence and approximate position. It was better to stick to a measured response, going to ahead flank only if required. At ahead full, the Kilo submarine would be forced to its maximum speed, at which it could remain for only a half-hour. If it was going to attack, it would have to do so before then.

VELIKIY NOVGOROD

"Command Post, Hydroacoustic. Hydroacoustic one-three has increased speed."

Tratnyek acknowledged the report, then examined the geographic display on the nearest fire control console. The American captain was forcing his hand. Tratnyek's submarine couldn't keep pace for long.

So be it.

He looked to Captain Third Rank Grigory Domashev, *Velikiy Novgorod*'s First Officer, who was hunched over the shoulders of the two men at the fire control consoles. Once their adversary's course was refined to within ten degrees and its speed to within a few knots, they'd be ready.

Domashev tapped one michman on the shoulder. "Set as Primary."

The michman complied and Domashev reported, "Captain, I have a firing solution."

Tratnyek announced, "Prepare to fire, Hydroacoustic one-three, horizontal salvo, tubes One and Two. Tube One will fire first."

He was shooting from long distance, increasing the American submarine's odds of survival. Even so, a two-torpedo salvo, with the torpedoes running side by side in the shallow water, would make it difficult for his adversary to evade. Plus, it gave him two weapons he could steer, using the thin guidance wire attached from the submarine's torpedo tube to the torpedo.

Domashev called out, "Solution updated."

"Torpedo ready," the Weapons Officer reported.

"Countermeasures armed," the Watch Officer announced.

Tratnyek gave the order. "Fire tubes One and Two!"

USS *MICHIGAN*

"Torpedo in the water, bearing three-five-five!"

Wilson responded immediately. "Helm, ahead flank. Launch countermeasures."

The Helm rang up ahead flank and Lieutenant Cody launched a set of *Michigan*'s decoys and jammers. White scalloped circles appeared on the geographic display, recording their countermeasure locations.

Wilson examined the geographic display. A red bearing line was radiating toward Sierra two-seven. With the torpedo approaching from the starboard stern quarter, *Michigan* was already on an adequate evasion course, assuming the torpedo was fired on a line-of-bearing solution.

No maneuver was required, so Wilson focused on getting a torpedo into the water. They were tracking Sierra two-seven, but Patzke hadn't determined a satisfactory firing solution. With *Michigan* increasing speed to ahead flank, they'd likely lose Sierra two-seven due to the turbulent water flow across *Michigan*'s bow array. They needed to launch a torpedo soon.

Wilson joined Patzke, examining the target parameters on the three combat control consoles. They were converging toward similar solutions. As Wilson estimated how long before Patzke felt comfortable with one of them, he was interrupted by another announcement by the Sonar Supervisor.

"Torpedo in the water, bearing three-five-eight!"

A purple bearing line appeared on the geographic display. Their adversary had launched a two-torpedo salvo. Wilson responded instantly.

"Quick Reaction Firing, Sierra two-seven, tube One."

Wilson implemented an urgent firing order, which forced his Executive Officer to send his best solution to the torpedo immediately. The Russian captain wouldn't know how well aimed the torpedo was, and it was better to give him something to worry about instead of letting him refine his target solution and send updates to his torpedoes over their guidance wires.

Lieutenant Commander Patzke shifted his gaze between the three combat control consoles, then tapped one of the fire control technicians on the shoulder. "Promote to Master."

Patzke announced, "Solution ready!"

Lieutenant Trevor Powers, seated beside another fire control technician at the Weapon Control Console, reported, "Weapon ready!"

"Ship ready!" Lieutenant Cody announced.

"Shoot on generated bearings!" Wilson ordered.

Wilson listened to the whirr of the torpedo ejection pump as the torpedo was impulsed from the tube, accelerating from rest to thirty knots in less than a second. Inside the sonar shack, the sonar technicians monitored the status of their outgoing unit.

"Own ship's unit is in the water, running normally."

"Fuel crossover achieved."

"Turning to preset gyro course."

"Shifting to medium speed."

Michigan's torpedo headed toward its target.

Wilson examined the red and purple lines on the geographic display, with new lines appearing every ten seconds. The purple torpedo bearings were marching steadily aft, which eased his concern until he evaluated the red lines. The bearings to the torpedo remained constant.

The Russian captain was well trained, firing a torpedo salvo with a *lead* torpedo fired slightly ahead of *Michigan* and a *lag* torpedo behind. When Wilson increased speed, he'd unwittingly put *Michigan* on an intercept course with the first torpedo. He needed to maneuver, but if he turned away from the first torpedo, he'd turn into the path of the second. If he turned the other way, he'd head toward the Russian submarine.

There were no good options.

Wilson decided to turn toward his adversary. The Russian captain would soon be occupied, forced to evade *Michigan*'s incoming torpedo.

"Helm, right full rudder, steady course three-one-zero. Launch countermeasures."

Michigan turned northwest as Lieutenant Cody launched a second set of torpedo countermeasures. Wilson watched the bearings to both torpedoes intently, and both started drawing aft.

So far, so good.

VELIKIY NOVGOROD

"Possible target maneuver, Hydroacoustic one-three, due to increase in frequency."

Captain Second Rank Tratnyek listened to the fire control watchstander's report. The American submarine had turned, attempting to evade the incoming torpedoes.

First Officer Domashev called out, "Confirm target maneuver, Hydroacoustic one-three."

Tratnyek approached his First Officer, standing behind the two fire control consoles. Both solutions were converging to a northwest track for their target.

"Insert steer, both torpedoes. Eighty degrees right."

The Weapons Officer sent the order to the two torpedoes over their guidance wires. Seconds later, both torpedoes acknowledged the order and turned sharply right.

USS *MICHIGAN*

"Conn, Sonar. Upshift in frequency, both torpedoes. Torpedoes have turned toward."

Wilson acknowledged the Sonar Supervisor's report, then examined the geographic plot on the nearest combat control console. The Russian captain had steered both torpedoes back onto a corrected-intercept path toward *Michigan*. The bearings to one torpedo were drawing forward, while the other torpedo drew aft. They had *Michigan* bracketed. Time to maneuver again.

With the Russian submarine to the north, Wilson decided turn away. "Helm, left full rudder, steady course two-zero-zero. Launch countermeasures."

The Helm complied and *Michigan* turned toward

the south again as Lieutenant Cody launched a third set of torpedo countermeasures.

As *Michigan* steadied on its new course, the Weapons Officer called out, "Tube One has enabled," informing Wilson that the torpedo launched from tube One had gone active. Hopefully, their solution was accurate enough for a kill. They'd likely lose the wire soon, as high-speed maneuvers put stress on the thin copper guidance wire.

In concert with Wilson's thoughts, the Weapons Officer announced, "Loss of wire, tube One."

They could no longer steer their weapon, not that it mattered. They'd lost the Russian submarine on sonar. The initial target solution would have to do.

Wilson returned his attention to the two pursuing Russian torpedoes, which were proving difficult to shake. He hoped there was enough time to maneuver out of the way before either torpedo closed to within detection range.

VELIKIY NOVGOROD

Captain Tratnyek monitored the situation with growing confidence. His crew had kept track of the evading American submarine, guiding their torpedoes toward their prey with a steer, and it wouldn't be long before both torpedoes reached detection range. Tratnyek had kept his submarine at a steady speed and course, so they didn't break the guidance wires to their torpedoes.

Hydroacoustic reported, "Possible target maneuver, Hydroacoustic one-three, due to downshift in frequency."

The American submarine was turning again, trying one last maneuver to evade the incoming torpedoes. Tratnyek focused on the geographic display and was assessing whether another steer was required when his

Weapons Officer made the announcement he'd been waiting for.

"Detect! Second fired unit!"

Tratnyek moved behind the Weapon Launch Console, observing as the second torpedo altered course to the left. The torpedo would send a few more pings before confirming the object was a submarine and not a decoy, and Tratnyek looked forward to watching it close the remaining distance.

A report from Hydroacoustic blared across the Command Post speakers. "Torpedo in the water, bearing one-seven-zero!"

Tratnyek spun toward the sonar display as a bright white trace appeared.

"Steersman, ahead flank!" he ordered. "Right full rudder, steady two-eight-zero. Launch countermeasures!"

Their adversary had counterfired while evading, and its torpedo had just gone active. Tratnyek hoped there was sufficient time to evade, but the next report destroyed his hopes.

"Torpedo is increasing speed. Torpedo is homing!"

Tratnyek's stomach knotted. The American crew had placed their torpedo expertly, providing insufficient time to evade. The Watch Officer was just now launching a decoy. He'd have to wait another minute to launch a jammer, placing a noise field between their submarine and the torpedo, leaving the decoy as bait.

But the incoming torpedo was too close. It would hold both the decoy and *Velikiy Novgorod* simultaneously, and would easily discern between the six-inch-diameter decoy and the three-thousand-ton submarine.

Tratnyek watched the American torpedo speed past their decoy, altering its course again as it closed on *Velikiy Novgorod*.

"Steersman. Hard left rudder!"

Tratnyek tried one last maneuver, putting a knuckle in the water to distract the torpedo, letting his submarine slip away. But the torpedo turned sharply left to a new intercept course.

They had only a few seconds left.

USS *MICHIGAN*

Michigan's torpedo had detected the Russian submarine and was now homing to detonation. However, Wilson was focused on his crew's survival. The second Russian torpedo had detected *Michigan* and they might soon share the same fate as their adversary. He glanced at the geographic display and listened for updates from Sonar.

"Torpedo is increasing speed and range-gating! Estimated range, two thousand yards."

The torpedo had detected *Michigan,* then adjusted the interval of its sonar pings to more accurately determine the target's range. It was homing.

"Helm, hard left rudder, steady course zero-nine-zero. Launch countermeasures."

Lieutenant Cody launched another decoy and jammer while *Michigan* turned east. Wilson had pointed *Michigan* toward shallower water for two reasons. The first was that torpedoes had a more difficult time looking upslope than downslope, as the shallowing water made things more difficult for the torpedo's sonar algorithms. In addition to sonar returns from the target, the torpedo would also receive reflections bouncing off the sea floor and surface, plus returns from rock formations on the bottom, clouding the sonar picture.

The second reason was a pessimistic one. Headed back toward shore, the water would get shallower rather than deeper. If *Michigan* went to the bottom, it was imperative that the intact compartments not implode from the sea pressure. The surviving crew members could then escape to the surface.

"Torpedo range, one thousand yards!"

Wilson examined the last set of torpedo countermeasures they had launched, annotated on the geographic display. The torpedo had passed both; the eighteen-thousand-ton submarine was too tempting of a target.

"Torpedo range, five hundred yards!"

Wilson gave it one last shot—an aggressive turn to starboard.

"Helm, hard right rudder, steady course one-eight-zero!"

Michigan was almost two football fields long and couldn't turn rapidly like the smaller fast attacks. The maneuver didn't fool the incoming torpedo.

As the torpedo closed the remaining distance, Sonar reported, "Explosion to the north. Correlates with Sierra two-seven."

Michigan's torpedo had done its job, sinking the Russian submarine. That was little consolation, however. The Russian captain had also accomplished his mission; USS *Michigan* was going to the bottom.

Wilson grabbed on to the Conn railing, preparing for the torpedo's detonation.

USS *MICHIGAN*

A deafening roar swept through the Control Room, accompanied by a jolt that knocked Wilson to the deck. Lighting fixtures shattered and anything not fastened down catapulted into the air. The intense burst of sound faded, replaced with a dull roar. As Wilson and other crew members picked themselves up, the oscillating wail of the flooding alarm filled the air, followed by a report over the 4-MC emergency circuit.

"Flooding in Missile Compartment Lower Level, starboard side!"

The Diving Officer responded as he was trained. "Thirty up. Full rise, fairwater planes."

The Engine Order Telegraph beside the Helm shifted, indicating the Throttleman in the Engine Room had adjusted the throttles to ahead full.

Michigan tilted to a thirty-degree up-angle, and despite the upward angle and the sail planes at full rise, the submarine sank rapidly. They had started out at 150 feet and were already past two hundred.

Wilson grabbed a 7-MC microphone, then overrode the standard flooding procedure. "Maneuvering, Conn. Ahead flank!"

The Engine Order Telegraph shifted back to ahead

flank, and Wilson felt tremors in the deck as the main engine turbines spun back to maximum. Despite the additional speed, *Michigan* kept sinking.

The Chief of the Watch stood and reached for the Emergency Blow levers, looking to Wilson for direction.

Based on the rapid depth increase, Wilson knew there was a large hole in the hull; they weren't dealing with a burst pipe or misaligned flange. There would be no way to stop the flooding, and with the entire Missile Compartment flooded, not even a full emergency blow would bring *Michigan* to the surface.

They were going down, and once they came to rest on the bottom, assuming the other compartments remained habitable, air would be a valuable commodity.

"Do *not* emergency blow!" Wilson ordered.

The Chief of the Watch returned to his chair and energized the trim and drain pumps, aligning both of the eight-foot-tall behemoths to the Missile Compartment bilges. But even against a hole only a foot in diameter at this depth, both pumps would be overcome. With a Russian heavyweight torpedo exploding a few feet from the hull, Wilson knew the hole would be much larger.

The Missile Compartment was lost.

Wilson shifted gears, transitioning from tactical to survival mode. There was no way to stop the flooding, so he had to get everyone out of the Missile Compartment before they got trapped inside. He grabbed the 1-MC microphone. "All personnel evacuate the Missile Compartment. Repeat, this is the Captain. All personnel evacuate the Missile Compartment."

His eyes shot to the fathometer. The last recorded sounding was four hundred feet. Despite *Michigan*'s unstoppable descent to the sea floor, relief washed

over him. The Operations and Engineering compartments would remain intact.

"Passing three hundred feet," the Dive announced.

Only a hundred feet to the bottom, and *Michigan*
was traveling at ahead flank. The last thing Wilson
wanted was to plow into a rock formation at full speed,
crushing the sonar dome and puncturing the pressure
hull. Wilson decided to arrange a soft landing.

"Helm, back full. Dive, zero bubble."

He wanted to stop *Michigan* and return it to an even
keel before it landed on the bottom.

The Helm complied, and the tremors through the
deck increased as the Throttleman spun the ahead
throttles shut, then sent steam into the astern turbines
while they were spinning in the wrong direction. The
main engines strained as the astern turbines slowed
the submarine's propulsion shaft, then reversed it. The
submarine's twenty-two-foot-diameter screw dug into
the water, gradually slowing *Michigan* as the deck leveled off.

Without an up-angle on the submarine and with
speed bleeding down, *Michigan* sank faster. But there
wasn't much farther to go.

As *Michigan* prepared to settle onto the bottom of
the Black Sea, Wilson's thoughts went to the Engine
Room. The main seawater suctions were at the four
and eight o'clock positions along the hull, and if the sea
bottom was silt-covered, the seawater intakes would
suck silt into the condensers, fouling them. They could
be cleared with high-pressure air, but that would be
noisy, revealing *Michigan* had survived, along with its
location. Months earlier, he'd witnessed the Russians
torpedoing a submarine on the bottom to ensure it was
destroyed. He didn't want another torpedo coming his
way.

Michigan's speed slowly subsided. When it reached zero knots, Wilson retrieved the 7-MC microphone. "Maneuvering, Conn. All stop. Shut the main seawater intakes."

Seconds later, Wilson felt tremors as *Michigan* settled onto the Black Sea floor. A deep rumbling and the sound of groaning metal filled the air. Then there was silence.

Wilson waited tensely, listening for another emergency report, but nothing came.

The tension slowly dissipated as Wilson sorted through the issues. His first concern was his crew. "Chief of the Watch. Get me a crew count."

The Chief of the Watch sent a request to all spaces via the sound-powered phone circuit. The reports filtered in, with the chief keeping a tally. When the last report was received, he relayed the information to Wilson.

"Captain, all personnel are accounted for. Twenty-four crew members are in the Engine Room. The remaining crew members, along with all sixty-one members of the SEAL detachment and President Kalinin, are in the Operations Compartment."

That was good news. Then Wilson keyed on the SEAL detachment. It was a sixty-six-man unit, not sixty-one. "Where are the other five SEALs and Navy divers?"

"Commander McNeil reports that five SEALs did not return to *Michigan*."

Wilson nodded. He'd been occupied in Control and hadn't been debriefed on the mission. He knew that only one of the two RHIBs had returned with President Kalinin, but nothing else.

"Where is Christine O'Connor?" Wilson asked.

The Chief of the Watch replied, "She didn't board, sir."

Wilson wondered what happened to her, but had more pressing issues to deal with.

"Secure from Battle Stations Torpedo," he ordered. "Have all department heads, the XO, and Chief of the Boat muster on the Conn."

The Chief of the Watch passed the word over the 1-MC, and soon only the normal Control Room watchstanders remained at their posts, although there wasn't much to do at the moment. Lieutenant Commander Patzke stepped onto the Conn, followed by the Navigator, Weapons Officer, and finally the Engineer, who emerged from Sonar. Battle Stations had evolved over the years, and it was now common practice to assign the Engineer, one of the most experienced officers aboard beside the Captain and XO, as the Sonar Coordinator. The Chief of the Boat was the last to arrive, coming up from the third level.

Captain Wilson addressed his submarine's senior leadership. "We need to get our arms around the situation. Determine the structural status of the hull and piping, life support systems, food and water, power, etc. Department heads, check on the systems within your purview. COB, put together a team and check every space in the Operations Compartment and Engine Room for structural integrity. Any leaks, hull deformations, etc. XO, get with everyone who evacuated the Missile Compartment and determine what kind of damage we're dealing with. Once we better understand our predicament, we'll discuss how to proceed."

The Engineer interjected, "Sir, I assume the reactor is still critical. Without main seawater and a vacuum in the main condensers, there is nowhere to send the steam. I recommend we shut down the reactor and secure unnecessary equipment throughout the ship, including all tactical systems. There's no need for sonar or fire control right now."

"I concur," Wilson said. "Shut down the reactor and all unnecessary propulsion plant equipment." To the Nav and Weps, Wilson directed, "Secure everything except atmosphere monitoring and minimum lighting. We need to reduce the drain on the battery to buy as much time as possible while we sort things out."

67

WASHINGTON, D.C.

Secretary of Defense Bill Dunnavant entered the Oval Office, accompanied by Colonel Dubose and Chief of Staff Kevin Hardison for the unscheduled afternoon briefing. All three men wore grim looks as they settled into chairs facing the president.

"What have you got, Bill?"

"I've got good and bad news, Mr. President. I'll start with the good news. Kalinin was rescued by *Michigan*'s SEAL team."

"That *is* good news. So what's the bad news?"

"We monitored communications between the SEAL team and *Michigan,* and the first piece of bad news is that only one RHIB returned. It's likely we lost several SEALs during the mission."

"Why don't we know?"

"This is where the news gets really bad, Mr. President. We haven't received a message from *Michigan* with the mission details, and SOSUS arrays in the Black Sea detected two torpedo explosions, with the bearings intersecting near *Michigan*'s rendezvous with the SEAL team. Based on acoustic analysis, one explosion was a U.S. MK 48 torpedo, while the other was a Russian torpedo. It looks like *Michigan* was engaged by a Russian submarine and both were likely sunk."

"When will we know for sure?"

"*Michigan* has been ordered to provide a mission status within the next four hours. If we don't hear anything by then, it should confirm our assessment."

"If *Michigan* was sunk, could some of the crew be alive?"

"Yes, Mr. President. It's likely many survived; whoever escaped to intact compartments. The water depth near the explosions is four hundred feet, so the other compartments wouldn't have imploded."

"Where do we stand on a rescue effort?"

"The Undersea Rescue Command in San Diego is preparing to transport its equipment and personnel to Turkey, where they'll load onto a support ship at one of their Black Sea ports. We've got two issues to deal with, though.

"The first issue is that it appears Russia has attacked the United States, and you'll need to consider our response. We can retaliate unilaterally or consider this one facet of Russia's aggression in Eastern Europe, tying our response to a coordinated NATO effort."

The president replied, "War hasn't broken out yet, and if we can force Russia to withdraw their troops without resorting to military conflict, we should do so. At this point, I'm inclined to delay a direct military response, but give me some options by tomorrow morning." The president paused, then shifted topics. "What's the second issue?"

"We believe the Russians sank *Michigan* because President Kalinin is aboard. They aren't going to sit around while we rescue him. The Russian Navy has already proclaimed the Black Sea off-limits to NATO forces, declaring they will sink any ship that violates their decree. Although the Undersea Rescue Command is on its way, it's unlikely the Russians will give us the opportunity to rescue *Michigan*'s crew and President Kalinin."

"Continue with rescue preparations and develop a plan to put pressure on the Russians. Let them know we'll hit them hard if they interfere with the rescue effort. Maybe a plan to destroy their Black Sea military and commercial ports. Something that gives us leverage."

Colonel DuBose took notes as the president continued. "Where do we stand on a full-scale NATO offensive against Russia?"

Dunnavant replied, "First Armored Division is the last division we're waiting on. Its equipment is aboard transport ships crossing the Atlantic. It'll be a few more days before they offload in Europe and are staged for battle. I'll provide an update on the timeline once I receive additional details from SACEUR."

The president nodded his understanding. The meeting was about to conclude when he commented, "You said Kalinin was rescued by the SEALs. Any word on Christine?"

"No, sir," Dunnavant said. "All we know is that she wasn't aboard the RHIB. We presume she shared the same fate as the SEALs who didn't return."

After a short moment, the president said, "I understand."

68

USS *MICHIGAN*

Murray Wilson stepped into the Officers' Wardroom, settling into the Captain's chair at the head of the table. The Wardroom was dimly lit, with only one-half of the submarine's lighting energized. Joining Wilson and already seated were his Executive Officer, four department heads, and Chief of the Boat. Also present were Commander McNeil and Doc Aleo, plus Russian President Kalinin and his executive assistant, Lieutenant Victor Clark, who had been assigned to "Kalinin's hip" to ensure the Russian stayed out of Sonar, the Radio Room, and the Engine Room, areas that were off-limits for foreign nationals.

Wilson went around the table, getting updates. The COB went first.

"The pressure hull in the Operations Compartment and Engine Room appears uncompromised, as are the piping systems. We didn't find any issues, sir."

The inspection result was welcome news. Now that their immediate survival wasn't a concern, Wilson focused on the long-term outlook. The submarine's Engineer, Lieutenant Commander Bill Harwi, went next.

"From an atmosphere perspective, we should be good for at least ten days. We've got a week of oxygen in the banks, plus another week of oxygen candles. Carbon dioxide is a bigger concern, as we have only a week of carbon dioxide curtains. Doc Aleo," the Engineer nodded in the medical officer's direction, "recommends we keep carbon dioxide level below one percent, so we can let it rise a bit. We're probably looking at ten days by the time we'll need to turn on a carbon dioxide scrubber.

"Power, on the other hand, is more of a concern. The good news is that the electrical grid hasn't been compromised by the flooding in the Missile Compartment. The battery is supplying the Engine Room without any grounds or electrical shorts. The bad news is the load on the battery. We've secured everything except partial lighting and intermittent propulsion plant equipment to keep the reactor cool.

"We've got four or five days of power at the current battery discharge rate. We could eke out another few days by putting the reactor on emergency cooling, but the recovery for reactor startup would be complicated. At this point, I recommend we leave the steam generators in hot standby, minimizing the time required for reactor and electrical turbine startup."

Wilson concurred. "Leave the steam generators in hot standby for now."

Lieutenant Commander Haas, *Michigan*'s Supply Officer, went next. "We have plenty of food; about two months. Water won't be a concern for a while either. All potable water tanks are full and uncompromised. We've done some calculations and we've got enough water for several weeks.

"That addresses the Operations Compartment. The Engine Room is another story. Personnel trapped in the Engine Room have access to potable water and can tap into the Pure Water Tank if required. But we have no way to feed them."

Wilson turned to Commander Aleo. "How long can they last without food?"

"Your crew is young and healthy, so they should last at least three weeks."

The Navigator and Weapons Officer went next. All navigation and tactical systems were in working order prior to being shut down. The XO went last, providing a damage assessment.

"The torpedo exploded on the starboard side of the Missile Compartment, between tubes Thirteen and Fifteen, at the five o'clock position looking forward. I couldn't get a good idea of the hole size, but it'd have to be fairly large based on the rate of flooding. Even if we gained access to the compartment, it'd be impossible to plug a large hole against the sea pressure we're dealing with. Pumping the water out is pointless, because more water will flood in. I'm afraid the Missile Compartment is a complete loss."

Wilson looked to Commander McNeil and Doc Aleo, to see if they had anything to add. Both men shook their head.

"Let's put things in perspective," Wilson said. "Don't expect a rescue. The Russians sank us for a reason, and I doubt they're going to let the U.S. Navy waltz into the Black Sea and rescue us, nor lend a hand themselves." He looked to Kalinin for input.

Kalinin replied, "That would be a reasonable conclusion, Captain."

Wilson continued, "That means we're on our own. I'm not thrilled about escaping to the surface. We've got the survival equipment to do so, but I don't want to put the fate of my crew in Russian hands. That means . . . we bring *Michigan* off the bottom. Any suggestions?"

There was silence around the table until the Engineer spoke. "We need to get the water out of the Missile Compartment. We can't pump it out, but we can push it out."

"Explain," Wilson said.

"The Missile Compartment isn't completely flooded," Harwi replied. "There's a bubble of air at the top of the compartment. Essentially, the flooding stopped once the pressure in the air pocket equalized with the surrounding sea. If we can add air and expand the pocket, we can push the water back out the hole."

"Salvage Air?" Wilson asked.

"Yes, sir. Based on our depth, we'd have to pressurize the Missile Compartment to about one hundred eighty psi. Our high-pressure air banks are still fully charged. A-Gang is looking up air flask volumes and verifying bank pressures, but my best guess at this point is that we can blow the water out until we reach the hole in the hull. The Missile Compartment would still be partially flooded, but we can compensate by pumping water out of the variable ballast tanks and doing a partial emergency ballast tank blow. We're still running the calculations, but we might have enough air to make it work."

"Sounds like a plan, Eng. Let me know when we're ready to give it a shot."

69

KRASNODAR KRAI, RUSSIA

Christine O'Connor felt the cool, wet earth beneath her body. Her eyes fluttered open and a sideways world came into view, sunlight streaming through trees pointing left, rising from the ground on her right. She realized she was lying on her stomach, the right side of her face pressed against wet sand. There was a sound of running water, and all around her, grass sprouted from the ground. She felt the sun's warmth on her back, contrasting with the cool earth beneath. As she tried to figure out where she was and how she got there, the memories slowly assembled. Harrison's eyes came into focus, staring down at her as she dangled from the cliff, her hand in his. Then he let go.

She relived the terrifying fall, ending with a plunge into cold water. She'd fought her way to the surface as the turbulent river swept her downstream. But her memories of the trip down the raging river were vague; clipped images of her struggling to keep her head above water and her legs aimed downstream so she'd hit the boulders with her feet instead of her head. She hadn't always been successful.

Her body ached all over, with sharp pain in both shins and left thigh, while the left side of her head throbbed. She felt her scalp, wincing as her fingers found a tender knot. She moved each limb cautiously, checking for broken bones. Everything seemed intact. She pushed herself to a sitting position, then inspected herself further. There were dark bruises along her shins, and her knees and elbows were cut and rubbed raw, as was her right shoulder. Her clothes hadn't fared much better.

She had no shoes and her skirt was torn down the left side up to the waistband, with a thin red cut along her thigh to match. Her shirt was in tatters, barely held together by an inch-wide stitch of material across her right shoulder. The left side had torn completely, exposing her breast and back. She gathered the loose material in front and behind, tying them together in a knot above her shoulder.

Looking up, she examined her surroundings. She was on a riverbank, with both sides sloping up into the thick forest. She had no idea where she was, other than some distance downstream from where she fell. As best she could tell, it was morning, with the sun just clearing the treetops on the opposite bank. She realized she still had her watch on. It was 7 a.m.

Christine waded gingerly into the river, cleaning her wounds and washing the dirt clinging to her body from lying on the ground. After assessing the terrain, she decided to head into the forest rather than remain exposed along the riverbank. She'd have to make it through the forest without shoes, and there was no discernible path to follow. Additionally, she had no weapon, no food, and no way to carry water. She cupped her hands in the clear river and quenched her thirst. Then she took a deep breath and headed into the woods.

It was slow going, since she had to watch every step, avoiding anything that might cut her feet. After a half-hour picking her way through the forest, she came across a path winding down toward the river. She followed it up, making better progress on the smooth ground. A house came into view in the middle of a small clearing.

The house was similar to the one she and Kalinin had spent a day in—a small log cabin, except this one was in good repair and inhabited. Light smoke rose from the chimney. After assessing the risk of revealing herself to the cabin's occupants, Christine realized she didn't have a choice. She needed help. Any kind would do for now, starting with food and shelter. Finding a way out of Russia would come next.

Christine approached the cabin and knocked on the door, which was opened by an elderly woman. A shocked expression appeared on her face as she examined the battered woman before her. She asked a question, which Christine didn't understand. As Christine tried to decide what to do next, the woman took her hand and pulled her inside the cabin—a kitchen on one side, a table and chairs in the middle, then a couch and small coffee table in front of a fireplace.

The woman guided Christine to a chair by the table, babbling question after question. Christine shook her head and answered in English.

"I don't understand."

The woman sat beside Christine for a moment, trying to communicate, and they eventually learned each other's names. The unintelligible dialogue continued until Tamara said something Christine understood.

"Tea?"

Christine smiled and nodded.

Tamara prepared tea, which was served with a shallow cup of jam. There was no bread to go with the jam, so Christine assumed it went in the tea. She took a small spoonful and held it over her cup, then looked at Tamara. She gave Christine a curious look, as if to say—*what a ridiculous question,* then nodded. *Of course the jam goes in the tea.* She then busied herself in the kitchen again, and aroma filled the air as she prepared a pot of hot borsch.

The cabin door opened and an elderly man entered. He stopped when he spotted Christine at the table. Before Tamara could explain, he asked a curt question.

Tamara guided him to the table, talking along the way, then pushed him down into a chair across from Christine. Tamara pointed to him and said, "Vasily."

Christine extended a hand. "Christine."

The man eyed her hand suspiciously, then shook it.

Vasily wasn't any better at communicating, but Christine figured he was trying to ascertain who she was and how she ended up in their cabin. But aside from her name, she was able to convey nothing.

Borsch was served and Tamara joined them, and the conversation ceased while they ate. After living off the meager backpack rations the last few days, Christine was famished. Tamara offered a second helping, which Christine eagerly accepted.

Christine was the last to finish, and after the dishes were cleared, Tamara and Vasily resumed their efforts to communicate. Christine finally conveyed she needed a phone by punching her finger in the air, and learned that they didn't have one.

Tamara went to the fireplace mantel and returned with a framed photograph of a young woman. She pointed to herself and Vasily, then to the picture.

"Anna," she said, punching her finger in the air. Christine understood; the woman in the picture was their daughter and she had a phone. Tamara then pointed to the door and then to her watch, offering a questioning gesture. Christine stood, then tapped her watch vigorously. She needed a phone as soon as possible.

Tamara and Vasily exchanged looks, then Vasily spoke. He pointed to himself, then the door. He would take Christine to his daughter.

70

USS *MICHIGAN*

"The piping systems are aligned," Lieutenant Commander Bill Harwi reported, standing by a watertight door to the Missile Compartment. Accompanying the Engineer were Captain Wilson and a chief machinist mate in charge of Auxiliary Division, along with a machinist mate second class on the sound-powered phones.

Wilson acknowledged Harwi's report. The piping systems had been aligned to port high-pressure air into the Missile Compartment, to expand the existing air bubble and force water back out the hole in the hull. The back-of-the-envelope calculations indicated the effort might succeed, depending on how high up the hole was in *Michigan*'s hull. If it was too high, air would spill out the hole before sufficient water was expelled, and the effort would fail. There was only one way to find out.

"Open Salvage Air," Wilson ordered.

The Engineer passed the order to the machinist mate second class who rotated the handwheel, and air began flowing into the Missile Compartment. The piping was only two inches in diameter, so it would take a while to force the water back out the hole. Meanwhile, other preparations were required.

The A-Gang chief remained at the Salvage Air valve with the other machinist mate, while Wilson and Harwi headed to the Control Room to monitor air bank pressures and ship's depth. The ballast and ship control panels, along with the other equipment in Control, were dark.

"Energize Sonar and the ballast and ship control panels," Wilson ordered.

The Officer of the Deck ordered the appropriate electrical breakers shut and a Sonar startup. The ballast and ship control panels energized, and the air bank pressures slowly decreased as air flowed into the Missile Compartment.

Sonar completed its startup, but communications were still down, so the Sonar Supervisor opened the door to Sonar. "Sonar, Conn. Sonar startup complete. Commencing broadband and narrowband searches."

Wilson entered Sonar, addressing the Sonar Supervisor. "We need to determine when we've pushed all the water possible out of the Missile Compartment and air starts spilling out the hole. We can't afford to waste any air."

"I understand, sir. We'll monitor broadband and the self-monitoring hydrophones for any change in sound signature. We should be able to determine when air starts exiting the compartment."

Wilson returned to the Control Room, settling into his chair on the Conn, waiting until the Salvage Air process was complete.

The minutes ticked by as air flowed into the Missile Compartment, pushing the water out. Finally, the Sonar Supervisor emerged from Sonar again. "Captain, we're detecting air bubbling into the surrounding water."

Wilson ordered the Salvage Air valve shut, then examined the air bank pressures; they were pretty close to what the Engineer had calculated. A glance at the Ship Control Panel revealed the expected information. *Michigan* was still stuck on the bottom. Too much water remained in the Missile Compartment.

He was about to proceed to the next step—pumping water from *Michigan*'s variable ballast tanks—when the Sonar Supervisor reported, "Sonar, Conn. Hold a new narrowband contact on the spherical array, Sierra two-eight, bearing two-five-zero, classified submerged. Analyzing."

Another Russian submarine was nearby, most likely another one of the three Improved Kilos.

Wilson ordered, "Man Battle Stations Torpedo silently." He didn't have a choice, with the shipwide communications systems secured.

The Officer of the Deck sent the Messenger and the LAN Technician of the Watch throughout the Operations Compartment while the Chief of the Watch informed personnel in the Engine Room via the sound-powered phone system.

To the Engineer, Wilson ordered, "Commence reactor startup. We'll wait until we're in the power range to come off the bottom and open the main seawater intakes for Engine Room startup. I want to minimize the time we're hovering above the bottom, more vulnerable to detection, until we have propulsion."

"Aye, sir," the Engineer replied, then relayed the order to the Engineering Officer of the Watch in the Engine Room.

Wilson then asked, "What do we have left in the battery?"

The Engineer queried the Engineering Officer of the Watch, who reported battery discharge rate and voltage. They had enough power to sustain the tactical systems for a few hours.

To the Officer of the Deck, Wilson ordered, "Bring

up Combat, Navigation, and all communication circuits."

Personnel streamed into the Control Room, taking
their positions at the dormant consoles, waiting as
the combat control and navigation systems completed
their start-up routines.

As the last console flickered to life, Sonar reported,
"Sierra two-eight is classified Improved Kilo class
submarine."

Wilson ordered, "Designate Sierra two-eight as
Master one. Track Master one."

There were two fire control technicians and a junior officer manning consoles dedicated to tracking
targets, and each man worked independently toward
a target solution. However, *Michigan* held Master one
only on passive sonar. With *Michigan* immobile, unable to change course and speed to alter the inputs
into the combat system algorithms, there were several
possible solutions for the Kilo submarine's course,
speed, and range, none of which were accurate enough
to launch a torpedo. Nor did Wilson want to, without
propulsion to evade counterfire.

The Chief of the Watch announced, "Officer of the
Deck. Maneuvering reports the reactor is critical."

Lieutenant Cody, who had relieved as Officer of the
Deck while Captain Wilson assumed the Conn, acknowledged. Control rods had been withdrawn from
the reactor core far enough to allow the nuclear fis-
sion reaction to become critical, which meant self-
sustaining, generating heat in the process. The fuel
cells were now heating up, transferring heat to the primary cooling water, which in turn transferred it to the
water in the steam generators. The next report came a
few minutes later.

"The reactor is in the power range."

Reactor power was now at one percent. The watch-standers in Maneuvering would slowly increase power, heating the primary and secondary cooling systems until both reached their normal operating temperatures. Wilson had left the steam generators in hot standby, well above 212°F, and with the reactor now adding heat, they could soon send steam to the propulsion and electrical turbine generators. But they had to open the seawater intakes first and start main seawater, which provided cooling water to condense the steam back into water after it passed through the turbines. The water would then be pumped back into the steam generators to repeat the process. To open the seawater intakes without fouling them, *Michigan* had to come off the bottom.

"Chief of the Watch," Wilson ordered, "pump all variable ballast and trim tanks to sea."

The Chief of the Watch complied, and Wilson waited as the trim and hovering pumps emptied the tanks that controlled the submarine's buoyancy while underway, along with its fore-to-aft tilt. He watched the nearest depth indicator, waiting for the numbers to change, but they remained steady.

"All variable ballast and trim tanks are empty," the Chief of the Watch reported.

Wilson assessed the situation, which wasn't unexpected. There was still a lot of water in the Missile Compartment, which would have to be offset. The variable ballast and trim tanks were dry, so that left the water in the main ballast tanks.

"Chief of the Watch. Conduct an emergency blow."

The Chief of the Watch stood and reached for the Emergency Blow levers. Although it was unlikely they'd blow too much water from the ballast tanks, Wilson wasn't worried. If *Michigan* became too light and started to float toward the surface, they could quickly flood water into the variable ballast tanks, reestablishing neutral buoyancy. The bigger concern, by far, was that there wasn't enough high-pressure air left.

The Chief of the Watch pulled the Emergency Blow levers, and the remaining air in the high-pressure air banks flowed into the ballast tanks. Everyone in Control focused on the depth gauges, waiting for the numbers to change. The red digital numbers and the needle on the analog gauge stared back at them ominously, both immobile.

Wilson examined the air bank pressures as they lowered until they stabilized at the surrounding sea pressure. His eyes went back to the depth readouts.

They were steady at 410 feet.

He waited another minute, hoping for a delayed reaction as the eighteen-thousand-ton submarine freed itself from the bottom.

Still no motion.

After another minute waiting without any change on the depth readout, Wilson accepted defeat. USS *Michigan* was stuck on the bottom of the Black Sea.

71

BEREGOVOY, RUSSIA

The sun was still climbing into a clear blue sky as Vasily led the way down a narrow path, ambling back toward the river. During this trek through the woods, Christine was better equipped, albeit not fashionably. Tamara had given her a purple and white floral dress, eight sizes too big, to replace her shredded blouse and torn skirt, a sash tied around her waist, and a pair of old boots plus socks. Tamara also offered a wooden hair clip, which Christine had used to bundle her hair behind her head.

Christine spotted the river through the trees, then the path turned and followed the river's course as it wound toward the Black Sea. They reached a wider but muddier dirt trail, which they followed until it connected with a paved, two-lane road. An occasional van and sedan passed by, to which Vasily paid no notice. They eventually reached the outskirts of a small town and turned down a side road. Vasily stopped at a two-story duplex and knocked on the right-side door. The woman who answered matched Tamara's picture. Anna hugged Vasily, then her eyes went to Christine. Vasily quickly explained.

Anna stepped aside, beckoning them to enter as she

peppered Vasily with more questions. Then she disappeared down a dark hallway, returning a moment later with a man in his mid-twenties, dressed in slacks and a sports jacket and collared shirt, whom Christine surmised was Anna's husband. His hair was damp and he smelled of cologne. He must have been getting ready for work. He extended his hand.

"I am Ruslan," he said with a heavy accent.

After Christine introduced herself, Ruslan said, "You need phone, yes?"

Christine answered, then he asked, "Who do you call?"

That was something she didn't want to reveal. Thus far, Christine had provided only her first name. Her new Russian acquaintances seemed friendly enough, but she had no idea if she could trust them. It was best if they didn't discover she was America's national security advisor, who wanted to call the president of the United States.

"A friend," Christine answered.

Her response didn't satisfy Ruslan, who asked, "In Russia, or out?"

Christine finally understood Ruslan's line of questioning. Did she need to make an international phone call? "Out," Christine said.

Ruslan shook his head. "Not possible."

"It's okay," Christine said, "I can call who I need, no charge. Do you have a smartphone?"

Ruslan pulled an Android phone from his jacket and handed it to Christine.

"I need to talk in private," she said.

Ruslan pointed to the kitchen opening.

Christine stepped into the kitchen, where she duplicated the procedure she'd used on the phone stolen from the pub; she downloaded the free app again and after entering her username and password, a man answered.

After Christine provided her full name and verification code again, the man asked in the same monotone voice, "How can I help you?"

Christine explained her situation quietly, to which the man said, "Please wait."

A moment later, he said "We have located you using your cell phone. Someone who can assist will call you shortly. Is this a good number?"

"Yes, but I have to return this phone. How long until someone calls."

"Not long," the man said.

Not a helpful answer, Christine thought. "Make it fast."

"I will see what I can do."

The man hung up and Christine returned to the living room.

When Ruslan extended his hand for the phone, Christine withheld it, saying, "I'm waiting for a return call."

"How long?" he asked.

"Not long," Christine replied, providing the same vague timeframe the man had.

Displeasure formed on Ruslan's face. "I work soon. Need phone."

"It won't be long," Christine said again. She looked to Anna and Vasily, hoping one of them would assuage Ruslan. Anna took Christine's cue and spoke with her husband, who looked at his watch with a disapproving frown.

"Ten minutes," he said to Christine.

"Thank you."

Anna hurried into the kitchen, returning with a tray containing a pot of tea, four cups and spoons, and a dish of jam. This time, Christine knew what to do with the jam. Ruslan asked a few questions about who she was and what happened to her. Christine made things up as she went, telling Ruslan she was an American tourist, traveling alone, who'd fallen into the river while hiking. She hoped Vasily hadn't mentioned that she'd arrived at his cabin wearing a shirt and silk blouse, definitely not hiking apparel.

Christine had almost finished her tea when Ruslan's phone rang. She excused herself to the kitchen again, then answered.

"Who am I speaking with?" a man asked.

"Christine O'Connor."

"Verification code?"

"851051."

"We have you at 140 Ulitsa Podgornaya in Beregovoy. Is this correct?"

Christine peered around the kitchen corner, repeating the address. Ruslan nodded.

"Correct," Christine said.

"A man named Maxim Anosov will pick you up in one hour. Do you have any questions?"

"I will no longer have access to this phone. Is that okay?"

"Yes," the man said. "We have the information we need. Maxim will knock on your door. Any other questions?"

Christine said no and the man hung up.

She returned to the living room and handed the phone to Ruslan. "Thank you."

Ruslan seemed pleased to have been of assistance, then checked his watch. "I must go," he said.

Once Ruslan departed, Anna surveyed Christine's disheveled hair, dirt-smudged face, and oversized clothes with a critical eye, commenting to Vasily in a disapproving tone. Vasily shrugged. Anna, who was much more Christine's size than her mother, disappeared into her bedroom, returning with a stack of clothes and shoes that would fit better than what Christine was wearing. She guided Christine down the hallway to a bathroom, grabbing a towel from the closet along the way.

Christine locked the bathroom door, then stripped off her clothes and stepped into the shower, letting the hot water run over her. She examined her cuts, scrapes, and bruises, noting that there were only a few areas of unblemished skin on her body. But she was still in one piece and in good health, as opposed to being splattered on a river boulder or riddled with bullets. She considered herself fortunate.

Her thoughts then went to others. Since awakening on the riverbank, she'd been focused on her survival and hadn't wondered about Kalinin, Harrison, and the other SEALs. Had they made it back to *Michigan*? Or had they been apprehended, or even worse, killed?

After her shower, Christine donned a pair of slacks and a blouse that fit fairly well, then brushed her hair. She felt refreshed and ready for the next and hopefully last leg of her journey—a car trip to a CIA safe house or perhaps directly to the airport. Only a few more hours, and the unpleasant trip to Kalinin's summer residence would be behind her.

A few kilometers away, Ruslan pulled his car over to the side of the road. He pulled his cell phone from his jacket and did an internet search, finding a news article about the television bulletin he'd seen a few days ago. After examining the woman's picture, along with the reward for information leading to her apprehension, he dialed the number provided and a man answered.

"The woman you're looking for," Ruslan said, "the American fugitive? I know where she is."

72

USS *MICHIGAN*

Events hadn't played out as Wilson had hoped. *Michigan* was supposed to be rising from the bottom right now, and he had prepared accordingly. Sonar and most of the Control Room systems had been energized, along with the equipment required to support reactor startup, which were placing a heavy drain on the battery—a battery they'd need for life-support functions now that they were stuck on the bottom. But before throwing in the towel and shutting everything down again, he decided to brainstorm one last time.

"XO, department heads, COB. Approach the Conn. Inform the Eng in Sonar."

The XO, department heads, and COB stopping at the Conn railing.

"It looks like we're stuck on the bottom," Wilson said, "unless someone has a bright idea."

The Navigator replied, "We need to push more water out of the ballast tanks."

That much was obvious, Wilson thought. "We don't have any more high-pressure air."

"Make more."

Wilson considered the Navigator's words, latching

on to his idea. Submarines recharged their air banks by running high-pressure air compressors, which sucked in air from the submarine compartments. While submerged, there was no way to replenish the air, so air pressure throughout the submarine lowered. That was okay as long as it didn't lower too much. But could they compress enough air before pressure inside the boat dropped too low?

Wilson directed the XO, "Have Commander Aleo report to Control."

The XO sent word over the sound-powered phones, requesting the SEAL detachment medical officer's presence. While they waited, the Engineer said, "We can offset some of the air loss by bleeding the low-pressure air reservoirs into the boat." *Michigan* had a low-pressure air system for various functions, including emergency breathing air during fires.

"Good idea, Eng. We'll tap into it if necessary."

Doc Aleo entered Control, joining Wilson and the others.

"We need to run the air compressors," Wilson said, "which take a suction on the internal compartments. How low can we drop atmospheric pressure before it becomes life-threatening or impairs our ability to function?"

Aleo replied, "The general rule is about one-half atmosphere before you become incapacitated. Results vary by individual and impairment occurs earlier, so I'd advise you to keep atmospheres above three-fourths."

"Thanks Doc." Turning to his XO and department heads, Wilson said. "I plan to run all compressors, simultaneously, until we reach three-fourth atmospheres or come off the bottom. If we're still on the bottom when we reach three-fourths, we'll evaluate how to proceed. Any objections?"

The Weapons Officer, in charge of Sonar, replied, "The air charge is going to be noisy."

"That's why I'm going with every high-PAC," Wilson replied. "If we're going to put noise into the water, I want to do it for as short a time as possible."

The Weps seemed satisfied with the answer, then Wilson asked, "Anything else?"

There were no responses, so Wilson turned to Lieutenant Cody, stationed as the Officer of the Deck. "Commence a high-pressure air charge with all high-PACs."

Wilson took his seat on the Conn while the other officers and COB returned to their battle stations positions. He decided to keep the emergency blow valves open, which let the compressors charge air directly into the ballast tanks.

Lieutenant Cody reported the air charge had commenced. Wilson requested battery voltage and discharge rate again, which Cody provided. The air compressors were putting a heavy drain on the battery, but it would last another hour or two at the present load. It was quiet in Control, aside from occasional communications between watchstanders as they tracked Master one.

The XO called out, "Possible target zig, Master one, due to upshift in frequency."

The Kilo's crew had detected the air compressor tonals and was turning to investigate. As the watchstanders tried to determine the Kilo's new course, the submarine lurched.

Metallic groans filled the air as the deck tilted downward. The stern was rising from the bottom. A moment later, the bow broke free and *Michigan* drifted upward with a ten-degree down-angle.

Wilson ordered, "Dive, zero bubble. Hover at three-eight-zero feet."

The Diving Officer ordered the Chief of the Watch to flood water into After Trim. As water flowed into the stern trim tank, *Michigan* leveled off until a zero bubble was obtained. The Dive then ordered the Chief of the Watch to hover at 380 feet.

The hovering system kicked in, flooding water into the variable ballast tanks, stabilizing *Michigan* at the ordered depth.

Wilson ordered, "Secure the air charge and start up the Engine Room."

Lieutenant Cody relayed the order to Maneuvering, and Wilson waited while the nuclear-trained machinist mates raced to bring up the electrical generators and propulsion turbines. To survive a duel with another submarine, *Michigan* needed power and propulsion.

73

BEREGOVOY, RUSSIA

As a white van sped down Highway E97, Maxim Anosov looked out the passenger window, searching for the exit to Beregovoy. His driver knew the area well enough and didn't need a map, but Anosov followed along on his smartphone, which indicated they were approaching the exit in a few hundred meters. The van slowed and made a left turn, then Anosov checked the map again; they were five kilometers from their destination.

Anosov resisted the urge to check the firearm in the holster beneath his jacket. It was loaded with the safety disengaged, and there was no point in checking it again. The CIA safe house in Sochi didn't have a detachment of tactical mercenaries, but Anosov was no stranger to firearms, and his driver was also armed. Additionally, today's assignment was as simple as it got. Swing by the designated address and pick up the package. Even though this package—America's national security advisor—was unusual, Anosov had been involved in far more delicate extractions.

As Anosov's van headed down the two-lane road, it was passed by two Russian military armored personnel carriers, traveling well above the speed limit.

The vehicles diminished in size as they sped into the distance, then turned left. A sick feeling formed in Anosov's stomach when he checked the map on his phone. The armored carriers had turned down Ulitsa Podgornaya, the road on which his package was waiting.

The van made the left turn and Anosov propped his elbow on the open window, projecting a nonchalant look as they traveled toward their destination. Ahead, the two personnel carriers had stopped and two dozen Russian soldiers were streaming forth, surrounding a duplex apartment. Anosov checked the map again, then swore under his breath. The Russian military had somehow tracked down Christine O'Connor.

"Continue on," Anosov directed his driver.

The van slowed, imitating the natural curiosity of passersby. One of the Russian soldiers, standing by the street, waved them on. As they passed 140 Ulitsa Podgornaya, Anosov spotted Christine O'Connor, in handcuffs, being led roughly from the duplex toward a personnel carrier. He discreetly took a picture with his smartphone.

After the van traveled another hundred meters, Anosov pounded his fist on the dashboard. If they'd arrived a few minutes earlier, O'Connor would've been safe in the back of his van.

74

USS *MICHIGAN*

"Confirm target zig, Master one," the XO announced. "Master one has turned toward. No anchor range."

Wilson listened to Patzke's report, then examined the three combat control consoles tracking Master one. All three consoles had converged on solutions with the target pointing directly at *Michigan,* but the solution range varied from four to ten thousand yards.

Determining the target's range was critical, since that would determine when the torpedo would enable, turning on its sonar. If it enabled too soon, the target would have advance notice of the approaching torpedo, improving its odds of evading. If the torpedo enabled too late, it would pass by the target, blind, before beginning its search.

"Attention in Control," Wilson announced. "I intend to initiate Firing Point Procedures, but won't shoot until we have propulsion. Hopefully Master one will give us the time we need. Carry on."

There was no doubt in Wilson's mind that the Kilo's crew had detected *Michigan*; the contact had turned toward them after the high-pressure air charge commenced. However, the Russian crew was probably still sorting out what they held on sonar. Air compressor tonals would not be easily correlated to an American submarine in combat, plus *Michigan* was stationary, contrary to tactical guidance. Submarines constantly maneuvered during combat, trying to prevent their adversary from gaining a firing solution while helping their combat system algorithms calculate the target's course, speed, and range.

Additionally, the Kilo was in deeper water, looking upslope toward shore, where shore-based tonals often interfered with sonar. Electrical power plants near shore, for example, often emitted tonals similar to submarine electrical generators. Although Wilson preferred to maneuver, their stationary predicament had its advantages.

"Firing Point Procedures," Wilson announced, "Master one, tube One, normal submerged presets, except set minimum run to enable." Since the target range hadn't been nailed down yet, Wilson ordered the torpedo to go active as soon as possible, so it didn't run past the target before turning its sonar on.

Patzke stopped behind each of the combat control consoles to examine the target solutions, then tapped the middle fire control technician. The watchstander pressed a button on his console and the XO announced, "Solution ready."

The fire control technician at the Weapon Control Console sent the course, speed, and range of their target to the MK 48 torpedo in tube One, along with the target search presets. A few seconds later, the Weapons Officer reported, "Weapon ready."

"Ship ready." Lieutenant Cody announced. The torpedo countermeasure launchers were armed.

Michigan was a single button push away from firing.

The Russian Kilo continued its approach toward *Michigan,* but the three combat control consoles still had markedly different ranges to the target.

The Sonar Supervisor's voice came across the Conn speakers. "Conn, Sonar. Mechanical transients from Master one. Contact is opening torpedo tube outer doors."

Wilson acknowledged Sonar's report, then turned on the 2-JV speaker on the Conn, listening to communications in the Engine Room. Main Seawater had been restored and they were drawing a vacuum in both main condensers, but it wasn't low enough yet. If they sent steam into the turbines before there was sufficient vacuum on the other end, the steam would back up, bringing the turbines to a halt.

A sonar ping echoed through *Michigan*'s hull, coming from the approaching Kilo. The Russian crew was dealing with the same question as Wilson's—what was the target's range? With a steady, bow-on approach, the Russian captain had skipped the valuable maneuvers his fire control algorithms needed to determine the target's range. He had two options: maneuver to the side to get a crossed-bearing range, or go active. Going active was much quicker, but would give his submarine's presence away. The Russian captain had guessed correctly; *Michigan* was already aware of the Kilo's approach.

Wilson moved to the front of the Conn, preparing to launch a torpedo, either when the Kilo fired or propulsion was restored. He listened intently to the Engine Room communications in the background, and the report he was waiting for finally came across the Conn speaker.

"Conn, Maneuvering. Ready to answer all bells."

Wilson announced, "Match sonar bearings and shoot!"

The Weapons Officer ordered the torpedo launched, and Wilson heard the whirr of the ejection pump impulsing the torpedo from the tube.

"Helm, ahead flank!" Wilson ordered. "Hard left rudder, steady course one-three-zero! Launch decoy, hold jammer!"

The Helm turned the rudder hard left and twisted the Engine Order Telegraph to ahead flank. The submarine's engines sprang to life, sending tremors through the deck. A few seconds later, a fire control technician called out, "Decoy away!"

The torpedo decoy had been launched none too soon, because Sonar reported, "Torpedo launch transients from Master one, bearing two-five-zero!" Seconds later, a report blared from the speakers, "Torpedo in the water, bearing two-five-zero!"

Wilson examined the red line on the geographic display, with new lines appearing every ten seconds. The bearing to the torpedo remained constant.

Either they weren't moving out of the way fast enough, or the torpedo had been fired from long range. Hopefully, it was the latter, which would give *Michigan* time to slip away before the torpedo approached within acquisition range.

Michigan picked up speed and completed its turn. Wilson glanced at the torpedo bearing again. It was drifting to starboard. A good sign. The torpedo hadn't yet acquired *Michigan* and was continuing on its preset course.

After *Michigan* moved far enough away from its decoy, Wilson ordered, "Launch jammer."

The fire control technician complied and an acoustic jammer was launched, placing a blinding field of noise between the decoy and *Michigan* in the hope the torpedo would see only the decoy and not the larger object speeding away.

Wilson confirmed the torpedo remained on its original course, then turned his attention to their weapon, which was inbound toward the Russian submarine at medium speed.

Lieutenant Commander Patzke announced, "Possible target zig, Master one, due to downshift in frequency."

The Russian submarine was mimicking *Michigan,* turning away and no doubt launching torpedo countermeasures to fool the incoming torpedo. The bearings to the Kilo submarine were almost steady despite *Michigan*'s speed and course change, which meant the Russian captain had turned in the same direction as *Michigan*. They were now on almost parallel courses, albeit slightly opening.

"Confirm target zig, Master one. Target turned to starboard and increased speed. Set solution anchor range at five thousand yards."

Five thousand yards. That was the last bit of information they needed.

"Weps, give me a steer recommendation."

The Weapons Officer studied the Weapon Control Console display, examining their torpedo's track and the updated target solution as the fire control technician simulated various steer commands.

"Recommend right six-zero."

Wilson ordered, "Insert steer, right six-zero, tube One."

The fire control technician sent the order to their torpedo over the guidance wire, and they watched the torpedo turn right.

"Tube One has accepted steer."

Although their torpedo had been set back onto an intercept course with the Russian submarine, it still had to deal with the decoy and jammer the Russian crew had undoubtedly launched.

"Sonar, Conn. Have you detected decoy or jammer deployment?"

"Conn, Sonar. Yes, sir. Decoy bears two-seven-zero and jammer bears two-six-two."

Patzke overheard the report and ordered one of the fire control technicians to insert symbols at the appropriate bearings, using the anchor range to the target before it maneuvered. The two symbols appeared on the display.

Michigan's MK 48 MOD 7 torpedo was quite capable, usually able to identify small objects pretending to be a submarine as decoys, and able to see through jammers to some extent. But Wilson didn't want to take a chance the Russian countermeasures were newer, more capable versions.

"Pre-enable tube One," Wilson ordered.

The Weapons Officer sent the command to the torpedo, which turned off its sonar and search algorithms. Wilson stepped from the Conn, stopping behind the Weapons Officer and fire control technician, watching the MK 48 proceed along its ordered course.

After the torpedo passed the decoy and jammer symbols, Wilson ordered, "Enable tube One."

The Weps complied, activating the torpedo's sonar. Their MK 48 was close to acquisition range. If the steer was accurate enough, not even another maneuver by the Russian captain would save him.

Wilson returned his attention to the incoming Russian torpedo, which appeared to be attacking *Michigan*'s decoy. However, it wouldn't be long before the Russian crew directed it onto a new intercept course with *Michigan*. Hopefully, the Russian crew would become preoccupied with their survival.

The Weapons Officer reported, "Detect!"

Their steer had been good enough, and Wilson's

decision to run the torpedo past the Russian counter-measures had worked superbly.

A few seconds later, the Weps announced, "Acquired!," indicating the torpedo had verified the detection was a submarine.

The torpedo surged to maximum speed and increased its ping rate to more accurately calculate an intercept course. It would close the remaining distance in less than a minute, making course adjustments while the target maneuvered, likely giving the Russian crew insufficient time to insert a torpedo steer.

Wilson focused on the Russian torpedo again, which was circling back for another attack on *Michigan*'s decoy. So far, so good.

The seconds counted down, and then the sound of an explosion rumbled through Control, followed by Sonar's report. "Torpedo explosion on the bearing to Master one."

Wilson examined the Russian torpedo, which was still preoccupied with the decoy. *Michigan* had survived.

He was about to order a slower speed when Sonar reported, "Conn, Sonar. Detect a loud flow tonal coming from own-ship, starboard side."

It must be the torpedo hole in the hull. As *Michigan* increased speed, the water flowing down the hull was interacting with the jagged metal surrounding the blast point, creating a flow tonal. With the Russian Kilo vanquished, it was time to slow down, blending into the Black Sea again.

"Helm, ahead two-thirds."

Michigan's speed tapered off and the adrenaline coursing through Wilson's body began to fade. He stopped by a combat control console and examined where they were in the Black Sea. As he evaluated where to head next, an urgent report blasted from the Conn speakers.

"Torpedo in the water, bearing zero-nine-zero!"

A red bearing line appeared on the display. *Michigan* had been traveling at ahead flank, reducing the range of its spherical array while putting a tremendous amount of noise into the water due to the high speed and flow tonal from the damaged hull. There was another Russian submarine out there, probably the third Kilo, which had tracked *Michigan* during its evasion and had developed a firing solution.

"Helm, ahead flank! Hard right rudder, steady course one-eight-zero. Launch countermeasures."

Michigan was still at high speed and it didn't take long to turn to the evasion course. Wilson listened for the reports of torpedo decoy and jammer launches, then focused on the enemy submarine. Unfortunately, they didn't hold it on sonar and had no idea where it was or where it was headed, except that it had launched its torpedo from the east.

"Quick Reaction Firing, tube Two, bearing zero-nine-zero!"

Lieutenant Commander Patzke tapped one of the fire control technicians on the shoulder, who entered the ordered bearing.

Patzke announced, "Solution ready."

The Weapons Officer followed. "Weapon ready."

"Ship ready," Lieutenant Cody reported.

"Shoot on generated bearings," Wilson ordered.

The torpedo was impulsed from the tube, then turned east. It was a shot in the dark, aimed at where the enemy submarine had fired from as opposed to where it was headed, but it would have to do. Wilson focused again on the incoming torpedo. The red bearing lines were stacking on top of each other. The torpedo was on an intercept course.

"Helm, hard right rudder, steady course three-zero-zero."

Wilson turned away from the incoming torpedo, reversing course to the northwest. As long as the torpedo hadn't acquired *Michigan* or it wasn't steered toward them, they'd escape. After *Michigan* steadied on its new course, the torpedo bearings drew steadily aft on the submarine's starboard stern. Then the bearing drift halted.

"Damn it," Wilson muttered. The torpedo had been steered back toward them. It was unclear how far away the torpedo was, but the rate at which it drew aft before it steadied indicated it was close and would acquire *Michigan* soon. Drastic action was required, beyond another course change.

Wilson glanced at the sound velocity profile recording by the Ship Control Panel, which reported the speed of sound as it varied by depth. During *Michigan*'s last trip to periscope depth to retrieve the SEAL RHIB, they had passed through a strong thermal layer, with its lower boundary at two hundred feet.

The thermocline was a thin layer of water where the temperature transitioned rapidly between the warm surface heated by the sun and the cold water beneath. Submarines used thermoclines to their advantage because the rapid temperature change bent sound waves as they traveled through the layer, reflecting the sound back toward its source like light reflecting off a window. Depending on the frequency and angle of the sound wave, some tonals wouldn't make it through. If *Michigan* could pass through the layer before the torpedo acquired, they'd have a chance.

"Dive, make your depth nine-zero feet. Use thirty up."

Wilson ordered *Michigan* shallow, placing the sail only fifteen feet from the surface. The massive stern planes rotated, tilting the submarine until a thirty-degree up-angle was achieved. With *Michigan* at ahead flank, the submarine shot toward the surface.

The Dive called out the depth change in one-hundred-foot increments, ordering a zero bubble as they passed through two hundred feet, hoping to arrest *Michigan*'s ascent at the ordered depth. The deck leveled off as the submarine passed one hundred feet, with the keel settling out at ninety feet as ordered.

Wilson monitored the water temperature as his submarine came shallow. There was a strong thermal layer, but there was no way to know if the gradient was sufficient without running sound-velocity profiles on the submarine's computers. There wasn't enough time.

"Helm, all stop."

The Throttleman in the Engine Room shut the ahead throttles, and the screw coasted down. Now that they were shallow and at a lower sea pressure, the submarine's screw would cavitate when spinning at ahead flank, serving as a beacon to enemy sonars. Wilson had traded speed for silence, hoping the torpedo passed beneath the layer without detecting them.

The first indication was positive; Sonar lost the torpedo after *Michigan* passed through the layer, which meant the torpedo engine sound waves were bending back down. Whether the torpedo's sonar would penetrate the layer and detect *Michigan* was unknown, however.

As *Michigan*'s speed bled down, Wilson calculated how long before the torpedo passed beneath them, using a worst-case range for the Russian torpedo shot. He checked the clock and when it approached the predicted time, he listened for Sonar's report that they had regained the torpedo, which would've been bad news; it'd mean the torpedo had followed *Michigan* through the layer.

The time passed and there was no Sonar report. Wilson waited another minute, then another. *Michigan* coasted to a halt, hovering at nine-zero feet.

Wilson was confident the torpedo had passed beneath them, so he stepped from the Conn and examined the geographic display on the nearest console. Wilson's best guess, based on the torpedo launch transient and subsequent maneuvering, was that the Russian submarine was still to the east. That meant it would head west to regain *Michigan*. If the layer was strong enough, Wilson would have a nice surprise for the Russian captain.

"Helm, ahead two-thirds. Hard right rudder, steady course zero-nine-zero. Sonar, Conn. Prepare to deploy the thin-line array."

As *Michigan* turned toward the Russian submarine, Wilson briefed his crew.

"Attention in Control." When all eyes were on him, he continued. "We've got a strong layer beneath us, which we'll use to our advantage. The Russian captain will likely head west in an attempt to regain contact, but we won't be where he expects us. We're heading east, and if things work out, we'll pass over him, then shoot from behind.

"We're going to deploy the thin-line array, letting it drop through the layer so we can get a look at what's going on below us. Hopefully, the Russian won't poke his head above the layer looking for us. But if he does, we'll shoot him in the face. Any questions?"

There were none, so Wilson announced, "Carry on." He then addressed the Weps. "Weapons Officer. Reload and make tubes One and Two ready in all respects."

Sonar reported they were ready to deploy the thin-line array, and it was soon trailing a thousand yards behind *Michigan*. Wilson checked the array scope—

its trailing distance—against ship's speed, verifying it would droop through the thermal layer, but not drag on the sea floor.

"Conn, Sonar. Hold a new towed array contact, designated Sierra two-nine, bearing one-zero-five, classified submerged. Analyzing."

Wilson announced, "Designate Sierra two-nine as Master two. Track Master two."

The Fire Control Tracking Party went to work, focused on generating a firing solution. While they worked on the target's course, speed, and range, Sonar provided additional information:

"Conn, Sonar. Master two is classified Improved Kilo class, traveling at high speed."

"Sonar, Conn. Aye," Wilson replied.

The Russian captain had increased speed, most likely using a sprint and drift tactic to rapidly close on *Michigan,* slowing on occasion for a detailed sonar search. During the high-speed sprint legs, the Russian sonar would be impaired and the submarine would remain deep so its screw didn't cavitate. Both of these factors played into Wilson's plan.

The XO announced, "I have a firing solution."

The Kilo was traveling at twenty knots, due west. The Russian submarine wouldn't pass directly beneath *Michigan,* but close enough. The contact's rapid closure, then opening, would result in an even more accurate solution.

As Wilson pondered the best tactic to employ, the Weapons Officer reported, "Tubes One and Two are ready in all respects."

"Firing Point Procedures, Master two, tube One. Set minimum run to enable."

While he waited for the required reports, Wilson announced, "I plan to remain on a course to the east, firing an over-the-shoulder shot at minimum range."

He watched as the three combat control consoles slewed to near identical solutions, showing the target passing just south of *Michigan*, six hundred yards away, still headed west.

"Helm, right twenty degrees rudder, steady course one-two-zero."

Wilson adjusted *Michigan*'s course to pass directly behind the Russian submarine at one thousand yards.

Lieutenant Commander Patzke tapped a fire control technician on the shoulder, who sent his solution to Weapons Control.

Patzke announced, "Solution ready."

The Weapons Officer reported, "Weapon ready."

"Ship ready," the Officer of the Deck announced.

Wilson monitored Master two on the geographic display. When it opened to one thousand yards, he ordered, "Shoot on generated bearings."

The torpedo was impulsed from the tube. Sonar then reported the status of their outgoing weapon.

"Tube One is in the water, running normally."

"Fuel crossover achieved."

"Turning to preset gyro course."

With a minimum pre-enable run, the torpedo went active once it stabilized on the ordered course, one thousand yards behind the Russian submarine.

A few seconds later, the first of the hoped-for reports was received. "Detect!"

It took only three more pings before the torpedo verified the object ahead was a submarine, and Sonar picked up the characteristic torpedo response.

"Tube One is increasing speed and ping rate," the Weapons Officer reported, confirming Sonar's observation as he read the telemetry data sent back to *Michigan* over the torpedo's guidance wire. "Tube One is homing! Telemetry range, eight hundred yards."

"Helm, ahead full." Wilson increased speed in case

the Russian crew counterfired. But with *Michigan*'s torpedo going active only a thousand yards away, it was unlikely they'd have enough time.

"Conn, Sonar. Burst of cavitation from Master two."

The Russian crew had detected the incoming torpedo, probably from a torpedo-warning hydrophone on the hull. But it was most likely too late.

Twenty seconds later, an explosion rumbled through Control.

Michigan shuddered as a shock wave passed by, followed by Sonar's report. "Explosion in the water on the bearing to Master two."

Another minute passed and Sonar reported, "Mechanical transient from Master two, consistent with bottom impact."

The watchstanders in Control let out a collective sigh of relief. *Michigan* had survived, and now they had to clear the area quickly. If there were other Russian submarines nearby, they would converge on the explosion.

Wilson ordered, "Helm, ahead standard. Left full rudder, steady course two-seven-zero."

Michigan slowed as it reversed course to the west.

75

MOSCOW, RUSSIA

In the National Defense Control Center, deep beneath the Main Building of the Ministry of Defense, General Andropov studied the thirty-meter-wide display on the far wall with growing confidence. Russian units had fortified key locations across the continent-wide defensive line, and although it stretched Russian units thin, it stretched NATO units even thinner. NATO simply didn't have the troops to cover such a wide front and concentrate sufficient forces for a breakthrough that could be leveraged to any significant extent.

The military campaign was going well, with Russian troops reinforcing their positions while Andropov consolidated his. Over the last two weeks, Colonel Generals Zolotov and Grachev, commanders-in-chief of Russia's Strategic Missile Troops and Airborne Troops respectively, had been pulled into Andropov's inner circle. Additionally, the generals in charge of Russia's four operational strategic commands—Western, Southern, Central, and Eastern—had been informed of the coup and had pledged their support. Andropov now had firm control of Russia's military down to the division and brigade level.

Finally, Colonel General Korobov, head of the

GRU—the military's Main Intelligence Directorate—had committed to the cause. The expanded tier of support was crucial due to Kalinin's escape. Andropov needed insurance against a possible public plea from Kalinin to Russia's military, government, and citizens. With the GRU and its Spetsnaz brigades aboard, any political or public opposition would be crushed.

The cover story for Kalinin's absence—his serious illness and recovery at Gelendzhik—had worked thus far, with the media focused on events unfolding as Russian forces advanced across Europe. With the report that the American submarine Kalinin was aboard had been sunk, it had appeared everything was in hand.

However, two additional Russian submarines had been sunk in the same vicinity this morning and Andropov's concern had rekindled. Although he was confident Kalinin's public emergence and denouncing of the coup could be handled, it was better if the matter was avoided.

Andropov's console phone buzzed and he answered. Colonel Savvin was on the other end. "We have the American woman," Savvin said.

"How is that possible?" Andropov asked. "She and Kalinin were rescued by the American SEALs and taken aboard their submarine."

"That's what we thought," Savvin replied. "We didn't come across her body and assumed she had accompanied Kalinin. However, she turned up in Beregovoy this morning."

"Send her to Moscow for interrogation," Andropov ordered. "As America's national security advisor, she's privy to NATO war planning. Any insight we can gain regarding NATO's pending offensive might prove valuable and be the difference between victory and defeat. We cannot leave any stone unturned."

"It's unlikely she'll talk," Savvin said.

"Leave that to me," Andropov replied. "We have methods that guarantee results."

None of them were legal, however, nor left those interrogated unharmed.

76

HAMBURG, GERMANY

During World War II, the city of Hamburg almost ceased to exist. In July 1943, after completing a five-month-long bombing campaign against Germany's Ruhr industrial region, the Royal Air Force Bomber Command and America's Eighth Air Force turned their attention to Hamburg. Employing over three thousand aircraft dropping nine thousand tons of ordnance over an eight-day span, Operation Gomorrah was at that time the heaviest assault in the history of aerial warfare.

The bombings killed over 42,000 persons, the majority on a single night that British officials later called the Hiroshima of Germany. On the evening of July 27, 1943, almost eight hundred aircraft bombed Hamburg. The concentrated bombing, combined with unusually dry conditions and inadequate firefighting resources, created a quarter-mile-high vortex of flames that incinerated eight square miles of the city. Scorching winds reaching 150 miles per hour swept people from the streets like dry leaves, while temperatures approaching 1,500°F vaporized those unfortunate enough to be sucked into the maelstrom.

The city recovered, and today the port of Hamburg

is Germany's largest and one of the busiest container ports in Europe, depositing cargo onto more than 2,300 freight cars per week. Located on the Elbe River and known as Germany's Gateway to the World, today it also served as the U.S. 1st Armored Division's gateway to Europe.

Major General Dutch Hostler stood beside his aide, Captain Kurt Wise, observing the offload of 1st Armored Division equipment from Military Sealift Command ships docked in the busy port. The equipment for two armored brigades—Old Ironsides and the Bulldogs—was being offloaded in Hamburg, while the 1st Stryker Brigade vehicles and supplies were being disembarked from additional ships in Bremerhaven, a short distance west. Once the equipment was offloaded at each port, it would mate up with 1st Armored Division personnel who had flown to Europe ahead of time.

After departing Hamburg and Bremerhaven, Hostler's brigades would rendezvous at the NATO assembly point near Kraków, Poland. South of the Vistula River and north of the Carpathian Mountains, the terrain to the east was mostly flat, with intermittent low, rolling hills.

Tank country.

77

CASTEAU, BELGIUM

General Andy Wheeler sat at his console in the command center at SHAPE—Supreme Headquarters Allied Powers Europe—examining the video screens along the front wall. The maps were annotated with symbols of various colors and designs, each representing a NATO or non-Alliance combat unit. The red symbols were static, representing Russian units digging in on the eastern bank of the Vistula River cutting south through Poland, covering the passes through the Carpathian Mountains, and fortifying the Siret River in northeast Romania.

The Russians had chosen their defensive terrain wisely, with much of NATO's advance blocked by wide rivers or mountain ranges. Only a small gap in southern Poland offered favorable terrain. The Russians understood the weak spot in their defense and had deployed the entire 1st Guards Tank Army to the fifty-mile-wide swath of land. Assigned to that flashpoint on NATO's side was the U.S. 1st Armored Division, the last American combat unit to arrive in theater, currently disembarking in Germany.

America's 1st AD would be joined by Germany's 1st and 10th Panzer Divisions and three British armored infantry brigades. Although they were a formidable force, history and conventional wisdom held that an attacker had to outnumber the defender by between two-to-one and five-to-one odds, depending on the composition of the opposing forces and defensive terrain. NATO didn't even have one-to-one odds, at least not along the entire front.

Wheeler planned to employ NATO's superior mobility to concentrate his forces for an attack, but even two-to-one odds would be difficult to attain without seriously weakening other sectors, providing Russia the opportunity to also redistribute forces. He'd have to rely on NATO's supposedly better trained troops and ability to control the skies. But neither were certain bets against the restructured and modernized Russian ground forces and their significant anti-air assets.

After NATO forces completed their buildup, Wheeler would have to select the best strategy for success. No one said it would be easy.

78

USS *MICHIGAN*

USS *Michigan* cruised at periscope depth, sucking fresh air in through its ventilation mast while the air banks were being recharged. Wilson sat at the head of the Wardroom table as lunch wound down, reviewing the outgoing message in his hands while a radioman stood patiently beside him. Most of the junior officers had excused themselves, and remaining in the Wardroom with Wilson were Russian President Yuri Kalinin, *Michigan*'s Executive Officer and department heads, and Navy SEALs McNeil and Harrison. And Lieutenant Clark, of course, still attached to Kalinin's hip.

The Russian president was getting around much better now; he could make it through the watertight doorways and up ladders without assistance, and his curiosity had increased along with his mobility. But he respected the boundaries put in place, prohibiting entry into restricted spaces. Clark was doing an admirable job as Kalinin's tour guide, filling him in on the workings of an American guided missile submarine. As far as events occurring throughout the world, Kalinin had become a fan of the Submarine Force's daily news summary, downloaded from the radio broadcast each day.

Wilson signed the message, authorizing its immediate transmission. The message provided details of Kalinin's rescue, along with the loss of five Navy SEALs and Christine, noting their deaths hadn't been confirmed. The topic had come up earlier during lunch. When Christine was mentioned, Kalinin's eyes had flashed to Harrison, but there'd been no reaction from the stone-faced SEAL. Wilson, however, hadn't miss the Russian's glance. Despite the short time spent with Harrison, Kalinin had picked up on the SEAL's special relationship with Christine.

Commander McNeil had shared the mission details with Wilson, including Harrison's decision to release Christine in the effort to save Kalinin. Wilson wondered how Harrison was taking his role in Christine's likely demise, but the SEAL had been unreadable since his return to *Michigan*.

After Wilson handed the message board back to the radioman, he asked the submarine's Navigator, Lieutenant Lloyd, "Where do you think we'll transfer President Kalinin off?"

Lloyd replied, "Most likely one of the Turkish ports."

At the mention of his pending debarkation, Kalinin asked, "Have you been informed of the details of my return to Russia?"

"*Return* to Russia?" Wilson asked. "We just extracted you *from* Russia."

"That was part of the deal," Kalinin said. "Your president agreed to help me overthrow the military coup. In return, I will withdraw my troops to Russia, avoiding war with NATO."

Wilson shook his head. "I haven't heard anything. But I'm not at the top of the food chain. I'm sure the president and his advisors are working on a plan."

"Time is critical," Kalinin said. "The longer General Andropov has to consolidate his power, the harder my job becomes." He glanced at Commander McNeil and Harrison, then turned back to Wilson. "I have developed a plan we can implement immediately."

"I suppose that plan has something to do with *Michigan*?" Wilson asked.

"Any effort to return me to power must be limited and strike quickly. We cannot take on the Russian military; we need to target its leadership. You have two platoons of SEALs aboard, the most highly trained men in your armed forces. If I can obtain the support of the SVR and perhaps the FSB—my country's Federal Security Service, I can defeat the coup and prevent the bloodshed throughout Europe."

"You have a point," Wilson replied, "but I can't do anything without direction."

"I understand," Kalinin said. "How can I help you obtain that direction?"

"Explain your plan and I'll send the details up the chain of command. If the president agrees, I'll receive the necessary orders."

Wilson paused, then asked, "So what's your plan?"

79

WASHINGTON, D.C.

"What do you think?"

The president surveyed his advisors gathered in the Situation Room beneath the West Wing. In addition to Kevin Hardison and others from the president's staff, SecDef Dunnavant and the Chief of Naval Operations were present, along with CIA Director Jessica Cherry. The image of Rear Admiral Justin Walker, head of the Naval Special Warfare Command, appeared on the video display on the far wall. Each person at the table had a folder before them containing a lengthy message from USS *Michigan*.

"This is pretty interesting," Director Cherry replied. "President Kalinin has provided a detailed data dump on the SVR and FSB Spetsnaz units: numbers, training, armament. It pretty much validates our intel and fills in a few holes, especially concerning Zaslon, the SVR's highly trained Spetsnaz unit."

"It's what we needed to know," Dunnavant said. "We need to understand the forces available on both sides, so we can plan accordingly."

"What are we looking at?" the president asked.

Dunnavant replied, "There are no regular military units in Moscow. General Andropov has sent all combat-ready units to the front line. The distribution of the various Spetsnaz units, as well as their loyalty, is a bit murkier, but Director Cherry has insight." He looked to Cherry.

Cherry answered, "Russia's Main Intelligence Directorate, the GRU, has assigned two Spetsnaz brigades to Moscow. As the foreign intelligence agency of Russia's armed forces, the GRU is staffed with numerous military personnel and is commanded by an Air Force general. President Kalinin would know better, but I agree with his assessment: the GRU Spetsnaz units will follow General Andropov's orders. That means you're going to have to deal with two Spetsnaz brigades once the assault on the Ministry of Defense building is discovered."

Dunnavant said, "That pretty much forces our hand. The SVR has only one Spetsnaz unit, Zaslon. It's five hundred strong per President Kalinin, with only one hundred presently in Moscow. That's not enough to cordon off the area surrounding the Ministry of Defense building and prevent GRU reinforcements from breaking through. Kalinin prefers we keep the mission held close for obvious reasons, limiting participation to the SVR. But we need the three FSB Spetsnaz units."

The president asked Cherry, "What's your assessment of the FSB risk?"

Cherry replied, "The SVR and FSB were main directorates within the KGB before it was dismantled after its participation in the 1991 Soviet coup. Both organizations report directly to President Kalinin, so both should be loyal to him. The difference is that Kalinin is a former SVR director and is good friends with Josef Hippchenko, the current SVR director, while the FSB director is a holdover from Putin's days. Kalinin isn't sure if he can be trusted. There's no indication he's in on the coup, nor anything to confirm he isn't. That's a problem for us, because the only way the mission will succeed is if the FSB Spetsnaz units assist, *and* we have the element of surprise on our side."

The president asked, "How do we determine whether the FSB can be trusted?"

"Ask Hippchenko," Cherry replied. "He's been in Moscow since the coup occurred and undoubtedly has his finger on the pulse of all critical issues. Even though the SVR's charter is foreign intelligence, they do a lot of domestic surveillance as well. He should be able to provide a decent evaluation."

The president nodded his understanding, then looked to the screen on the far wall. "Admiral Walker, what's your assessment of mission success?"

"It's risky, sir. We don't have enough intelligence to adequately plan the assault. We don't have schematics of the Ministry of Defense building after its renovation and we have no idea of internal security aside from what Kalinin provided, which is sketchy at best. We'd be going in blind for the most part."

"I understand we're going in with limited intelligence. But is it probable the mission will succeed?"

"It's possible, sir, but I recommend we proceed only if we obtain adequate intelligence. Going in without building schematics and the ability to pass through security perimeters without setting off alarms is a potential disaster."

The president's chief of staff, Kevin Hardison, said, "I hate to play devil's advocate, but if we return Kalinin to power, there's no guarantee he'll pull his troops back to Russia."

"Do you have a better plan?" Dunnavant asked. "One that doesn't involve a full-scale continental war?"

"I don't," Hardison said. "I'm just pointing out there's a lot of risk involved to achieve an uncertain outcome."

Director Cherry joined in. "If the SVR commits, it's likely they'll have the intelligence we need and methods to bypass some of the security systems."

The president asked, "What if we go with a partial plan? What if we extract President Kalinin to someplace safe where he can make a public appeal to Russian citizens, explaining there's been a military coup? He can then order all troops to return to Russia."

"We looked at that," Dunnavant answered, "but we don't think it will work. The Russian officer corps heavily stresses loyalty up the military chain of command, but that loyalty doesn't extend to the president like it does here. Although we think that approach would work if you made a similar appeal to the U.S. military, we doubt if Kalinin's appeal, made from exile, would be effective.

"President Kalinin is right," Dunnavant added. "He has to appear back in control, having defeated the coup, for the individual units to disregard the orders of their superior officers."

After absorbing everyone's remarks, the president said, "Here's what we're going to do. We'll proceed with the SEAL mission on three conditions: *if* Hippchenko agrees to support, *if* he thinks we can trust the FSB, and *if* he's got the intel we need. Any objections?"

There were none, and the president asked, "How do we contact Hippchenko without tipping off the GRU? We should probably avoid official channels."

"I agree," Cherry said. "We can call him on his personal cell phone."

"Good idea," the president said. "Let me know when you run his number down."

"That's easy," Cherry said. "I've got his number in my contact list." Cherry pointed to the door; they'd placed their cell phones in lockers outside the Situation Room, since they weren't allowed in classified meetings.

Hardison asked, "You've got his number on your cell phone?"

Cherry shrugged. "We talk."

"About what?" Hardison asked.

"About *stuff*," Cherry replied with an edge to her voice, making it clear it was none of Hardison's business.

The president glanced at the Moscow clock on the wall. It read 4:30 p.m. "Let's give Hippchenko a call."

80

YASENEVO, RUSSIA

It was late afternoon in the Moscow suburbs when Josef Hippchenko, seated at his desk in the Y-shaped headquarters of Russia's Foreign Intelligence Service, scrolled through the afternoon update on his computer. Russia's military and political landscape were in upheaval, and Hippchenko was proceeding cautiously as events unfolded, analyzing the issues extensively.

Although the SVR focused primarily on issues beyond Russia's borders, one of its mandates included the authorization to *Implement active measures to ensure Russia's security.* The authorization was broadly worded, deliberately using the term *active measures,* which was a Soviet term for political warfare. Although the SVR's political warfare was supposed to be waged against other countries, the recent turn of events within Russia left Hippchenko pondering his options.

Hippchenko's personal cell phone vibrated. He retrieved it from his jacket pocket and checked the number on the display.

Unknown.

He pressed the *Accept* button. "Director Hippchenko."

"Good afternoon, Director Hippchenko. This is the

president of the United States." The man paused, waiting for a response.

"One moment, please," Hippchenko replied.

He muted the cell phone microphone, then pressed the button on his desk phone for the SVR operations center. When the supervisor answered, Hippchenko said, "Trace the call to my personal cell phone immediately."

After the supervisor acknowledged and hung up, Hippchenko decided to stall for time, concocting a flippant response, but with a sound premise. It was unlikely the president of the United States was on the other end. Hippchenko unmuted his cell phone.

"Not likely," Hippchenko replied. "You're the third American president who has called me today."

There was a muffled laugh on the other end of the phone.

The man replied, "How can I convince you?"

"There are protocols in place for the United States president to communicate with Russian officials. Calling my personal cell phone isn't one of them."

A different person responded. "Josef, this is Director Cherry." Hippchenko immediately recognized the CIA director's voice. She continued, "Considering what's going on right now, we can't use official channels. We can't afford to take a chance our plan is discovered."

"What plan?" Hippchenko asked.

"We have President Kalinin."

Hippchenko leaned back in his chair. The intelligence reports had been accurate. A U.S. Navy SEAL team had been sent into Krasnodar Krai to extract Kalinin. Whether the effort was successful hadn't been determined. Until now.

"What do you plan to do with him?"

"That depends."

"On what?"

"On whether you help."

"How can I assist?"

"Kalinin needs your help to defeat General Andropov's coup."

"What do you have in mind?"

Cherry outlined the plan, then waited for Hippchenko's response.

It didn't take long to decide. Yuri was one of his closest friends, plus General Andropov's invasion had gone too far. Andropov was convinced NATO was too weak to wrest back control of the occupied territories, but that didn't mean NATO wouldn't try. Hippchenko was dedicated to furthering Russia's ambitions, but in a more civilized manner. Andropov's plan would spill blood needlessly, plus the long-term ramifications for Russia were too complicated to accurately predict.

Hippchenko's desk phone buzzed. "One moment," he said, then muted the cell phone again. He picked up his desk phone handset. "Hippchenko."

It was the SVR operations center. The call had been traced to the Oval Office in the White House. It was useful information, but he'd already convinced himself he was talking to the American president and his CIA director. He hung up and unmuted the cell phone.

"I will provide the requested support and evaluate whether the FSB units can be trusted."

The American president responded, "Thank you, Director Hippchenko. What is the best way to coordinate our efforts?"

There was a secure conference room in the SVR operations center, where Hippchenko could confer with his most trusted subordinates and communicate with American and FSB leadership. He provided the number to the direct line.

Before ending the call, the American president said, "We need you to keep the plan limited to the fewest people possible until the last moment. We can't afford to alert any of General Andropov's sympathizers."

"I understand, Mr. President."

81

MOSCOW, RUSSIA

Inside the main Ministry of Defense building, on the third floor underground, Christine O'Connor sat on the edge of her cot in a dark cell. The accommodations were spartan: a cot, toilet, and sink, plus a locker at the foot of her bed for personal items, although she had none. It was dead quiet inside the eight-by-eight-foot room, one she concluded was soundproof. Whether that was to prevent sound from entering or exiting, she wasn't sure.

When Anna opened the door to her home in Beregovoy yesterday, soldiers stormed inside. There was little Christine could do aside from lying on the floor as directed. Her hands were handcuffed and she was led into an armored personnel carrier, enduring a bumpy half-hour ride. She was then transferred to a military helicopter, and after a long transit north, the chopper touched down on one of two landing pads atop Moscow's main Ministry of Defense building.

Her interrogation had started this morning, and the day-long event had gone as well as she could have hoped. She'd refused to provide any information concerning NATO war planning and hadn't been harmed. After being threatened and cajoled, with neither tactic producing results, she'd been returned to her cell a few minutes ago. Before departing the interrogation room, however, the GRU colonel in charge had informed her that tomorrow's interrogation would go much differently. She had no idea what that meant, but had imagined a few scenarios.

She was about to settle into her cot for the night when her cell door opened. Two soldiers entered, while the GRU colonel who'd led the interrogation effort waited by the doorway. Christine was handcuffed and escorted down the corridor, then shoved inside another cell that looked more like a hospital room, with two more soldiers inside. What caught her attention immediately were the straps attached to the bed for her feet and hands.

Her handcuffs were removed and she was forced onto the bed by two soldiers, then held in place by all four as they strapped down her wrists and ankles. Christine considered resisting, but didn't see the point. She'd be overpowered and the result would be the same.

Another man entered the cell, wearing a white lab coat. After a short discussion with the colonel, he stopped by Christine's bed.

"My name is Andrei," he said in English. "I understand you've refused to provide the requested information. I've been directed to make you more *pliable*. Unfortunately, there are severe side effects to this process, and you will not be the same afterwards. There will be a window of lucidity, about eight hours, after which you will be permanently insane. You won't know who or where you are. You will merely exist in a vegetative state."

"Your scare tactics won't work, doc," Christine replied, trying to quell the rising fear as she evaluated the man's claim.

Andrei frowned. "I'm not trying to scare you, Christine. Only provide you with accurate information so you may make a wise decision. I have done this many times and do not enjoy it. I don't want you to end up a drooling shell of your former self."

Andrei leaned closer, lowering his voice. "Tell them what they want to know. Your silence isn't worth what this will do to you."

Christine stared at him, her mind reeling at the scene created by his words—an image of herself sitting in a chair in an insane asylum, drool being wiped from her chin as she gazed into the distance with vacant eyes.

Okay, the scare tactics are working.

Andrei saw the indecision play across her face and waited patiently while she vacillated, alternately deciding to tell them what they wanted to know, then immediately admonishing herself for the thought. Her resolve gradually crumbled and she was about to acquiesce when she reminded herself that the issue was bigger than herself. Providing the requested information would cost countless lives and jeopardize the NATO offensive. Although she didn't know what strategy General Wheeler would employ, she knew the options.

She turned away from Andrei and looked at the ceiling.

"Well, then," he said. "Let's get started."

Andrei went to a small refrigerator and retrieved an IV bag containing a clear solution, which he hung from a stand beside Christine's bed. He disinfected her arm, although Christine wondered what the point was, then inserted a needle into a vein. He attached the IV tubing to the needle, then adjusted the drip rate. Christine felt the cool liquid enter her bloodstream.

"This will take some time," Andrei said. "The

solution entering your body contains two drugs. One will reduce your inhibitions, making you more likely to talk in the morning, while the second drug is preparing the receptor sites for the chemicals you will receive if the morning's interrogation fails. You'll have until then to change your mind. Once the next chemicals are injected into your bloodstream, there is no turning back."

Andrei pulled a syringe with attached needle, plus a small vial from a cabinet, placing them on a tray which he set on a table beside her. He exchanged a few words with the GRU colonel, then the men left, turning off the lights and closing the door.

Christine tested her restraints, trying to break free. When that failed, she tried to slide her hands through the straps, but her wrists were securely fastened. After trying both options again several times, she gave up. There was nothing more she could do except wait until morning. She stared at the ceiling as the drug dripped into her bloodstream.

82

USS *MICHIGAN*

The tension in the air was palpable.

Throughout the day, as the twenty-eight SEALs prepared for combat, Captain Wilson sensed an eerie quiet seep throughout his submarine. The SEALs had entered the two missile tubes that had been converted to ammunition magazines, each containing thirty tons of munitions, extracting the desired weapons and ordnance for tonight's operation. All twenty-eight SEALs were now in the Battle Management Center behind the Control Room, with Commander McNeil having just completed the mission briefing. Wilson lingered in the BMC as the SEALs huddled around the dual-display workstations in groups of four, reviewing the plan in more detail.

SVR Director Hippchenko had provided schematics of the Ministry of Defense building, and Zaslon operatives would provide the SEALs with security cards that would allow access through the building's security features. If everything went as planned, the SEALs and President Kalinin would gain access to the control center fourteen minutes after entering the building. Entry was the biggest challenge, as all entrance points were monitored with cameras and would be secured at the projected 3 a.m. ingress time. During the mission brief, Wilson listened with fascination to the plan McNeil briefed, outlining their route on a map provided by Russia's SVR.

While the SEALs penetrated the National Defense Control Center, a two-block perimeter would be established by SVR Zaslon forces and three FSB Spetsnaz brigades. Director Hippchenko had concluded the FSB could be trusted and the FSB director had committed the three Spetsnaz units under his purview to the effort.

Hippchenko had considered including Russia's Federal Protective Service, the counterpart to America's Secret Service, but decided otherwise. Although the organization as a whole would be loyal to Kalinin, it lacked a large, central unit that could be maneuvered into place around the Ministry of Defense perimeter. Too many individuals would have to be brought into the plan, increasing the risk it might be discovered by those loyal to General Andropov. For similar reasons, incorporating the Interior Ministry forces was rejected. Russian National Guard units were also considered for the perimeter, but Hippchenko was unsure where Director Karakayev's loyalty resided.

Finally, a combined SEAL and Zaslon assault team had been discussed but discarded due to language barriers—only Harrison and two other SEALs spoke Russian, plus the communication gear wasn't interoperable. If the schematics were accurate and security cards worked as promised, twenty-eight SEALs would be more than enough.

The four-man fire teams completed their review of the building schematics, along with primary and backup contingency plans, then filtered from the BMC to suit up for deployment. For tonight's mission, the SEALs would exit via mass lockout from the two Dry Deck Shelters. There was insufficient room to fit all twenty-eight SEALs in the two shelters at once, since the shelters still held the SDV mini-sub and one RHIB, so two lockouts would be required.

When McNeil finished the review with his fire team, he approached Wilson, and the two men were joined by Harrison. Wilson had requested their presence after the mission preparations had been completed.

"Captain," McNeil said, "what did you want to discuss?"

"I received a Personal For message today, which contained good news and bad news." Wilson's eyes shifted to Harrison. "The good news is that Christine is alive."

"What?" Harrison asked. "Where is she? How is she?"

"She's fine as far as we know; she was walking on her own. Unfortunately, that's where the bad news starts. She turned up in a town called Beregovoy yesterday and requested assistance. A CIA team was sent to pick her up, but the Russian Army got to her first. She's been transported to Moscow, most likely for interrogation. However, it seems her fate and ours remain intertwined. She was taken to the main Ministry of Defense building."

Harrison asked, "Do we know where she's being kept?"

"Zaslon operatives will provide that information to you tonight if they've obtained it."

The two SEALs exchanged glances. McNeil spoke first. "There will be no deviation from the mission plan. Once we've gained access to the control center and Kalinin has regained control over the Russian military, we can search for Christine. Until then, she doesn't factor in. Is that understood?"

"Yes, sir," Harrison replied. "No argument."

Although Harrison had provided the proper response,

Wilson was certain the wheels were churning inside his head.

McNeil and Harrison left the Battle Management Center to gather their gear and suit up. *Michigan* was already in shallow water, approaching the launch point. Wilson checked the time. They'd arrive on station in less than an hour. As the last SEAL fire team left the BMC to prepare for the mass lockouts, Wilson entered Control and settled into his chair on the Conn.

"Dive, prepare to hover."

Moments earlier, *Michigan*'s main engines had gone silent and the submarine was now coasting to a halt at periscope depth. *Michigan* was in water only 130 feet deep, allowing the eighteen-thousand-ton submarine to approach within two miles of shore. *Close enough,* Commander McNeil had said. The SEALs would swim underwater to the coast from there.

"Ready to hover," the Diving Officer reported.

"Hover at eight-zero feet," the Officer of the Deck ordered as he circled on the port periscope.

The Diving Officer ordered the Chief of the Watch to engage hovering, and Wilson waited as the system took control, keeping the submarine on ordered depth.

The first fourteen SEALs had climbed into the two Dry Deck Shelters and were awaiting permission to flood down the hangars. The evolution was directed from Control, as *Michigan* would become heavier as water flooded into the shelters, with neutral buoyancy maintained by pumping water from the variable ballast tanks. The hovering system would handle things automatically, but on occasion the system lost control and manual intervention by the Chief of the Watch was required.

"Hovering is engaged," the Diving Officer reported. "Steady at eight-zero feet."

The Officer of the Deck, still circling on the periscope with his face pressed against the eyepiece, addressed Captain Wilson. "Sir, hold no sonar or visual contacts. Request permission to flood down the port and starboard shelters."

"Flood down both shelters," Wilson ordered.

Inside each shelter, a Navy diver flooded down his respective hangar. The hovering system kicked in, and Wilson watched the Ballast Control Panel as valves on both variable ballast tanks shifted from shut to open as water was pumped out at a rate matching the water flooding into the shelters. The shelters were soon flooded down and Control received the expected communication.

"Request permission to open hangar doors, port and starboard shelters."

Wilson replied, "Open hangar doors, both shelters."

The order went out and Wilson watched from the camera mounted on the aft Missile Compartment deck as both nine-foot-diameter hatches swung slowly open in the murky water, faintly illuminated by the fading light above. A mass lockout would normally have been conducted at night, but the SEALs had a long transit ahead and would need a head start to arrive in Moscow on schedule. By the time they reached shore after their two-mile swim, however, darkness will have fallen.

The fourteen SEALs exited the two shelters and collected on the missile deck as the hangar doors swung shut in preparation for the next mass lockout.

Draining the hangars was easier than flooding them down, as the water drained into additional ballast tanks installed in the missile tubes beneath the seven-pack Tomahawk launchers, keeping *Michigan* neutrally buoyant. The shelters were quickly drained and made ready for the next group of SEALs.

"Request permission to enter the port and starboard shelters," the Battle Management Center requested.

Wilson gave permission, and the second batch of SEALs and President Kalinin entered the Dry Deck Shelters. Once inside, the flood-down process was repeated. Wilson watched the SEALs and Kalinin exit the hangars and the twenty-nine men kicked off from the missile deck, disappearing into the darkness.

83

THE BLACK SEA

In a semicircular cove along the shore, Lieutenant Harrison emerged from the water in the darkness, his MP7 held ready. Beside him, the other twenty-seven SEALs, clad entirely in black, worked their way up the gentle slope until they reached the beach, then moved quickly into the nearby foliage. In the distance, the rubble of an open-air villa loomed atop a thirty-foot-high rock outcropping overlooking the Black Sea.

This was the second time Harrison had entered the cove containing the summer villa. Two months ago, he'd led a SEAL squad on an extraction mission, pulling Christine O'Connor from the water, destroying the villa in the process with a shoulder-fired rocket launcher. According to satellite intelligence, the cove had remained abandoned since the attack, offering ideal ingress along the Black Sea's cliff-lined shore.

After moving into the lush foliage, Harrison removed the closed-circuit rebreather facemask, letting it hang around his neck; he'd need it for the third leg of their journey. Beside him was Commander McNeil and President Kalinin. The Russian had insisted on swimming on his own during the underwater trek toward shore. He was in remarkably good shape, but he hadn't gone far before two SEALs had to pull him along the rest of the way.

As Harrison waited to begin the second segment of his transit, he heard the faint beat of approaching rotors. Two Kasatka stealth helicopters descended, touching down on the narrow strip of sand. After the awaited green signals were flashed from both helicopters, Commander McNeil ordered the SEALs forward.

Harrison's platoon boarded one helicopter and Lieutenant Acor's boarded the other, with McNeil and Kalinin climbing into Harrison's Kasatka. The helicopter rose rapidly from the beach, flying low over the cliffs framing the secluded cove.

In addition to the fourteen SEALs and President Kalinin, there was a Russian Zaslon operative aboard, who greeted President Kalinin, then asked for the man in charge. He was pointed toward Commander McNeil, who was sitting between Harrison and Senior Chief Stone. The Russian Spetsnaz approached them.

"Commander?" the Spetsnaz asked. McNeil nodded and the Russian handed him a pouch of security cards, which could be clipped to their equipment. "These cards will provide access through all security barriers and into the National Defense Control Center. I need to confirm your ingress route."

Harrison pulled out a laminated printout of the building schematics, with the selected route annotated.

The Russian examined it. "This is correct. We've made arrangements; at 3 a.m. exactly, the cameras along this route will freeze, delivering a static image to the security center. Your transit to the command center will not be detected. Zaslon and FSB units will cordon off the area around the Ministry of Defense building at 3 a.m., so your entry must be timed to match."

The Spetsnaz handed two military radios to McNeil, who handed one to Harrison. "These radios will communicate with the Zaslon commander, who will be along the perimeter with our unit. If you run into difficulties and need help, we will do what we can. Be advised that the signal will be blocked once you descend to the control center; you will be too deep underground. Do you have any questions?"

McNeil turned to Harrison and Stone. After both men shook their heads, McNeil replied, "Nothing at this time."

The Russian said, "I have one more piece of information I was directed to pass along. Can I see your schematic again?"

Harrison opened it.

"Your national security advisor is on the third floor underground, but we do not know exactly where she is. This is her cell block," the man pointed to a row of rooms along one corridor, "and these are the standard interrogation rooms. She may be in one of these if they are interrogating her through the night." Finally, he pointed to another room. "This is the chemical interrogation cell."

"Chemical interrogation?" Harrison asked.

"For those who refuse to talk, we have methods to extract what we want."

McNeil and Harrison exchanged glances. The SEAL commander didn't have to say a word. Christine wasn't part of the mission. Once Kalinin was back in power and the Ministry of Defense building was secured, they would search for her.

Harrison tried to keep his thoughts focused on the mission and not Christine as he settled in for the long flight to Moscow, with one refueling stop along the way.

84

MOSCOW, RUSSIA

The Moskva River, which winds its way through the heart of Moscow, is fed by numerous small tributaries. During Moscow's centuries-long expansion, many of these tributaries were paved over, the water flowing into the Moskva River through underground tunnels. One of the well-known tributaries, the Neglinnaya River, flows through a five-mile-long series of tunnels beneath Moscow streets, with one branch running directly beneath Red Square, just outside the Kremlin. The Neglinnaya was too far north to be of use, but there was a smaller tributary flowing into the Moskva River near the main Ministry of Defense building. The tributary tunnel, running northwest beneath the streets, would be their entry point.

It was 2 a.m. when the Kasatka stealth helicopters reached Moscow, leaving the countryside behind as buildings began passing by on both sides of the low-flying aircraft. When they approached the center of the twelve-million-strong megalopolis, the helicopters intersected the Moskva River, then followed its winding course toward the main Ministry of Defense building. When the Krymsky Bridge appeared in the distance, the doors on each side of the helicopter cabins opened and both choppers slowed.

Harrison and the other SEALs had donned their rebreathers and were ready for the drop. Senior Chief Stone held Kalinin by one arm, having explained the water entry procedure to the Russian president. The Zaslon operative communicated with the Kasatka pilots over his helmet communication gear, then began counting down the time, starting with five fingers extended, retracting one at a time.

When his hand curled into a fist, the SEALs and Kalinin stepped from both sides of the helicopter at one-second intervals, splashing into the Moskva River twenty feet below. Harrison swam underwater toward the west bank, where the tributary emptied into the river. He spotted the tunnel ahead, along with two dozen dark shapes moving through the water toward the opening.

Moments earlier, from his top-floor perch overlooking the Moskva River, Major Leonid Egorov held binoculars to his eyes, scanning the river in both directions. Egorov was a member of Russia's GRU, the military intelligence agency of the general staff of the armed forces. When most people thought of Russian spies, the SVR came to mind. But the GRU deployed six times as many spies and had informants embedded in every critical domestic organization. One of their informants, high up in the FSB leadership, had provided a crucial tip. Tonight, President Kalinin would accompany an American SEAL assault on the National Defense Command Center.

Major Egorov lowered his binoculars. He'd seen enough. The two helicopters had been difficult to spot, since the sound of their stealthy rotors blended in with the city's night sounds and their radar signatures were hard to detect. But knowing the Americans would need air transport to Moscow and that Navy SEALs were involved had focused the GRU's surveillance.

Egorov raised the radio to his mouth. "They have arrived."

"Understood," the voice said over the radio. "Primary units, remain in place until they reach the control center."

The plan had been hastily hatched, since the GRU learned late this evening of the pending assault. Two GRU Spetsnaz companies, each with 120 men, had been prepositioned: one inside the Ministry of Defense building and one outside, within the perimeter that the SVR and FSB Spetsnaz units would establish. To prevent tipping off the Americans, the GRU troops had moved into position using Moscow's underground tunnel system. Above ground, in view of spying American satellites, there had been no indication that their mission had been compromised.

85

MOSCOW, RUSSIA

The SEALs moved in single file in the darkness, up a narrow, arched-brick tunnel, with Harrison in the lead and President Kalinin in the middle. Each man had removed his rebreather, replacing the facemask with a helmet, which had a communication headset built in and night vision goggles attached and lowered into place. The water from the paved-over tributary river was waist-high and fast-running, and the dank smell of centuries-old stone walls hung in the air.

Harrison checked the map on occasion with a green flashlight, examining the labyrinth of subterranean river and drainage tunnels, abandoned Soviet bunkers, and Metro-2, a secret four-line underground rail system linking the Kremlin with strategic sites. He guided the SEAL formation through the network of concrete and brick-clad tunnels, through several junctions and past numerous sluices dumping rainwater into the tunnel. After several turns, they reached the first obstacle in their journey: an arched entryway on the left, sealed off with concrete.

McNeil called two of the SEAL breachers—demolition experts—forward, to attach explosives to the concrete barrier. They were still a fair distance away from the Ministry of Defense building, so this operation wouldn't be as delicate as the next one. Explosives were put in place and the concrete barrier was reduced to rubble. Just enough explosives had been used to crack through the one-foot-thick wall, so significant tremors weren't sent underground, warning others of their approach. The SEALs removed the concrete chunks by hand, clearing the entrance.

Leaving one fire team behind, led by Lieutenant Acor, guarding the entrance, the SEAL column entered a dark and musty corridor—a drainage duct that had been sealed off when the Ministry of Defense building was constructed. The new tunnel ran straight, but was smaller, forcing the SEALs and Kalinin to duck their heads. After a few hundred yards, they arrived at a dead end. The tunnel was sealed with another layer of concrete. This barrier, four feet thick according to the drawings, was part of the outer wall of the Ministry of Defense building.

Harrison checked his watch. They had thirty minutes to break through. The two breachers stepped forward again, attaching a prefabricated web of detonating cord and small C-4 charges to the concrete. Everyone moved back and the contraption was detonated. The sound was deafening in the small tunnel, but Harrison knew the explosion was small in comparison to most.

When the dust cleared, the breachers examined the result; they'd penetrated three inches into the concrete wall, exposing the first layer of metal bars reinforcing the concrete. The breachers repeated the process, demolishing another three-inch layer, fully exposing the metal bars. Two other SEALs stepped forward with hydraulic bolt cutters, snipping the bars away.

The process was repeated, with the SEALs eating their way through the wall in three-inch increments, cutting away each layer of reinforcing metal bars as they were exposed. After the fifteenth detonation, gaps appeared in the concrete wall. The SEALs pulled the remaining concrete apart with their hands, cutting away the last layer of bars.

The opening provided access to a storage room, with light leaking under a closed door in the far wall. One of the breachers pushed aside a stack of storage containers partially blocking the opening, then entered the room, followed by Harrison and McNeil. Harrison checked his watch. It was 2:58 a.m. The storage room supposedly opened to a corridor, with the nearest camera fifty feet to the left, mounted above a security door. McNeil waited until 3:01 a.m., then opened the door.

The SEALs entered a well-lit hallway, with closed gray-metal doors along both sides. According to the map provided by the Zaslon operator, they'd entered the Ministry of Defense building on the second floor underground. They had to go much farther down. The control center was three hundred yards below ground, almost one-fifth of a mile. The only access to the facility was via several elevators and emergency stairways.

Harrison led the way to the security door, glancing up at the camera. He swiped his badge on the door access panel. The small red light on the panel turned green and he heard a click as the door unlocked. They passed through, and after another fifty-foot journey down the corridor, they reached a stairway. It was unlocked from the outside, as was every stairway door. Once inside, however, the only unsecured exit was on the main floor, just above ground.

They descended the stairway, passing exit doors on the next few levels, then continued their descent level after level finding no exits whatsoever. Peering over the railing, Harrison watched the bottom of the stairway rise toward them, and they eventually reached the first of three doors opening to the tri-level command center. The door was secured and Harrison swiped his badge.

The door opened to another well-lit hallway that turned right after a short distance. McNeil left a second fire team behind at the corner. They continued on, reaching a set of four elevators facing a pair of sealed metal doors with a seam down the middle. The SEALs took station on both sides of the control center entrance, with President Kalinin behind the SEALs on one side. McNeil swiped his badge on the door panel.

Nothing happened.

He tried again. It still wouldn't open.

McNeil stepped aside and let Harrison try with his security card, but the result was the same. Senior Chief Stone also tried. The doors remained sealed.

"We got company."

Mendelson peered through his night vision goggles, looking around the corner into the tributary tunnel, watching a column of Russian soldiers, their weapons drawn, moving toward them. Mendelson waited for a response from Lieutenant Acor as he stood at the edge of the arched opening, with Robert Lee crouching near Mendelson's legs. Both men aimed their MP7s at the approaching Russians.

Lieutenant Acor joined the two SEALs, looking briefly around the corner before pulling back. "Arrington," Acor said, and the fourth SEAL in his fire team joined them.

Acor tapped his and Arrington's chest, then pointed across the tunnel. Acor and Arrington would *go long,* stepping out past Mendelson and Lee so all four SEALs could engage the Russians at once.

While they waited for the Russian column to advance closer, Acor changed channels and spoke into his headset, but there was no answer. McNeil and the other SEALs were too deep underground.

When the control room door failed to open, the SEALs shifted to their backup plan. McNeil sent another fire team down the corridor to the corner, mirroring the fire team positioned behind them, monitoring the approaches from both directions.

Two breachers stepped forward, pulling blocks of C-4 from their backpacks. As they attached the C-4 to the entrance doors, shots were fired at both ends of the corridor. Reports streamed over Harrison's headset from both fire teams. Russian soldiers were advancing down both corridors. McNeil sent the remaining SEALs to the corners, split evenly on each side, retaining only Harrison, Senior Chief Stone, and the two breachers.

They were caught between two opposing forces. Even worse, they couldn't blow the doors to the control center without pulling back around one of the corners, where the Russians were advancing. The amount of C-4 it would take to blow open the heavily fortified doors would kill anyone in the immediate corridor. As Harrison and McNeil evaluated their dilemma, explosions occurred first at one corner, then the other.

SEALs tumbled through the air, blown backward by the explosions. The Russians had launched or thrown grenades. As the smoke cleared, seriously injured SEALs were pulled to safety. Others scrambled back toward the corners, trading fire with the Russians and targeting anyone who exposed themselves, attempting to launch or throw additional grenades.

A few Russians learned the hard way, dropped to the floor when they stepped out, their grenades detonating nearby. Others tried to heave them from around corners, but the grenades landed short and skidded

down the floor, stopped by ceiling debris from the
earlier blast, detonating harmlessly between the two
forces. The SEALs had halted the Russians, creating a
temporary stalemate, but they were trapped and would
eventually run out of ammunition.

They needed another way out. McNeil tried the
Zaslon radio, but there was nothing but static. They
were too far underground. Harrison examined the four
elevators opposite the control center doors. Based on
the floor indications, all four were at the main lobby
level of the building. He was loath to use one, but also
didn't want one to open behind them, full of Russian
soldiers. He pressed the *Up* button, hoping to pull each
elevator down to their level and lock it in place, but
none moved. The red L glowed from the indicator
panels. The Russians had beat them to it, locking the
elevators above them.

Another idea occurred to Harrison. The security
center, which controlled the codes to the security
locks, was on the third floor underground. If Harrison
could gain access to an elevator shaft, he could climb
up to the third floor and attempt to enter the security
center, forcing personnel to open the National Defense
Control Center doors from there. He explained the
plan to McNeil, who directed him and Senior Chief
Stone to proceed.

Harrison requested C-4 and associated detonating equipment from a breacher, which he placed in
his backpack, except for the detonator cord snips,
which he jammed into the elevator door seam. Stone
did the same and the two men pried the doors open.
They peered into the dark shaft. On the right side was
a metal maintenance ladder attached to the wall that
ascended into darkness, but there was no easy way to
get to it. Harrison took his backpack off, then went in
first. He worked his way around the entrance, his back

to the elevator doors, his heels on a small ledge. When he could advance no farther, he leapt for the ladder.

His hands slipped down two rungs before grabbing hold. Stone tossed him his backpack, then Harrison climbed a few feet, making way for Stone, who accomplished the same feat. The two men began their climb, which Harrison figured was about a thousand feet. The light faded and both SEALs lowered their night vision goggles into place. They passed no exits for a while, then reached a set of doors with the number 5 painted on them. They continued up two more levels, stopping when they reached the third level underground. Exiting the elevator shaft would be more difficult than entering, however.

They couldn't jump from the ladder onto the door ledge. Instead, Harrison grabbed the nearest elevator cable and swung to one closer to the door. From there, he gained a foothold on the narrow door ledge, then pushed himself to an upright position against the door. He worked his way to the other side as Stone followed, and the two men were soon standing with the door seam between them.

They repeated the process with the detonator snips, but more carefully this time. They didn't have much leverage and if they fell backward, it'd be a long drop to their deaths. They gained a finger hold, then slowly pried the doors apart, flooding the elevator shaft with light. After lifting up their night vision goggles and retrieving their MP7s, they peered past the doorway into the corridor. It was empty.

After stepping into the hallway, Harrison checked the schematics again, then led the way to the security center. When they reached the last intersection, they halted and Harrison peered around the corner. Down the hallway was the door to the security center. A badge panel was affixed to the wall and a camera was mounted above the door. Harrison took aim at the camera and fired his MP7, destroying the camera with a single round. With so many cameras in the facility, hopefully it would take a while for someone to realize this one wasn't working, and even longer to investigate.

Harrison moved swiftly toward the door and swiped his security card. The light remained red. He tried again and it still glowed red.

Senior Chief Stone tried his card, to no avail. It looked like their security cards were now worthless.

Harrison examined the door, evaluating where to place the C-4. The door was heavily reinforced and he had no idea if the amount of C-4 he'd brought with him would do the job. As he evaluated his options, an alternative came to mind.

He pulled out the building schematic again and examined the ventilation system. There was a duct running overhead down the corridor, with a branch entering the security room.

Senior Chief Stone said, "We can't fit. The duct's too small."

"We can't," Harrison said, "but Christine might."

They were on the same floor as Christine. Harrison examined the schematic again, recalling the Zaslon operator saying she'd be in either the cell block, the standard interrogation rooms, or chemical interrogation room. He decided to check the cell block first.

They moved swiftly down the hallway, entering the prisoner cell section. There were small windows in each door, and Harrison peered through each one as they passed by. They were empty. They swept by the normal interrogation rooms, which were also empty. That left one place. The SEALs approached the door and peered through the window. The faint light entering the room from the hallway illuminated a woman in bed.

Both SEALs entered the room and Harrison turned on the light, revealing Christine strapped to a bed, with the contents of an IV bag dripping into her arm. Her eyes fluttered open and she turned away from the harsh overhead lights while her eyes adjusted. Both SEALs stopped beside her bed, and Stone unstrapped her ankles as Harrison examined the IV bag. There was no telling what was inside. He removed the needle from her arm and she turned toward him. Her eyes met his and several emotions played across her face as he unfastened her wrist straps.

After both hands were freed, Christine sat up, then punched him in the face.

"You dropped me!"

He knew she'd be angry when they met again, and also knew her well enough to know her rage wasn't spent. He grabbed her wrist.

Christine swung her left hand, but Harrison caught her fist in his palm.

"We'll talk about this later."

"You're damn right we'll talk about it later! You—"

"Shut up and listen, Chris." Harrison spoke in a tone he rarely used with her, and Christine clamped her mouth shut. "We're pinned down and need your help. Got it?"

Christine nodded tersely, then yanked her hands from his grip.

Harrison went on to explain, and he could tell she was struggling to push her anger aside and focus on the information. When he finished, he asked, "Do you understand?"

Another nod.

"Follow me," he said.

Christine fell in between Harrison and Stone as they entered the corridor.

When they reached the ventilation vent near the

security center, Harrison lifted Stone up and the senior chief removed the vent, revealing a two-foot-wide opening.

He dropped Stone onto the floor and turned to Christine. "Head that way," he said, pointing toward the security door, "and take the first ventilation shaft on the right. The duct into the security room is even smaller, but I think you'll fit."

Harrison gave her his pistol, which she slid inside her waistband into the small of her back. Then she removed her shoes, so her bare feet would give her traction in the confined space.

"Ready?" Harrison asked.

Christine nodded and Harrison grabbed her waist with both hands, then lifted her until her head and arms were inside the ventilation shaft. Then he slowly released her as she pulled herself inside and disappeared.

MOSCOW, RUSSIA

Christine pulled herself through the ventilation duct, getting a feel for how fast she could move without creating noise. It was a tight fit, but there was enough room to pull with her arms and assist with her feet. After a twenty-foot crawl, she reached the opening to her right, as Harrison had predicted. She studied the opening for a few seconds. It was too small, even for her.

She rested her forehead on the ventilation duct as emotions swirled inside her. Moments earlier, her anger had ignited when she'd seen Harrison standing over her bed, looking down at her, just as he'd done while holding her hand as she dangled from the cliff. She hadn't planned to hit him, but it felt good nonetheless.

Her anger was dissipating, replaced by frustration. If Kalinin didn't gain access to the command center and assert control over his military, countless lives would be lost. She examined the opening again, then decided to give it a try. If she angled her shoulders at a forty-five-degree angle, she might fit. Getting out might be a problem; she could end up stuck in the ventilation shaft like a canned sardine.

She inserted both arms into the shaft and tilted her body. Slowly, she worked her way into the duct, forced to remain at an awkward forty-five-degree angle. Once inside the smaller duct, her progress slowed. Her arms were fully extended in front of her, so she couldn't use them to pull herself through. That left only her toes to propel her forward.

Wriggling like an earthworm, she moved forward inches at a time, keeping her movements slow to avoid making noise while traveling through the metal conduit. Fortunately, the hum of electrical equipment and cooling fans in the background helped mask the sound of her transit.

Up ahead, light filtered through a vent cover. She worked her way toward it, eventually reaching the opening. Through slits in the vent cover, she peered down at two men seated at control consoles, monitoring several dozen video displays.

The duct opening was the same width as the ventilation shaft and she concluded she could fit through. She grabbed the cover with one hand, holding it in place, then pushed back the retaining clips. Carefully, she tilted the cover and pulled it into the shaft, placing it gently on the other side of the opening. Now came the hard part—getting out.

Ideally, she'd drop down feet first. But she was on her stomach, and even if she moved forward and placed her feet above the hole, her knees didn't bend that way. There wasn't enough room in the ventilation shaft to turn over, either. That left headfirst, crashing onto the hard floor ten feet below. Unfortunately, there wasn't another choice.

She stuck both arms through the opening, followed by her head, then looked around. The two men were seated with their backs to her. Christine focused on remaining as quiet as possible until the last moment. She worked her way forward until her upper body hung from the opening. With one last wriggle, she fell from the ventilation duct like a fish squirming free from a fisherman's grasp. She arched her body at the last second to avoid landing headfirst, bracing her fall with her hands. She hit the floor with a loud thud.

Both men swung around, surprised to find a woman lying on the ground. Christine reached behind her back and retrieved the pistol, then leveled it at the nearest man. He'd risen from his chair, but froze when he saw the gun. Christine shifted her aim toward the other man, who remained seated, then back to the first man while she pushed herself to her feet.

Christine kept the gun pointed at the nearest man as she backed away. When she hit the wall, she found the knob and opened the door. Harrison and Stone surged inside, aiming their MP7s at the two men.

Harrison spoke in Russian as he advanced, and the man who was standing returned to his chair and faced his console. Harrison was ordering them to do something, but both men remained seated, staring straight ahead. He repeated the same order, this time with an angry tone. When neither man complied, Harrison put a bullet in one man's head.

The man fell sideways onto the floor, a red pool spreading out beneath his head. Harrison swung his MP7 toward the second man and spoke again. This time, the man entered several commands in his keyboard. There was movement on one of the displays. Two large doors slid open, revealing Commander McNeil and two other SEALs. They passed through the entrance, their MP7s drawn, followed by President Kalinin. Other SEALs, retreating from both ends of the corridor toward the opening, also entered, dragging their wounded along.

Harrison spoke again. When the last SEAL passed

through the opening, the doors began to close, sealing the entrance as Russian soldiers arrived.

One of the soldiers swiped his badge on the security panel, but the doors remained closed.

87

MOSCOW, RUSSIA

As McNeil led the two breachers and President Kalinin into the control center, they took immediate fire. Three bullets struck his tactical vest, stopped by the armor plate, while the two other SEALs were hit as well. Kalinin dove for the floor, rolling against the nearest console. McNeil and the other two SEALs likewise ducked for cover on the third level, which consisted of a balcony tier running along the back and both sides. Russian soldiers were firing from both ends and from the ground level below. When the soldiers spotted Kalinin, some stopped shooting. The incoming fire eased, then stopped. McNeil ordered the same for his men.

The Russian soldiers spoke among themselves, some of the conversations becoming heated. McNeil concluded the rank-and-file Russian soldiers had no idea what they were defending the control center from, aside from an armed assault. When President Kalinin had appeared amongst the black-clad SEALs, his presence had given them pause.

An officer on one side was berating his men, ordering them to open fire again. McNeil aimed his MP7 and put a bullet in his head, while another SEAL did the same to an officer on the other side. Additional SEALs surged into the control center, fanning out along the back balcony as the control center doors closed behind them. McNeil ordered them to hold their fire.

Kalinin poked his head above the console and grabbed a microphone at the station, pulling it to the edge of desk. He spoke in Russian, giving a short speech, then one by one, the soldiers placed their weapons on the floor and stood. The SEALs moved swiftly along the top tier, gathering the weapons and ensuring the Russians were disarmed. McNeil looked over the balcony; the soldiers on the main floor had also put down their rifles.

McNeil signaled to Kalinin that it was clear and the Russian president slowly stood. He pulled the microphone to his mouth again and talked for a short while. In addition to the Russian soldiers, there were two dozen personnel on watch on the ground floor, wearing the green, blue, and tan jumpsuits of their respective military branches. The watchstanders turned to their consoles, and McNeil spotted a supervisor moving behind them, giving direction.

Kalinin took a seat at the center console on the third level, and the one-hundred-foot-wide video screen on the far wall morphed into sixty black squares arranged in five rows. Images of military commanders slowly replaced the dark squares, with most of the video being grainy headshots of army and aerospace generals, some rubbing the sleep from their eyes. When the final black square was replaced with video, Kalinin spoke for several minutes.

When he finished, every square went black again, but not until each officer repeated the same phrase, which McNeil translated to "Yes, sir."

President Kalinin spoke into the microphone again

and the supervisor on the main floor looked up at him, then gave additional directions to his watchstanders. A list of Russian four-letter codes appeared on the left side of the screen, the text color of each switching from red to green. McNeil beckoned to a SEAL who spoke Russian, who approached and translated. Kalinin had directed the command center to activate the emergency broadcasting system, tapping into every Russian television and radio station feed so he could address the entire country. It was 4 a.m. in Moscow, but the president's speech would be broadcast repeatedly throughout the day.

When the final television station on the list switched to green text, the supervisor below reported that they were ready. Kalinin sat up in his chair, then began.

88

WASHINGTON, D.C.

It was quiet in the Situation Room as the president and his advisors followed the events in Russia. They'd gathered seven hours ago as *Michigan*'s SEALs began their journey ashore, watching satellite images as they emerged from the Black Sea into a secluded cove. Two helicopters landed and the infrared images of Navy SEALs and President Kalinin had boarded them. It'd been a long wait during the transit to Moscow, then the unit dropped from the helicopters skimming low over the Moskva River. Nothing had been heard from them since.

Things took a turn for the worse at 3 a.m., when the SEALs were supposed to enter the Ministry of Defense building. Russian soldiers emerged from a nearby building, inside the perimeter of the SVR and FSB forces and hidden from their view. Several dozen soldiers rappelled over the concrete embankment of the Moskva River, then entered the same tributary tunnel the SEALs had. There was dead silence in the Situation Room; the mission had been compromised.

The president waited, the tension ratcheting up when GRU Spetsnaz brigades arrived at the perimeter of the Ministry of Defense building. The GRU

troops halted when confronted by the SVR and FSB
Spetsnaz, content to form a perimeter around them.
The SVR and FSB troops would not escape either.

The information technician's voice came across
the Situation Room speakers. "Mr. President. General
Wheeler from NATO's Allied Command Operations
center is requesting a videocon."

"Put him through," the president said.

The satellite video display on the far wall was replaced with General Wheeler's image. "Mr. President," he began, "I have good news. Russian troops are
starting to retreat."

Wheeler's report injected a jolt of energy into the
Situation Room. The president's advisors sat up at the
table and in chairs along the cramped room's perimeter.

"If you'll go to split screen," Wheeler said, "we'll
send you an additional feed."

The president ordered the monitor on the far wall
split in half. Wheeler's image moved to the left and a
map of Europe appeared on the right, with red icons
along the Vistula and Siret Rivers and the Carpathian
Mountains, opposed by blue icons of various shades.
The image zoomed in on the Vistula River, where several red icons were moving eastward. The image shifted
to a satellite view and zoomed in further, showing
armored personnel carriers and tanks forming into
convoys on nearby roads, headed east.

General Wheeler added, "The Russians are pulling back along the entire front: Poland, the Carpathian
Mountains, and Romania."

The president replied, "Thank you for the update,
General. We believe President Kalinin has defeated
the military coup and ordered the withdrawal."

"I understand, sir," Wheeler said. "We'll monitor
the situation."

General Wheeler's image faded from the display,

along with the NATO satellite feed. The president was about to address his staff and cabinet when the IT specialist's voice came across the speakers again.

"Mr. President. Director Cherry is on the line. She has a video feed she'd like to send us."

Cherry was monitoring events from the CIA operations center in Langley.

"Patch it through."

President Kalinin appeared on the Situation Room display, sitting at a control console as he spoke to his countrymen. His speech was repeated in English by a CIA translator, who voiced over Kalinin's remarks as he explained what had occurred: a military coup, which had been defeated. The men responsible would be held accountable.

89

MOSCOW, RUSSIA

In the upstairs study of his two-story home in the Moscow suburbs, Colonel General Viktor Glukov glanced at the pistol on his desk. He was partially dressed in his ceremonial uniform; everything except for his jacket, which hung from a hanger on the door. It had just come back from the cleaners and Glukov was pinning his medals back on, paying meticulous attention to the spacing and alignment. In years past, his wife would've done this for him, but she had passed away not long ago. They had no children, so Glukov had dedicated the rest of his life to his one remaining love. His country.

Upon seeing President Kalinin's image on the television this morning, he knew it wouldn't be long before the Interior Ministry or FSB forces apprehended him. Kalinin would have his head, but not before making a public spectacle of him, sending a message to those who might entertain similar treasonous thoughts. That was something Glukov would not allow. He had served his country admirably and would do what he could to prevent his name from being dragged through the mud. Yes, he'd supported the coup, but for all the right reasons.

Like the Germans in World War II, NATO would eventually want what Russia had—enormous reserves of oil and natural gas. It was only a matter of time before natural resources ran low, and Western European countries struggling for their economic survival looked east. Although NATO was currently weak, it was a twenty-nine-country alliance against—Russia. It wouldn't take NATO long to rebuild their militaries, or worse yet, resort to tactical nuclear weapons to take what they wanted. Glukov supported the coup for the sole purpose of protecting Russia. There was no personal gain involved, only risk.

There was a screech of tires outside. Glukov went to the window and pulled back the curtain. Interior Ministry police were streaming from several vehicles, encircling his house. There was a heavy pounding on the front door.

Glukov put on his dress uniform jacket and buttoned it slowly, then sat at his desk. He heard the front door splinter into pieces, followed by men shouting and running. As heavy boots surged up the stairs, he reached for the pistol on his desk. He placed the barrel in his mouth, then pulled the trigger.

90

SAN JOSE, CALIFORNIA

NCIS Special Agent Joe Gililland rode in the passenger seat of the black Buick headed east on Interstate 280, having landed at San Francisco International Airport an hour ago with his driver, Kelly Lyman. Local law enforcement officials had arrived at their destination this morning and confirmed the presence of their suspect, who had reported to work as expected. Gililland reviewed the information on his laptop computer in preparation for today's arrest.

After Clark Curtain Laboratory identified the culprit microprocessor chip, NCIS had opened an investigation into DavRoc Enterprises, the company that manufactured it. DavRoc had the requisite bona fides: an American-owned company managed by American citizens, and a preliminary review of its employees identified no one noteworthy. Gililland had been prepared for a laborious investigation into every employee's background to identify the traitor, but the answer had been tossed into his lap yesterday.

Russia's GRU had contracted for the microprocessor alteration, and after President Kalinin regained power, he'd ordered the new director to cough up the details. Gililland reviewed the information on his laptop one final time, then closed the lid as the Buick pulled into the parking lot outside DavRoc's main building. Gililland called the specified number on his cell phone, and several detectives and uniformed police officers crossed the street toward the black Buick. Gililland and Lyman stepped from their car, then led the entourage into the lobby.

"Fifth floor," one of the detectives said.

Keith Vierling heard a buzz of commotion and looked up from his cubical desk. It wasn't hard to figure out the walking suits exiting the elevator were detectives, as they were followed by uniformed police officers. He felt a rising trepidation when he spotted the officers, then panic stabbed into him as they turned toward his cubicle. Vierling looked straight ahead at his computer monitor, then took a deep, shaky breath and tried to focus. The sick feeling in the pit of his stomach was slowly replaced by anger. He would never be discovered, Ed Sutton had told him.

Making the requested changes had been easy; just a few subroutines added to the chip circuitry. The quick work had returned dividends over the last ten years, although he was certain the Russians paid him that long to keep him quiet during the decade-long navigation update to America's nuclear weapons. Nothing would come of it, Vierling had convinced himself, justifying his actions. A full-scale nuclear war was too horrifying to imagine, something neither side would resort to.

A man and woman stopped at the entrance to his cubical.

"Keith Vierling?" the man asked.

Vierling considered, just for an instant, denying

who he was. But the question was merely a formality. He nodded.

"I'm NCIS Special Agent Joe Gililland, and this is Special Agent Kelly Lyman. We'd like you to come with us."

91

WASHINGTON, D.C.

Seated behind his desk in the Oval Office, the president pressed the intercom button on his phone, connecting him to his secretary in the adjacent office.

"Send SecDef Dunnavant in."

The door to the Oval Office opened and SecDef Bill Dunnavant entered, along with Chief of Staff Kevin Hardison and Colonel DuBose.

"What have you got, Bill?" the president asked as the three men sat before him.

"As you're aware," Dunnavant began, "the mission to restore Kalinin to power was a success, although it didn't go exactly as planned. We lost six SEALs inside the Ministry of Defense building, plus eight wounded. Add to that the four Delta Force and five SEALs killed during Kalinin's extraction from Russia, and we're looking at fifteen dead, of which we've recovered thirteen bodies. The two Delta Force soldiers ejected from the Black Hawk before it crashed remain unlocated.

"The remaining SEALs, along with Christine, are on their way back to Washington aboard a C-32 we sent over, along with thirteen coffins in the cargo hold. We're making arrangements for a coordinated burial ceremony in Arlington National Cemetery.

"Regarding Russia's invasion of Ukraine and NATO countries, Kalinin kept his word. All troops have been withdrawn to Russia, although he did leave an additional battalion of his newest anti-air missile batteries in Kaliningrad Oblast, something NATO previously objected to. I recommend we not quibble over it, considering what we were looking at a few days ago.

"Kalinin dealt swiftly with the military coup, and four of the five commanders of the Russian military branches have been arrested, with the fifth, Colonel General Glukov, committing suicide. The arrests include General Zolotov, in command of Russia's Strategic Missile Troops. The idea to divert American ballistic missiles was his brainchild, although it was envisioned for defensive purposes only. Russia has had this capability for the last ten years, increasing to one hundred percent as we rolled out our navigation upgrades to our ballistic missiles and B-2 bombers.

"In addition to the heads of the five main military branches, the four military district commanders have been arrested, along with the generals in charge of the GRU and national guard. Kalinin is ferreting out whoever else was involved in the coup, but it looks like they've got the main players except for General Andropov, whose whereabouts remained unknown until the SVR tracked him down yesterday, hiding out in a dacha in Siberia."

"When do they plan to take him into custody?" the president asked.

"That's the interesting part," Dunnavant said. "It turns out that President Kalinin has as wicked of a revenge streak as you."

The president leaned back in his chair, evaluating whether Dunnavant's comment was a compliment or not.

Dunnavant continued, "President Kalinin wants us to take General Andropov out in a unique way."

"What does he have in mind?"

"Andropov implemented the Zolotov option, eliminating our nuclear ballistic missile capability. Kalinin has proposed we kill Andropov with one of our conventional ballistic missiles."

"How does he know we have that capability? It's a Top Secret, compartmented program."

"It is. But they've obviously figured it out."

"It could be a ruse," Hardison said. "An attempt to figure out whether we have the capability or not."

"That's true," Dunnavant answered. "But it's not critical, in my opinion. These missiles are difficult to employ against countries with intercontinental nuclear weapons due to the inability to distinguish between incoming conventional and nuclear-warhead-tipped missiles. It's unlikely we'd ever use these missiles against Russia."

"So Kalinin wants us to kill Andropov with a conventional strategic missile strike?"

"Yes, sir. We'd coordinate with Russia's missile troops so they'd be aware of the launch, and they'd verify the missile's trajectory takes it into remote Siberia where Andropov is hiding."

"I like it," the president said. "Proceed with the preparations and brief me when we're ready."

92

USS *MARYLAND* • SIBERIA, RUSSIA

Commander Britt Skogstad stood on the submarine's Conn beside the Group Ten admiral, waiting for the expected message. USS *Maryland* was at its normal patrol depth with one of its communication buoys deployed a few feet below the surface, keeping *Maryland* in continuous receipt of the Very Low Frequency broadcast. Skogstad checked the clock in Control. If satellite surveillance confirmed the target was at the specified location, *Maryland* would receive the Emergency Action Message, although this one would be a conventional version.

He'd been informed of the plan two days ago, directed to pull *Maryland* into one of the explosive handling buildings for yet another on-load, this time for a Trident missile carrying conventional warheads. There were two variations of conventional Trident warheads, which provided long-range strike capability quickly without having to wait for ships or aircraft to transit within range. The missile loaded aboard *Maryland* carried tungsten rod flechettes, which would rain down on the target, destroying everything within a three-thousand-square-foot area. The other conventional warhead type could destroy hardened bunkers deep underground.

Although the missile being launched today carried conventional and not nuclear warheads, the launch procedure would be similar due to needing access to one of the launch keys, which was contained in a safe the crew didn't have the combination to. In the Cold War days, the crew possessed every key required to launch its nuclear missiles, but someone must have woken up at night in a cold sweat, realizing there were a dozen American submarine crews at sea that could initiate a nuclear war if they chose to, with no safeguards in place other than training and procedures that said they couldn't. One of the keys was now kept locked in a safe in Missile Control Center, with the combination provided in the launch message.

The message Skogstad was waiting for finally arrived.

Alert One! Alert One!

Radio's 1-MC announcement reverberated throughout the submarine, reporting they'd received an Emergency Action Message. Junior officers streamed into Control as they were trained, not yet knowing what type of EAM had been received.

Unlike nuclear EAMs, the message was transmitted in plain text, so the extra steps of decoding the message, validating it against the authorized message formats, and verifying the nuclear release codes wouldn't be required. However, the message would contain the pertinent launch details and the combination to the launch key safe.

Two junior officers, each holding the message, approached Skogstad. Since the message contained the combination to the launch key, two-man control was required.

The senior of the two officers reported, "Sir, we

are in receipt of a conventional strike message. No authentication is required."

Skogstad replied, "What are the launch instructions?"

"Missile tube Two-one, carrying conventional warheads, has been released."

The two officers placed the message where Skogstad and his XO, standing beside him, could read it, and both men verified the message released the missile in tube Twenty-one.

"I concur," his Executive Officer said.

Skogstad picked up the 1-MC microphone. "Man Battle Stations Missile for strategic launch. Spin up missile Two-one."

The two junior officers departed with the message, headed to Missile Control Center to retrieve the launch key as the crew manned battle stations. Meanwhile, the section on watch made the initial preparations for missile launch.

"Helm, all stop," the Officer of the Deck ordered. "Dive, bring the ship to launch depth. Prepare to hover."

The Helm and Diving Officer acknowledged, and the main engines went quiet as *Maryland* took a ten-degree up-angle, coming shallow and slowing in preparation for launch.

Maryland's angle leveled off as the submarine coasted to a halt. After the Chief of the Watch engaged the hovering computers, the Diving Officer announced, "The ship is hovering at launch depth."

The Chief of the Watch reported, "Battle Stations Missile is manned."

Skogstad picked up the 1-MC again. "Set condition 1-SQ for strategic launch. This is the Commanding Officer. The release of conventional weapons has been directed."

Skogstad left Control and opened the safe in his stateroom, then returned with one of the twenty-four keys in his safe. He handed it to a missile technician waiting to arm missile tube Twenty-one's gas generator, which would launch the missile above the ocean's surface, where the missile's first-stage engine would ignite.

The two junior officers with the message returned to Control with the CIP launch key, which they handed to Skogstad, who inserted it into the Captain's Indicator Panel. He turned the key ninety degrees, then flipped up the Permission to Fire toggle switch. The panel activated, illuminating the status lights for all twenty-four missiles.

Only missile Twenty-one was brought on line, spinning up its inertial navigation system. Skogstad monitored the progress as the indicating light for missile Twenty-one illuminated, indicating it had successfully communicated with the submarine's navigation system. It now knew its starting location. The next indicator toggled from black to red as the missile accepted its target package, carrying the impact coordinates for its warheads.

The light in the third column of the Captain's Indicating panel turned red as the missile techs in Missile Compartment Lower Level armed the explosives in the gas generator.

USS *Maryland* was ready to launch.

Skogstad turned to the watchstander beside him. "Phone-talker to Weapons. You have permission to fire." The phone-talker passed the order to Missile Control Center over the sound-powered phone circuit.

Skogstad listened to the orders going out over the MCC communication circuit.

"Prepare Two-one."

The light for Missile Tube Twenty-one's muzzle

hatch turned red, indicating the hatch was open and locked in place. The starboard missile team relayed its report back to MCC.

"Two-one, ready."

Seconds later, Skogstad felt *Maryland*'s deck flex when the Weapons Officer squeezed the trigger, ejecting the sixty-five-ton missile from the tube. Missile Techs checked the panel indications and the small glass portal in the side of the tube, then reported to MCC.

"Two-one, away."

General Andropov turned off the television, then placed the remote control on the couch beside him. A few days ago, upon learning of the pending American assault on the main Ministry of Defense building, he'd considered being in the National Defense Control Center in the middle of the night, if nothing more than to greet the crestfallen former president of the Russian Federation. However, Andropov was a cautious man and he'd hedged his bets, choosing to visit a Moscow suburb for the evening. Based on how things unfolded, he wondered if he would've been better off if he'd faced Kalinin in Moscow. Perhaps he could have put a bullet in him.

The whole thing was infuriating. He shouldn't have been forced to take matters into his own hands in the first place. Had Putin still been president, he would have realized the wisdom of Andropov's plan. Russian forces would still be in possession of half of Poland, the Baltic States, and a portion of Romania. In the coming weeks, Putin would have negotiated a compromise, ceding Poland and Romania back to NATO in exchange for friendly Russian governments in the Baltic States and Ukraine. A simple plan, lacking only a Russian president with the guts to see it through.

Andropov pondered his future. He had few allies left, but there were some who could be counted on. Former Fleet Admiral Georgiy Ivanov, fired by President Kalinin after the events at Ice Station Nautilus, harbored a grudge, and there were several generals who had served under Andropov who would demonstrate their loyalty if given the proper opportunity. As the evening wore on, while staring at a dark TV, General Andropov plotted his revenge.

Above Andropov's dacha in the Siberian hinterland, five Trident warheads, already separated from the missile's third stage, descended through the atmosphere at four miles per second. Just before impact, the warhead nose cones separated, releasing dozens of heavy tungsten rods, which spread evenly in a circular pattern centered around a single dacha. The tungsten rods impacted the ground with the destructive force of over one hundred tons of TNT, obliterating everything inside a three-thousand-square-foot circle.

93

WASHINGTON, D.C.

Inside the White House, there are three dining rooms: the President's Dining Room in the West Wing, often referred to as the Oval Office Dining Room; the first family's private dining room in the Prince of Wales Room on the second floor; and the most formal of the three, the Family Dining Room on the first floor. It was just before noon when Christine O'Connor followed the president into the Prince of Wales Room, where they sat opposite each other at a round mahogany table. Servants brought in their lunch; nothing lavish, just Caesar salad with a grilled chicken breast cut into strips.

Christine concluded that the choice of venue for today's lunch indicated something important was on the agenda. The president was likely to make one final effort to convince her to withdraw her resignation. The extra effort wouldn't be required, however. She'd already decided to continue serving as his national security advisor.

The last few weeks had been hectic overall, but the quiet hours hiding in the forest with President Kalinin and the long flight back from Moscow had provided Christine with the opportunity to reflect on everything she'd done over the past three years. What crystallized her thoughts was watching Harrison put a bullet in the head of a defenseless man in the Ministry of Defense security center to coerce the other watchstander into opening the control center doors. It was no different than what she'd done in China.

Her actions during the last three years, except in one instance, had been driven by the desire to save lives. The singular case, putting a gun in Gorev's mouth and pulling the trigger, had been driven by revenge alone and had been the catalyst for the crisis that led to her resignation. However, President Kalinin's assessment during dinner at Gelendzhik had been correct. She was holding herself to too high a standard, one requiring her to make the correct decision every time, regardless of the circumstances. That she had trouble dealing with why she'd killed Gorev was a good thing, she concluded.

Christine had finally worked her way through what she'd done over the last three years. She was about to inform the president that she was pulling her letter of resignation and was looking forward to working for him another five years—after his reelection next year, of course—when the president spoke first.

"I've hired a new national security advisor who will start next week."

Christine was at a momentary loss for words. She dropped her eyes to her plate and poked her fork through her salad. She hadn't expected to be replaced so easily. The president had often commented on how valuable her insight was and how fortunate he was to have her as his NSA. Now, she'd been tossed aside. She had only herself to blame, though. She'd handed him her resignation.

The president continued, "We've both held up our end of the agreement. You've completed the nuclear arms negotiations with Russia, and I've accepted your resignation."

Christine searched for an appropriate response, settling on, "Thank you, Mr. President." She forced a smile.

The president was silent for a while, watching her as she brought a piece of chicken to her mouth and chewed slowly. The president said, "I think it's for the best."

She didn't know what else to say; she just wanted to leave before her voice or face betrayed her feelings. She placed her fork on her plate and wiped her mouth with her napkin, then placed it on the table, signaling she was done. She'd have to wait for the president, however, who still had a fork in one hand and knife in the other.

The president cut into a strip of chicken as he asked, "Have you given much thought to what you'd like to do next?"

She had, but wasn't about to tell him she'd decided to pull her resignation. "I've received several offers over the last few years. After I've turned matters over to the new NSA, I'll look into them." She considered asking who the new NSA was, but decided otherwise. She'd rather not think about who would so easily replace her.

The president chewed his chicken thoughtfully, then said, "I've got an idea." Instead of explaining, he took a sip of water.

Christine knew the president well enough to know he was dragging the discussion out. To what end, she didn't know. She played her part.

"Something interesting?"

"I think so." The president brought another forkful to his mouth. After swallowing, he smiled.

Christine's curiosity was piqued. But before she

could ask her next question, the president said, "Director Cherry is retiring next month."

Another sip of water.

Christine wondered about the sudden change of topic, from discussing her next job to the CIA director's retirement. Unless—

She stared at the president in disbelief. "You're not serious."

"I am," the president said.

"Let me get this straight. I offered my resignation as NSA because I've been getting into too much trouble, and your solution is to make me the director of the CIA?"

"Exactly. You'll be well-insulated in your white palace at Langley. You'll have plenty of operatives around the world to do the heavy lifting and keep you out of trouble. But I'll expect you to immerse yourself sufficiently in the details to keep tabs on what the agency is actually doing. That's why I'm offering you the job. I'm not saying I don't trust the CIA, but I *am* saying I need someone I can trust inside the organization."

"You want a spy inside your spy agency?"

"You could put it that way."

"What's going on?"

"Career spies are very good at hiding things, and I need someone smart and persistent enough to separate the wheat from the chaff. Cherry was excellent at it, and I need a replacement just as good."

Christine considered the proposal. CIA directors were political appointees, their exposure to CIA operations often limited to their time on a House or Senate intelligence committee. She had more relevant experience than many of her predecessors. Plus, as CIA director, no one would touch her, which offered protection against her current SVR death sentence.

"I need some time to consider," Christine said.

"I'd like to have your answer by Monday."

"How about Tuesday? I have a date this weekend, flying back into the country on Monday."

"An international date? With Kalinin?"

Christine nodded. "There are a few things we need to discuss."

94

MOSCOW, RUSSIA

In her twenty-seventh-floor suite in the Swissotel Krasnye Holmy, Christine O'Connor examined herself in the full-length mirror before heading out. She was wearing a black V-neck evening dress with an hour-glass cutout across her back, filled in with see-through gold mesh spreading across her shoulders, narrowing in the middle, then wrapping around her slender waist. Armed with black pearl earrings and pendant necklace set in eighteen-karat gold, along with black-and-gold heels and matching purse, she was dressed to kill.

Christine checked her watch. It was a few minutes before the appointed time. Kalinin's executive assistant, Andrei Yelchin, who'd met her at the airport this afternoon, had requested she be ready at 7 p.m. Someone would stop by her room to escort her to dinner with President Kalinin. No further details were provided. As she waited the last few minutes, her thoughts drifted to her pending dinner with the Russian president.

Following his return to power, she hadn't heard from him until a few days ago, requesting she join him in Moscow. He regretted not being able to spend time with her in a more romantic setting, but he thought it unwise to leave Moscow while dealing with the aftershocks of the military coup. He'd finally carved a weekend free and would be pleased if she could join him.

The secrecy shrouding their relationship remained in place. Kalinin sent a private jet, which she boarded at Reagan National Airport on Friday evening for the overnight flight to Moscow, where she was driven by limousine to the Swissotel, a luxurious five-star hotel in the heart of the Russian capital.

There was a knock on her door at exactly 7 p.m. Christine grabbed her purse, then opened the door to be greeted by Yelchin again, who escorted her to the elevator. They stepped inside, but instead of descending to the lobby, they ascended to the thirty-fourth floor where they were met by an attractive woman wearing a full-length red dress and holding two menu boards, standing between two Federal Protective Service agents in black suits.

"Welcome, Miss O'Connor," the hostess said. "Please follow me."

As the hostess escorted them down a short corridor, Christine whispered to Yelchin, "How does she know who I am? I thought my visit was supposed to be discreet."

He replied, "The staff have signed confidentiality agreements. There will be no word of your or President Kalinin's visit here tonight."

"What about others having dinner?"

As Christine stepped from the corridor into the restaurant, there was no need for Yelchin to answer. Two things struck Christine immediately: the restaurant was empty, aside from a bartender and Kalinin at the bar, and the view was breathtaking.

They had entered the Space Bar and Restaurant, a flying-saucer-shaped, glass-encased restaurant with an elegant, modern decor, offering a stunning 360-degree panoramic view of the city. Christine had learned of its reputation during previous visits: a stylish, glamorous hot spot with pricey custom cocktails made by mixologists instead of bartenders, where wealthy men could be found with a beautiful woman on each arm, or where one could observe a man on one knee before his girlfriend, ring in hand, on an almost nightly basis.

Kalinin stood as Christine approached, while Yelchin departed. The hostess escorted Kalinin and Christine to their table on the outer rim of the restaurant with the glass exterior an arm's length away. After Kalinin helped Christine into her seat and took his own, the hostess handed them menus, and a waiter arrived with two custom cocktails. Christine took a sip. She had no idea what it was, but it was absolutely delicious.

Dinner was ordered and quickly served, along with a bottle of wine—Cabernet Sauvignon, which Christine preferred and Kalinin remembered. They talked throughout dinner, the conversation remaining light except when Kalinin offered details on the recovery from the military coup. Surprisingly, he never steered the discussion toward their personal relationship. It seemed he would let things play out naturally, or perhaps let her be the one to broach the subject.

When dinner was finished, Kalinin escorted Christine to the bar, ordering two glasses of champagne. As Christine sipped her drink, Kalinin led her around the panoramic restaurant, pointing out the sights in the historic city. They concluded their circular tour with a view overlooking the Kremlin and Red Square.

"Now, where were we?" Kalinin asked, "the night we were having dinner, when we were rudely interrupted by General Andropov?"

"I believe we were about to put the past behind us and drink to the future."

"I remember." Kalinin raised his glass of champagne and Christine touched their glasses together. "To the future," he said.

Christine had spent a great deal of time contemplating her future with Kalinin. He was an attractive man, and as far as wealth and power went, he didn't leave much to be desired. But wealth and power had never mattered to Christine. There were far more important factors to be considered, with the most important being chemistry. She liked Kalinin and had to admit she was physically attracted to him, but there was no spark.

Over the last several weeks and during the long flight to Moscow, she had contemplated how to break the news to him. She was unsure how he'd respond, as men and women were unpredictable when spurned.

"About us. Our future." She fell silent for a moment, then finally said it. "I don't think we have one."

Christine went on to explain her feelings for him, concluding that there wasn't enough to sustain a serious relationship.

Kalinin nodded. "Your response is not unexpected. It is easy to see that your heart is elsewhere."

Christine gave him a curious look.

"Your SEAL friend Harrison."

Christine turned away, staring out across the city. *Harrison*. There was no future there.

Kalinin continued, "I had to pursue you to the end, just to be sure. Plus, there is another reason I wanted to see you. There is something I wanted to tell you in person."

Christine turned back to Kalinin as he said, "I never thanked you for rescuing me in Gelendzhik. I must show my appreciation."

She waited for him to explain.

"What you did to Gorev," he said, "is forgiven. The

SVR death sentence levied against you has been vacated."

As Christine absorbed the news, it felt like a burden had been lifted from her shoulders.

"Is Director Hippchenko on board with my clemency?"

"It was his idea."

"Thank you," Christine said, "and please pass my appreciation on to Hippchenko."

Kalinin nodded.

No words were exchanged for a while as they looked over the darkening city.

"This man, Harrison," Kalinin said, "Are you dating him?"

Christine shook her head. "He's married."

Kalinin gave her an odd look. "Things are more complicated than I suspected."

Christine laughed. "That's an understatement. I probably won't ever talk to him again."

Kalinin fell quiet, and she could tell he was evaluating where to take the conversation next. Finally, he asked, "So what becomes of us? Good friends and nothing more?"

Christine pushed Harrison from her mind and turned to Kalinin. "We could be friends or friendly adversaries. Depends on your point of view."

"I know what you mean. I'm aware your president has asked you to become the new CIA director."

Christine's eyes narrowed. "How do you know that? We had a private lunch."

"I have sources in many places. There isn't much you Americans can do without me learning about it." After a short pause, he asked, "Do you plan to accept?"

"Maybe I already have," Christine replied. "Maybe I'm wired right now, recording every word you say."

Kalinin grinned, then set his champagne glass down.

He stepped closer, placing his hands on Christine's waist. "Now where do you suppose those wires are hidden?"

Christine rested her forearms on Kalinin's shoulders. "I'm sure you'd like to find out."

Kalinin smiled, then leaned in for a kiss.

95

ARLINGTON, VIRGINIA

Two weeks after returning from Russia, Christine exited CIA headquarters at Langley and pulled onto the George Washington Parkway, traveling south against the early evening traffic leaving Washington, D.C. It'd been a long day and tomorrow would be even longer. She'd spent the day continuing her turnover with Director Cherry and would spend tomorrow attending the burial ceremony for the SEALs and Delta Force personnel killed in Russia. The thirteen-casket interment would be long, followed by a reception for the grieving families afterward, and she wouldn't have time to see her parents. Today was more appropriate anyway, since it was her mom's birthday. It was a half-hour before sunset; just enough daylight left to spend a few minutes with them.

After exiting onto Memorial Avenue, Christine pulled a worn yellow envelope from her glove compartment and retrieved a car pass, which she placed on her dashboard. She turned onto Eisenhower Drive, where a sentry examined the pass and waved her into Arlington National Cemetery. She continued down Eisenhower past the Tomb of the Unknowns, turned left on Patton Drive, then pulled to a halt beside section 70. She headed across the grass, passing gravestone after gravestone before stopping in front of headstone 1851.

There were two names on the marker: Daniel O'Connor on the front, and Tatyana O'Connor on the back. The lawn had been freshly cut and grass clippings were clinging to the headstone. She kneeled before the gravestone and brushed the grass off. She'd never known her father, who died before she was born, and Tatyana had passed away when Christine was in her twenties. It seemed so long ago. Christine was fresh out of college when her mom died, and Tatyana had never seen the woman Christine had become or what she had accomplished.

Childhood memories flooded her thoughts, and Christine smiled as she recalled her mom's exasperated efforts to transform her from a tomboy into a proper girl. Nature had eventually taken care of things, and the boys that used to consider her one of the gang began to treat her differently. She remembered the first time Jake Harrison tried to hold her hand. As they sat on the edge of the barn loft overlooking his father's farm, she had no idea what he was doing. When his hand touched hers, she moved hers away to make room for his. She remembered the crestfallen look on his face before he suddenly stood and left.

A reddish-orange light reflected off her parents' white gravestone. The sun was slipping beneath the horizon, irradiating the cirrus clouds in a pink, red, and orange hue. She pushed herself to her feet, then headed to her car. In the distance, she spotted a man standing beneath a tree, watching her. She slowed her pace, trying to discern who he was. He moved toward her. When Christine finally recognized him, she stopped where she was. It was Jake Harrison.

On the C-32 flight home from Russia with the Navy

SEALs, she'd arranged for a seat far away from Jake, then sank into it and closed her eyes. But instead of falling asleep, she relived those last few seconds dangling from the cliff, her hand in his, over and over. When the flight landed, she left without saying goodbye. In fact, they hadn't spoken since they'd departed Russia's Ministry of Defense building.

Christine waited until Jake stopped in front of her. She wasn't sure what to say.

It looked like he was at a loss for words as well. Both stood quietly for a long moment.

"What are you doing here?" she finally asked.

"I stopped by to say hi to a few friends, then I saw your car. You've been avoiding me and I thought we should talk."

"There's nothing to talk about." Christine considered leaving, but her words belied her true feelings.

"You haven't forgiven me yet," Harrison said. It was more a statement than a question.

"How can I? The odds of surviving that fall were near zero."

"I didn't have a choice. Extracting Kalinin was the primary mission. You were secondary."

"So that's it? The job came first and I meant nothing?"

"You know that's untrue. Letting go of you was the hardest thing I've ever done."

Christine heard the remorse in his voice. From a logical perspective, she realized he'd done what he was trained to do; saving Kalinin was more important. Emotionally, however, she hadn't been able to reconcile his actions with those of a man who had once loved her; a man she thought—up until that moment—still did.

Her stoic facade began to crumble. She looked away, searching for words.

Jake stepped forward and pulled her close, wrapping his arms around her. She reacted instinctively, hugging his waist and resting her face on his shoulder as she'd done so many times while they dated. Neither one spoke as they stood there, and Christine fought to hold back the tears. She had many regrets in her life, but one stood out from the rest.

He said he would wait.

Jake broke the silence. "I hear you're going to be the new CIA director."

"So it seems," Christine answered, her face still resting on his shoulder.

"That's an odd career choice, considering everything you've been through."

Christine shrugged, then repeated the president's line. "I'll have a lot more help staying out of trouble."

She felt Jake's arms relax, releasing her from his embrace. She didn't want to let go. She held on for a while, then acquiesced and stepped back.

"What are your plans?" she asked. "Rumor has it you're retiring soon."

"I haven't decided. But I plan to make a decision before *Michigan*'s next deployment."

"If you get out," Christine said, "let me know when you start looking for a job."

"You offering?"

Christine smiled.

COMPLETE CAST OF CHARACTERS

AMERICAN CHARACTERS

UNITED STATES ADMINISTRATION
BOB TOMPKINS—vice president
KEVIN HARDISON—chief of staff
DAWN CABRAL—secretary of state
BILL DUNNAVANT—secretary of defense
CHRISTINE O'CONNOR—national security advisor
BILL DUBOSE (Colonel)—senior military aide
LARS SIKES—press secretary

MILITARY COMMANDERS
OKEY WATSON (General)—Chairman, Joint Chiefs of Staff
BRIAN RETTMAN (Admiral)—Chief of Naval Operations
ANDY WHEELER (General)—Supreme Allied Commander, Europe
BOB ARONSON (Admiral)—Commander, U.S. Strategic Command
DUSTY RHODES (Vice Admiral)—Director, Strategic Systems Programs
DUTCH HOSTLER (Major General)—Commanding General, 1st Armored Division

JUSTIN WALKER (Rear Admiral)—Commander, Naval Special Warfare Command

USS *MICHIGAN* (OHIO CLASS GUIDED MISSILE SUBMARINE)-CREW

MURRAY WILSON (Captain)—Commanding Officer

AL PATZKE (Lieutenant Commander)—Executive Officer

BILL HARWI (Lieutenant Commander)—Engineer Officer

KELLY HAAS (Lieutenant Commander)—Supply Officer

ED LLOYD (Lieutenant)—Navigator

TREVOR POWERS (Lieutenant)—Weapons Officer

VICTOR CLARK (Lieutenant)—Junior Officer

CAROLYN CODY (Lieutenant)—Junior Officer

USS *MICHIGAN*-SEAL DETACHMENT

JOHN MCNEIL (Commander)—SEAL Team Commander

JAKE HARRISON (Lieutenant)—SEAL Platoon Officer-in-Charge

BOB ACOR (Lieutenant)—SEAL Platoon Officer-in-Charge

JOE ALEO (Commander)—SEAL Team Medical Officer

JEFF STONE (Special Warfare Operator Senior Chief)

RICHARD MENDELSON (Special Warfare Operator First Class)

TUCK ROSENBERRY (Special Warfare Operator Second Class)

ROB MAYDWELL (Special Warfare Operator First Class)

BILL STIGERS (Special Warfare Operator Second Class)

TONY RODRIGUES (Special Warfare Operator First Class)

Wayne Brown (Special Warfare Operator Second
  Class)
Robert Lee (Special Warfare Operator First Class)
Brian Arrington (Special Warfare Operator Second
  Class)

USS *MARYLAND* [OHIO CLASS BALLISTIC MISSILE SUBMARINE]

Britt Skogstad (Commander)—Commanding
  Officer
Tom Martin (Lieutenant)—Weapons Officer
Andrew Wells (Lieutenant)—Junior Officer

OTHER MILITARY CHARACTERS

Joe Martin (Captain)—Delta Force team leader
Kurt Wise (Captain)—1st Armored Division aide
Carole Glover (Major)—B-2 bomber pilot
Bill Houston (Captain)—B-2 bomber co-pilot

OTHER CIVILIAN CHARACTERS

Jessica Cherry—Director of the Central Intelligence
  Agency
Mark Johnson—Russian translator (American em-
  bassy)
Barry Graham—aide to the U.S. ambassador to the
  Russian Federation
Diane Traweek—Clark Curtain Laboratory chief
  executive officer
Jacinta Mascarenhas—Clark Curtain Laboratory
  division director
Rich Underwood—Clark Curtain Laboratory execu-
  tive assistant
Steve Kaufmann—Clark Curtain Laboratory soft-
  ware engineer
Keith Vierling—DavRoc Enterprises hardware
  engineer

KELLY LYMAN—NCIS special agent
JOE GILILLAND—NCIS special agent

RUSSIAN CHARACTERS

RUSSIAN FEDERATION ADMINISTRATION

YURI KALININ—president
ANTON NECHAYEV—defense minister
ANDREI LAVROV—foreign minister
SERGEI IVANOV—national security advisor
MAKSIM POSNIAK—director of security and disarmament, Ministry of Foreign Affairs
JOSEF HIPPCHENKO—director of the Foreign Intelligence Service (SVR)
ANDREI YELCHIN—President Kalinin's executive assistant

MILITARY COMMANDERS

SERGEI ANDROPOV (General)—Chief of the General Staff
ALEXEI VOLODIN (Colonel General)—Commander-in-Chief, Aerospace Forces
VIKTOR GLUKOV (Colonel General)—Commander-in-Chief, Ground Forces
OLEG LIPOVSKY (Admiral)—Commander-in-Chief, Navy
ANDREI ZOLOTOV (Colonel General)—Commander-in-Chief, Strategic Missile Troops
VLADISLAV GRACHEV (Colonel General)—Commander-in-Chief, Airborne Troops
IGOR KOROBOV (Colonel General)—Chief of the Main Intelligence Directorate (GRU)
LEONID SHIMKO (Admiral)—Commander, Northern Fleet

DMITRY SOKOLOV (Lieutenant General)—
    Commanding Officer, 4th Guards Tank Division
VIKTOR KARAKAYEV—Director, Federal National
    Guard Service

K-561 *KAZAN* (YASEN CLASS ATTACK SUBMARINE)
ANATOLY MIKHAILOV (Captain Second Rank)—
    Commanding Officer
ERIK FEDOROV (Captain Third Rank)—First Officer

B-268 *VELIKIY NOVGOROD* (IMPROVED KILO CLASS DIESEL ATTACK SUBMARINE)
JOZSEF TRATNYEK (Captain Second Rank)—
    Commanding Officer
GRIGORY DOMASHEV (Captain Third Rank)—First
    Officer
BOGDAN GOLOVIN (Captain Lieutenant)—Central
    Command Post Watch Officer

OTHER RUSSIAN CHARACTERS
VAGIT SAVVIN (Colonel)—General Andropov's aide
PAVEL LEBEDEV (Major)—assigned to Colonel Savvin's
    unit
LEONID EGOROV (Major)—assigned to GRU Spetsnaz
    unit
DANIL VASILIEV—Traktir na Petrovke (tavern) owner
GEORGIY ABRAMOV—Traktir na Petrovke patron
TAMARA LEBEDEV—Krasnodar Krai cabin inhabitant
VASILY LEBEDEV—Krasnodar Krai cabin inhabitant
ANNA ORLOV—Tamara and Vasily's daughter
RUSLAN ORLOV—Anna's husband
MAXIM ANOSOV—CIA operative in Sochi, Russia
ANDREI POPOV—GRU chemical interrogator

OTHER CHARACTERS

NATO

Johan Van der Bie—secretary general
Susan Gates—United Kingdom prime minister
François Loubet—French president
Lidwina Klein—German chancellor
Dalia Grybauskaitė—Lithuanian president

BELARUSIAN

Alexander Lukashenko—president

AUTHOR'S NOTE

I hope you enjoyed reading *Treason*!

Treason was a fun book to write, but I did so with some trepidation. The plot structure of each book in the Trident Deception series determines which characters play dominant roles, and Christine O'Connor is forefront in *Treason*. Although the Trident Deception books don't have a true main character—the novels use a montage approach featuring Captain Murray Wilson, SEAL Jake Harrison, Christine O'Connor, and the president—if you had to hang your hat on someone, it'd be Christine, because she's the only one of the four main characters who can move around. Wilson and Harrison are tied to USS *Michigan* and related SEAL operations ashore, and the president isn't going to head out on any exciting missions. As a result, much of the Trident Deception story lines are told through Christine's eyes.

This is problematic, in my opinion, because most military thrillers feature strong male leads, typically Special Forces types, which Christine isn't. She's also completely untrained. She's not a character you'd design as a lead for a military thriller series. The reason for this is that I never intended to publish more than one book. However, when St. Martin's Press offered to buy *The Trident Deception,* their first question was— Are you writing a sequel? My answer was—Of course! I threw a proposal together that night and plugged in the characters who survived *The Trident Deception,* and sent it in. St. Martin's Press then offered a two-book deal.

So there I was, with a character set ill-suited for sequels, but for which I've been contracted for five so far, with many more hopefully to come. Under normal circumstances, a White House staffer like Christine would attend meetings and brief the president, and that's about it. But that's pretty boring and readers would soon be flipping past every page Christine appeared on. To keep things exciting, I gave Christine a few useful character traits—she's impulsive and vindictive—which gets her into situations most people would walk away from. She's also deadly with a pistol (as long as the target is stationary and inside twenty-five feet) and very athletic, being an Olympic-level gymnast. (Both of my daughters were gymnasts, and I'm amazed at the things they can do.) Neither of those skills came in handy in *Treason,* although they've been useful in previous novels and perhaps will be in future ones as well.

Anyway, this is a long-winded explanation of why Christine O'Connor is featured so heavily in *Treason.* Primarily, it's just the way the plot turned out. It also turns out that Christine is the favorite character in the Trident Deception series, based on reader feedback, followed by Wilson. One of the questions I frequently get is—When are Christine and Jake Harrison going to get together? Harrison is married, I remind everyone. However, hold that thought. The next book paves the way, and Harrison's marriage isn't going to be dissolved by a simple divorce. (I write thrillers, and courtroom drama doesn't count.)

Finally, the usual disclaimer—some of the tactics described in *Treason* are generic and not accurate. For example, torpedo employment and evasion tactics are classified and cannot be accurately represented in this novel. The dialogue also isn't one hundred percent accurate. If it were, much of it would be unintelligible to the average reader. To help the story move along without getting bogged down in acronyms, technical details, and other military jargon, I simplified the dialogue and description of operations and weapon systems.

For all of the above, I apologize. I did my best to keep everything as close to real life as possible while developing a suspenseful (and unclassified), page-turning novel. Hopefully it all worked out, and you enjoyed reading *Treason*.

ACKNOWLEDGMENTS

Many thanks are due to those who helped me write and publish this novel:

First and foremost, to my editor, Keith Kahla, for his exceptional insight and recommendations to make *Treason* better. To others at St. Martin's Press—Martin Quinn and other members of my marketing and publicity team—who I relied upon in many ways as *Treason* progressed toward publication—thank you for your support. And finally, thanks again to Sally Richardson and George Witte for making this book possible.

While writing each book, I've relied on subject matter experts to ensure I get the details correct. While I can handle most of the submarine parts, other areas require assistance. For *Treason,* thanks are due to Murray Gero, Eric Mason, Sam Carver, Matt Fulton, and LynDee Walker.

Finally, every book needs fine-tuning, and I owe thanks to those whose keen eye made *Treason* better—to Jeff Porteous, Sam Carver, Michael Williams, George Vercessi, Adelaida Lucena-Lower, and Rick and John Schwartz.

Thanks again to everyone who assisted, and I hope you enjoyed *Treason*!

Turn the page for a look ahead to

DEEP STRIKE

the next explosive novel by Rick Campbell,
coming soon in hardcover
from St. Martin's Press!

INDIAN SPRINGS, NEVADA

"High value target. That's all you need to know."

It was already ninety degrees at Creech Air Force Base, the morning sun burning down on several dozen trailers neatly arranged in four rows. Captain Mike Berger, seated inside one of the dimly-lit, cramped, and chilly trailers, kept his right hand on the joystick and his left on the throttle as his eyes scanned one of the fourteen displays built into the two-man control station. Beside him and sharing a center console was First Lieutenant Dee Ardis, likewise studying the pertinent screens.

Berger and Ardis were seated inside an MQ-9 Reaper Ground Control Station, controlling a Reaper drone, with Berger piloting the aircraft while Ardis operated its sensors. For the last twelve hours, the Reaper had been circling high above Khyber Pakhtunkhwa, a Pakistani province bordering Afghanistan. This section of the province was mainly no-man's-land, sparsely populated with sporadic villages containing only a dozen or so families each, a region where the Pakistani government had ceded authority to tribal warlords. In the center of Berger's visual display was a single dwelling at the end of a long dirt road, if you could call it that—more like a trail worn into the rugged terrain, snaking through the wilderness.

Most days, it'd be just the two of them in the control van during their six-hour shift, even during combat missions taking out the bad guys. But Berger had been surprised this morning when he'd arrived to relieve the off-going team, finding an entourage of four high-ranking Air Force officers—his supervisor and his boss, plus a colonel and brigadier general he hadn't seen before—further cramping the small trailer as they monitored the mission. Berger sensed the tension in the air the moment he stepped into the trailer. When he was briefed on the operation, he'd been told, "High value target. That's all you need to know."

Thus far, it'd been a boring four hours, with Berger keeping the MQ-9 Reaper at ten thousand feet to keep it out of sight and earshot of anyone inside or approaching the isolated dwelling. It was clear that today's mission was combat-related and not just surveillance, and the Reaper was well-equipped for the task, carrying four Hellfire missiles and two Paveway II five-hundred-pound bombs, all laser-guided to their target by equipment in the sensor ball mounted beneath the Reaper's nose.

Although Berger and Ardis flew the drone, operated its sensors, and released its weapons, the mission was controlled by an attack controller, a special operations type that Berger figured was probably stationed in a windowless concrete bunker somewhere in the Middle East. In the past, different attack controllers had provided Berger and Ardis with varying degrees of freedom over their attacks. Some were micromanagers, directing the drone approach angle, weapon selection, and impact point. Other attack controllers were more hands-off, simply saying, "Kill these two targets," letting Berger and Ardis make the optimum selections. Berger still didn't have a feeling for this attack controller, as they'd had few interactions thus far. Things started to pick up, however, when Berger noticed movement on his visual display.

A white bongo—similar to a pickup truck but with a wider body—appeared on the left edge of his optical display, dust billowing behind the vehicle as it traveled up the dirt road toward the dwelling. From ten thousand feet and a thirty-degree offset, he could tell there were two occupants inside the vehicle, but nothing more.

The attack controller's voice emanated from Berger's headphones. "Request visual target confirmation."

Berger acknowledged, then titled his joystick, sending the Reaper closer to the ground so the drone's camera had a low enough angle to get a good look at the faces of whoever was in the pickup truck.

The Reaper leveled off at the new altitude as the truck stopped beside the dwelling. When the two men, both wearing white dishdashas—long white robes traditionally worn by Middle Eastern men—stepped from the vehicle, they were greeted by two other men who emerged from the building. Ardis zoomed in, taking a picture of each man's face.

Berger waited as the facial-recognition algorithms worked in the background, watching the percentage under each photograph churn until the reading under one of the pictures stopped at ninety-three percent. The man's name remained blank on Berger's display, but a green *Target Confirmed* appeared beneath the image as the four men entered the dwelling.

"We have confirmed jackpot," the attack controller declared. "You are cleared for weapon release. Paveway in the center of the building."

Berger selected one of the Reaper's two Paveways, a laser-guided five-hundred-pound bomb, then waited as Ardis slewed the laser designator onto the building.

Release solution valid appeared on a display in the center console.

Berger armed the Paveway, its status also appearing on the display—*Master arm on*.

Finally, *Ready for release* appeared.

After a final glance at the laser designator, verifying it was locked onto the center of the building, Berger pressed the red button on his joystick, releasing the five-hundred-pound bomb.

As the Paveway descended toward its target, Berger assessed the probability of mission success. A five-hundred-pound bomb would normally kill everyone inside a dwelling that size, but they had no building schematics and no idea of the structure's internal layout or composition.

Berger watched as the Paveway completed its journey, hitting the building dead-center. An orange fireball erupted, billowing upward above a trail of black smoke as debris rained down on the surrounding landscape. As Berger studied the screen for signs of survivors, two men ran from the building.

"We've got two squirters," Ardis announced.

Berger focused on the squirters, a drone term for someone who runs—squirts—from the scene of an explosion.

"Kill the squirters," the attack controller ordered. "Payload your choice."

Berger selected a Hellfire missile, which could be guided more effectively toward nimble targets on the move. The two men were close together and headed in the same direction, so Berger directed Ardis to guide the missile between the two men. After Ardis adjusted the laser designator to the escaping pair, Berger released one of the Reaper's Hellfire missiles.

As the Hellfire began its journey, Berger evaluated the advance warning that'd be given to the two targets. An incoming Hellfire missile would create a sonic boom, with the time delay between boom and impact up to eight seconds depending on the azimuth—the angle the laser designator was aimed toward the target. In Afghanistan, especially, after years of drone strikes, the bad guys had learned—if you hear a boom, it's time to run. Ideally, Berger would have maneuvered the Reaper to reduce the azimuth before firing the Hellfire, but the squirters had been unexpected and there hadn't been time to reposition the Reaper.

"Four second warning," Ardis announced, having done the mental calculation.

Four seconds ought to be short enough between boom and detonation, Berger figured, providing insufficient time once the targets heard the boom, for them to realize what it was, change direction, and open far enough from the impact point to survive.

The Hellfire streaked toward its targets, and just before impact, the two men altered their escape route, turning abruptly and splitting up. The Hellfire detonated a few seconds later, filling the center of Berger's visual display with another explosion, albeit much smaller than the Paveway's.

Ardis waited for the dust to clear, then zoomed in on the area, searching for the targets. Both men were lying immobile not far from the impact point, one man on his back with his eyes frozen open, and the other face down with red splotches spreading through the sand, outward from his body.

Post-mission analysis would be conducted to assess the results of today's mission, but Berger was confident the man's status on his display would be updated from *Target Confirmed* to *Target Deceased*.

The attack controller's voice came across Berger's headphones again. "You are released for further duties."

Berger tilted his joystick, altering the Reaper's course, sending it toward Kandahar Airfield in southern Afghanistan for refueling and rearming.

THREE YEARS
LATER

1
NEW YORK CITY

Standing at the back of the United Nations General Assembly Hall, Mel Cross surveyed the 1,800 men and women in attendance as they listened to the man at the podium. Like many of the attendees, Cross wore an earpiece, although for a decidedly different reason. There was no need to translate the speech being delivered by the American ambassador to the United Nations; Cross was one of the Diplomatic Security Service agents assigned to the ambassador's detail. In the other rear corner of the assembly hall, DSS agent Jill Mercer also kept a watchful eye as they waited for Ambassador Marshall Hill to finish his speech, the topic of which had been publicized a week in advance, and which was just now becoming interesting.

"Over the last several months," Ambassador Hill continued, "there has been an increase in terrorist attacks around the world. The United States has direct evidence of Iran's involvement, providing both funding, arms, and training to organizations intent on harming those who do not align with Tehran's ideology. Additionally, we have proof that Iran has recommenced refining uranium for its nuclear weapons program. Evidence of Iran's transgressions will be provided to the

Security Council, and the United States will be working with member nations to strengthen the sanctions already in place.

"Let me be clear—if Iran's leadership continues its belligerent and aggressive behavior, developing weapons of mass destruction and supporting those who harm others, the United States will work with its allies to address the situation. Various military options are within the realm of potential responses."

There was a low murmur throughout the assembly hall as some of the attendees commented to others. Cross paid no attention to the murmuring. His eyes continued their sweep across the congregation, searching for that one small detail that seemed out of place. His gaze stopped on Agent Mercer, whose watchful eyes also surveyed the occupants. Cross's thoughts dwelt for a moment on Jill, an attractive brunette who'd been assigned to the ambassador's detail two months ago. A recent widow with two young kids—her husband had been a NYPD cop, killed a year ago in the line of duty. Jill had remained aloof since her assignment to the ambassador's detail, failing to provide Cross with an opportunity to determine whether she was ready for, or even interested in, a relationship with him.

Cross forced his eyes to keep moving, admonishing himself for the lapse in his duties. He'd dwelt on Jill far too long. However, the United Nations General Assembly Hall was about a safe a place as any in the city.

Upon completing his speech, Ambassador Hill stepped away from the podium, and Cross moved to intercept him, as did Jill. The ambassador was on a tight schedule, heading to LaGuardia Airport for a flight to spend time with his family in Rhode Island, instead of returning to his penthouse condo a few blocks away. Jill reached the ambassador shortly after Cross did, and the two agents bracketed the diplomat as they headed toward the exit.

Cross received a report via his earpiece. He responded quietly into his sleeve, then informed Ambassador Hill, "Transportation is ready."

The ambassador nodded his understanding. He had already been briefed on the enhanced security measures. Based on the administration's position against Iran and its aggressive response to the recent wave of terrorism, along with Hill's role as a primary messenger, his security detail had been augmented. The ambassador would travel with two DSS agents in the second of three vehicles, with two more agents in the lead SUV and Cross and Jill in the third.

The convoy was waiting as they exited the General Assembly Hall lobby, and Ambassador Hill stepped into the middle of three black Lincoln Navigators while Cross and Jill slipped into the vacant third, whose original driver had moved to the lead vehicle. The lead SUV pulled out, with the second and third SUVs following close behind. The convoy turned quickly onto 2nd Avenue, beginning the short trip to LaGuardia Airport.

A few blocks from the United Nations headquarters, Lonnie Mixell waited patiently in the driver's seat of a rented Buick Enclave, parked alongside the curb on East 37th Street, a hundred feet from and offering a clear view of the 2nd Avenue and East 37th Street intersection. After evaluating several locations over the last week, he'd selected this intersection because at this time of day, in the middle of rush-hour, the traffic backed up at the red light. The vehicles of interest would be either stopped near the intersection or moving slowly through it.

Normally, after a day at work, Ambassador Hill would have returned to his residence within walking distance from the UN headquarters, offering Mixell a slim chance of completing his assignment in the manner desired by his employer: a method that would be captured on video—the aftermath, that is—and played repeatedly on news channels throughout the world. Mixell had eventually connected with one of the ambassador's aides who, for the right price, had shared his boss's schedule. It had taken more money than Mixell had planned, but it didn't really matter; he wasn't the one paying the bills.

Inside the Buick, Mixell's eyes were fixed on the video playing on his cell phone, relayed from a small wireless camera placed on a windowsill inside the Millennium Hilton, across the street from the United Nations headquarters. The hotel room was rented under an alias, of course, and provided a clear view of everyone exiting the UN General Assembly Hall. Mixell watched the three-car convoy of interest pull away from the building entrance, then turn left onto 2nd Avenue.

Jill Mercer sat in the passenger seat of the third SUV while Cross drove, scanning the traffic and passerbys for anything out of the ordinary. It was a beautiful day, a clear blue sky with the temperature in the mid-seventies, unusually pleasant for this time of year. The forecast for the next few days was comparable, likely the last patch of reasonable weather before the winter set it.

She planned to take advantage of the warm afternoons, spending time outdoors with her children this weekend. The last year had been difficult for the kids, adjusting to the loss of their father. It'd been tough on her as well, and as she approached the one-year anniversary of her husband's death, she wondered whether it was time to move on, or if pursuing another relationship so soon would dishonor his memory.

As her eyes scanned left across the traffic, she noticed Cross's thumbs tapping on the steering wheel. It was a nervous habit of his, she'd noticed, and wondered what the issue was. Today's transit was as straightforward as they came and there were no indications that anything was amiss. After reflecting on the issue for a moment, she realized his nervous glitch appeared only when it was just the two of them, alone in a vehicle. It was clear that Cross was attracted to her, as she frequently caught him gazing in her direction. Thus far, however, he'd made no advance.

"So," Cross said, interrupting Jill's thoughts, "do you have plans for the weekend?"

Jill repressed a smile. Cross had finally worked up the courage to ask her out.

"The weather's going to be nice," she replied, "so I plan take the kids to Central Park one day. Other than that, I'll probably just relax and spend more time with the kids."

"Care for company when you visit the park, or perhaps dinner one night?"

Her reaction to Cross's question was unexpected. She was hit with a wave of grief and guilt, and a lump formed in her throat. She'd been wondering whether she was ready for another relationship, and she had the answer. She turned away, looking out the side window, hoping Cross hadn't noticed her reaction.

"Not this weekend," she replied. She tried to phrase her response delicately, not shutting the door completely on him. She was interested, but now wasn't the right time. "I'm not ready yet. I hope you understand."

"Of course," he said quickly. "I can only imagine how difficult things have been for you. Whenever you're ready, let me know." He offered a smile before returning his attention to the traffic, slowing for the red light ahead.

Mixell checked his watch. He'd timed the route from the United Nations headquarters several times, and the three-car convoy should arrive in the next fifteen to forty-five seconds. He spotted the lead black Lincoln Navigator not far from the intersection, stopped for a red light, but the other two vehicles were hidden behind a corner building. It wouldn't be much longer, however. He slid the driver's door window down, ostensibly to enjoy the nice weather, although the real reason was so he'd have a clear shot.

Beneath a blanket on the passenger seat was an M79 grenade launcher—a single-shot, break-open, shoulder-fired weapon—which could fire a variety of 40mm rounds. This M79 was loaded with an XM1060 thermobaric round, a fuel-air explosive consisting of a fuel container and two explosive charges. The first explosion would burst the container open and disperse the fuel in a cloud, which would mix with atmospheric oxygen as it expanded. The second charge would detonate the cloud, creating a massive blast wave, killing anyone nearby and destroying equipment and even reinforced structures.

On the seat beside the M79 was a 40mm grenade belt holding twelve additional thermobaric rounds. However, if things went as planned, he'd need only the round in the launcher, plus two more.

The light along 2nd Avenue turned green, and Mixell waited as the traffic began moving again, the vehicles establishing the desired spacing between them like an accordion stretching out. He'd have only one shot at the target as it passed through the intersection, which if successful, would bring the three-car-convoy to a halt.

Accuracy wasn't a concern, as the M79 had a maximum effective range of four hundred yards and he was about thirty yards away. Reload time was an issue, however, as the M79 was a single-round-capacity weapon. But reloads were relatively quick and likely well within the response time of the agents in the lead and trailing vehicles. For his escape plan to work, he couldn't afford to have DSS agents charging up the street toward him.

When the lead Navigator began moving, Mixell pulled the blanket from the passenger seat and lifted the M79 to his shoulder, taking aim at his primary target.

It happened almost simultaneously. A thin trail of white smoke appeared before Jill as the ambassador's Navigator erupted in an orange fireball, the explosion sending glass fragments and metal shards pelting off Jill's SUV. Cross slammed on the brakes, bringing their Navigator to a screeching halt, as did the driver of the lead vehicle.

Jill turned toward the origin of the attack, spotting a man in an SUV about thirty yards away, focused on something in his lap instead of the burning hulk in the intersection. As he lifted and aimed a shoulder-fired launcher at the lead Navigator, Jill shouted, "Weapon at two o'clock!"

The words left Jill's mouth a second before a projectile slammed into the lead car, detonating before either agent was able to exit.

"Get out!" Cross shouted.

His warning was unnecessary, as Jill was already kicking open her door. She darted from the SUV and circled behind the vehicle, joining Cross as he

squeezed off a three-round volley. The bullets missed
the perpetrator, shattering his vehicle's front window
instead. Jill added another three-round burst while
Cross fired again. This time, the assassin ducked
down inside his SUV and slipped from the vehicle via
the passenger door, then fled up the sidewalk as pedestrians scattered, searching for cover.

Cross directed Jill to take the right side of the street
while he headed left, and they crossed the remaining lanes of 2nd Avenue and sprinted up both sides
of East 37th Street toward the suspect. Jill traveled up
the sidewalk on the opposite side of the street as the
suspect while Cross ran up the road on the other side,
keeping parked cars between him and the suspect.

Mixell had planned to leave the grenade launcher and
belt in the SUV, strolling away from the scene with his
hands in his pockets, headed toward his escape vehicle
parked not far away. Unfortunately, the two agents in
the third vehicle had reacted more quickly than he'd
hoped. They had a bead on him and were already
charging up the street. Mixell shifted to plan B.

He reloaded the M79 on the run, then stopped beside a parked SUV, swinging the grenade launcher
back toward the two agents pursuing him: one male,
one female, with the man in the lead. Before Mixell
was able to target the man, both agents fired their
weapons. He ducked behind the vehicle and waited
until the hail of bullets pinging into the car stopped.
He popped over the hood again and fired a round into
the car closest to the lead agent, then dropped back
behind the vehicle before either agent returned fire.

The XM1060 detonated once it pierced the car
and the explosion shredded the vehicle, sending glass
and metal fragments in every direction. Nearby pe-

destrians had taken cover, either behind vehicles or in nearby stores, but those unfortunate enough to be near the explosion were hit by shrapnel. The lead DSS agent was one of the casualties, his smoldering body writhing on the sidewalk.

After a quick assessment of the results, Mixell continued his sprint up the sidewalk, hoping to slip away from the last agent.

Jill noted Cross's fate as she moved up the sidewalk, shifting her thoughts from wondering whether he'd survive to getting a clear shot on the perpetrator. As she traveled up the street, she periodically regained her target, glancing between the parked cars she used as cover. She heard the faint sirens of approaching law enforcement; assistance would arrive soon, cutting off the man's escape routes. However, he was moving up the street faster than she was, opening the distance between them. She couldn't let him slip away before assistance arrived.

She picked up her pace, moving as fast as she could while staying in a crouched position, shielded by the parked cars. In an effort to make up some ground, she decided to skip checking on the man's progress between each vehicle, sprinting past a dozen cars before pausing to take a look.

As she peered over the hood of a Chevy Blazer, her eyes scanned the other side of the street, focused on where the man should've been if he'd kept up his pace. Just to the left of where she expected him to be, not quite as far up the road, she spotted the suspect. The man had the rocket launcher on his shoulder, aimed at her.

Jill's gaze shifted to the burning and shredded car near Cross, suddenly realizing her peril. The projectile the man was firing would rip apart the Chevy Blazer she was hiding behind, turning the vehicle into a four-thousand-pound fragmentation grenade.

Bad place to take cover.

The realization coalesced in her mind a moment too late. She saw a thin white exhaust trail streak toward her as the projectile slammed into the side of the Blazer.

Time seemed to slow down for Jill after the round detonated. An orange, blossoming cloud expanded from the vehicle as it shattered the windows and shredded the car body, enveloping her in a scorching inferno as shrapnel penetrated deep into her face and torso. The pressure transient from the explosion knocked her from her feet, blasting her backward until she slammed into a building's brick façade, where she crumpled to the ground. Unbearable pain sliced through her body as she lay there, while a pool of blood spread slowly across the concrete. The last thing she realized as her world faded to darkness, was that the agonizing scream piercing her ears was her own.